SAND CREEK

A NOVEL BY
KEVIN CAHILL

LoneWolf

This edition published by KC Lonewolf, 12/15/2018
admin@kclonewolf.com
ISBN 13: 978-0-9969544-5-7
ISBN 10: 0-9969544-5-7

First edition published 07/27/05 by
Author House, Bloomington, Indiana USA
ISBN 13: 978-1-42-087043-5
ISBN 10: 1-4208-7043-2
Library of Congress Control Number: 2005906773

Photo & Illustration Credits: Dedication page - *"Keeper of the Lighting"* - sculpture by J. Mark Snowdon, from the Author's private collection - Illustration by Kevin I. Cahill ©2005 All Rights Reserved. Page 0 - *"Of Dogman Scalps"* illustration by Kevin I. Cahill ©2005 All Rights Reserved. Photos, pages 3, 21, 25, 59, 183, 191, 212 courtesy Western History/Genealogy Department, Denver Public Library. Pages 362, 364, 365, 367-371, 373, 376, 377, 387 illustrations by Kevin I. Cahill ©2005 All Rights Reserved rendered from photos courtesy Western History/Genealogy Department, Denver Public Library. Page 374, Ellenbecker, John G. - *Oak Grove Massacre, (Oak, Nebraska), Indian Raids on the Little Blue River in 1864.* Marysville, KS: Marysville Advocate-Democrat, 1927. Pages 39, 41, 51, 349, 383, 385 from the private materials of Byron Strom, Anne E. Hemphill Collection.

Maps pages 12, 42, 83, 174, 237 copyright ©2005 by Kevin I. Cahill. All Rights Reserved

Author contact information: admin@kclonewolf.com
Or go to **www.kclonewolf.com** and click on "contact" link.

Published and printed in the United States of America
This book is printed on acid-free paper.

Kindle and Audible book available on Amazon.com

This book is dedicated to the memory of
J. Mark Snowdon

Acknowledgements

I wish to extend my warmest appreciation to:

The staff of the Denver Public Library, Western History/Genealogy Department, for their help in searching an astounding collection of Colorado history.

And my sincere thanks to Mr. William Dawson, for providing the bibliography that opened the trail, and for allowing me to wander that quiet prairie along the banks of Sand Creek in search of spirits – and rabbits.

Special thanks to:

Colorado State Historical Society, Stephen Hart Library

Kansas State Historical Society

Christopher H. Wynkoop, Edward Wanshaer Wynkoop Collection web http://freepages.genealogy.rootsweb.com/~wynkoop/webdocs/ned-

wkp.htm

Deana Moller – Many thanks for introducing me to Lisa

Lisa Coberly Cyrus - Many thanks for introducing me to the Coberlys

Byron Strom (Anne E. Hemphill Collection) –
    Thank you for sharing a glimpse into the Soule

KC

Other Books by Kevin Cahill
Letters to a Rose
The Last Cafe
Knights of Harvest
Simon Sez (with Garry Lambert)

For information on these titles, and the
massacre at Sand Creek, visit:
www.kclonewolf.com

AUTHOR'S NOTE

A large portion of this book is derived from official reports, testimony, and personal written accounts of those who were directly involved in the incident at Sand Creek on November 29, 1864. In the case of all historical novels, an author must take certain liberties to dramatically portray events and characters within the framework of a true story. This work is the result of ten years of extensive research into the individuals involved in the affair at Sand Creek. I have made every effort to portray events and characters based on the historical record. With the exception of a few minor "extras" that fill out certain crowd scenes, every person in this story is a non-fictional character. In the case of incidents in which an unnamed person was involved, a true, historical name was given to that character. Obviously, because individual interviews of the participants were impossible, I invoked "literary license" in most instances of character dialogue, although some quotes and hearing testimony are taken from official government transcripts and written accounts of witnesses or participants. I, too, have made certain assumptions as to the personal lives of some, where no historical record exists. Every effort has been made to make logical and fair deductions based on known facts, but the reader must consider that this is a dramatic presentation based upon my own interpretation and personal opinion.

To this day, the Colorado Third Volunteer's attack on the Cheyenne and Arapaho Indians camped at Sand Creek is the subject of controversy, accusation and recrimination. To justify the barbarous acts of John M. Chivington's militia is no less ludicrous than the attempts of others who try to cleanse the reputation of the warrior societies that rampaged across the Great Plains in the 1860s. Responsibility for the affair at Sand Creek lies on both sides of the river, and the consequences were deadly for all . . .

KC

"A nation is not conquered
Until the hearts of its women
are on the ground.

Then it is finished,
No matter how brave its warriors
Or how strong their weapons."

Cheyenne proverb

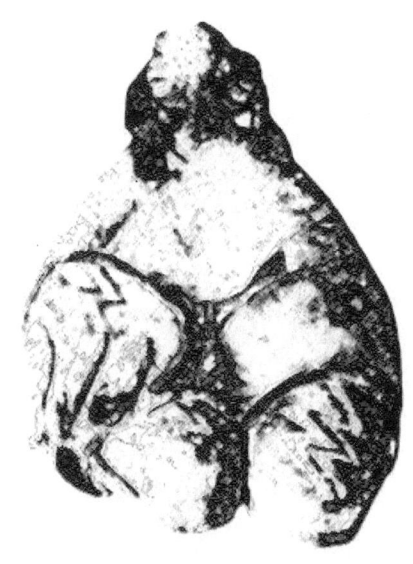

1

THE BEGINNING...

I t happened in the spring of 1858, "the time when the horses get fat," as the Cheyennes called it. A ragtag prospector's heart twisted like a knotty rope as he pulled his rusty pan from the waters of Cherry Creek. It was a notion lodged between dreams of wealth and fears of destitution.

"Can it be?" he wondered aloud.

After four agonizing years of toil in merciless winter cold and arid summer heat, what he saw rolling in the sand and pebbles sparkled like the first star at twilight. He blinked his parched eyes and swirled the river water until the nugget reappeared.

"Please, God," he whispered, "please..."

In short order, hundreds of like dreamers dotted Cherry Creek at the confluence of the South Platte River, scouring hopes for a better life from the muddy creek bed. Like a mountain wildfire, word quickly spread: Gold's been found, not in the treacherous Rocky Mountains, not another twelve hundred hellish miles across Death Valley, but here on a high plains creek bed 70 miles north of Pike's Peak - just a week's trip west of the Kansas plains. New camps sprung up along the banks of Cherry Creek and the South Platte like prairie grass, unceremoniously staked and claimed with little legal precedence beyond a ratty flag and a loaded rifle. Claims were christened *Montana, Auraria* and *St. Charles*, and wary eyes scanned for bushwhackers looking to ransack dreams of riches beyond the wealth of kings.

It didn't matter this was a vacuous dream. It didn't matter that the coveted nuggets regurgitated from the mountains produced a nominal yield to those lucky to be in the right place at the right time. The story passed from prospector to prospector, messenger to messenger, swiftly working its way east on hopeful tongues. When the tale eventually reached impoverished families along the Missouri River, the Pike's Peak gold claim was but a burgeoning fantasy. By the time word finally reached Washington, the banks of Cherry Creek had become the Mother Lode. More truthful accounts of sub-zero blizzards, rugged box canyons and dangerous Indians were conspicuously absent from rumors about the Pike's Peak territory. Stories of the gold camp along Cherry Creek declared St. Charles a gilded paradise. The claim was situated fifteen miles due east of the Rockies on a high plateau, so they said, a mild and forgiving climate on both seasonal extremes, friendly Arapaho Indians of agreeable demeanor, and enough gold gushing from the river to pay a king's ransom.

Inevitably, Union power brokers arrived with their formidable benefactors' influence in tow, pushing the Arapahos away from the South Platte's fertile basins. The St. Charles claim was soon poached by Jayhawker partners of the Kansas political base, led by a salty young land broker by the name of Edward "Ned" Wynkoop. Before the name St. Charles could be inked upon a map of this high plateau in the heart of what would soon be known as the Colorado Territory, the growing river encampment was renamed to honor Kansas Governor James Denver.

By the early 1860s, 140,000 white settlers descended on the eastern Colorado prairie like summer locust. Riding on dreams of riches, the hopeful nomads drove prairie schooners in vast trains across the perilous plains of Bloody Kansas, putting further strain on the relationship with Plains Indians already engaged in fierce intertribal wars over dwindling hunting grounds. Before the grossly exaggerated tales of Denver City's gold reached the East, the Indians begrudgingly co-existed with the white men, who although sparse in number were firmly entrenched and often had valuable goods to trade. Until then, the Pike's Peak Region was best suited to the rugged adventurer with a knack for surviving among traders, prospectors, loggers, and trappers - many of questionable character seeking asylum in the wilderness from crimes committed in the States or abroad. But now the Union expansionists pushed toward the Rocky Mountains, moving on territories previously promised to the Indians through governmental treaties, among them the Kiowa, Comanche, Sioux, Cheyenne and Arapaho.

Gold fever raged across the Pike's Peak Region, officially named the Colorado Territory in 1861, infecting all hope for peaceful cohabitation among the red and white man. And it wasn't just the diminutive white immigrant who arrived with modest dreams of wealth. The territory, once considered a desolate wilderness, was beginning to draw the ardent attention of politicians and other like opportunists in the States, whose bitter dispute over slavery had exploded into a bloody war of rebellion, splitting the nation's heart in two. The Union, now immersed in a genocidal civil war of power and providence, dispatched agents to fulfill its self-proclaimed Manifest Destiny by gaining control of this gateway to the vast mineral wealth of the West before the Confederate States could establish a military foothold. Among the new emigrants were Dr. John Evans of Chicago, appointed Colorado's second Territorial Governor by President Abraham Lincoln; and Colonel John Milton Chivington of

Ohio, a towering, grizzly bear Methodist preacher-turned-warrior, who was known to sling his six-guns as often as his Bible. Colonel Chivington's reputation exceeded his 6-foot-4, 250-pound frame, celebrated by locals for turning back the Texans in a savage battle at La Glorieta Pass, New Mexico Territory. For his resounding defeat of the Confederates' drive toward Colorado, Chivington earned command of Colorado's military district, and with it the admiration of Denver's anxious settlers.

Governor Evans, saddled with the secondary, bureaucratic title of Superintendent of Indian Affairs, did not enjoy such adoration. The governor precariously teetered along the top rail of a rickety fence, attempting to balance the tenuous relationship between his white constituents and the increasingly belligerent Plains Indians. Washington was more concerned with the war in the States than the neglected, pre-gold land treaties granted to the Indians. It turned a deaf ear to Evans' warnings of a brewing Indian revolt against settlers invading the lands that were legally promised them. Evans and Chivington, both ardent Union abolitionists, cast imposing shadows over Denver City, by now a volatile and lawless town surrounded by five surly Indian nations growing more hostile toward the disregarded treaties.

Inevitably, all bets were off now that Colorado was a proven Union asset worthy of statehood. The government never truly intended to satisfy the Indians of the plains with treaties. It believed European monarchy far outmatched dog-eating savages who beat drums, scalped enemies, and incessantly wailed at the moon. The Indian, as white Christian reasoning went, was after all a soulless predatory

Governor John Evans

animal barely evolved to its hind legs. Unlike the African slave, who had a propensity for accepting white Christianity, the unshackled Indian took no such stock in a pale savior. Therefore, government treaties were intended to merely pacify the savages until Indian fighters operating under the government sanctioned "war of extermination" could summarily dispatch them to their heathen Happy Hunting Ground. There, the red savage could wallow in godless eternity and no longer hinder Anglican progress in the New World...

It was now 1863. The shots fired on Fort Sumter barely echoed across the Colorado Rockies, but the large Union-sympathizer population knew who buttered its bread. Those who arrived years earlier in search of gold found mostly dust, but they were survivors determined to forge a life on the High Plains. It was a treacherous proposition. Colorado's military ranks were stretched thin, leaving a handful of camps or forts in the territory to maintain a defense against a Confederate invasion or Indian raid. If either happened, the citizens of Denver City were left on their own hook to defend themselves.

In reality, the sight of graybacks thundering into Denver was a farfetched notion, but a boiling sea of red savages in war bonnets was an all too real and frightening possibility. One could not toss a stone across Cherry Creek without hitting an Arapaho lodge, but in earlier years the Arapahos were cautiously tolerant of the ever-growing number of white faces in the territory. Southern Arapaho Principal Chief Little Raven was a man of feisty nature and sound judgement. He spoke English fluently, having mastered a colorful cache of cuss words often bantered with his white friends over cigars and whiskey. He was considered a tough but fair negotiator when treating with his white brethren, and he and Governor Evans maintained a civil rapport. Evans pacified Little Raven and his people with material goods in exchange for their friendly disposition and allowance of gold prospecting in Indian territory.

Many young warriors of the Cheyenne and Arapaho military clans, however, considered the white intrusion on their land a growing illness that required immediate and forcible action. This division of opinion among Indians, combined with similar dissention among whites, created a myriad of problems for which conventional diplomacy had no solution. The Arapahos rarely interacted with the whites, other than to occasionally show off bloody scalps taken in land skirmishes with their primary nemesis, the mountain-dwelling Utes. As more whites moved on Colorado, the Indian-white relationship grew increasingly volatile through frequent skirmishes between Indians camped around Denver and nomadic mountain prospectors passing through town in search of whiskey and whores. Arapaho sub-Chief Left Hand was incensed when a pack of miners, led by a hard-drinking scalawag called Big Phil the Cannibal, went on a drunken spree through Left Hand's Arapaho camp, raping several squaws while the Arapaho men were out hunting. Left Hand and his warriors might have set Denver City in flames if not for the intervention of his friend Jim Beckwith. The old mulatto mountain man talked Left Hand out of the reprisal, but he wrote a letter to the

Rocky Mountain News, warning the settlers of Denver City that further blatant mistreatment of Indians by "drunken devils and bummers" would lead to certain disaster. Beckwith tried to impart upon the whites that Indian culture dictates swift and vicious revenge against the perpetrators of crimes against their people.

Although the occasional Denver skirmishes were troublesome, the Arapahos were not Governor Evans' only concern. In 1862, the Sioux, betrayed by broken government promises, went on a four-month rampage of abduction, rape and murder at New Ulm, Minnesota, resulting in the deaths of nearly 1,400 citizens and soldiers before the uprising was finally subdued. The Comanches and Kiowas, as well, were conducting vicious raids on remote white settlements, but their numbers were more concentrated far south and east of Denver. What troubled Evans most was the near proximity of the most formidable and fearsome of the Plains tribes - the Cheyennes. In addition to hunting the eastern Colorado plains formerly reserved for them under the 1851 Ft. Laramie Treaty, the Northern and Southern Cheyennes, with their Arapaho allies, roamed lands from the Republican River in Nebraska to the southern regions of the Arkansas in Kansas.

The Cheyennes and Arapahos had maintained a civil relationship with the whites under the former treaty, freely hunting buffalo, trading with whites along the wagon routes, and subsisting on government annuities. The gold invasion of Denver, however, forced a new treaty on the Cheyennes and Arapahos in 1861, a fanciful land swindle conducted at Fort Lyon (formerly Fort Wise) on the Arkansas River, 250 miles southeast of Denver.

The new Fort Wise Treaty, by which the government reclaimed valuable ranch and farmland from the Indians, voided the Fort Laramie Treaty and cut Arapaho and Cheyenne land in Colorado by more than half. The Indians were ordered to live on the remaining reservation along the Big Sandy – the *Ponoeohe* or "Little Dried River" - with a hollow promise to help them cultivate the barren parcel of land substantially devoid of water and game. No government assistance ever materialized, and the Cheyennes and Arapahos, many who opposed the new treaty from the beginning, began to wander away and conduct raids against whites who settled on their former hunting grounds.

In an attempt to head off more trouble, Governor Evans established a tenuous dialogue with the Indian tribes both on the plains and in the mountains, but he found the Cheyennes to be most enigmatic and unbending. The Cheyenne Nation was comprised of a complex political structure ranging from conservative and peaceful bands, to the mysterious military societies of young and volatile warriors, among them the Bowstring Soldiers, Kit Foxes, Red Shields, Elkhorn Scrapers and the infamous Dog Soldiers. Understanding the dynamic political composition of the Cheyenne Nation escaped Evans, who for all his intentions of maintaining a red/white détente was a victim of inbred European chauvinism. Evans considered the Indian a creature incapable of quantum reasoning.

His mistake would twist the American West down a long and dark trail for decades to come...

By the spring of 1864, the number of Indian attacks on isolated white settlements near the Kansas/Colorado border grew from the tens to hundreds. Although most attacks involved only a few Indians and whites at a time, a shadowy message nipped at Evans' neck. He would never admit his frustration with the treaty violations by his government, but he knew even a savage could decipher the intent of Union lies. In a weak moment, Evans admitted he knew the Indians wouldn't simply go on a targeted killing spree against the whites without good reason. Colonel Chivington had orders to hunt down and kill the Indian raiders, but rumors drifted in suggesting Chivington's troops weren't wasting time trying to determine which Indians were hostile, and which were not. In one such instance, Cheyenne Dog Soldier Chief Lean Bear was shot dead by troops under the command of Lieutenant George Eayer, after the chief allegedly made a hostile advance on the soldiers. Evans knew Lean Bear had recently traveled to Washington with other peaceably inclined chiefs as honored guests of President Lincoln. Word filtered back to Major Edward Wynkoop that Lean Bear was shot without provocation while wearing a peace medal presented to him by "The Great Father" Lincoln.

As both a governor appointed to support the Union's informal declaration of war on the Indians, yet also charged with the duty of pacifying the red man, Evans was hopelessly pinned between ambiguous government policy and ancient native culture. His problem was compounded by Chivington's ferocious attacks on those leaders who might be instrumental in stopping the Cheyenne war parties. Chivington was a hero in the eyes of Denver settlers, further shaking the tightrope that Evans walked. The governor had few friends with sympathetic ears, and numerous enemies with one hand outstretched and the other ominously hidden behind the back.

The Cheyennes held the key to Colorado's fate. Certainly, the warlike Kiowas, Utes and Comanches were an imposing threat who during councils never fully satisfied Evans of the safety of the territory; but there was something about the enigmatic Cheyennes that made him see shadows where there should be light. A simple gesture or dark stare from a Cheyenne chief made Evans' blood run cold. Councils with other tribal leaders often turned to shouting matches - Evans with his perfect King's English and the Indians with their strange and staggered tongue bombarding hapless interpreters. Most angry words from both sides dissolved into a handshake and nebulous promise of food, a parcel of land, or material goods in exchange for tempered behavior. But the stoic Cheyenne chiefs rarely threatened, hollered, or compromised.

Cheyenne Principal Chief, *Moke-tav-a-to* – "Black Kettle," as the whites called him - sometimes conveyed elegant diplomacy, and other times, vicious certainty. Black Kettle, the elderly gentleman, convinced Evans he wished to call the white man his brother. Conversely, Black Kettle, the Principal Chief, equally convinced Evans he would find no more formidable foe on any Confederate battleground. Black Kettle had led his people on devastating raids against the Utes and Pawnees, taking scalps and leaving adversaries to die on the battlefield, and yet, he professed his sound intention to keep peace with the white man. Black Kettle was present when his friend Lean Bear was shot by Eayer's troops, but he nonetheless intervened and pulled his angry young warriors back. The incident concluded with both sides backing away from a major battle, but the seed of war had been planted as far as the Dog Soldiers were concerned. Although Black Kettle's word was law, Major Wynkoop and other officers noted that the young warriors' anger over Lean Bear's killing indicated a division in the Cheyenne ranks.

Subsequent Dog Soldier raids on supply trains led Evans to conclude that the Cheyennes were a dangerous commodity. Should their warriors, numbering in the thousands, suddenly advance just a hundred miles west from the Kansas plains, the massacre at New Ulm could repeat itself on the streets of Denver City. This wasn't simply an ephemeral nightmare that brought Evans upright in his bed at night. The Fort Wise Treaty, endorsed by Black Kettle and other elder Arapaho and Cheyenne chiefs, drove a wedge between tribal elders and the younger chiefs, who were neither consulted, nor present at the treaty's signing. Although Black Kettle professed a desire to maintain peace with the whites, the military clans were stubbornly determined to avenge Lean Bear's death. Dog Soldier leaders steadfastly insisted that no peace could *ever* be made with the white man.

Clearly, the forceful younger generation of Cheyenne and

Arapaho warriors were ranging from the control of the elders. Additionally, an alarming rumor passed by one of Evans' Indian spies claimed that the Dog Soldiers were holding councils with other tribes – in particular, Sioux warrior clans that participated in the Minnesota uprising. The war councils, as the rumor went, proposed to unite all five Plains Indians tribes in a war to run every white man out of Colorado for good. In November 1863, Governor Evans received a dispatch from his spy, Robert North, a "squaw man" (a white man married to an Indian woman), who related details of the council that North claimed he witnessed. His dispatch included this ominous warning:

"The Comanches, Apaches, Kiowas, the northern band of Arapahoes, and all of the Cheyennes, with the Sioux, have pledged one another to go to war with the whites as soon as they can procure ammunition in the spring. I heard them discuss the matter often and the few of them who opposed it were forced to be quiet and were really in danger of the loss of their lives.

I saw the principal chiefs pledge to each other that they would shake hands and be friendly with the whites until they procured ammunition and guns, so as to be ready when they strike. Plundering to get means has already commenced, and the plan is to commence the war at several points in the sparse settlements early in the spring.

They wanted me to join them in the war, saying that they would take a great many white women and children prisoners, and get a heap of property, blankets, &c. But while I am connected with them by marriage and live with them I am yet a white man, and wish to avoid bloodshed. There are a great many Mexicans with the Comanche and Apache Indians, all of whom urge on the war, promising to help the Indians themselves, and that a great many more Mexicans would come up from New Mexico for the purpose in the spring.

Evans took North's warning seriously, despite denials by many Cheyennes and Arapahos, who declared North's claims were outright lies. They characterized North as a dishonorable white man who was often at odds with the Indians. However, continued signs of an impending Indian war arose throughout the Colorado Territory. In the spring, Evans received another letter from a settler regarding alleged Cheyenne and Arapaho depredations along the Arkansas near Camp Fillmore, where Lieutenant George L. Shoup was in command:

BOONEVILLE, COLO. TERRITORY
Hon. JOHN EVANS
SIR:

May I beg of you, in behalf of my own family and others in this settlement, if not incompatible with the public interest, to allow the present military or an adequate force to remain at Camp Fillmore for defense of our border. It is at this point the Indians cross to and from the Ute fights, and it is here that women have been grossly abused, cattle killed, farmers driven from their lands, and fear and danger have run riot. Had I the honor of Colonel Chivington's acquaintance I would write him, but Shoup advises me to lay the matter before you, and views it as I do, a matter of importance. Leaving my family here alone, as I am forced to, I am in constant dread that they may be abused by the Indians that pass and repass at this season of the year. I am not naturally timid, nor would I thus plead did I not know whereof I affirm. In this I am expressing the views of the whole settlement, and I am, faithfully, yours,

H. M. FOSDICK.

Evans immediately forwarded Fosdick's letter to Colonel Chivington, requesting additional troops to be pulled in from Kansas to protect Booneville. Upon receipt of Evans' dispatch, Chivington requested a report from Lieutenant Shoup. While Shoup acknowledged several Cheyenne attacks against settlers and wagon trains that resulted in death and the loss of supplies and stock, he reported that these incidents were on the Kansas frontier in the vicinity of Fort Larned, some 250 miles east of Booneville. Shoup claimed there were no reports of Indians near Booneville at all, but he would allot a few of his men to patrol the area in response to Fosdick's request. Colonel Chivington then replied to Evans:

...as a soldier I am compelled to obey the orders of my superior officers. These orders are to concentrate all my available forces on the extreme southeast corner of this district, from which you will readily perceive, what I write with regret, that I cannot comply with the above-named request.

Since my assuming the command here it has always been my aim to protect all our population from all possible danger, and from the orders under which I am acting, part of which are above quoted, you will readily see that I cannot keep the company now in the neighborhood of Booneville at its present station and obey my orders to send it to the extreme southeast part of the district...

Frustrated by the Colorado First Cavalry's dispersal toward Kansas in defense against Confederate troops, Governor Evans took his case to Major General Samuel Curtis, commanding the Military District of Kansas at Fort Leavenworth. Evans sent several dispatches, pleading for more adequate protection:

It will be destruction and death to Colorado if our lines of communication are cut off, or if they are not kept so securely guarded as that freighters will not be afraid to cross the plains, especially by the Platte River, by which our subsistence comes. We are now short of provisions and but few trains are on the way. I would respectfully ask that our troops may be allowed to defend us and whip these red-skin rebels into submission at once.

...In the name of humanity, I ask that our troops now on the border of Kansas may not be taken away from us, just as they have been specially prepared to defend us by the Government and at the time of our greatest need of their services since the settlement of the country. I ask, as the best protection to our settlements and the best economy to the Government, that at least half of the regiment go up from their present place of rendezvous on the Arkansas River, which is not very far from the Indian's haunts on the Smoky Hill and Republican, and chastise them severely until they give up hostilities, and I make these requests, feeling as deep an interest in the suppression of the infernal rebellion against the Government as any other man, and also feeling as ready to send out for that purpose every available man at this most trying time in the history of our country. I do it, too, entirely independent of any political or personal considerations. If the permission for the expedition asked for is granted please telegraph me, and I will do my best to co-operate along the line of the settlements and the stage route by distributing arms to the ranchmen for their own defense under our militia regulations...

With the majority of Union troops committed to the conflict in the States, Evans knew that an Indian war could not be won. If just the Arapahos and Cheyennes declared war on the whites, Evans thought, we would die with barely a whimper. If the Kiowas, Comanches and Sioux waded in, God help every white soul from here to St. Louis. General Curtis soon thereafter wired Evans that he would do whatever he could to summon additional federal troops, but if the Indians were indeed mounting a consolidation as Evans feared, then the governor could act upon his own authority to initiate a local call for volunteers...

From its modest beginning in 1858, Denver City had become a racial powder keg on the verge of holocaust. With meager military protection, a compromised governor, and a military commander zealously carrying out his government's order to exterminate Indians, the fuse was now set. Most agreed the final match was struck on April 12, 1864, at a small ranch near Fremont's Orchard on the South Platte northeast of Denver. A rancher named Ripley reported that Cheyennes were cutting telegraph lines, stealing stock, and running settlers off their farms. Colonel Chivington ordered Lieutenant Clark Dunn from Camp Sanborn, with two companies from the Colorado First Regiment, to investigate. Dunn encountered a small band of Cheyennes on the Platte driving a herd of reportedly stolen horses and cattle north. From that point, the truth of what happened lies somewhere in-between the telling. Dunn had orders to confront all Indians, disarm them, and retrieve stolen stock in their possession. The military viewed this a simple punitive measure, but the Indians considered it an act of war. The whites claimed the Indians drew into a line of battle to defend their booty, and the Indians claimed they had found the stock and were willing to negotiate a trade. A heated argument ensued, and angry words turned to powder, arrows and lead. When the brief battle subsided, both sides retreated with several wounded or dead. A month-long search for the horses ensued, culminating in the death of Cheyenne Chief Lean Bear, who was shot from his horse by soldiers, and shot again as he lay dying on the ground.

The question of who started the initial fight at Fremont's Orchard would be forever disputed, but from the seed of anger grew reprisal, and upon reprisal bloomed black petals of vengeance. Governor Evans' nightmare had just materialized from the Cheyenne Spirit World. First blood was drawn. It ran into the Platte and spread through its spiny tributaries, eventually drifting to the Bijou Basin and into the Big Sandy – or, as it was more commonly known - *Sand Creek*.

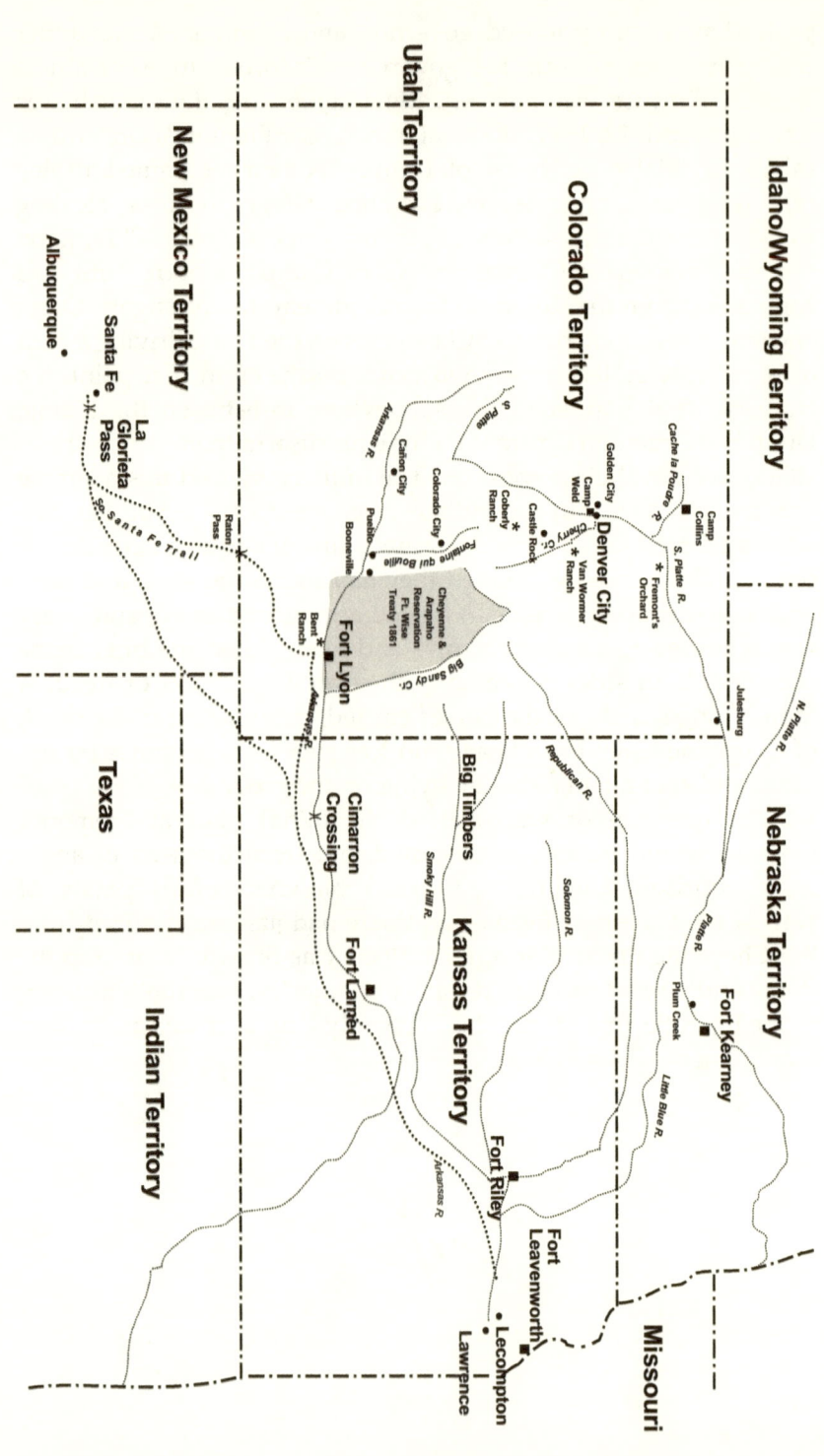

2

Governor John Evans swirled his glass before taking a healthy belt. He measured William Byers as the trail-hardened newspaper editor twenty years Evans' junior matched him ounce for ounce.

Evans was born in 1814 to Ohio farmers, a staunch conservative and religious couple who taught the young boy the values of hard work and morality. He received a medical degree from Lynn Medical College and practiced medicine in Indianapolis, where he developed revolutionary theories and procedures for treating the mentally ill. He moved to Chicago in 1847 and taught at Rush Medical College, while taking an interest in real estate and the railroads. Evans had an astute instinct for business, and he eventually changed careers, devoting all of his time to investing in Chicago land and railroads. He was instrumental in turning Chicago into a large railroad hub, and soon entered politics as a strong supporter of Abraham Lincoln. He helped found the town that bore the name Evanston in his honor, as well as spearheading the creation of Northwestern University. When Lincoln was elected President, Evans was sent to replace William Gilpin as governor of the fledgling Colorado Territory. With the burgeoning gold rush to Denver City in full swing, Lincoln relied on Evans' expertise in the railroads to blaze a trail of iron rails to Colorado.

When Evans arrived, he quickly enlisted the support of fellow Ohioan, Bill Byers, a brash young journalist with an adept skill at fashioning lies and rumors into fact. In 1859, Byers created Denver's first newspaper, the *Rocky Mountain News*, and quickly became one of the early promoters of the fool's gold rush to Cherry Creek. He now signed on to the Evans' political team, looking to cash in on the upcoming campaign for statehood.

"That's fine whiskey," Byers said, the back of his throat still tingling. "How did you lay your hands on this?"

Evans bit the tip of a cigar and spat it out with a chuckle.

"Dead men tell no tales?" Byers said.

Evans lit his cigar and fiercely puffed with a leer. He propped a leg up on his desk, sending a plume of fine dust into the air. "Damn, I'm never gonna get this goddam silt out of here."

A devastating flood on Cherry Creek a month previous had

washed much of Denver into the Platte Valley. The governor's office was soaked but spared, and remnants of the disaster permeated every wall. Bill Byers was lucky to be alive - he and his wife and children for that matter. His home and office disintegrated in the wash, and they were plucked from the raging waters by rescuers in rowboats.

Byers gazed out the window. "I can't thank you enough for putting my family up in your home."

"Forget it," Evans said, dismissing Byers with a brush of his hand. "You'd do the same for me."

"No I wouldn't," Byers smirked.

Evans laughed. "No, I guess you wouldn't, you bastard!"

"I have to remain impartial," Byers chuckled. "However, I *can* be bought, you know."

"I already own you, chum," Evans said. "You, and that Rocky Mountain rag of yours."

"In the biblical sense, I guess," Byers grinned. "But it's mine on paper – a muddy, wet paper right now."

"Eh - don't fret. You've survived fires, bandits and bullets. Hell, you'll be up and muckraking in no time."

They silently toasted with their whiskey glasses.

Outside, Denver City was wickedly alive, its streets still scarred from the flood. A spring cloudburst sent a twenty-foot wall of water down Cherry Creek, guzzling everything in its path, including a few still-lost and presumed dead souls. But, as usual, the valiant township proved once again its indestructibility. It was as if Denver itself was alive with the mysterious spirits the redskins talked about. Despite one of nature's more formidable blows, the muddy town defiantly emerged from the receding waters as if to say, "Hey, God, is that all you got?"

Byers wandered the dusty office and finally perched in a crusty leather chair across from Evans. "Can we get down to business?"

"It's your interview," Evans puffed.

"Let's start with the obvious," Byers said. "What are our chances in the election this fall?"

"Slim to none," Evans said. "Don't print that. Let's say I'm cautiously optimistic."

"Don't sell yourself short. Chivington could be elected king around these parts."

"Chivington *is* king, my friend," Evans said. "Just ask him. But being king is a mile short of senator, and Chiv hasn't mastered the fine art of politics yet. You're not printing that either, by the way."

"Understood," Byers said. "But Chiv *is* a hero around here."

"Granted - when it comes to killing rebels. But Chiv is accustomed to giving orders, not taking them. You don't mold a political career with a sword; and when it comes to bull and barter, he's as graceful as a buffalo on an icy pond. The voters don't want him drinking cocktails in Washington until every Indian and Texan is securely buried and forgotten. And as Chivington goes, so goes Yours Truly. Folks in Denver see Chiv and me locked at the hip."

"You aren't?"

"Of course," Evans said. "But I'm about as popular as a rattlesnake in this town right now. I need Chivington, and he needs me. It doesn't sit well with that titanic ego of his, but he'd probably admit it if you put a gun to his head."

Evans and Byers laughed and saluted again with their glasses.

"Alright," Byers continued, "so you don't hold much hope for us calling you Senator Evans-"

"I didn't say that. I'm just saying that statehood may not pass in this election. You gotta crawl before you walk. I've got plenty of enemies looking to send me back to Illinois, whelping with my tail between my legs. It will take time to crush them, but rest assured, they're dead men who just don't have the good sense to lie down."

"So, you're saying it's out of the question?"

Evans warily eyed Byers. "You should have been a trapper."

Byers smiled. "You don't trust me, do you?"

"I didn't get where I am by trusting newspaper men," Evans said, his mood suddenly darkening. "But I like the cut of your jib, Bill. You're a smart boy - smart enough to come out here and build your little newspaper while harpooning every tenderfoot and go-back in the territory. I admire your spunk, and I trust you're smart enough to back the right horse - especially one who could buy that *Rocky Mountain News* of yours and burn it down just for sport."

Byers tried to hold his smile, but a chill bit his anus. He *was* smart - and not about to cross this heavyweight who not only owned most of Chicago, but was also one of Abe Lincoln's closest cronies.

"Statehood will come in due time," Evans said, easing up on the young editor. "But I don't think voters are overly optimistic about self-governing in Indian country without help from Washington. And you know, they may be right. We have to get the goddam war over with, and we sure as hell can't attract substantial commerce with the mail strewn across Kansas, and every settlement between here and Leavenworth in flames. Chiv's gonna have to kill a slew of Indians first, and he won't get that done until we draw more troops from the East."

"Tall order," Byers agreed.

"You just stick with me, son," Evans said. "Denver's still a bucking mustang, but I'll tame her, you watch me. With your help, we'll get the university's charter in place before Christmas. And mark my words, in ten years time the main rail will come through here if I have to drive every damned spike myself."

"You aren't giving me much copy I haven't already printed, Governor," Byers cautiously chided.

Evans winked. "I'm sure you'll think of something."

"Look, I'm trying to get the paper back on its feet. Just throw me a bone - a scrap."

"Alright, let's talk about the Indians. Your readers are interested in them, I'd say."

"Terrified describes it better," Byers said. "Any word from Washington about your request for more military protection?"

Evans took a hard drink. "Nothing. The war is eating the States alive right now. I've wired the commissioner too many times to remember, asking - no - goddam *begging* him for more troops, but all I get is a handful of soldiers, most of whom immediately marched down to Fort Lyon and right on out to Kansas."

"How about a volunteer regiment?" Byers asked.

"Who's gonna volunteer to risk his neck against a Dog Soldier, when all we can give him is a broken-down musket and a swayback mule?"

"What about private funding? I should say a call to the citizens to put up or shut up might be in order."

"Well, it *is* your newspaper," Evans said. "But you don't see many people wandering around here flush. The farmers are barely feeding themselves, the miners can't make grub, and those goddam red thieves are cleaning out supply trains regularly."

"There are plenty of able-bodied miners out there – out of work, and able-bodied," Byers said. "If we outfit them properly, I think their empty stomachs just might override the fear of Indians."

"You got no argument from me," Evans said. "I'll raise a regiment and set Chiv to work on them in a wink if I can just procure the funds."

"Any more rumors about the rebs recruiting Indians?" Byers asked.

"The rumors are as thick as thieves," Evans said. "Sorting them out isn't easy. I've heard talk that Texas has operatives in Cheyenne territory, but I'm more concerned about North's claim that Black Kettle and Little Raven are sidling up to the Kiowas and Comanches - maybe even the goddam Sioux."

"That sidewinder has a few axes to grind, you know. I wouldn't trust that bastard."

Evans nodded in agreement. "I've never known an Indian agent who hasn't damn-near lost his hair cheating the redskins at one time or another. I *don't* trust North, but I can't afford to ignore him. The Dog Soldiers are raising hell in Kansas, and they've been spotted as far south as the Arkansas - clear over to Fort Lyon in recent months. I'd say it's damning evidence that they're riling up the Arapahos at the very least."

"What's the word from Fort Lyon?" Byers asked.

"Major Wynkoop's dispatches say it's fairly quiet down there, but the Santa Fe Trail is too inviting to Texans and Indians alike. If any more trails are cut off, we'll bleed to death. Chivington took more men from Camp Weld and headed for Lyon this morning."

"Damn," Byers said. "Camp Weld is practically empty as it is."

Evans re-lit his cigar and looked at Byers in pensive acknowledgment.

From the window, the sounds of a commotion wafted into the room. The intermittent hollering at first barely caught Evans' attention, since a drunken brawl was hardly front-page news in Denver City. But now the clamor grew frantic.

"What the hell's going on out there?" Evans said.

Byers curiously walked to the window, the sounds now mixing with an occasional woman's scream. He peered out, furrowing his brow to the afternoon sun.

"What is it?" Evans asked.

Byers' face grew pale. "What the hell - is that what I think it is?"

Evans popped up and walked to the window. It took his mind a moment to sort out what he saw. "Mother of God," he finally whispered.

Evans and Byers bolted outside...

A freight wagon stood in the city square. A pack of burly freighters unloaded a heavy wooden crate, led by a bull of a man named Johnson. Two more crates stood upright near a tree, Johnson nailing them up in a fine display. In the first crate, the ravaged corpse of Nathan Hungate was strapped in, his butchered head dangling with tufts of blood-caked hair draping over his swollen, purple eyes. His waxy body looked like a pincushion. In the crate next to him was the corpse of Hungate's young wife, Ellen, her blood-caked scalp split open, exposing her skull. Her dress was crusty and peppered with black-red holes.

The gathering crowd cried out in horror as the freighters

cracked open the third crate containing the bodies of two infant female children, their throats cut and hideously gaping. Johnson carefully nailed the crates together and secured them for all to see. Many women in the crowd screamed and turned away, some scurrying their shell shocked children from the grisly scene.

"What in God's name!" one man cried.

"God ain't got nothing to do with it!" Johnson bellowed, his drunken anger boiling over the crowd. He wielded his hammer, threatening to brain anyone who challenged him. "This is the work of those goddamn redskins the governor's been feeding!"

Johnson rounded the wagon and faced the crowd as Governor Evans and William Byers pushed through. Evans gasped when his eyes alighted on the Hungate children.

"What the hell is this!" Evans demanded.

"This is *your* goddam doing!" Johnson said.

"What happened?" another man asked.

"This here is Nate Hungate and his family - what's left of them. Nate was Ike Van Wormer's ranch foreman. We found the poor woman splayed out and raped! Her babies' throats cut! Injuns butchered them and burned Van Wormer's ranch to the ground!"

"Indians?" Evans said. "How many?"

"Had to be a pack of 'em." Johnson said. "Looked like Nate gave 'em a fight."

The crowd erupted.

"Van Wormer?" a man cried. "That's only twenty miles from here!"

"You satisfied, Governor?" Johnson railed. "You gonna give them more whiskey and coffee for this, you bastard?"

"See here, mister!" Evans barked. "You take those crates down and cover the poor souls!"

"Not on your life!" Johnson snapped his fingers, and a freighter aboard the wagon tossed him a rifle. He leveled the weapon at Evans. "They stay right here until everybody in town takes a good look at what you done by coddling them goddamn redskins!"

The crowd's anger turned on Evans. Some of the more level-headed men stepped in to keep order, but Evans knew he was whipped. He slowly backed away, protected by his few sympathizers. Johnson and his boys set up guard around the bodies, chiding everyone to stare at the corpses, but there were few takers.

Evans and Byers continued to back away from the mob as Sheriff Steck rode in.

"Amos," Evans said to Steck. "Disperse this crowd!"

Steck couldn't take his eyes off the corpses.

"Sheriff!" Evans ordered.

"Get back!" Johnson hollered. He waved his rifle, scattering people in all directions.

"Looks like that old boy's doing a pretty good job of dispersing," Steck said.

"Arrest him," Evans said. "Lock up every one of those goddam bummers!"

"You gotta be kidding," Steck said.

"John," Byers said. "Better to back off and just let them run their course."

The crowd suddenly turned its attention to a rider, who frantically rode in from the east as if the devil was on his tail.

"Indians!" he cried. "Indians!"

The rider was Bill Shortridge, who was followed by a stampede of wagons and horses carrying frightened ranchers and their families. His horse nervously danced. "Raiders!" Shortridge cried. Many took off in all directions, snatching wives, children and stock. Shortridge barely gathered another breath. "There's hundreds of injuns coming this way!"

"Are you sure?" Evans said.

"I seen a huge cloud of dust on the horizon!" Shortridge said.

"You saw Indians?" Evans asked.

"I wasn't gonna ride out and ask, if that's what you mean! We just barely had time to pack up and pull foot!"

Rifle shots rang out behind Evans. Johnson shot in the air two more times as he and the other freighters scrambled for their wagon, ordering everyone to arm themselves and run for cover.

Denver exploded in uncontrolled horror.

Shortridge reined his horse westward.

"Wait!" Evans hollered. "I need more information!"

"You got your information!" Shortridge hollered over his shoulder. "I risked my neck to warn you! I got a family to protect!"

Four or five soldiers from Camp Weld quickly rode up. They had little time to sort out the situation before Evans pounced on the soldier in charge.

"Corporal!" Evans shouted. "Round up some help!"

"Help?" the boy said. "Governor, you're looking at it!"

"Damn!" Evans spat. "Alright, wire Castle Rock and see if Colonel Chivington's been there yet!"

"Injuns cut the wires again, sir!"

"Then send a messenger!" Evans snapped. "*You* go! Find Chivington and tell him to get his ass back here, pronto!"

"Yes, sir!" The corporal spurred his horse south.

Evans turned and looked across the square. Hundreds of people, horses and wagons bounced off each other, retreating to their homes and families.

He looked up the long, wandering vein of Cherry Creek that disappeared into the oblivion of Cheyenne country. He couldn't see them, but he felt the Dog Soldiers' spirits rising from the distant cottonwoods on the horizon. "Son of a bitch," Evans whispered.

He turned and looked into Byers' frightened eyes.

"Pray to God that boy finds Chiv," Byers said.

Evans gritted his teeth. "Where's your family, Bill?" Evans said.

Byers' hands shook. "I - I don't know."

"Find them!" Evans said. "Find my wife!" He pushed off.

"Where are you going?"

"I'm gonna get some of these fools organized! Go on and find our families! I'll meet you at my home directly!"

Byers watched Evans push into the rolling ocean of humanity, and then he turned in the direction of the governor's house.

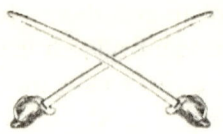

3

The moon's white light cascaded down the Smoky Hill River, turning the water into a sea of fireflies. Black Kettle and his wife, Medicine Woman Later, sat on a small rise overlooking the water. In the darkened distance, the sounds of singing lilted over the warm, dry air. Black Kettle, son of Swift Hawk Lying Down, was born in the early 1800s in the Black Hills. As a young man, Black Kettle had many dealings with the whites and was befriended at an early age by William S. Harney, a career soldier who rose to the rank of general over the years of their friendship. Indian storytellers called Black Kettle a good warrior, leading his tribe to victories over Kiowas and Utes in interim years. He lost his first wife to the Utes, and later married Medicine Woman Later, of the Wotap band of Cheyennes. According to Cheyenne tribal custom, he lived thereafter with her people. Black Kettle rose to power and became Chief of the Wotapio sometime in the 1850s.

At the time of the Fort Wise treaty, Black Kettle's influence among the Cheyennes was recognized by white leaders, which did not go unnoticed by the Union military hierarchy. In 1863, his friend and warrior chief, Lean Bear, accompanied chiefs from the Arapaho, Comanche and Caddo tribes to Washington, at the invitation of President Lincoln. They were awarded peace medals and taken on excursions intended to demonstrate the great wealth and potential the white man had to offer. In council with Lincoln, the chiefs in turn pled their case regarding the growing conflict over land with the white settlers. The president related to them the great benefit that the white man could offer them, showing them a globe and telling them of the far reaches of the world from which their pale brothers had come to spread civilization to their land.

Cheyenne Chief Black Kettle

Lincoln told them that he, too, did not want his "white children" to encroach upon Indian lands, but he, much like a father, sometimes could not always prevent his children from behaving badly. He insisted that, in deference to tribal customs, he must nonetheless reiterate that for the Indians to thrive and prosper, they must change their ancient ways and adapt to the customs of their white brethren. Lincoln assured them, if they would use their influence to bring a cessation of Indian hostilities against white settlers, he would do everything in his power to honor treaties and help them learn how to farm, cultivate their land, and subsist on their own hook.

The chiefs were encouraged to consider new concepts of trade and commerce that could ensure a brighter and more productive future for their children. Lean Bear returned with optimism and great resolve. He impressed Black Kettle with tales of his journey, and inspired the Wotap chief to lead all Cheyennes toward a lasting peace with his white brothers. But the awe inspiring journey to the East quickly paled in Lean Bear's mind, as he returned to the reality of disease and famine suffered by his people, and to the violent conflicts escalating between his young warriors and the Colorado soldiers. Soon thereafter, Lean Bear fell to a soldier's bullet, and it seemed to Black Kettle that The Great Father Lincoln's promise to take the Cheyennes by the hand and lead them to a bright new world may have died with his old friend. He knew it would take all of his wisdom and experience to reason with the raging hearts of the young warriors in light of this...

Medicine Woman Later rubbed her leathery hand along Black Kettle's arm and rested her head on his shoulder. Black Kettle tried to smile.

"You are so quiet tonight," Medicine Woman Later said.

Black Kettle silently watched the river flow.

"What is bothering you?" she asked.

"I have too many thoughts," Black Kettle said. "They make my head hurt."

"Tell me..."

Black Kettle heaved a sigh. "Buffalo. War. White men. Our people. Our grandchildren."

"*Tsis Tsis Tas*," Medicine Woman Later whispered, referring to the ancient Cheyenne word, 'The People.'

The old Cheyenne chief nodded as he listened to the war songs of young warriors that pierced the cool night air. "I wonder if those young boys care what that means."

"Can you blame them? They have not seen what we have. They do not know the world as we know it."

"Perhaps that is what makes my head hurt."

Medicine Woman Later gently touched Black Kettle's face. "You try too hard to change things that will never change."

"The earth *is* changing," Black Kettle said. "What choice do I have?"

"I do not think you will ever convince the young people that there are no choices left for them. Our world is the earth, but theirs is the sky."

"Listen to them," Black Kettle said, turning an ear to the distant singing. "A war dance - when they should be dancing for the buffalo hunt."

"Without the war dance, they do not believe they will *find* a buffalo."

Black Kettle didn't speak.

"I am right," Medicine Woman Later said. "You know I am."

"That does not mean I have to be happy about it," Black Kettle muttered.

Medicine Woman Later looked at him first with a hint of anger. Then, when his smile warmed her, she gave him a playful shove.

"You always think you know everything," Black Kettle said.

Medicine Woman Later shrugged, as if she really didn't need to answer that.

They perked as Chief White Antelope pushed through the brush. "Moke-tav-a-to? Are you out here?" The rickety old chief, once a fierce Dog Soldier warrior, groped through the darkness.

"Over here," Black Kettle called.

White Antelope muttered as he stumbled forward, his old legs but a shadow of what they once were. "What are you two doing out here in the dark?"

"We were hoping to think of something," Black Kettle said.

White Antelope mumbled again as he clumsily sat. He took a moment to gather his breath. Black Kettle and Medicine Woman Later patiently waited.

"Did I interrupt something?" White Antelope finally said.

"Yes," Black Kettle said.

White Antelope stared at the river. "I have bad news from a messenger."

Black Kettle waited.

"Hook Nose and they say maybe Medicine Man – their bands raided a white man's lodge not far from where the big rivers meet. It turned into a fight, and the white man killed two braves before the braves rubbed out the white man and his woman. They found two children – babies – and they cut their throats."

Medicine Woman Later put her hand to her mouth. Black Kettle clenched his teeth and cursed under his breath.

"They burned the white man's lodge and took all the ponies," White Antelope said.

"Hook Nose tells me he wants peace?" Black Kettle angrily said. He looked at his wife. "He tells me he controls his men - that he and the Arapahos will help make peace with the Long Knives? Then he cuts the throats of their children? That coyote!"

"They said they just wanted ponies, but the white man fought back. When he rubbed out the braves, the others shot him and made him watch them take his women and kill his babies before they took his hair."

Medicine Woman Later took Black Kettle's arm and tried to calm him, but he was inconsolable. He looked to the black sky for an answer, but the Great Spirit was in no mood for talking tonight.

White Antelope slowly pulled himself to his feet and walked away.

"White Antelope?" Black Kettle called.

The old chief stopped and looked back.

"What kind of medicine makes someone cut the throats of babies? What have we not taught *our* children?"

White Antelope stared at the ground. "They are angry. And they are not children anymore." He turned and disappeared into the brush.

Black Kettle looked across the Smoky Hill. The moonlight danced across the water...

4

Colonel John Milton Chivington sat astride a huge black stallion, his 250-pound frame as solid as the granite face that sprouted a bushy, red beard. He led a somber company of blue-clad soldiers down Denver's Ferry Street, Captain Silas Soule riding by his side. The strikingly handsome Soule stood out among the troops. He normally garnered stares from many women who rarely hid their admiration whenever he passed. But the Denver streets were deserted this morning, and Soule's mood was far from his usual playfulness that placed him among the most popular officers of the Colorado First Regiment. Soule and the boys of D Company warily scanned the boarded-up buildings and curiously watched heads and rifle barrels bob in and out of doorways. Some of the braver citizens occasionally scooted in and out like cockroaches seeking safety in shadows. The arrival of Chivington and D Company gradually lifted the black veil of terror that held Denver City hostage since the day before, when a virtual riot turned the city into a boiling cauldron.

Many townspeople emerged from homes and businesses to hail Chivington, who passed an occasional wave or salute like treasured gifts from a royal potentate. Many cheered the men, believing they certainly had beaten the Indian raid back somewhere in the Cheyenne netherworld. The soldiers spurred down Cherry Creek, stopping for a moment to curiously survey the armory, which was ransacked last night. Chivington hailed his men onward toward City Hall, abruptly stopping when they came upon a macabre sight that repulsed even these war-hardened soldiers.

A small crowd gathered around the bloody crates containing the ravaged Hungate corpses, still propped against a cottonwood tree. Some covered their mouths with

Colonel John M. Chivington

kerchiefs, and the few women who dared to look hid their noses from the stench that attracted flies and rodents from the creek. A grimy, out of work freighter busily fastened the crates together with piano wire. He bustled about like a fastidious museum curator as he collected money from those who stepped within a few feet for a more thorough inspection of the bodies. He turned a suspicious eye as Chivington and his soldiers approached.

Chivington raised his hand to signal the troops to halt in front of the ghastly display. He struck a wooden match and lit a half-smoked cigar as the freighter cautiously maneuvered between the burly colonel and the Hungate remains.

"Morning, Colonel," he said.

Chivington exhaled a cloud of smoke. "You have a name, sir?"

"Joe Cobb, at your service."

"Mr. Cobb," Chivington said. "Is there some explanation for this - spectacle?"

"It's the doings of that Indian-lover bastard Evans and his Cheyenne friends. A couple hundred redskins raided a farm a mile from here and raped the woman and babies before torturing them - right in front of her husband's poor eyes - then they stuck *him* full of holes just for fun."

"You didn't answer my question, Mr. Cobb," Chivington said. "What are *you* doing with them?"

"I bought them," Cobb said.

Chivington abruptly stopped puffing his stogie. "Pardon me?"

"Bought and paid for this morning, Colonel. Do you and your boys want a closer peek? Only one thin dime apiece."

Chivington incredulously stared at Cobb and then turned his eyes to Captain Soule, whose cynical smirk spoke volumes. "Can you believe this, Silas?" Chivington softly spoke.

"Sorry to say I can," Soule said.

"Hey, Chiv!" one of the onlookers called. "Did you get 'em?"

"Get who?" Chivington asked.

"The injuns who did this."

"We just arrived," Chivington replied. "But I assure you, the perpetrators of this despicable crime will be hunted down and killed, you have my word."

"What about the raid?" the man asked, tightly clutching his rifle.

"What raid?" Chivington asked.

"The Dog Soldiers! They was bearing down just outside of town last night!"

"Dog Soldiers?" Chivington said. "There are no Dog Soldiers within two hundred miles of here, so I'd feel much better if you'd stop waving that weapon around and go home to your family."

The small gathering exchanged disgusted glances, as if they had just been subjected to a rather distasteful joke.

"Ladies and gentlemen," Chivington continued, "I don't know precisely what transpired here, but I *will* find and punish the Indians who killed these poor souls. As for this sideshow here, this is certainly not what good Christians should do with their idle time."

A shroud of embarrassment befell the crowd, and everyone quickly retreated from Chivington's scolding glare.

"Tell your friends!" Cobb called out. He looked back up at Chivington. "You ain't too good for business, Colonel."

"Mr. Cobb, cover those bodies and take them to the undertaker."

"I can't do that," Cobb said.

"And why is that?"

"I paid a goodly sum for them. You're running for Congress, so you know it's important to help a small businessman."

Chivington measured the ratty man and pierced him with his steely eyes. "I'm not going to tell you again, sir. You will cover those bodies right now, and you will deliver them to the undertaker."

"Hey, I ain't one of your sojer boys that you can order around!" Cobb said.

"But you're a God-fearing man, are you, Mr. Cobb?" Chivington said.

"God?" Cobb chuckled. "I don't see no evidence of God 'round here."

"Uh-oh," Captain Soule said to the boys.

Chivington sighed. "Captain Soule, would you kindly review Mr. Cobb's options for him?"

Unlike Chivington, Soule was a bit playful. "Mr. Cobb, healthy agnosticism is welcomed for debate; however, in this instance you put yourself in a precarious position by defying both God *and* the colonel."

Cobb pulled his rifle. "I don't give a good god *damn* if you're the Fightin' Parson or not. I'm ready to debate whenever you are."

Instantly, Cobb found himself staring at a company of rifles pointed directly at him. His knees rattled, but he stood his ground without drawing aim. "I ain't scared of you just because you got your fancy uniforms! You ain't got no right to go murdering honest citizens!"

Chivington shook his head and tossed his cigar to the ground. He slowly dismounted and approached, towering over the little man. "Now you take caution, you little toad. I am the military commander of this district, and you will obey my order; or I swear to almighty God that you will rue the day your mother brought your sorry carcass into this world. Savvy?"

Cobb's answer didn't come fast enough. Chivington swiftly snatched the rifle from Cobb's hand and struck him in the jaw with the butt end. Cobb's head snapped back, and he hit the ground hard. Captain Soule winced and looked away, shaking his head. Many of the soldiers watched in stunned silence as Chivington stalked the injured man with sadistic glee. He viciously kicked Cobb in the groin. The little man cried out and curled into a ball, his throat gurgling a painful cry. Chivington cocked his pistol and pointed it at Cobb's forehead.

"Captain Soule!" Chivington snapped.

"Sir," Soule responded.

"I find this man in contempt of military authority. How say you?"

"Guilty as charged," Soule said.

Cobb trembled in horror as Chivington playfully drew circles on his forehead with the pistol barrel. "What do you think, Captain? Should I blow his brains up to Central City?"

"Naw," Soule said. "Too messy."

Chivington glared into Cobb's teary eyes, and for a moment, Cobb believed he would pull the trigger. Then, Chivington slowly let the hammer down and pulled his weapon away. "Okay," he nonchalantly said.

Cobb cried out. "Jesus Mary God!"

"There are easier roads to salvation, but it will do," Chivington smirked. He stepped over Cobb and tore the crates down with his bare hands, gently lowering each to the ground. He knelt before the bodies and whispered, "Heavenly Father, I commend these, your children, to your charge. May you have mercy on their souls, amen."

A few soldiers softly spoke "Amen" with Chivington, but Captain Soule stared at the ground without a word. Chivington then grabbed Cobb by the collar and pulled him up.

"Do we understand each other now, Mr. Cobb?" he said.

Cobb blindly nodded.

"Good," Chivington said. "Make no mistake, if you *ever* make a violent gesture at me or any brave soldier again, I *will* kill you, so help me God. Savvy?"

Cobb's ruptured insides belched as he managed another weak nod.

Chivington threw him to the ground. "I knew we could work this out."

He rounded Cobb's crumpled body and mounted his stallion, throwing a glance at Captain Soule. "Stick with me, Silas; I'll make a Christian out of you yet."

Soule glanced at Cobb for a moment. "I don't know, Colonel. I have high hopes of fathering a few children someday."

Chivington rolled his head back and threw a good laugh. He turned to Lieutenant Joe Cramer. "Lieutenant Cramer, take charge and deliver these poor people to the undertaker. And have someone take Mr. Cobb to a doctor - I believe he's taken ill."

"Yes, sir," Cramer said, not entirely pleased with what he had just witnessed. He dismounted and set the men to cleaning up.

"Let's find Governor Evans," Chivington said to Soule.

They reined their horses across toward Cherry Creek, crossing the bridge to McGaa Street, where they found Evans directing a small group of men in the process of cleaning up a ransacked feed store. The governor spotted Chivington and Soule and angrily raised his arms. "So, where the hell have *you* been?"

Chivington and Soule dismounted. "I was obeying orders to take D Company to Fort Lyon until a messenger intercepted us and said Denver was about to go up in flames. What in God's name went on here?"

"It's been a madhouse," Evans said.

"Obviously," Chivington said. "You want to start with those four poor dead people nailed to a tree back there?"

Evans paced. "They were butchered on Ike Van Wormer's ranch. Indians burned the place to the ground and ran off the stock. Some goddam whiskey-soaked bummers set them on display."

"You're the *governor*, John!" Chivington said. "What possessed you to allow that abomination?"

"They put a gun to my head when I tried to take them down! What the hell am I supposed to do? I didn't get any support from the sheriff, and you and your boys were off playing soldier in the wilderness!"

"Well, that hideous display has been taken care of," Chivington said.

"Thank God."

"This attack on Van Wormer's ranch. Any witnesses?"

"One of the boys who brought the bodies in claims he saw a large raiding party," Evans said. "I'd bet they were Dog Soldiers."

"Unlikely," Chivington said. "We met some trappers on the road who saw four Arapahos leading horses north from that vicinity. One of them thought he recognized Roman Nose. If it was him, he's probably heading north to the Cache La Poudre."

"Only four? Were they sure of that?" Evans asked.

"It's all they saw. I'd reckon that family was attacked by more than four redskins, but it's more likely they were a small band of Arapahos."

"Son of a bitch," Evans mumbled. "Those freighters made it sound like the entire Cheyenne Nation raided that ranch."

"Look, John, I have serious doubts that this crime was the result of the Dog Soldiers. This Roman Nose character may be responsible; or perhaps some other small band of Arapahos who roam these parts. I'll set Captain Davidson after them directly and we'll have an answer."

"I want them, Chiv," Evans said. "I want their damned heads on a platter!"

"They're as good as dead, I assure you. Good lord, those poor little babies," Chivington said.

"Those goddam Indians!" Evans bellowed. "Goddam liars! I look like the dumbest sonofabitch in the territory with my peace councils and annuities!"

"Oh, that's fine," Soule chimed in. "I imagine if them little babies were still alive, they'd be embarrassed as *hell* for you."

"Easy, Silas," Chivington said.

"Two little babies with cut throats, and all you care about is your political profile?" Soule snapped.

"I care about them!" Evans said. "And who asked your goddam opinion?"

"You don't have to ask, Governor; I'm happy to oblige!"

"Boys, boys," Chivington said. "Let's keep a Christian tongue here."

"You keep your own tongue, Chiv!" Evans barked. "I have a goddam uprising here, and what the hell support do I get from you? You're prancing down to Lyon!"

"Calm down, Governor," Chivington said.

Evans sucked a hard breath. "I *am* calm." He glared at Soule, but he got one right back.

Chivington broke the silence. "So what else went on here last night? What's this about a raid on Denver?"

Evans sighed. "Aw, some fool came into town, screaming he saw a raiding party heading this way. It was pandemonium, Chiv - people stampeding over one another – breaking into stores. They kicked in the armory and stole every weapon in sight. Last night we hunkered down, waiting for an attack that never came. Damned idiots all over town were shooting at anything that moved."

"Any casualties?"

"A few stray dogs," Evans mumbled.

Soule chuckled, and Chivington gave him a good-natured elbow in the ribs.

"Look," Evans said, "I'm in fear for my life here!" He put his hands out to emphasize the loaded six-shooter strapped to his side.

"Nice touch, Governor," Chivington joked.

"Half the town has threatened to string me up!" Evans said.

"So," Chivington said, "I gather this report of Indians storming into town was a slight exaggeration?"

Evans nodded. "I sent scouts out last night. They found some Mexicans juiced up on mescal who said they lost control of a herd of cattle. The herd was running every which-way."

"Were you able to ascertain if the cattle were friendly or hostile?" Soule asked.

"Silas," Chivington chuckled.

"Due respect, sir," Soule said, "but there ain't nothin' more frightening than a riled-up Mexican heifer!"

"I fail to see the humor in this, Captain!" Evans fumed. "In fact, I don't think anybody in this *town* is interested in your renowned shenanigans today!"

"Silas, run on back and help Cramer," Chivington said, biting his lip to keep from laughing.

"Yes sir," Soule said. He bowed to Evans. "Your Majesty..."

Soule hopped on his mount and rode away.

"You'll have to excuse Silas," Chivington said. "He's a Jayhawk wiseacre, but that Dutchman's a fine soldier."

"I don't think you appreciate the gravity of the situation," Evans said. "We're on the verge of an all-out war that could level this town, and what protection do we have? You and that smart aleck sidekick of yours heading two hundred miles south to the Arkansas!"

"I apologize that we weren't here last night, but General Curtis ordered me to Fort Lyon to hunt down rebels at Cimarron Crossing."

"That's in goddam Kansas!" Evans railed. "Washington sends me soldiers by the thimbleful, and when I get them, Curtis snatches them to cover his flank!"

"I'm doing my best to convince Curtis of our situation," Chivington said.

"Are you, Chiv? Well, your best isn't good enough! I for one don't intend to see any more women and children butchered in their homes. And I sure as hell will not allow millions in gold to stay in the dirt because of these murderous savages!"

"Alright," Chivington said. "What you need to do is calm the citizens and assure them they're safe."

"Lie to them, you mean?"

"Look around, John," Chivington calmly said. "This is Denver City. There isn't a buffalo within fifty miles of here. No buffalo - no Indians; it's as simple as that. I intend to continue to press those red devils until every last one is rotting on the prairie. By God, through starvation or for simple want of breath, they will be driven from this territory by the end of winter."

"What if the rumors of a confederation are true?" Evans asked.

"Nonsense. Those savages don't have the intelligence to consort with their enemies; besides, they'll have little time for anything but running from me. All I ask is your support."

"There's so much I can do, Chiv," Evans said. "I need you *here* - not at Fort Lyon; and I need more soldiers."

"Then use your clout, Governor," Chivington said. "Raise me a regiment of volunteers, and I'll kill every Indian from Fort Lyon to Camp Collins."

"You don't think I'm trying?" Evans said.

"Of course, John, I know you are. And now more than ever you have the opportunity to prick some ears in Washington."

"What do you mean?"

"You have two dead infants in your lap, for God's sake. Cheyennes raiding a train or stealing horses mean nothing in Washington; but two children with their throats cut cannot be ignored. Now is the time to make your play, John. Do it while the stench of those dead babies still hovers over this town..."

5

Yellow Wolf sat with Black Kettle and Dog Soldier Chief Bull Bear in the council lodge at the Cheyenne encampment on the Smoky Hill River. Old Yellow Wolf looked tired and worn, his craggy skin layered from winters too many to count on the harsh prairie. Black Kettle and Bull Bear accorded Yellow Wolf the respect the elder had earned over his seventy-plus years of life. Black Kettle and Yellow Wolf well knew that Bull Bear was a smart and tested warrior of an emerging generation of Dogmen grown wiser with age. They also knew that any attempt to secure a lasting peace with the Long Knives was impossible without the cooperation of Bull Bear's hot-blooded constituency.

Yellow Wolf's old eyes squinted in the firelight, passing from the young Dogman leader to his old friend, Black Kettle. For many years he had watched Black Kettle mature into a prominent Cheyenne leader. He never doubted his leadership skills, and now, more than ever, was no time to start. But times were changing. Bull Bear's presence at this council was evidence of the emerging Dogmen's ascent in the complicated Cheyenne hierarchy. Once a banished Cheyenne band of renegades, the Dogmen had very little political influence among Northern or Southern Cheyennes. The surly warrior clan had splintered from the Cheyenne Nation decades earlier, when Porcupine Bear, an undisciplined and malevolent warrior, killed a fellow Cheyenne in a drunken brawl - an unforgivable crime among the *Tsis Tsis Tas*. Porcupine Bear's crime resulted in his banishment from the Cheyenne tribe, but he and his followers survived, attracting other renegade warriors to the Dogman clan.

In the 1830s, the Cheyennes and Arapahos maintained a civil relationship with the white trappers and explorers. The tribes migrated throughout the middle and northern plains and rarely competed with whites for buffalo hunting ground or grasslands that fed their ponies. The whites were a source of information, weapons and valuable trade goods, and many Cheyenne and Arapaho bands carved a friendly relationship with them, but the Dogmen suspiciously kept their distance. In his prime, Yellow Wolf gained the respect and trust of the whites, but now that gold fever drew so many new whites to the territory, the old chief's successor had an entirely new white man with whom he must treat. With the overwhelming consumption of buffalo and land by thousands of white settlers descending on the prairie, the Cheyennes and Dogmen were drawing closer to confront this new enemy, which was far more formidable than any Indian competitor. The children of Porcupine Bear's generation, who held contempt for the older Cheyenne leadership's acquiescence to white dominance, were now emerging as the only hope for survival in the minds of many in the Cheyenne Nation. Consequently, Dogmen power could no longer be discounted or ignored.

Black Kettle, as much as any chief in the Cheyenne Council of Forty-four, was aware of this. He believed that Bull Bear, a dynamic and intelligent warrior chief, held the key to reconciliation between the Cheyennes and whites. The recent killing of Lean Bear, however, would make this all the more difficult. Rumors filtered back to Black Kettle that the Dogmen declared an all-out war on the whites in response to Lean Bear's death. Depending on who related the story, Lean Bear may or may not have provoked a fight, but soldiers under Chivington's command were under direct orders to hunt down Indians and kill them at every opportunity. Black Kettle's band was camped nearby when Lieutenant Eayer's soldiers shot Lean Bear, but the chief did not witness the incident. He did intervene afterwards and prevent the warriors from going after the fleeing soldiers. Lean Bear, who once met President Lincoln, always carried documents to indicate his peaceful intentions, and he clearly stated this to Black Kettle. In light of Lean Bear's death, quieting the spirit of war in the young Dogmen might be impossible now, but Black Kettle would not relent. This council, in Yellow Wolf's presence, signified Black Kettle's resolve, for Lean Bear was the brother of Chief Bull Bear...

"Do you know of this fight at the white man's lodge?" Black Kettle asked.

"Yes," Bull Bear said.

"Is there anything you can tell me about it?"

"Do you mean, am I responsible?"

"I want the truth," Black Kettle said.

Bull Bear defiantly glared at the elder chief. "I will kill a soldier who tries to kill me or my people. I will kill a soldier who burns my village or threatens our women and children. But I do not kill children, no matter their color. And I know that if any Dogman did this thing, I would have heard about it by now - *that* is the truth."

"Do you know who did it?" Yellow Wolf asked.

"I heard it was Arapahos," Bull Bear said.

"Any names?" Black Kettle said.

"Medicine Man and Hook Nose. There is talk that one of them had a quarrel over ponies. Another story is the white man provoked a fight and killed two braves for no reason. But these are only words, and I do not know what the truth is."

"Dogmen are provoking a war with the Long Knives," Black Kettle said.

"And your warriors are *not?*" Bull Bear said. "Can you look me in the eyes and tell me that none of your people have white blood on their hands?"

Black Kettle measured Bull Bear. "Rubbing out innocent children, no matter what wrong their people have done to us, is unforgivable. I do *not* condone it, no matter the circumstances."

"Nor do I!" Bull Bear snapped.

"The truth we do know is that many Dogmen are committed to war now, in reprisal for Lean Bear," Black Kettle said. "May I assume, if *any* Dogmen had a hand in killing those children, that you would tell me?"

"You have my word. Despite what you may think, I do not support the war with the whites. I gave my word to Lean Bear that I would help him seek peace, and I intend to keep it."

"I want to believe you," Black Kettle said.

"Black Kettle and Yellow Wolf, I respect you, and I never lie, for it would not only make bad blood with the Great Spirit, it would be bad medicine between you and me. I promise, if I choose to avenge my brother's murder, the individuals who killed him will pay. You will not have to ask me who is responsible - you will know. But cutting the throats of white women and children would not give Lean Bear reason to smile on me from the Spirit World. If whoever attacked that white lodge thinks he did it for Lean Bear, he did not act with my approval."

Satisfied, Black Kettle nodded. "We will say nothing more about it."

"What was done to the woman and children is wrong on its own accord," Bull Bear said, "but in the bigger world it is bad medicine for all of us. The Long Knives do not ask questions of Indians before they act, and that means everyone will pay for this. The woman and children could have been taken and used in trade."

A quiet moment passed as Black Kettle gazed on Yellow Wolf. The old chief was still wise, but the years had dulled his senses. "I want to propose a council with the whites," Black Kettle said. "I think I should try to talk to Bent."

Yellow Wolf nodded. "You can try, but Little White Man is not a big chief. And I fear it may be too late for a council now."

"Perhaps," Black Kettle said. "But we cannot remain silent about this. We will surely have a war on our hands if we do not attempt to right this wrong."

"I agree," Yellow Wolf said. "But we ignored their requests for council on many occasions of late. They may not be willing to listen to us now."

"This Evans chief sends messages demanding councils during the buffalo hunt - to locations too far for us to travel. The last time, we had so much sickness among our people that no one could travel," Black Kettle said. "Evans knew that. I cannot hide my suspicion that he organizes these councils simply to justify his own cause."

Bull Bear agreed. "So what good will it do to talk to them now?"

Black Kettle shook his head with frustration. "I am open to ideas, Bull Bear. To not attempt a council with them will surely seal a war. This is your chance to prove the Dogmen are willing to negotiate instead of attacking white lodges."

"I *told* you I am with you," Bull Bear said.

"Then offer some ideas!"

Bull Bear drew a long sigh. He shrugged. "If you want a council, I will join you."

"If I arrange it, will you support me?"

"*My* support - yes. I see no benefit in a war with the Long Knives, but it will not be easy for me to convince all of the Dogmen - not until the white soldiers stop attacking *their* camps."

Black Kettle nodded. "Yellow Wolf, can William Bent be trusted?"

"In the older times, I would say without hesitation, yes," Yellow Wolf said. "I tell you now to trust your own instincts, but Bent is a good white man. His wife is Cheyenne, and his children live with the People. Little White Man is wise, and he speaks both the white and the Cheyenne words."

"Bent has no influence over the white soldiers," Bull Bear said. "They took his trade lodge for their fort and gave him an honorary rank as payment."

"I am aware of that," Yellow Wolf indignantly said. "But he has respect of the soldiers at Fort Lyon. It is due to his influence that they once treated peaceably with us, unlike the soldiers from the big camp Denver."

"Then it is settled," Black Kettle said. "I will send messengers to apprise the other chiefs of my intentions, and to gain their approval. Bull Bear, I need your help – more from you than the other chiefs. You must convince the Dogmen to cease hostilities and respect my efforts."

"I do not make a promise I cannot keep, but I will do my best," Bull Bear said.

"No, I want more than that," Black Kettle said. "I want your word."

"You *have* my word, but understand – for me to confront the younger warriors and demand an end to their hostilities, I must offer something in return."

"What do they want?"

"They want assurance that they can live and hunt without fear of returning to their camps to find their villages burned and their families scattered in many directions."

"I cannot guarantee that until I secure a treaty with the soldiers," Black Kettle said. "As I see it, we have two choices. We treat with them peaceably and try to reach an accord; or, we go to war. We can sustain a war and scatter them for a time, but they have far too many soldiers to come from the east for us to ultimately win. With your help, we must use words first to try to make peace. I believe the soldiers will listen."

"But what about Kiowa? Comanche? Lakota? Does anyone know what they have in mind for the soldiers? We can talk peace for as long as the soldiers will listen, but if other tribes attack, no white man with any sense will stop to ask who is a good Indian, and who is bad."

"I cannot worry about them," Black Kettle said. "The other tribes fear us for good reason, and the white chiefs know that. If you and I show unity, perhaps we can offer as barter our protection of the whites from the bad tribes. The soldiers know we have numbers and strength to run every other tribe away from their lodges. They will understand that show of force."

"Which soldiers will listen?" Bull Bear said. "Yellow Wolf is right – the soldiers at Fort Lyon may talk peace, but the soldiers in the Denver camp have shown the most desire to strike us. They have as much trouble agreeing among themselves as we do."

Black Kettle nodded with a sigh.

"Give me my due, Black Kettle," Bull Bear said. "You and I are not so distant in what we want for our people."

"That may be true, but your young warriors show no respect for the Cheyenne ways."

"Because many of you resist a fight, even when the Long Knives attack for no reason."

"Then show your men the way, Bull Bear. Avoid the soldiers if you can."

Bull Bear agreed. "Many bands scattered after Lean Bear was

killed. They headed north, and it will be difficult to convince them to stay away from the white lodges up there. I do not lie to you - many of them are out for white blood. Tall Bull said he will never again trust them, and he will fight to the death."

"Then it is up to you to stop him," Black Kettle said. "I know that many Dogmen like you respect the *Tsis Tsis Tas*. If the whites bring war on our people, we must be united to fight them. But I do not want it to come to that."

"If they bring war," Bull Bear said, "it may not matter what you want..."

6

Silas Stillman Soule was born on July 26, 1838, in Bath, Maine, the third-born of Sophia and Amasa Soule. Silas adopted his father's abolitionist principles in his teens, when Amasa, an agent for the Emigrant Aid Society of Boston, moved the family to Coal Creek near Lawrence, Kansas, to aid in the struggle to establish Kansas as an anti-slavery state. Amasa, with sons William and Silas, took up with the "Jayhawkers," a self-appointed anti-slavery band of guerillas that plundered political enemies in the vicious pre-rebellion border war between Kansas "free-staters" and Missouri slave owners. The Jayhawk was a fictitious creature, deriving its name from two predatory birds that unmercifully stalk prey before devouring it, much like the free-state Jayhawkers that hunted and terrorized the despised Missouri aristocracy. In the early 1850s, 17-year-old Silas helped his father spirit slaves to freedom via the Underground Railroad, a clandestine network of escape routes and safe houses throughout the States established to assist Negro slaves flee their captors.

Irish immigrants claimed the Jayhawk was a real predatory bird from their homeland, which suited Soule, who fancied himself a feisty Irishman, although his family was of Dutch descent. Soule's adopted heritage was the result of exposure to Irish laborers with whom he worked in eastern factories before moving to Kansas. Soule's devilish sense of humor, minced with an Irish brogue he loved to mimic, usually endeared him to chance acquaintances, but sometimes provoked a fistfight – something from which any good Irishman worth his salt would never back down. In fact, Soule delighted in a lively brouhaha from time to time, for he believed it sharpened the knuckles and cleansed the blood. Soule was neither a malcontent, nor a bushwhacker, as some pro-slavery proponents suggested. Yet, he could slither under the thickest skin of pro-slavery or Union supporter alike, with his sharp tongue, cynical nature and charming wit. He would lay his life on the line for a just cause, but was no partisan lackey by any means, for the young man was wise beyond his years and able to separate the wheat from the chaff on matters of politics. The same held true of his spiritual agnosticism. On religion, he was a healthy skeptic, not overly convinced of the existence of a higher spiritual power, but not foolish enough to fly in the face of a God that he could not altogether refute. An adept gambler with cards and dice, Soule understood the rationale of hedging one's bet, or folding his hand when licked.

In a letter to his younger sister, Annie, Silas lamented:

You and Mother write for me to be a Christian and not to be too wild, etc., but the Army don't improve a fellow much in that respect. And you know I never was much of a Christian and am naturally wild, but I have seen so much of the world and are not much changed. I think there is not much danger of my spoiling – our Colonel is a Methodist Preacher, and whenever he sees me drinking, gambling, stealing, or murdering, he says, he will write to Mother or my sister Annie, so I have to go straight...

The Jayhawkers of the 1850s, led by Colonel James Montgomery, were both regarded as honorable abolitionists or renegade thieves, depending upon which side of the racial firestorm of slavery one resided. Soule, as usual, was in the thick of the fight, and in 1859 he joined a rescue party that set out to free Dr. John Doy, a fellow Jayhawker captured near Lawrence as he escorted 13 escaped slaves bound for freedom. Doy was arrested and taken back to Missouri, charged with abducting slaves from that state. Sentenced to five years in prison, Doy was soon freed in a daring rescue by Soule and a band of Jayhawkers, who managed to get Doy out while driving back a hoard of other hopeful prison escapees, whom the Jayhawkers considered true murderers and thieves worthy of just punishment.

The Jayhawker rescue of a man considered innocent by free-state sympathizers was considered an ultimate act of heroism. Soule's cunning leadership under fire led Jayhawkers to call upon him to attempt yet another rescue of John Brown, a fanatical Calvinist anti-slavery proponent. Brown led a retaliatory raid in 1856 for the bloody sack of Lawrence, resulting in the killing of five pro-slavery men near the Pottawatamie River. Brown's fanatical and violent war against slavery persisted, as he recruited likeminded followers and amassed arms with the plan to lead an invasion of southern states. In

1859, Brown's guerillas tried to capture the arsenal at Harpers Ferry, Virginia, but Brown was captured in a battle that killed or wounded most of his men. He was tried and found guilty of the crimes of treason, conspiring with slaves to rebel, and murder, and was sentenced to death by hanging. Soule and his derring-do Jayhawkers intended to rescue Brown, but the plan was aborted when Brown let it be known he would refuse rescue in favor of the martyrdom afforded by his death. Undaunted, the pesky Jayhawkers devised an elaborate plan to rescue two other Brown followers also captured at Harpers Ferry. Similar to the Doy rescue, the plan called for Soule to get himself arrested in the guise of a drunken Irish laborer, and then charm his captors into allowing him to contact Brown's men. The plan worked, and Soule found the prisoners, but to his dismay they also favored martyrdom over flight. Brown and his men were hanged, and Soule returned to Kansas a bit wiser and more cynical to the ways of God and divine providence.

After the death of his father in 1860, Soule found the rumors of Denver's gold strike far more appealing than midnight raids and a potential rifle ball in the back. He ventured to Geneva Gulch in the Colorado mountains, only to find the dream of riches as fleeting as a faint sparkle in the mud. By now the wind of war in the States blew westward, and the Colorado Territory, still under governance of Kansas, was ripe for the picking. Soule could only hope his mining claims would remain secure while the more pressing issues of war called him to service. Southerners and Northerners drew a line across the Rocky Mountains, but the Jayhawk spirit was stronger, and Union sympathizers flocked to recruiting stations. Soule enlisted in the First Regiment Colorado Infantry Volunteers as a First Lieutenant, K Company. There, his path crossed with Colonel John Chivington's, a twist of fate that would forever alter the course of both lives...

Reverend John Milton Chivington preached to the Methodists throughout the Midwest for fifteen years before coming to Denver's First Methodist Episcopal Church as a Presiding Elder in 1860. A fierce, fire-and-brimstone abolitionist, Chivington shunned a commission of Chaplain of the Colorado First Regiment when the war in the States broke out, instead demanding to fight rather than preach. In 1861, the then Major Chivington helped organize the Colorado First when the mountains of the New Mexico Territory swarmed with Texas confederates. The rebels began a meticulous campaign, capturing Albuquerque and then Santa Fe. They then set their sights on Colorado, and the Colorado First was called to help New Mexico units defend the territory. Under Colonel John Slough, Chivington joined in the first battle with the Texans at Apache Canyon in 1862, fighting to a draw. Two days later, Slough made a fateful decision to advance over the mountains at La Glorieta Pass in order to draw up behind the Texans, while Chivington took his command in a direction intended to support Slough's flank. Either by the mercy of God, as Chivington surmised, or sheer luck, Chivington's troops came upon the rebels' main baggage train and quickly pounced, sacking the enemy's entire munitions and supply line and dispatching the Texas heathens to a place in Hell reserved especially for them. The bloody battle ended when the train was burned and hundreds of Confederate horses and mules were bayoneted. Decimated and left without military sustenance, the surviving Texans fled back to the south. Chivington was celebrated as the savior of New Mexico and Colorado, leaving the hapless Colonel Slough to return to Denver and resign in Chivington's formidable shadow.

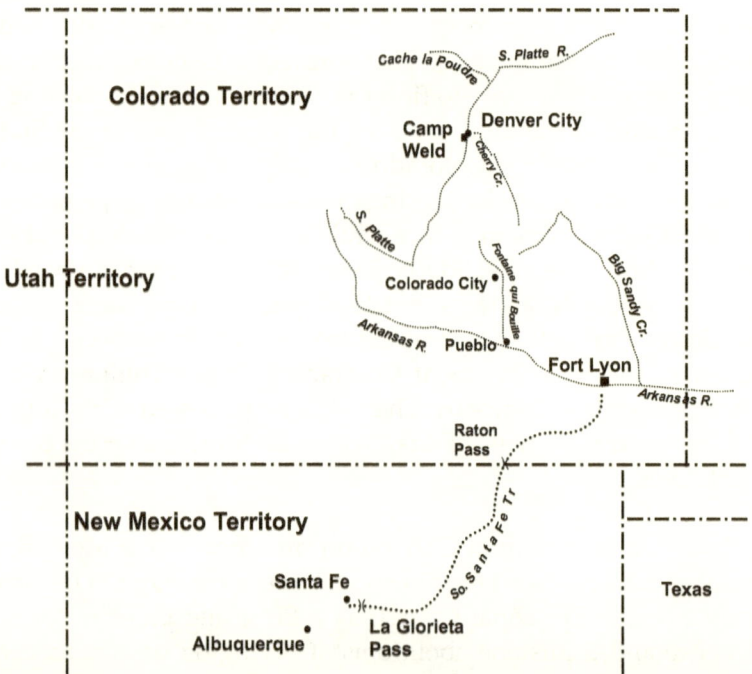

Chivington was promoted to Commanding Colonel of the Military District of Colorado, and the men who fought under his command at La Glorieta reaped the benefit of his success. Among the honored soldiers were Edward "Ned" Wynkoop, Samuel Tappan and Silas Soule, now regarded by Denverites as military royalty. But they, too, would forever be linked to the infamous spirit of the Jayhawk. With such regard, they would be honored by allies, and fiercely hated by their pro-slavery enemies.

Lurking in the vast Kansas Territory, which stretched from Missouri to the farthest reaches of the Rocky Mountains, was an enemy unconcerned with the plight of the Negro slave, the providence of white men, and the destiny of an emerging new nation. This enemy, driven by a Great Spirit unknown to Christians, had roamed the territory for centuries long before any European paleface had gazed upon it, and no land so long possessed would be willingly yielded without a fight…

Captain Soule entered Colonel Chivington's Denver office and saluted.

Colonel Chivington put the finishing touches on his mid-day meal as he passively waved. "At ease, Captain. Did you eat?"

"You might call it that," Soule said.

Chivington offered Soule a cigar as he lit one for himself. "Join me in a smoke?"

"Thanks," Soule said. "Colonel's ration is a far sight better than what I manage to find."

Chivington smiled and peered out his window. "Enjoy it, son. It's probably the last taste of civilization you'll have for awhile."

Soule puffed and curiously raised an eye.

"Ned Wynkoop's neck-deep in problems at Fort Lyon. Texas rebels are still thick at Cimarron Crossing, and the Indians are swarming the Arkansas. Ned needs you. I'm sending you and D Company, as originally planned. You'll leave at sunrise."

"You're not going with us?"

"No. There's a change coming. Lyon's going to be placed in the new Upper Arkansas District and will no longer be under my command. I have orders to remain here and see to the Indian problems in Denver."

"Due respect, Chiv, but it don't seem likely the Dog Soldiers are going to storm City Hall just yet; not unless a few hundred buffalo roll in anytime soon."

"It's a bit more complicated than that, Silas. This Hungate business turned everything on its ear. We're going to find Evans shot in the back if I don't give some reassurance to these people. I have to exert some military persuasion over the idiots masquerading as the law around here."

"There's a tall order," Soule said. "Since when has Denver ever abided any law? Hell, this place makes Bloody Kansas look like bloody England."

"General Curtis seems to think I'm not taking the Indian threat seriously. I just received a dispatch from him that implied I might be back passing a collection plate if I don't straighten matters here, pronto."

"Not a very good political platform to stand on, is it?"

Chivington stopped short. "How's that?"

Soule smiled. "The voters want to send the Fighting Parson to Congress, not the praying one."

Chivington's face soured. "Smart aleck."

Soule chuckled and puffed a good smoke ring. "So, with our departure, the ranks are stretched pretty thin at Camp Weld, aren't they?"

Chivington nodded with a sigh. "No thinner than anywhere else in this territory. With the war back east escalating every day, we're on our own here. The governor's lobbying for a volunteer regiment to reinforce Denver. When that comes to pass, I'll be preoccupied with organizing and whipping them into shape."

Soule tossed that impish grin. "No honor among thieves..."

"Amen to that," Chivington said. "But right now, I'm inclined to take any warm body with a pulse and a rifle. Redskin attacks on trains and settlements are moving this direction. I'm afraid we're in for a long hot summer with the Cheyennes."

Soule shook his head. "It's a hot bed we made for ourselves."

"Oh, don't start with me, son."

"Sir, you've always allowed me to speak my mind in private quarters. If that's changed, I'll abide."

"Nothing's changed, Silas, but that self-righteous Jayhawk attitude with regard to Indians simply doesn't wash. Old darkie has a soul to save, but a redskin has nothing salvageable. They're born of devils – they can't be rehabilitated."

"I don't know much about devils, Chiv, but one thing I do know is that if you take food from a man's family, you're gonna have a fight on your hands. The government swindled the Cheyennes and left a handful of us to fight the whole boodle."

"Look," Chivington said, "we're not here to litigate, approve or amend. Our job is to enforce, and that's what we'll do."

"We're in a fix if we expect to recruit and arm the half-baked miners around here to do our enforcing. Hell, some of them would just as soon shoot a white man as an Indian."

Chivington nodded. "I'd prefer a regiment of Ned Wynkoops and Silas Soules, but beggars can't be choosers, son."

"I may be out of line, sir, but has Washington given any thought to sitting down with Black Kettle and trying to make nice with him? Before he burns down the whole territory?"

"Silas, the red rebels don't make nice, as you put it."

"I don't know about that, sir. I'm just a lowly captain, but I've sat down with a few Indians around here, and I found once you give them a little straight talk instead of lies, they're willing to talk. Can't be any worse than what we got right now."

"No offense intended, son, but your carefree prospecting days in Colorado prior to joining the army hardly qualifies you as an expert in Indian affairs. Experience with the ragtag Arapaho beggars around Denver is a far cry from treating with a Cheyenne war chief. Governor Evans has been dilly-dallying with councils and treaties far too long. I didn't see the results of straight talk on the Hungates, did you? They're murdering children now. If they think that will force us to the table, they have another think coming."

"Sir, the Hungate raid has all the earmarks of a few murderers on their own hook. The governor's in a panic. I don't think it's too awful smart to take stock in rumors about the whole Cheyenne Nation lining up with other tribes to go on the warpath. They chew up the Utes, Kiowas and Pawnees like bitter tobacco."

"Point taken," Chivington said. "But Evans is in a tight spot here. He banked on diplomacy with the heathens, and his short-sightedness got him bit on his backside. Granted, the Hungate atrocity probably *was* committed by a few renegades, but as far as the people of Denver are concerned, it might as well have been a thousand Dog Soldiers. And the larger picture must be considered – if we don't respond to this crime swiftly and decisively, we're all but admitting we can be whipped into submission. The time to act is now, before the Cheyennes do decide to overwhelm Denver."

"Something else to consider, if you don't mind me sayin' it," Soule said. "You know yourself there's a peck of lunatic white raiders roaming this territory. The rebs might be behind some of these raids."

Chivington smiled at his brash young protege. The boy was worth his salt, but he had a tendency of pushing where a superior officer didn't care to be pushed. "Well, m'boy, we didn't sign up with any misgivings that we'd be on furlough out here, did we?"

"I signed on to defend the Union," Soule said. "The rebels are my enemy. The Indians would do us a favor by taking Texas scalps. Maybe somebody ought to offer something to persuade them to take our side."

"You may have to reevaluate your position sometime soon when one of those red heathens has a knife to *your* scalp, son. I don't recall any Dog Soldiers expressing interest in carrying the stars and stripes into Texas."

"In their position, Colonel, I'd do whatever it took to protect what I considered to be mine. If we gave them some guarantee of viable hunting grounds, instead of dumping them in the wilderness, they might be apt to defend it."

"Perhaps you'd like to resign now and strip naked and go join them? Eat dogs for supper - plunder farms and rape white women for entertainment!"

"Easy, Chiv..."

"Easy, my keister! Good Lord, Silas, didn't the sight of those horrible children lying dead with their throats cut turn your stomach?"

"Of course it did!" Soule said. "And if you set me on the trail of the perpetrators, I'll accord them similar treatment with a few added surprises. But to rile this town into thinking *every* Indian intends to butcher white babies is inviting trouble. It's something we can't afford – not if you and the governor want to go to Congress."

"Ah, here it comes – the accusations of politics and power driving motivation. I swear to the almighty, you are your father's son, God rest his soul."

"Thank you, sir," Soule said. "I couldn't be paid a higher compliment."

Chivington couldn't help but laugh. "I hope, just for my sake, he didn't spare the rod on you."

"Hell, no! He wore out several straps!"

"It's a shame it didn't take!" Chivington and Soule shared a good laugh. "Look, son, I admire your pluck, and your opinion is not without merit, but you need a bit more experience in Indian country to find out that there is only one way to tame them - and that is to show them the light of God. If they're unwilling to accept the almighty, then we must escort them to hell. It simply is not possible for Indians to obey or even understand any treaty. To kill them is the only way we will ever have peace and quiet in Colorado."

Soule tossed a heavy sigh. "Just your obedient servant, sir."

"And as long as you keep it that way, I won't have to take a strap to you myself. Now, enough personal chatter. It's time to pull rank. Major Wynkoop needs you, and I'm counting on you to lend a hand.

You will be second in command down there."

"Are we free to negotiate with the Indians if the opportunity arises?"

"I'm not opposed to taking prisoners, but no compromise. Wynkoop is under orders to kill any Indian who so much as casts a shadow near Fort Lyon, so don't get any ideas of chatting with them unless they clearly surrender as prisoners and submit to your authority. They must know that they no longer rule this territory, and anything less than full obedience to our laws will be considered an act of war. Governor Evans intends to issue a proclamation to them, leaving no room for negotiation on this point. We may be able to treat with some who are willing to lay down their arms and obey, but most will accept nothing less than death. You will accord them, savvy?"

"Yes, sir, but the Cheyennes stand above the other tribes in this territory. I've never met Black Kettle, but I hear he's a reasonable man. You'd be hard-pressed to convince me that he was behind the Hungate murders. If we could find him and hold council, we might put a stop to the trouble before it gets its head."

"That's a fine idea, Silas, but that reasonable man, as you call him, hasn't stayed put at Sand Creek as he agreed to do. If you'd like to go track him down out there in a thousand square miles of hostile Indian country to have a chat, I'll tell your dear mother you died the way you lived – with your eyes closed. Now, just be a good soldier and get yourself down to Fort Lyon."

Soule tossed a sigh. "Right..."

"And don't let me hear any rumors of your practical jokes stirring up the troops down there."

"So, with the change of districts, you're not my boss anymore?" Soule said.

Chivington smiled. "I'm *always* your boss, boy, and don't you forget it. If you have any difficulties, you know who to come to. In fact, I want you and Wynkoop to keep me abreast of all activities down there. I want to know what the Indians are doing, and who the agents are screwing. With Agent Colley and John Smith at Lyon - trading away anything that isn't nailed to the post - our boys are lucky they aren't sleeping in the dirt. I want regular reports, understood?"

"Bucking orders, aren't we?" Soule said with a grin.

"Oh, yes, Captain Wiseacre, I know *you* are very concerned with military protocol. Just like your concern with keeping the governor's feathers unruffled."

Soule laughed. "I did have him going there, didn't I?"

"Indeed you did," Chivington said. "You knucklehead – I

should have at least dressed you down for show, but I couldn't help but enjoy watching his collar get tight!"

"Politicians need a tight collar now and again," Soule said.

"I have a tight rope around *my* neck now. I need you to be my eyes down at Lyon. I've managed to rid the camp of that little weasel Anthony, and I expect Ned Wynkoop to shape the post up in short order."

"Are you and the good major speaking again?"

Chivington chuckled. "Sometimes even the best of friends spat now and again. That trigger temper of his gets him into deep water, but he's a fine soldier, and he knows who's in command. Ned steps out of line sometimes just to rankle me – much like you – but I trust him."

"I'd wager old Ned will talk his way into commanding *both* of us someday," Soule said.

"Wouldn't surprise me," Chivington said. "But, for now, you two answer to me, and I'll come down there and tie a knot into both of you if warranted. I admit I may need to have my head examined putting you together, but I trust you and Ned can run Lyon without burning it down?"

"That depends on how much whiskey Ned's managed to procure," Soule said.

Chivington winced and rubbed his eyes with his palms. "Silas, do your old Colonel a favor – just humor me here – give the almighty a try. And while you're at it, see if you can convince your chum Wynkoop that wild young men like yourselves can become wise old men, but they have to give it a hardy go. With God on your side, the going is much easier."

"I'll try to remember that, sir," Soule grinned. "I'll be sure to tell Ned."

"Do that," Chivington said. He stood and came around his desk to meet Soule with a handshake. "I have full confidence in you and Major Wynkoop. Don't let me down."

"You didn't answer my question about the whiskey," Soule said.

Chivington gave Soule a gentle slap. "Out of my sight, heathen."

Soule stood back and saluted. "Be well, sir." He walked to the door.

"Oh, Silas, by the way," Chivington said. "There's a fresh allotment of supplies at Halfway House. Pick it up on your way down."

Soule's eyes twinkled. "Ah, the luck of the Irish!" His brogue was thick and sassy.

"Luck, my keister," Chivington chuckled.

"How's that?"

"The requisitions have been there for a week. Don't let Wynkoop know I delayed delivery just so you could pick them up. I thought you might want to look in on Mr. Coberly and his family – his eldest daughter, in particular."

Soule smiled. "Thanks, Chiv. I appreciate it."

"How she was bitten by the love bug, thanks to a smart aleck Union captain under my command, I'll never know."

"Nor will I, but I ain't about to question it."

"Don't ever question the love of a good woman," Chivington said.

"I don't know," Soule said, "I had a mind to marry a wealthy girl from the east who could retire me while I still have my looks. Miss Coberly has the heart of an angel, and she's the finest sight my eyes have ever seen, but I don't think there are any kings or queens in her family. Being naturally lazy, I was hoping not to have to work after I left the service."

"Being naturally lazy is just the reason why Miss Coberly is perfect for you, Captain. The devil resides in the idle soul."

"Idle Soule, that's me," Soule said with a grin.

"Get out of here."

Soule saluted. "So long, Colonel."

"Godspeed, Silas. I promised your dear mother I would someday return her boy in a breathing condition. You keep your eyes skinned and your head down."

"Believe me, I have no intention of disappointing either one of you."

"See to it. And remember, I want to know what goes on at Lyon...everything..."

D Company rode for a good portion of the day, traversing the rolling hills of Castle Rock and approaching Huntsville by afternoon. Activity in the area had increased since the Hungate murders, as citizens rallied to help construction of a military fort to protect settlers and the mail line. Originally dubbed "Oakes Folly" when D.C. Oakes first began fortifying his business interests two years earlier, the new Fort Lincoln was now under earnest construction in light of frequent Kiowa raids in the vicinity.

James and Sarah Coberly packed up and left Iowa for the Pike's Peak Region in 1858, joining a westbound wagon train with their children, William, Joseph, Hersa, and Mattie. They settled in Spring Creek Valley west of Huntsville, where Spring Creek dumps into West Plum Creek. Coberly claimed a homestead on a fine piece of land and built two cabins with the help of D.C. Oakes, one of the region's early promoters and owner of the local lumber mill. Coberly was an experienced farmer and cattleman, who immediately went to work raising crops and stock. Bill and Joe were adept cowboys and hunters, and Hersa and Mattie were both excellent riders who helped build the Coberly ranch into a profitable enterprise in short order.

Sarah and the girls cooked meals for the numerous settlers passing through, and before long the Coberly ranch became a stage stop and boarding house for government and military officials traveling between the territorial capital of Golden City and Colorado City. Coberly's also served as a sutler for distribution of provisions to troops traversing the Cherokee Trail between the Arkansas and Platte rivers. Known throughout the eastern Colorado Territory as "Halfway House," or by its more appropriate name, the "Pretty Women Ranch," Coberly's hosted civic meetings and social gatherings for the citizens of Spring Creek Valley.

The elder Coberly and young Joe were accomplished fiddlers who played at square dances, where young bucks patiently waited in line for a chance to dance with Hersa and Mattie. Captain Soule first laid eyes on Hersa at one such event, and the beautiful 19-year-old immediately stole his heart. Hersa was the crown jewel of the Coberly clan, a bright and lovely young lady whose sweet disposition captivated Soule. His happy-go-lucky mien was a perfect match for Hersa, who was blessed with the devilish sense of humor of her father. It was a mutual infatuation from the beginning, and a loving courtship followed, but the misfortunes of circumstance kept Hersa and Silas apart for long and lonely periods. Whenever the good captain had the opportunity, he'd find a reason to pass through Spring Creek Valley, sometimes detouring on his own at the risk of being counted absent from his duties at Camp Weld...

Hersa wasted little time when she looked out the kitchen window and saw D Company ride over the rise. It was a prayer answered, for 'Silie' had dominated her thoughts all day. As her mother and Mattie cooed and laughed, Hersa tossed her apron and relinquished the day's chores to the girls, first checking her hair in the looking glass before bolting out the door. She didn't have to wait to make sure this was indeed D Company riding in. She knew. Of course, it might have been more romantic had a divine premonition beckoned her, but the plain fact was that Silas was easy to spot. Not to be outdone by his old pal Ned Wynkoop's taste in whimsical apparel, Soule abandoned mundane military issue and instead wore a beautiful white hat that he recently won in a Denver poker game.

Hersa's heart leapt when she saw her dashing captain, the most loving and honorable young man she had ever met – the man she was
determined to marry. Soule tossed a wave, and Hersa returned it,
running down the porch steps
and out to the gate.

As D Company cantered in,
Lieutenant Cramer, at Soule's
side, tossed a heavy sigh. "How
come captains get the best
girls?"

"Rank has its privilege, Joe,"
Soule said. "Do something stupid, and you can be a captain,
too." All the boys within earshot
had a good chuckle.

"Did Hersa put in a good
word for me with Mattie?"
Cramer asked.

"She did, but you have
some pretty hard competition
here. And don't forget, Mattie's

Hersa Coberly

just sixteen – still young enough to draw buckshot your direction
from big Jim and the boys."

"Gentlemen!" Cramer called. "You heard the captain. Hands off
Miss Mattie! I'll stand guard of her, sir..."

The boys shouted Cramer down with a chorus of catcalls.

"Nice try, Joe," Soule said.

The company rode up to the gate. "Dismount, gentlemen!"
Soule called. "Miss Coberly, I have some hungry heroes here, can
we get some hay? Oh, and my men wouldn't mind some grub, too!"

Hersa's laugh was catching, and it always tickled the boys.
"Heroes are always welcome here, Captain," she said. "You fellows
are just in time, too. Look down the road – I think that's the mail boy
coming!"

As if on cue, Soule followed up, "That don't look like no mail
boy to me, Miss Coberly."

"Well," Hersa said with a wry smile, "with all you handsome
soldiers here, let's hope he ain't a female boy!" She let out that infec-
tious laugh again.

The boys of D Company howled. A pretty girl around these
parts was as rare as icicles in July. A proper lady delivering one-lin-
ers like a saloon girl on top of that brought nothing but delight. Joe
Cramer called a happy hello to Hersa as they dismounted. "Miss

Hersa," Cramer said, "it's good to see you again!"

"Hello, Joe," Hersa said.

Soule removed his hat. "I'll second that opinion. You look like a queen fit for a king." He began to dismount, but he caught his foot in a stirrup and tumbled into the dust, drawing wild laughter and applause.

"Hail to the King!" Cramer yelled.

Hersa covered a giggle as the boys led their mounts to the feed yard. "Very graceful, Silie!" she laughed.

Soule dusted himself off. "I wish you hadn't seen that."

Hersa walked up and gently wiped the grit from his face. Soule tossed a look to see that the men were tending their own business now. He smiled and took her hand. "I hope you still love me; otherwise, I just wasted thirty-two days of heartache."

"Thirty-four days," Hersa said with a sad smile. They suddenly fell into each other with a warm embrace...

The early summer night was warm, and the vast Colorado sky yielded a million twinkling stars. Soule and Hersa sat in rocking chairs on the front porch, their hands tightly entwined. They both laughed uncontrollably, for Soule had just spent the better part of five minutes telling a tedious joke that just ended with a resounding bang. Soule had so amused himself in the telling that tears welled in his eyes, and Hersa now held her sides to keep them from splitting.

"Silie," Hersa cried, "that is the *dumbest* thing I ever heard!"

"Then why are you laughing?"

"It's funny!"

She laughed so loudly that some of the boys in the camp outside the gates curiously stopped and looked up at the porch. Big Jim and Joe played their fiddles, and a dance continued among neighbors and the soldiers by a large campfire.

Silas and Hersa finally retrieved some sense of dignity.

"You should act on the stage," Hersa giggled. "Oh, my sides hurt."

Soule lit his briarwood pipe - a gift from his daddy. Beyond the gates, the firelight of Company D's encampment bathed the ranch in a security rarely enjoyed in this part of the territory. Laughter arose from the camp, as the soldiers and neighbors sang, played cards, and enjoyed libations provided by Coberly. Big Jim sauntered up to the porch, fiddle in one hand and a jug in the other.

"Don't get up, son," Coberly said. "You look too comfortable there. Here, wet your whistle." He handed Soule the jug and sat on the porch swing, lighting a cigar.

"Much obliged," Soule said. He took a drink and nearly choked.

Coberly laughed. "Sorry. Homemade stuff. It's hard to get anything with a label on it these days."

"It's fine," Soule barely whispered. He winced and convulsed, to the great amusement of Hersa and big Jim.

"What in the world have you two been laughing at?" Coberly said.

"You missed a good one, Papa," Hersa said. "Silie's in rare form tonight."

"Oh no. Not another infamous Soule tale," Coberly said.

"Oh, yes sir," Soule said with a thick Irish brogue. "You see, it all began one fine evening – not unlike the one we're enjoying tonight - when a fine young Irish suitor by the name of Lucky McFluckley went a-calling on the local fat woman of ill repute – by the name of Hora Mc–"

"Stop!" Hersa cried. "I can't take another one!"

"Wait!" Coberly said. "I wanna hear this!"

"No!" Hersa snatched Soule's pipe and covered his mouth.

"Alright," Coberly conceded, "but you owe me one later."

"Give me my mouth back, girl," Soule mumbled.

Hersa giggled and poked Soule's pipe back in his mouth. "Now, stop with the tall tales for awhile."

Soule resumed his smoke. "I can't thank you enough for that fine meal, Mr. Coberly. It was mighty generous of you to provide those steaks for the boys, too."

"My pleasure, son."

"I don't think we'll see the likes of such a fine supper for months to come. We're much obliged to you, sir."

"Nothin's too good for the boys of the First, Silas. I'm just trying to figure a way to bribe you into staying here permanently. I can't remember when's the last time we sat out here come candlelight and felt safe."

"Well, you wouldn't have to bribe *me* to stay, sir." Soule gave Hersa a wink. "And if you keep the boys fed on steaks and green beans, you'll have to shoot 'em to get rid of 'em. Unfortunately, we ain't the ones to bribe. The governor's the expert on those matters."

Coberly laughed. "Governor – ha! That old peckerwood."

"Papa," Hersa scolded.

"Well, hell, he is a peckerwood. Might as well call him one."

"Oh, Papa, everybody's a peckerwood to you."

"Watch your language, girl. And not everybody – just politicians. Right, Sile?"

"Can't argue with you, sir."

"So, how's your momma doing?" Coberly asked.

"She's well, thanks," Soule said. "She and my sisters are still in Maine."

The town of Lawrence was attacked by Confederate raiders in late August the previous year, led by William Quantrill, a gambler, thief and murderer by trade. Town Marshal, William Lloyd Garrison Soule, Silas' older brother, valiantly led a defense, but some 180 men were executed, and virtually every home was either ransacked or burned to the ground. "I don't really know if Mother's ever gonna go back to Kansas in light of what happened."

"Can't say I blame her," Coberly said. "She must have suffered a serious fright. How's the house?"

"My brother Wil fixed it up, but we had some serious damage and loss. I sent my mother some money, but I ain't got much to live on myself. I wanted to transfer to Kansas and go after some of those Missourians. They're worse than Indians. I hope the Kansas boys will desolate Missouri and not leave a house standing."

"Those damn bastards," Coberly said.

"Papa," Hersa said.

"Well, that's what they are. They ransack Lawrence, putting good people from their homes for what? So's they can break the Union? Those Missouri pukes will have another think comin' when the Jayhawkers get ahold of them. Shoot 'em all in the head and string those pro-slavers up till they're done squirmin', that's what they ought to do."

"Papa!"

Soule laughed, but it turned to a choke when he took another drink.

"You ok, son?"

Soule took a breath. "I don't think I've ever drank anything like this. What is it?"

"You don't want to know."

Hersa snatched the jug from Soule. "You're gonna kill him, Papa."

"Not if he drinks slow," Coberly said.

Soule reached for the jug. "I think I'm getting the hang of it. Let me try just a little more..."

Hersa slapped Soule's hand and set the jug out of reach. "You've both had enough."

Coberly laughed. "Silas, let me give you a little advice about Coberly women. They're in charge. You ain't got nothing to say about it, neither."

Silas shrugged. "I've been taking orders from my mother and

two sisters for twenty-five years, now. I reckon I'm prepared."

"So, tell me, son, you got any advice for me regarding the Indians?" Coberly said.

Soule looked at Hersa. "Take a mighty caution, sir. I wish I had better news, but I'm afraid things will get worse before they get better. We're in for some hard fights with them."

Coberly blew cigar smoke in frustration. "Breaks my heart what's happening to this country. Look at this beautiful night – so warm, and ain't a drop of stickiness. Ain't a spot on God's earth any finer than Colorado."

Soule nodded. "Indians think so, too."

"I guess I just ain't smart enough to understand how things got so bad. Old Little Raven, him and me was friends going on five years. There was a time around here when we conducted business with the whole lot, traded, shook hands and then they went along their way without any trouble. Hell, they'd chase the Utes and Kioways off so we could all get along. Then, all a-sudden, we got a sea of greedy bastards coming in and grabbing up a thousand acres at a time."

"Colorado's a mighty big asset to the boys with deep pockets, sir," Soule said.

"I reckon. I figure a man's got a right to chase a dream, so long as he don't trample on somebody else's. You know, I don't cotton to them killing folks – but they're all puckered up over what the government's done to them. We're the ones left holdin' the bag."

"Well, I ain't a politician. I'm a soldier, and I got a duty to protect this territory."

"I know," Coberly said. "It's just a damn shame. They was here a long time before us, and hell, at first glance, I thought I'd walked in on the devil himself when I seen the way they live - fighting and stealing and scalping one another. But they behave the only way they know how, and what nobody seems to realize is they's damn smart people. They can learn a different way of living, but it ain't gonna happen overnight."

Soule agreed. "It's just their bad luck to have no choice in the matter. They either have to learn directly, or they're going to be killed. Colonel Chivington's an impatient man."

"Eh, Chivington," Coberly said. "There's another big fat peckerwood."

A smile curled Soule's lips. "Mr. Coberly, you're a hard man to please."

"Amen," Hersa said.

"Oh, Chivington was a hell of a soldier once, I'll credit him that," Coberly said. "But he should have *stayed* a soldier."

"How's that?" Soule said.

"Son, when you rode with Chiv at Glorieta, he was a first-rate commander. His tactics were second to none. But he came back a changed man, once Denver wrapped him in glory. What he done was trade his soul for gold and politics. Nowadays he spends all his time stumping for that Congress seat, using his military clout and garnering votes with every Indian he kills. These days, his word ain't worth a fart in a whirlwind."

"Papa!"

"Well it ain't!"

"I don't know, sir," Soule said. "I agree that Chiv has his eye on Congress. Don't be surprised if he's got even bigger game to stalk – maybe the presidency. But we got an Indian problem here that's more than anybody bargained for. Sure, Little Raven is a good man – a lot of 'em are - but some ain't nothing but hard killers. It ain't easy separating the good from the bad when they move in and out of the shadows like they do. I lost one of my men and had two wounded in a fight just last week – all because my boys hesitated."

"I know...I know," Coberly said. "It just taxes a man when he ain't got no say in matters. I don't reckon nobody's gonna ask me, neither."

Hersa broke the conversation with a heavy sigh. Her eyes rolled, and Coberly suddenly stood. "Yes, ma'am," he said.

"What?" Soule asked.

"My daughter just informed me that politics do not properly mix with matters of a woman's heart," Coberly said. "I'll just wander on back to the fire and let you two be alone." He kissed Hersa on the cheek.

"Goodnight, Papa."

"Goodnight, Mr. Coberly."

Hersa scooted her chair next to Soule's, and she wrapped her arm in his.

"Your father's a good man," Soule said. "He's a lot like my daddy was."

"He talks about you all the time," Hersa said. "He's proud of you."

Soule puffed and polished his fingernails. "After all, what's not to like?"

Hersa slapped his arm. "So modest, Captain."

"It's hard to be modest when you're in love with an angel."

They shared a long kiss.

"Do you *have* to go tomorrow?" Hersa asked. "I miss you so much."

Soule touched her lovely cheek. "I don't think you'll ever know how much I miss you, too, darlin'. But I have to go."

Hersa put her head on his shoulder, blinking a tear. "I wish things were different."

"They will be," Soule said. "I promise."

"When will you be back?"

"I don't know. I don't have any control over that. But the first chance I get, I promise I'll come see you."

They would hold each other for several more hours, talking of things that could be, and dreaming of a time when the world might hold limitless fortune. At a very late hour, they shared one last kiss, and Soule sadly returned to the camp. Before leaving, he held her gaze for a moment.

"I loved you, even before I knew you," he told her. "I love you more than life itself... Now and forever..."

Hersa awoke at the first light of dawn, quickly moving to her bedroom window. Her heart dropped when she looked out, for the soldiers were gone...

Camp Fillmore
Boone, Colorado Territory
Dear Mother,

I know you are worrying about me because I have not written for so long, but I am getting out of the notion of writing and have been busy for the last month fixing up my papers and just as I got them fixed my office was swept away by the flood and I lost everything I had – papers, letters, clothing, and all – wasn't I in luck? Blessed are the poor for they have nothing to lose!

I am now in command of my Company, a hundred brave warriors, ain't I proud? I am on my way to Fort Lyon. I do not know where I shall go from there. I may go fight Indians; if I do I will write first so you can be worrying while I am gone. I received a letter from Em a short time ago; she told me that you was going to stay awhile in Bangor. I would send you some money by this mail but I am afraid to as the Indians are bad along the road and may take the coach. I will send some the first safe opportunity...

I don't know what more to write, there is nothing I know of that would interest you. I still suffer with pleasure. Give my love to all the folks and when you write let me know how you and the girls get along, if you need money, etc.

I have some claims in the mountains that I could have sold a few weeks ago for ten thousand dollars if I had been there, but if they are worth anything they are worth $50,000. I think I can sell them for that much in a *year from now if they work the mines as they have begun to and they pay as well. Lewis Tappan sold some he had for $500,000 – just a half million dollars – that was pretty good wasn't it? Who knows but we are rich! I own fifty mining claims and there ought to be some good ones and if one of them is good it is a fortune for any one. I will send you my photograph when I write again.*

From your Sonny,
Sile

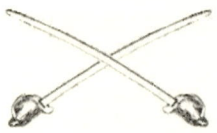

7

Edward Wanshaer Wynkoop was born in Philadelphia on June 19, 1836, the youngest of eight children. The great-grandson of Continental Congress member, Judge Henry Wynkoop, Ned came from a family of noble ancestry, many of his predecessors having honorably served in military or public service. His grandfather was a physician, and his father John, who died when Ned was an infant, ran a successful iron smelting business in Pennsylvania. Raised in a family of relative wealth and honor, Ned was educated in the finer schools of Pennsylvania, an intelligent young man blessed with an impressive vocabulary, and a quick study in the art of political discourse and diplomacy. In his childhood, he was a peacemaker in the face of childish skirmishes, and yet he administered more than a few black eyes to bullies uninterested in civil negotiation.

At the age of twenty, the ambitious Wynkoop saw little opportunity by trailing three substantially older brothers in the family business. He opted to venture west with his fourth brother, George, to Lecompton, Kansas Territory, in the employ of their sister Emily's husband, General William Brindle, an agent for the United States Land Office. There, Ned and George were tutored in the sale of former Indian reserves, eagerly honing their skills in the business of land trade. Brindle was a strict Calvinist Democrat, whose beliefs were firmly entrenched in the divine right of slavery, leading to certain philosophical conflicts with Ned, who was generally ambivalent to the fiery power struggle between Jayhawkers and pro-slavery advocates. Although his sympathies leaned toward the free-soilers, Ned believed that Kansas, and the entire country for that matter, was better served if the issue were resolved nonviolently.

Wynkoop, a tall and athletic man, had a short temper and a quick wit, a volatile combination in a place where

Major Edward W. Wynkoop

mere insult often resulted in bloodshed, but his innate ability to resolve conflicts with resolute diplomacy was a far cry better than resorting to powder and lead. Publicly, he remained neutral on the subject of abolition during his years in Bleeding Kansas. While maintaining a civil rapport with advocates on both sides, Wynkoop wisely became proficient with his fists and firearms as a matter of necessity in those dangerous days. He wouldn't meet Silas Soule until later, when he entered service of the Colorado First, but the brash young Wynkoop was well aware of Soule and the Doy Gang, or the "Immortal Ten," as they were known in legend. Although Wynkoop never officially took up with the Jayhawker cause, he shared a kindred spirit with Soule.

In 1857, President Buchanan appointed James Denver to the office of Kansas Territorial Governor, Denver's primary mission to end the conflict between free-soilers and pro-slavery advocates that violently split Bleeding Kansas. Like Wynkoop, the elder Denver was a well-liked and highly skilled negotiator who formerly served as Commissioner of Indian Affairs under President Franklin Pierce. Wynkoop wasted little time seizing the opportunity to introduce himself to Denver, and he became an advocate for the new administration. At the time of Denver's appointment to the Kansas Territory, news of the gold discovery in the Pike's Peak Region swept through Lecompton like a raging wildfire. Wynkoop, not immune to the ravages of gold fever, lobbied Denver for an expedition to the Pike's Peak Region, offering his excellent negotiation skills and experience in land trade as a valuable tool for securing commercial interest in the Rocky Mountain gold fields. A partnership between Denver, Wynkoop, Brindle and other prominent Kansas businessmen was struck, and Wynkoop was selected to journey west to establish a town company on Cherry Creek. Wynkoop was appointed Sheriff of Arapaho County, at that time a virtually mythical moniker assigned to the western hinterlands of Kansas, and he set out for Colorado in September 1858 with a party of 16 unofficial 'Officials' charged with securing legal authority over other prospective land owners. The Lecompton party followed the Santa Fe Trail on the Arkansas, encountering hundreds of Indians along the route, among them the Cheyenne, Arapaho, Comanche, Kaw and Kiowa, who acted with a guarded but friendly disposition. At that time, the Indians were yet unaware of the gold lust that would soon rage over their sacred hunting grounds.

In November, the Lecompton Party reached the confluence of the Fontaine qui Bouille and Arkansas rivers at El Pueblo, where they determined to camp, rather than make a treacherous winter march north over Palmer Ridge. Soon thereafter, a second party of Jayhawk partners from Lawrence, led by William Larimer, the newly appointed Arapaho County Treasurer, reached El Pueblo. Larimer urged Wynkoop's party to forge ahead with them to Cherry Creek due to rumors that independent prospectors might gobble up the region before spring. The combined parties braved a winter march over the pass, and arrived at Cherry Creek later that same month, where they discovered Charles Nichols and William McGaa warily guarding a claim they had staked out and named 'St. Charles.' McGaa's partners had just departed for Lecompton, for the purpose of obtaining a town charter from the Kansas State Legislature, and Nichols and McGaa drew a line in the sand when Wynkoop and Larimer's boys moved in. A rival band of Georgians, led by William Green Russell, had already staked the claim of Auraria across the creek, and the greedy prospectors of both claims had no interest in sharing their booty with the Kansas intruders. Skirmishes broke out like bickering sparrows fighting over tiny crumbs, but the ragtag Colorado "Pike's Peakers" were no match for the strong-armed Jayhawkers of Bleeding Kansas. Larimer "negotiated" a deal with Nichols and McGaa, who under threat of hanging agreed to add their new Kansas partners to the original St. Charles incorporation.

Over the objections of McGaa, the Jayhawkers suggested that the new town be renamed Denver City. A vote was held, and McGaa, either by proper vote or at gunpoint, was overruled, and the race was now on to add the Jayhawkers' names to the new town charter. With McGaa's partners already en route to Kansas, Wynkoop and A. B. Steinberger volunteered to immediately march for Lecompton, this time taking the South Platte route through wicked winter weather. Along the perilous 700-mile journey, Wynkoop and Steinberger survived frostbite, accidents and exhaustion, encountering numerous Indians, bandits, and none other than the infamous Charles "Big Phil the Cannibal" Gardner, an escaped prisoner from Philadelphia who had taken refuge with an Arapaho clan. Legend held that the half-man-half-ape Big Phil was once employed by General Harney to deliver army dispatches to Fort Laramie. Big Phil embarked on his mission with an Indian scout, but they soon became lost in a raging blizzard. For several weeks, Big Phil and his red companion wandered the frozen wilderness without adequate provisions. Just when the two were about to be given up for dead, Big Phil, as the story went, finally arrived at Fort Laramie alone, well fed and carrying the last edible remnants of his Indian companion. Big Phil, who years later almost provoked

Arapaho Chief Left Hand into burning down Denver City, would continue to live with the Arapahos for a decade, known to his adopted clan as "Big Mouth."

Beaten, hungry, half frozen, but fortunately not consumed by Big Phil, Wynkoop and Steinberger survived their journey to Lecompton, only to discover that the original St. Charles partners had already arrived and introduced their charter proposal to the Legislature. Undaunted, Wynkoop lobbied Governor Denver to use his influence to get his name, with the partners of the Lecompton/Lawrence parties, added to the St. Charles charter proposal. Denver successfully intervened, and the bill subsequently passed. Wynkoop spent the rest of the winter recovering in Lecompton, foolishly spreading exaggerated rumors of the Pike's Peak Gold Rush to everyone he encountered. He printed blank stock certificates for the new Denver town charter, and in the spring the cocky young entrepreneur charged citizens $100 dollars each to join his large wagon train headed back to the supposed Promised Land.

Wynkoop returned to find that William Larimer had ignited a real estate boom on both sides of Cherry Creek, which were now lined with cabins and businesses. Although the new city charter bore the name St. Charles, the Jayhawkers, with no legal precedence, ruled that the name Denver City would now and forever remain. If any former St. Charles or Auraria settlers disagreed, their objections were never voiced within earshot of a Jayhawker, and eventually all of the townships up and down both Cherry Creek and the South Platte would merge with Denver City. The Kansas boys, however, for a time suffered the wrath of many unsuccessful prospectors who accused them of fabricating the Pike's Peak Gold Rush just to line their own pockets. On several occasions after his return to Denver, the gilded-tongued Wynkoop talked his way out of a sound beating or possible lynching.

Wynkoop's former honorary title of Sheriff held no significance after Denver's incorporation, leaving him free to head for the mountains to stake a placer mining claim on Clear Creek, where richer veins of gold were more likely to be found. He courted Louisa Brown Wakely, the stepdaughter of an English photographer who recently moved his family to the territory. Wynkoop worked his claim with modest success, later selling his interest at the outbreak of war. During their mining days, Ned and Louisa spent idle time participating in philanthropic efforts and performing in the theater. Louisa was an accomplished actress, and Ned took a shine to the craft himself, once stealing scenes in a play with his hilarious portrayal of a drunkard. He laughingly credited the accuracy of his portrayal to working as a bartender during times when mining yields were thin.

Although Louisa had refined and rehabilitated Wynkoop to a degree, he remained a reckless adventurer, joining several militias charged with keeping the peace among the hoards of cantankerous prospectors flooding into town. He always seemed to be nearby whenever a fistfight, duel, or all-out gun battle broke out on the crude and uncivilized streets of Denver, and he never backed down from his duties to arrest, try and hang any 'bummers' that ran afoul of the law. On one occasion, Wynkoop himself accepted a challenge to a duel over a dispute with Denver's postmaster, but his adversary, after hearing about Wynkoop's deadly proficiency with a pistol, relented and apologized at the moment of truth. Wynkoop's flair for dramatics was evident upon his enlistment as a Second Lieutenant in the Colorado First Cavalry in 1861. Unsatisfied with the simple uniform of the First, he had Louisa embroider bold red designs on his uniform to show defiance of his enemy, much in the same spirit as the Indians who painted themselves for battle. He married Louisa soon after his promotion to captain, and he proudly displayed his embellished attire in a photograph taken by his new father-in-law, George Wakely, prior to participating in a heroic battle that would catapult him to fame.

Wynkoop rode with the Colorado First to La Glorieta, under the command of Colonel Slough and Major Chivington. For his bravery in that battle, he was promoted to major, replacing Chivington, who took command of the Denver Military District. Wynkoop spent a year of duty commanding his company in defense of Santa Fe, where he and Louisa celebrated the birth of their first son, Edward Estill Wynkoop. Wynkoop and his command returned to Denver with their families in 1863, receiving a grand welcome from a grateful citizenry that bestowed gifts and adoration upon the major. Wynkoop delivered an emotional speech to the adoring crowd, declaring his devotion to the Union and, more specifically, the newly established Colorado Territory.

Wynkoop took command of Camp Weld, ordered to protect Denver City from the growing threat of Indian reprisals, which by now had reached a fevered pitch in Kansas. He spent endless weeks hunting Ute Indian war parties along the Platte with little success. During these fruitless missions, Wynkoop learned a valuable lesson about the cunning intelligence of the Indians, who moved in utter silence and eluded capture when escape seemed impossible. By 1864, the raging war in the States required Chivington to send more troops away from Denver, and Wynkoop was given command of

Fort Lyon that spring. Wynkoop deemed it no longer safe for Louisa to accompany him, for Lyon was a desolate hellhole surrounded by hostile Indians and Confederate bandits. She stayed in Denver with their son and newborn daughter, Emily, and Wynkoop ventured southeast to the Arkansas. He found Fort Lyon in a dilapidated condition, occupied by troops ravaged by scurvy and demoralized by the arrogance of its former commander, Major Scott Anthony.

Wynkoop dispatched an urgent message to Colonel Chivington, requesting reinforcements and an experienced officer to serve as his second in command. He made no idle request on who specifically would fit the bill. He wanted an officer of tested courage - one he could trust with the lives of his men and the harassed settlers on the Arkansas. He demanded his friend and fellow warrior, Captain Silas Soule...

Fort Lyon sat on the far outskirts of the Colorado Territory, 240 miles southeast and a nine-day trip from Denver City. The fort was built on the north bank of the Arkansas River in 1860, but its roots took earlier from the seeds sown by William Bent, a St. Louis businessman who built a trading post on the Arkansas with his three brothers in the 1830s. Bent, dubbed "Little White Man" by Southern Cheyenne Principal Chief Yellow Wolf, took a Cheyenne wife, Owl Woman, and between 1838 and 1847 had two sons, Robert and George, and two daughters Mary and Julia. Owl Woman died giving birth to Julia, and Bent later married her sister, Yellow Woman, who gave him another son, Charles. Bent raised his family during the years when fur traders and explorers were the only white faces in the territory. He regularly traded with the Cheyennes, Arapahos, Kiowas, Sioux, Comanches and Prairie Apaches. Although the Cheyennes and Arapahos lived together, the latter tribes were their avowed enemies, but Bent's Fort was generally considered neutral ground. Bent held regular council with tribal leaders, gaining their acceptance and trust in matters of trade and peaceful relationships with the growing number of white emigrants moving in on the sacred hunting grounds.

During the Mexican-American War of '46, Bent's Fort served as a staging area for Union soldiers. The Indians had never seen so many white soldiers before, and they warily began to migrate toward the western Kansas plains to steer clear, taking away a large portion of Bent's trade business. In 1849, the army offered to purchase Bent's Fort, but Bent rejected the paltry offering price. Rather than giving in to the government, Bent destroyed the fort and moved 30 miles east, where he built a new post closer to the Indians.

By now, the fur trade had all but disappeared, and Bent began hauling Indian annuities for the government in addition to trading his own goods with the Indians. Throughout the 1850s, Bent lost all three brothers - one killed in the Mexican war, one murdered by Comanches, and the third who died of sickness. Bent's children were sent to Westport and educated in white schools during the same decade. At the outbreak of war, George Bent impulsively joined the Confederate Army in St. Louis, but he quickly changed his allegiance at the urging of his older brother Robert, returning to Indian country to live with his late mother's Cheyenne clan. Robert married into the Cheyenne tribe, and Julia Bent married Edmund Guerrier, the son of a white mountain man and a Cheyenne woman. Mary returned to live with her father, and young Charlie lived with Yellow Woman's clan.

Bent's Fort was the center of commerce for Indians and the white settlers traversing the Santa Fe Trail, and Bent was a master of diplomacy, delicately maintaining the peace between his adopted kin and the burgeoning number of settlers who emigrated during the late 1850s. As hostilities grew between Indian tribes and whites, coupled with the growing threat of a Confederate invasion, the fort's longstanding neutrality slowly deteriorated. William Bent continued to counsel and advise the Cheyennes and Arapahos, however, urging them to keep peace with the white chiefs.

In 1859, the War Department once again approached Bent with an offer to purchase his new fort, and this time Bent agreed. The army commissioned him to stay on with the honorary rank of colonel, and to serve as Indian agent and interpreter. He promptly sent a dispatch to the Commissioner of Indian Affairs, A. B. Greenwood, warning that a war with the Indians was inevitable unless something was done to stop the growing line of emigrants from taking land and pushing them to starvation. In a terse reply, Greenwood lamented that there was little alternative but to propose a treaty, for the easier solution of extermination was an affront to justice and humanity. Greenwood negotiated individual treaties with the Comanches, Kaws and Kiowas, and proposed the Fort Wise Treaty to the Cheyennes and Arapahos in 1861, which, due to few of the promises made by the government ever being kept, remained the subject of controversy between whites and Indians alike for its duration.

Fort Wise was renamed Lyon in 1862, to honor General Nathaniel Lyon, who held the dubious distinction of being the first general to die in the Civil War. Fort Lyon was rebuilt closer to the fertile Arkansas basin, and after Chivington led the Colorado First to victory at La Glorieta, a series of encampments sprang up along the Upper Arkansas to support Lyon's defense of the growing settlements up and down river. The fort was a desolate outpost by 1864, often isolated and deprived of supplies due to marauding Indian raiding parties. Like their Indian counterparts, many Lyon soldiers suffered from maladies brought on by the lack of proper nutrition.

Captain Soule's boys of D Company, fresh from a relatively healthy life in Denver City, knew they had dark days ahead on their assignment to the Upper Arkansas...

Major Wynkoop sat on the edge of his desk, meticulously rolling some precious tobacco into a smoke. If it were any other man, the task would be hasty and without much attention to finer details. But this was Ned Wynkoop after all. Enough said. By the time he finished, the cigarette looked like a finely manufactured cheroot. In fact, cigarette duty had so consumed Wynkoop that he didn't hear Silas Soule come in behind him. Soule planned a boisterous entrance, but he couldn't help but stand mesmerized by his persnickety pal. An Irish grin crept across Soule's face as he silently approached Wynkoop from behind. Wynkoop struck a match and touched the flame to his smoke.

"Captain Soule reporting for duty, sah!" Soule hollered.

"Jesus dammit to hell!" Wynkoop cried, snorting smoke from his nose. He jumped and turned, instinctively reaching for his gun.

"Don't shoot!" Soule laughed.

Wynkoop swatted the burning embers from his tunic. "Dang, you son of a bitch!"

Soule rolled with laughter. "Oh, I'm sorry, Major. Did I scare you?"

Wynkoop caught his breath and tried to salvage his smoke. "Not at all. Just a quick change of trousers and I'll be good as new." He plugged the cigarette in his mouth and tossed a hand at Soule. "How are you, ya little sidewinder?"

Soule shook his hand. "Perfect as ever, Neddy. You?"

"What's it look like? Welcome to hell."

"Boy, you ain't a-kiddin'. What'd we do to deserve this rathole?"

"The rats moved out before I got here – complained about the living conditions."

"They probably followed Anthony to Ft. Riley."

Wynkoop laughed and poured a whiskey for Soule and himself. They clinked their tin cups and took a drink. "Pull up a crate and take a load off. Your boys getting situated?"

"No, they went on east to see if the Dog Soldiers have better accommodations."

Wynkoop sat and tossed a sigh. "I tell ya, Sile, the place is a sight better now than when I got here. Three-quarters of the boys were half dead of sickness, and the others were on the verge."

"Hell, I'm more fearful of them mosquitoes we saw by the river. Dang gallnippers were big as robins."

"They don't eat much," Wynkoop said. "None of us around here is fat enough for them to poke into."

"Chin up, big fella. We brought some provisions that should ease the agony. I got more potatoes than an Irish grocer out there."

Wynkoop took a drink. "That's news I was hoping for. Some of the boys are so full of scurvy, you can't walk around here without stepping on a tooth."

"I don't know – a few looked pretty smart when they met us at the gate just now."

"Yeah. They're doing better now that we're cultivating a few greens. I also ran some midnight raids and found Sam Colley had a cache of army supplies and Indian annuities for sale out the back door."

"That son of a bitch," Soule chuckled. "I reckon old Honest Abe's virtues didn't rub off when he appointed Sam as Indian Agent."

"I heard tell Sam's wife was baking pies with flour that was allotted to the Cheyennes - she was selling them to the boys here at the post."

"Permission to kill him, or just stake him out where the Indians can find him?"

Wynkoop didn't laugh. "Let's just say I made it clear – if any more of my boys get the fever from lack of food, Agent Colley's gonna be happy if the Indians get him before I do. God damn his sorry ass; it's no wonder the Indians are starving and want our scalps."

"So, what other surprises do you have for me?"

"I tell ya, old friend, you're a sight for sore eyes. I'm sorry to pull you from Hersa, but I need you in the worst way."

Soule raised his glass. "Well, I'm here to give my worst." He toasted Wynkoop, and they tossed the last of their drinks. "I called on Louisa before I left, and she asked me to give you a big fat kiss. Hope you don't mind if a toast will suffice, cause it's all I got to offer."

"I don't know," Wynkoop said. "I been without for awhile... you're looking pretty good right now..."

"You just back off, there, Nancy-boy," Soule said.

Wynkoop laughed. "This place is getting to me. How's Louisa getting on?"

"She and the little ones miss you dearly. I swear, for such a little lady, she's strong as a bear. It's like she was born to be an officer's wife."

"That's why I married her."

"Chiv looks after them, so you can set your mind at ease."

"Thank God for that. How is Hersa and the Coberlys?"

"She's new to this army life, but I'm grateful she's got her daddy and brothers looking after her. Poor sweet little gal took my leaving hard. Hell, so did I. It's like ya have to put my broken bones in traction whenever she's outta my sight."

Wynkoop gave his old pard a wry smile.

"What?" Soule said.

"Oh, nothing," Wynkoop smirked. "Sometimes I just think I need to clean out my ears when I hear you talking about a woman like that. It wasn't so long ago that you were breaking hearts from here to Lawrence. As I recall, you declared nobody was gonna put a brand on you unless she had a mighty large dowry."

"Lordy, don't I know it," Soule said. "Hersey's just got me all in a twist, Neddy. I never figured any gal could pack up so much love in such a dainty package. That little girl can make me laugh with a twitch of her nose or one simple wisecrack, and she's the best audience I ever played."

"She's a pip, that's for sure," Wynkoop said.

"You're an old married man," Soule said. "Tell me, how do you know for sure that you've found the one for you?"

"Pretty easy, pal. How much pain are you in right now?"

"Dang – even my *hair* hurts."

"I'd say it's time you get on it, then."

"Yeah? I got *you* to thank for delaying a proper proposal. It wouldn't do to ask Big Jim for her hand, and then run off and get scalped."

"I'm sorry about that, pal. I wrote Louisa and told her to look in on Hersa when she could."

"Thanks, Neddy."

"We're lucky boys, Sile."

"Lucky? Right now I feel like Indians gone and shot me full of arrows."

"Well, now that you're here, we're gonna see to that problem. My boys, they're good down to the last man. They just need discipline and direction. I'm counting on you to boost their spirits."

"Not to worry. I got a whole new line of shines I been dying to cut on fresh meat."

"Just make sure you find some time to turn them into Irish brawlers, too. I'm afraid we're gonna lead them into some nasty scrapes this summer."

"Where do we stand?"

Wynkoop rolled another cigarette while Soule lit his pipe. They had a second drink. "Chiv told you we're under General Blunt's command now?"

"Yeah. But he told me my hide would be his if we don't clear everything through him."

Wynkoop sighed and shook his head. "Yeah. I don't like it, but I'm not too sure what to do about it. Granted, Chiv knows more about this territory, but he's essentially telling me to ignore my District Commander. We're the only line of defense against the Indians, but we have to guard Fort Leavenworth's flank as well."

"Blunt's fighting rebs. Chiv's fighting Indians. I guess we gotta split our loyalty, depending on who's shooting at us."

"There's no shortage of enemy fire in this direction, that's a certainty. The past month, I've had scouts running the Arkansas and down to Red River. A couple of weeks ago, a rebel gang hit a train at Cimarron Crossing – killed a few boys and got away with 70 head of mules – pilfered their harnesses, wagons, gear, and about ten thousand in cash."

"Did you catch up to 'em?" Soule asked.

"Not a one. The wagon master said they headed southwest, but I heard rumors to the contrary, saying we might see a swell of Texans heading this way. I sent Lieutenant Hardy on a scout that didn't amount to anything more than chasing rabbits."

"If they're stealing stock and equipment, they're either forming an army, or lining their pockets."

Wynkoop nodded knowingly. "I'd bet on the latter. In fact, Colley and Bent think it's Jim Reynolds, and I'm beginning to suspect it myself."

"Oh, shit," Soule said. "Reynolds? Hell, he ain't no Texan."

"No, but word is he took up with the rebs after his jailbreak from Denver."

"You should've shot him back in '62 when you had the chance, Mr. Sheriff."

"I couldn't shoot *everybody* back then," Wynkoop smiled. "Didn't have enough ammunition."

"I figured Reynolds to hightail to Mexico and die in a tequila whorehouse."

"No such luck. From what I understand, he hooked up with a

party of rebs and set out to recruit under sanction of the Confederates."

"Now there's some brilliant military strategy," Soule said. "Commission a horse thief and murderer to do your bidding."

"Naturally, they've been making a good living off the settlers and trains ever since. They're selling their booty to reb gangs and Indians, which makes my job a hell of a lot harder. We gotta find that bastard and take him down."

Soule nodded. "What about the Indians? Any idea where Black Kettle is?"

"We haven't seen hide nor hair of him since Eayer killed Lean Bear."

"What the hell happened out there, Ned? All I heard in Denver was a conglomeration of rumors, some of which were pretty ugly."

Wynkoop pensively smoked. He shook his head. "It was uncalled for. George Eayer was on the hunt with Chivington's orders to shoot first and ask questions later. When he came up on Lean Bear, he gave the order to shoot without regard to anything else. It was goddam reckless, because there were several hundred Cheyenne lodges out beyond his sight line – a good portion of them Dog Soldiers. It was lucky for him that Black Kettle was there, too, otherwise Eayer and his entire command would've been cut to ribbons."

"Black Kettle stopped them?"

"He pulled them back – the majority, anyway. Eayer exchanged fire with a few in a retreat to Larned, but most of the Indians ranged to the north and didn't pursue."

"Well, ain't *that* a pip," Soule said. "Brings a man to laugh how somehow out in the prairie a story gets just a tad distorted before it finds its way back to civilization."

"What do you mean?" Wynkoop asked.

"Neddy, your report to Chiv made it sound like Eayer was attacked. You said he killed Black Kettle – not Lean Bear. Hell, word was already coming back to Denver about Black Kettle sightings after Eayer's supposed fight with him. It didn't do much for Chiv's confidence in what's going on out here."

Wynkoop stamped his cigarette out, perhaps to salve the sting of Soule's jab. "Look, I reported what Eayer told me, Sile. Chivington had him out chasing Indians since the fight at Fremont's Orchard in April - with orders to kill them on sight. Eayer covered hundreds of miles, scouring both Colorado and Kansas in heavy spring rains and snowstorms looking for Indians with stolen stock, and he came up with nothing. He had mules dying in the harness, and his boys were dropping from exhaustion by the time he finally stumbled on that Cheyenne camp. It was only recently that word filtered back to me about what really happened out there, but it's obvious Eayer couldn't come back after all that time, telling Chiv that he finally found an Indian but had to run for his damned life!"

"Okay, okay," Soule said. "I was just making friendly conversation."

Wynkoop threw a frustrated sigh. "Yeah? After you start eating hardtack and dried prunes for supper and sleeping on a cloth bed-sack - *and* getting ordered around by three different commanders with entirely different agendas - maybe you'll learn how the world doesn't make much sense out here."

"Hell, to me it don't make sense here or on a feather bed," Soule said. He raised his cup in toast and downed his drink.

"Amen to that," Wynkoop said.

"So, let me ask again in a way that won't get you all puckered up. How can I help you, pard?"

Wynkoop took Soule's fine smile. "Help me keep Curtis, Blunt, and Chiv happy. In between time, help me figure a way to keep the Cheyennes from killing every white soul down here."

"Well, hell! Why didn't ya say so in the first place? This is gonna be easy duty."

The boys had a laugh and another smoke...

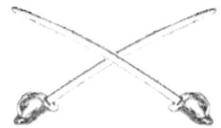

8

William Bent received word from Black Kettle's messengers, requesting a parley, and Bent immediately set out to confer with his old friend. They met on Coon Creek and discussed the killing of Lean Bear, the disposition of the Dogmen, and the potential for war. Although Black Kettle had many questions, Bent was unable to provide satisfactory answers other than to warn him that the white chiefs from both Kansas and Colorado considered the relentless Indian attacks on settlements and trains to be an act of war. Accordingly, the big chief Chivington had issued a standing order for his troops to kill any Indians they encountered. Black Kettle now had to gamble on the promise made by Bull Bear, and without knowing for certain that the Dog Soldiers would comply, he insisted that all of the Cheyennes wanted to end the hostilities. He asked Bent to relay this to the white chiefs along with a proposed council for the purpose of negotiating a peace treaty with the Cheyennes and Arapahos.

Bent promised Black Kettle he would do everything he could, a pledge upon which Black Kettle knew he could rely since Bent's wife and children had the blood of the *Tsis Tsis Tas*. The old friends parted with optimism, and Bent set upon the trail for Fort Leavenworth to apprise General Curtis of his meeting with Black Kettle. Shortly after he left, however, Bent had a change of mind. Leavenworth was several days farther to the east, and Bent also knew that Chivington was still the dominant military commander in Colorado. Bent decided that expediting a suspension of the army's advance on the Indians might happen faster if he took his case directly to Chivington, a mistake he would later regret. With that, he immediately turned around and headed back to Fort Lyon, where he hoped to enlist the help of Major Wynkoop to request a meeting with Chivington. When he arrived, he believed the Cheyennes' spirits just gave him an extraordinary blessing of good fortune, for Colonel Chivington had just arrived at the fort to check on his boys. Chivington planned a brief stay before heading back to Denver, so Bent acted quickly and seized an opportunity that just might put an end to the Indian problem...

"Colonel Bent!" Chivington said, greeting Bent at the council room door. "Long time no see!"

Bent, still weary from his journey, did his best to ward off Chivington's vice grip. "Colonel Chivington. Hello, Ned."

Major Wynkoop stepped forward and shook Bent's hand with a little more respect for his elder. "It's good to see you breathing and healthy, sir. We were getting a bit concerned when you were out so long."

"Hell – ain't no reason to worry about me. I'm too ornery to scalp."

Chivington blurted a laugh and offered a seat to Bent. The old trader looked around and saw Captain Soule, a man Bent regarded faintly familiar. Also present were the Indian Agent, Sam Colley, and John Smith, who was perched and sharing a bottle of whiskey. Smith was one of Bent's oldest acquaintances on the Arkansas. Originally from St. Louis, Smith ventured to the Rocky Mountains in 1830 and lived with the Blackfeet and Sioux Indians while making a living as a fur trapper. He eventually worked his way down the Arkansas and hired on with Bent as a trader. He quickly befriended the Cheyennes and married into the tribe, soon becoming a member and earning a respected position as sub-chief. Although the craggy-faced "Uncle John" Smith looked more like a mountain man born in a cave and raised by bats, he was possessed of a remarkable intellect and instinct for human nature. In addition to a strong command of the English language, he spoke Cheyenne, Blackfeet, Sioux, French and Spanish fluently, and had a photographic memory, enabling him to regale his white cronies with the many historic and sacred tales of Indian storytellers.

Smith's unique understanding of the Indians made him invaluable to the military, having served two decades as an interpreter in treaty councils. Most whites, however, concluded that Smith's unique abilities were of benefit, but his reputation as a liar and a cheat made him a man who could not be fully trusted. Despite his adept ability to speak so many languages, Smith could turn the air sour with purely English profanities and had the disposition of a rattlesnake, which endeared him to few. He was once run out of Denver City by none other than Ned Wynkoop when he got liquored up and beat his wife for getting too friendly with some miners at a dance. As enemies on the prairie were far less preferable to friends, Smith let bygones be bygones, but Wynkoop warily kept Smith at arm's length. Smith later returned to Bent's Fort with a new Indian wife in 1860, where he was enlisted to assist the army in quieting the Indian problems on the Arkansas...

"I believe you know everyone here, with the exception of Captain Soule," Chivington said to Bent.

"Silas Soule," Bent said. "I suspected that was you. Hell, I remember all the boys of La Glorieta, not to mention a Jayhawker."

Soule shook hands with Bent. "Don't know if a Missourian wants to shake hands or shoot me, but it's a pleasure to meet you anyhow."

"Hell, I been out here so long, my allegiances are to you Union boys."

"Gentlemen, down to business," Chivington said. "Daylight's burning, and I have to get back to Denver. Colonel Bent, I understand you met with Black Kettle?"

"That's right, Colonel," Bent said.

"And where is our savage friend camped?"

Bent measured Chivington. "What say we just talk about the problem at hand for now."

Chivington warily looked at Wynkoop. "Spoken like a true squaw man. Alright, Colonel, what's on your mind?"

"I had a long talk with the chief," Bent said. "Bottom line is, he wants a peace council."

"Indeed?" Chivington said.

"He wants to put a stop to this war."

"On whose terms?"

"Ain't no terms. He wants to know why the army's attacking his people."

"That's peculiar," Chivington said. "I thought the reason was pretty clear. Of course, Black Kettle wasn't present last month when I presided over a funeral for a man and his wife and children who were butchered beyond recognition. Perhaps he's forgotten about dozens of other people who've been killed, or maybe he didn't know his boys have been stealing stock and setting fire to trains strewn across Kansas. Maybe your red rebel friend is just suffering from some form of memory loss!"

"He sure as hell remembers Lieutenant Eayer shooting Lean Bear for no reason!" Bent snapped.

"No reason?" Chivington said. "Eayer searched the prairie for those horse thieves going on two months. He fought off attacks and the elements, and at one time I feared he and his entire command were dead. When he finally found that miserable savage, he carried out his orders."

"Lean Bear was a peace chief and you know it! He met with Lincoln, for Christ's sake, and he was wearing his peace medal when he was murdered! He approached your boys with one brave by his side, and he clearly offered himself for a parley when one of them sumbitches shot him dead!"

"Obviously, this is the story offered up by Black Kettle," Chivington said. "Let me tell you something, sir, Lieutenant Eayer bravely carried out his duty to my satisfaction."

"Brave?" Bent laughed. "He ran like a chicken in a storm! If it weren't for Black Kettle holding the Cheyennes back, the vultures would be picking his bones!"

"Where are you getting this? Eayer took the fight to *them!*"

"Eighty soldiers against five hundred Indians? Eayer is nothin' but a goddam liar!"

Chivington looked at Wynkoop. "Major? Do you want to add anything here?"

Wynkoop nervously puffed a cigarette. "Colonel, I have to admit I'm suspicious of Eayer's original report. I think Black Kettle's story is a little closer to the truth."

Chivington seethed. "Regardless, I'm convinced that the perpetrators of the depredations committed at Fremont's Orchard have been punished. And I intend to continue hunting down these red rebels until the last one is dead."

"Now, hold on," Bent said. "There's five tribes between the Republican and Red River, thousands of Indians roaming over hundreds of miles. You got Kiowas, Cheyennes, Arapahos, Sioux and Comanches – some hostile, but others trying to keep peace with us. You go and kill one for something another has done, then you just make the problem worse!"

"Did you call this meeting to give me a sermon?" Chivington said. "I have no concern what an Indian calls himself! In my book, they're all murdering renegades! They take a human head and wave it about as if they just bagged a rabbit! They rip the scalps from white women and decapitate children with no regard for humanity or justice. If one calls himself a Dog Soldier or a Sioux or a Kiowa, it makes no difference! I will call him dead, and leave his identification to the devil who created him!"

"God damn you," Bent said. "If that's where you stand, then we're gonna have a war on our hands that's gonna get us all killed!"

"Oh, I know where you stand," Chivington said. "You claim allegiance to us, but I happen to know that half-breed son of yours joined the rebel army!"

"Son of a bitch!" Bent stood and confronted Chivington, who met him with a glare.

Wynkoop and Soule quickly stepped between the two. "Gentlemen," Wynkoop said. "Let's just back down and take a breath."

"My family ain't for you to judge!" Bent said. "George is just a boy, and boys can afford a mistake now and again! Besides, he ain't a reb no more! He lives here with his dead mother's people, helping them hunt to stay alive."

"And just what - or *who* is he hunting?" Chivington said. "How do we know he isn't recruiting his renegade friends to take up with the Texans?"

"Because I goddam say he ain't, you arrogant sonofabitch!"

"Gentlemen!" Wynkoop said. "Colonel Bent, please have a seat." Bent complied, his hot eyes still locked on Chivington. "Colonel, I can vouch for George Bent. He's a good boy; and I've found no evidence to suggest that the Cheyennes have any interest in aligning with confederate troops."

"Evidence or not," Chivington said, "I am acting on orders to protect Colorado. When I see a squaw man with grown children serving the Confederate Army and living among Indians, I *will* question his motives!"

"And I ain't gonna say it again – George ain't a rebel," Bent said. "He fought for them and got hisself captured. The Union soldiers knew who he was, and they knew my older son Robert. George promised them he'd come back here and behave himself, and Robert brought him home. He was a young boy, which is the same as to say a stupid boy, but I knocked the stupid out of him. As for the Cheyennes, I'll tell you exactly where they stand on the war with Texas. Two years back, Black Kettle himself told me they parleyed with the Texans, and they had a damn good offer that would have given them land and annuities. All they had to do in return was fight for the rebels. Black Kettle asked me what he should do, and I told him to steer clear. I told him he'd have the whole Union army on his people, and they'd get rubbed out."

"He's right," Agent Colley said. "I haven't seen any sign of the Cheyenne interest in the rebels. They're too destitute right now to do anything but search for buffalo."

"Oh, this *is* rich, Colley," Chivington said. "It's a big territory, but not too big for me to hear interesting tales about the way you and Smith are wheeling and dealing down here."

"Look, I don't know where them rumors got started –"

"They started with *me*, goddamit!" Bent said. "I seen the way you two sold the Cheyennes the annuities that was legally theirs in the first place! You and Smith have made a tidy profit down here, puckering up the soldiers *and* the Indians!"

"That ain't true!" Colley said. "Uncle John, you tell 'em."

"Hey, I ain't sayin' a goddam thing," Smith spat.

"Shut up, both of you," Chivington said. "I don't care what

either one of you have to say, because I do the talking down here. God as my witness, if I hear one more word of either of you swindling any soldier at Fort Lyon, I will play thunder with the both of you. Savvy?"

Colley meekly nodded, but Smith cursed and hawked a load of tobacco on the floor.

"Uncle John," Chivington said, "I'll gladly fit you for a set of leg irons right now!"

"Gentlemen!" Wynkoop said, again trying to take the floor. He looked to Soule for help, but the wise Dutchman simply rolled his eyes to the window with a grin. "We aren't getting anywhere by sniping at one another. Colonel, I have this post in order, and I give you my personal assurance of Mr. Bent's loyalty."

Bent was still angry. "Them are my children, Colonel. They stand to die just as much as any other."

"I'm sure Colonel Chivington understands," Wynkoop said. "He has a family, too."

Chivington took a deep breath. "Colonel Bent, you're correct. It was not my intention to impugn your family. We're all under enormous stress here. I offer my apology."

Bent pulled a cigar and lit it. He took a moment. "Accepted."

"This situation has put our shins to the fire," Chivington said. "I've witnessed firsthand the grief and suffering of the people of this territory. It makes a man's blood boil." He suddenly and unexpectedly looked at Soule.

John Smith slopped some whiskey and broke the tension. "Then why in hail don't you ninnies figure a way to put a damn cork in this thing?"

Soule laughed. "Thanks, Uncle John. Why didn't *we* think of that?"

"Wah – ya bunch of stupid bastards," Smith said.

Chivington didn't share Soule's amusement, but he relented nonetheless. "Colonel Bent, I appreciate your efforts, but coming to me with word that Black Kettle demands answers for our course of action is hardly a prelude to a peace council. He's not in a position to dictate policy to me."

"He ain't dictating nothing," Bent said. "He just wants to know what's led us to the brink of war. He's lookin' for a solution. I know him, Colonel, and he's a good man. You think he's a murdering scoundrel, but there ain't nothin' farther from the truth."

"Respectfully," Chivington said, "his actions belie your description."

"It ain't *his* actions, Colonel! He's the Principal Chief of a council of forty-four chiefs of the southern and northern Cheyennes. They quarrel over damned near every issue that confronts them. Each chief leads hundreds of Cheyennes that are scattered from here to the Black Hills, and they only get together to council in a coon's age. It's a damned complicated society that don't get along any better than we do."

"So, what do you want from me?" Chivington asked.

"Black Kettle's trying to stop the warrior clans – particularly the Dogmen - from fighting the whites, but it's a troubling proposition. I think if we back off and stop attacking them, he just might be able to convince them to make peace."

"I will *not* back down," Chivington said. "General Curtis clearly defined my obligations in this matter. I am free to cross district lines to pursue and punish those red rebels."

"Then tell Curtis about my meeting with Black Kettle," Bent said. "He wants to meet with him face-to-face and tell him he wants peace for the Cheyennes and Arapahos. He is willing to submit to your terms, and he only asks that you stop attacking them."

"I don't have the authority to negotiate a peace treaty with Black Kettle," Chivington said.

"But Curtis has that authority."

"Curtis has given me orders to kill all Indians, wherever and whenever I find them. He is not interested in discussing peace with Indians that have declared war on us!"

"That just don't make sense," Agent Colley interrupted. "I hear tell that Governor Evans is gonna send out a proclamation that tells the Indians to approach the forts and surrender. If your boys have orders to kill them, how in hell do they surrender?"

"You'll have to take that up with the governor, not me," Chivington said.

"Then who's in charge? Curtis or Evans?"

"I'm in charge, Mr. Bent! The Indians are on the warpath, and so am I."

"Jesus sonofabitch!" Smith said. "That makes a hell of a world, don't it?"

"Mr. Smith," Chivington said. "Your blasphemy notwithstanding, you were not called to this meeting to voice your opinion. You are employed to provide strategic information and serve as an interpreter. If any Indian prisoner is still breathing and able to communicate vital information, I expect you to report it to Major Wynkoop. Do you understand your obligations?"

"Yeah, I understand," Smith said. He stood and walked to the door. "And you can go shit in your hat."

Chivington blasted a sigh as Smith slammed the door behind him. "Well, gentlemen, with that, I can't think of anything more that needs to be said."

"A shame the old boy has so much trouble expressing himself, ain't it?" Soule said.

Chivington turned to Bent. "Colonel, I'm going to ask you once more, and I want a straight answer this time. Where is Black Kettle camped?"

"I don't know, and that's the truth."

"Where did you meet with him?"

"He was in the vicinity of the Smoky Hill. He's been treating with Major Anthony out there, and he says Anthony and him have kept things civil for now."

"With due respect, sir," Chivington said, "may I trust your word that you cannot precisely tell me where Black Kettle is now?"

"I know what you got in mind, Colonel," Bent said. "But if you think Black Kettle would tell me where he's headed next, then you're just showing how little you know about Indians. I told ya, he ain't stupid."

"Very well," Chivington said. "Thank you for your time. This meeting is concluded."

Bent looked at Wynkoop and Soule, who provided little consolation. "Colonel, I ain't one that takes a liking to beg, but if I have to, I will. Please ask Curtis to consider a meeting with Black Kettle. This is probably our last chance to stop this war."

"It's too late for that, sir," Chivington said. "The Indians declared war on us, and I have no intention of letting them down."

"What about the trains heading to New Mexico? What about the settlers along the Arkansas? There ain't enough soldiers down here to protect them."

"They're going to have to protect themselves," Chivington coldly said. "Now, Colonel Bent, Mr. Colley, if you'll excuse us, I need to speak with my officers before I depart for Denver."

Exasperated, Bent shook his head and walked out with Colley.

Chivington sat at the table and blew a sigh into his hands. He furiously rubbed his eyes, and now that the others were gone, his guard dropped. "Ned, nothing has changed from this. I expect you to carry out your orders as they stand."

"I don't know, Chiv," Wynkoop said. "I don't see any harm in talking to Black Kettle. What have we got to lose?"

"I said you have your orders, Major!"

Wynkoop held his temper in check. "Yes, sir."

Chivington bit his lip. He blew another sigh. "I didn't mean to bite your head off, Ned. Just be a good lad and do what I say."

"Chiv?" Soule said. "You ok?"

"No, son, I'm not." He looked at Soule, who had watched most of the proceedings from a safe distance. "Silas, come sit down with me. You, too, Ned."

Wynkoop and Soule complied and gathered around Chivington. "Boys, I count on you to hold this post together. We've fought battles together, and we've watched gallant men die, sometimes taking their last breath in our arms. The two of you are like sons to me, and I have to tell you something that I would give my right arm to avoid."

"What's wrong, Chiv?" Soule said.

Chivington looked at Soule. "Silas, I wanted Ned to be here, because I know the two of you rely upon each other. I didn't want to tell you this until now, when the two of you will have some time together. I have terrible news for you, son."

Soule's heart suddenly raced. "What? Is it my mother?"

"No, son."

"Oh, shit," Soule said. "Hersa?"

"No! Hersa is fine, Silas. It's her father. He's dead."

"What?" Soule breathed a short gasp. His eyes welled, and he gritted his teeth. He tried to speak, but the words simply dropped from his mouth.

"Jesus Christ," Wynkoop whispered.

Chivington put his hand on Soule's shoulder. "I'm so sorry."

Soule, choked with tears, managed a whisper. "What happened?"

Chivington took a deep sigh. "Indians," he said. "They caught big Jim in his wagon. Nobody saw what happened. He was found... on the ground...the wagon was looted and burned."

Soule simply closed his eyes and took a moment. Finally, he sucked his tears back. "Hersa – her mother?"

"I sent some soldiers down to Halfway House." He looked at Wynkoop. "My wife and Louisa went with them. They're holding up. The Coberly boys are good men. Joe's taking it very hard. He took me aside and tried to enlist, but I told him to stay with his family for the time being. They'll look after the ladies. Hersa sent a message with me, son. She sends her love, and she told me to tell you she's alright. She is a strong young lady, and God will help her through this."

"I'm sorry, Sile," Wynkoop said. "Chiv, is there any trace of who did it?"

"Does it matter? Several other ranches were hit - two others killed. I assure you, Silas, I will hunt the renegades down, and payment will be made..."

9

By order of Hon. John Evans, Governor, Territory of Colorado
This 27th day of June, 1864
To the Friendly Indians of the Plains:

Agents, interpreters, and traders will inform the friendly Indians of the plains that some members of their tribes have gone to war with the white people. They steal stock and run it off, hoping to escape detection and punishment. In some instances they have attacked and killed soldiers and murdered peaceable citizens. For this the Great Father is angry, and will certainly hunt them out and punish them, but he does not want to injure those who remain friendly to the whites. He desires to protect and take care of them. For this purpose I direct that all friendly Indians keep away from those who are at war, and go to places of safety.

Friendly Arapahos and Cheyennes belonging on the Arkansas River will go to Major Colley, U.S. Indian agent at Fort Lyon, who will give them provisions, and show them a place of safety. Friendly Kiowas and Comanches will go to Fort Larned, where they will be cared for in the same way. Friendly Sioux will go to their agent at Fort Laramie for directions. Friendly Arapahos and Cheyennes of the Upper Platte will go to Camp Collins on the Cache la Poudre, where they will be assigned a place of safety and provisions will be given them.

The object of this is to prevent friendly Indians from being killed through mistake. None but those who intend to be friendly with the whites must come to these places. The families of those who have gone to war with the whites must be kept from among the friendly Indians. The war on hostile Indians will be continued until they are all effectually subdued...

Governor Evans called it a "proclamation." The Cheyennes had no word for it in their language, but any white interpreter worth his salt could tell you that the message Evans dispatched was more of a "declaration." The governor drew a line in the sand, leaving the Indians to decide if they should cross it. But just as things in the Spirit World were never black and white, neither were they easily discernable in the real world. Evans dispatched Indian agents, traders and interpreters to relay his proclamation to the tribes, demanding that his message make clear to every Indian on the plains that his word was law. With little knowledge of the intricate and autonomous political structures of Indian nations, Evans assumed that the words Cheyenne, Arapaho, Sioux and Kiowa were synonymous with "Indian." His notion was no less ludicrous than Black Kettle equating Abraham Lincoln with Jefferson Davis simply because they were both "white men."

In July 1864, the scribbled words of Evans' proclamation were passed along to Indian chiefs throughout the Colorado and Kansas territories, and subsequently passed by word of mouth through mounted messengers whose interpretations were left to chance. That hot summer month ushered a blight of locust across the plains. The blight, coupled by frequent Indian raids on outlying settlements inexorably drove many whites to the brink of financial ruin. Many Sioux and Dog Soldier bands roamed northwest along the Solomon River and up to the northern regions above the South Platte in central Nebraska. They attacked and looted settlements, raided stock and supplies, killed every white man and took white women and children captives for barter or enslavement. The settlers offered little resistance against the vast numbers of warriors bent on war, and army troops were too sparse in number to mount an adequate defense.

By mid summer, militant warrior parties overwhelmed the South Platte, virtually cutting off all supply trains headed for Denver City. Although the majority of Indian depredations occurred in Kansas, the settlers of Colorado were certain that a massive Indian strike was imminent. Governor Evans and Colonel Chivington baked in the political firestorm over Colorado statehood, as their respective bids for higher office in the autumn congressional elections hinged on a swift and decisive solution to the burgeoning problems befalling the Colorado Territory. The Denver settlers' rage over the Hungate massacre was unrelenting, for several other families had since been murdered by marauding Indians on the South Platte, and Governor Evans was continuously under pressure to act. Exacerbating the worrisome Indian revolt was the infiltration of Confederate operatives bent upon ultimate capture of the gold-rich western territories.

Among the peaceful Indian tribes that migrated south and away from the depredations on the South Platte, the Civil War between the whites did not go unnoticed, but their fundamental need for food and survival trumped all else. The big white chief Evans' demands of friendly Indian surrender to the white forts held no guarantee of safe passage to their hunting grounds, and many were starving and infested with disease for which Evans' proclamation offered no relief. Some Indians surrendered at the Kansas forts, but they were coolly received by the soldiers - mostly turned away and ordered to designated areas, where they hunted small game for sustenance. The majority of Indians of all four nations dispersed in many directions, some individuals venturing north to join the war parties avenging Lean Bear's death, while others fled to far reaches of the Kansas and Oklahoma prairies, trying to avoid the violence.

Black Kettle kept his Wotap band with Little Raven's Arapahos in the central vicinity between Forts Larned and Riley. Not yet aware of Governor Evans' proclamation, they camped with a large band of Indians and began their buffalo hunt. Other peaceful Cheyenne and Arapaho bands roamed southward and well away from any fort. The vengeful Dogmen bands indiscriminately attacked settlements and trains, despite Bull Bear's attempt to call them in for a council to consider Black Kettle's proposals. Black Kettle awaited word from Bull Bear regarding united cooperation from the Dogmen in his bid for a peacemaking council with Union soldiers, but the process was painstakingly slow due to the large range over which both Southern Cheyenne and Dogmen tribes were scattered. In the meantime, the Indians in Black Kettle's village participated in the ceremonial Sun Dance and renewal of the Sacred Arrows, ancient rituals performed when times of hardship and death befell the People...

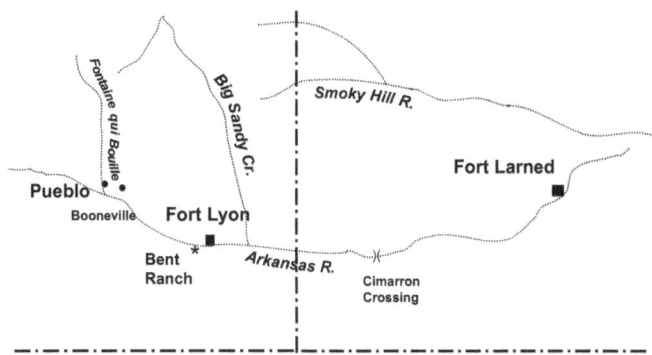

Fort Larned was established as the central stopping point between Fort Leavenworth and Fort Lyon, located on the Pawnee River near the confluence with the Arkansas. This leg of the Santa Fe Trail across the barren Kansas Territory was oppressively hot and humid in the summer and bone-chillingly cold in the winter. Larned's conditions were even more Spartan than Fort Lyon's, with crudely built hovels and tents for quarters, and a defense consisting of pits protected by nothing more than earthen mounds. The troops at Larned rode escort for trains, and protected a large amount of corralled stock for the passing stages. The fort was an easy target for marauders, and since the killing of Lean Bear, Larned's commander, Captain J. W. Parmetar, requested reinforcements from Fort Riley.

Cheyenne war parties had filtered down and sacked several ranches and killed ranchers and stage drivers. Settlers in the area mounted a defense, but they needed Parmetar's assistance. He ordered officers at the post to venture out to council with various Indian tribes in the vicinity, hoping to cull information regarding hostile war party positions.

The peaceable Indians in the Larned area, among them Left Hand's Arapaho clan, confirmed that many Arapaho and Cheyenne warriors were on the warpath, and although many Sioux, Kiowa and Comanches were averse to fighting the soldiers, some formed war parties on their own hook. Alarmed by Left Hand's ominous warning, Parmetar immediately ordered scouting parties out to search for and attack war parties. General Curtis sent Major T. I. McKenny from Fort Leavenworth to ascertain the severity of Parmetar's problem. McKenny soon returned a dispatch to Curtis, informing the general that the Indian depredations were indeed increasing around the Arkansas. This was hardly news to Curtis, but what troubled him was McKenny's evaluation of Captain Parmetar's judgement and ability to command.

Parmetar, McKenny reported, "is reported by every officer and man that I have heard speak of him as a confirmed drunkard..."

McKenny went on to report that the scouting parties Parmetar had dispatched were likely to attack any Indian without regard to their disposition toward the whites. McKenny warned that these indiscriminate attacks would serve to further unite more Indians in a war, many of whom had been at peace for years. Curtis, still more preoccupied with the protection of Kansas from Confederate forces, took McKenny's warning under advisement but did not remove Parmetar from his command. Soon, a band of Kiowas camped near Fort Larned forced Curtis to move on Parmetar.

Fort Larned's corrals were brimming with the horses and mules of Lieutenant Eayer's company, still garrisoned at the post. Kiowa Chief Satanta found the stock too inviting to pass up, and he approached the fort with a plan to steal them. Although Left Hand had warned Captain Parmetar not to trust the ornery Kiowa warrior chief, Satanta was allowed to approach the fort with several braves and a few squaws. Parmetar, eager to accept Satanta's offer to parley over whiskey and tobacco, drank with the chief while the women danced for the soldiers. While the troops were distracted, Satanta's warriors stormed the corral, killed a sentry, and stole over two hundred of the post's horses and mules. During the ensuing melee, Satanta and the women quickly disappeared into the darkness, leaving the enraged Parmetar to take out his wrath on his hapless troops, most of whom had enjoyed the free flow of liquor during Satanta's parley. Satanta, never one to allow his achievements to go without notice, sent word back to Parmetar, complaining about the quality of army horses and requesting that better stock be made available for his next visit...

Left Hand was hunting with a small party when word reached him of Satanta's attack on Fort Larned. The Arapahos, who maintained a civil but wary peace accord with the Kiowas, knew Satanta's stunt had just endangered every Indian within range of Parmetar's troops, and a council was immediately called to assess the situation. Chief Little Raven and Left Hand's brother Neva met Left Hand in his lodge.

"Have you heard any more from your messengers?" Left Hand asked Neva.

"Just that Satanta is still crowing," Neva said.

"Then he is not going to return the stock to Parmetar?" Left Hand said.

"He said to tell you he will trade some to us for food."

Left Hand disgustedly looked at Little Raven. "We have to do something about this."

"Do you want to kill him, or shall I?" Raven grumbled.

"Just what we need – a war with Kiowas *and* the soldiers," Left Hand said. "Parmetar will be on the war path."

"If the drunk bastard can stay on his pony," Little Raven said.

"It is not funny, Raven. They will come after us."

"I know," Raven sighed. "The only thing we can do is go to Parmetar and try to convince him we had nothing to do with Satanta's raid."

"I will go," Left Hand said. "I speak their words better than anyone else. This will require serious talk, and I do not want any misunderstanding."

"I speak their words, too," Little Raven said. "Do you want me to go with you?"

"It would be better if I go without you," Left Hand said. "After all, I was the one who warned Parmetar about Satanta. The soldiers there know me better than you, and we might not look as if we are joining forces if I approach them with just a few of my men."

"Agreed. Tell him we will get the horses back. We will go to Satanta and demand their return. If the Kiowas refuse, tell Parmetar we will take them back with force."

"Have you talked with Black Kettle about this?" Left Hand asked.

Little Raven chuckled. "I talked. He yelled."

"I take it he was not pleased."

"You might say that. He was ready to smoke the war pipe and rub out every last one of the Greasy Wood People."

"From that I assume he will help us if we have to go after Satanta."

"I have no doubt he will lead the war party if it comes to that..."

The next morning, Left Hand left his village and set out for Fort Larned with 25 braves. The band cautiously approached the fort, stopping when they were within a quarter mile of the post and in full view of the sentries. Left Hand held a long pole with a white flag attached, raising it high to be certain the sentries saw it. Neva flanked the Arapaho chief. They watched the sentries, who milled about for a moment before several turned their horses toward the Indians.

"Stay alert," Neva said to the men behind him. "If they raise their weapons, be prepared to fight."

"We will not fight unless they attack. Is that understood?" Left Hand said.

The braves acknowledged.

"I know these men, and I can talk with them," Left Hand said. "Everyone just keep your mouths shut and do not make any hostile movements. I will do the talking."

The three sentries, led by Lieutenant Hardy, slowed their horses when they were within 50 feet of the Arapahos. Hardy recognized Left Hand, and he gave a slight wave to show his intentions were non-aggressive. They slowly approached.

"Halloo, Left Hand," Hardy said.

Left Hand spoke in English. "Lieutenant Hardy."

"What are you doing here?"

"I want to talk with Parmetar."

Hardy blew a cautious sigh. "I gotta tell ya, Chief, you boys showing up here ain't such a good idea right now."

"We heard about your troubles with Satanta."

"Trouble don't describe it. That dirty little fice dog came in here with whiskey and women – slappin' Parmetar on the back, and them women cavortin' around like saloon gals - and he played us for goddam fools. Captain Parmetar caught the wrath of God from headquarters, and he's been in a conniption ever since. It's gonna be directed your way just as soon as he gets some horses from Fort Riley."

"Hardy, you heard me tell Parmetar not to trust Satanta. You were there."

"Yeah, I was. Trouble is, you got to catch him pretty early 'tween hangovers to make anything stick."

"Satanta asked me to join him," Left Hand said, "and I told him we would not. I told him not to do it, but he lied to me. It is the truth, Lieutenant."

"Okay, Chief, I believe ya."

"My people will not fight you. We do not want war, and we do not condone the Indians who are attacking your lodges and trains. I speak for Little Raven and Black Kettle, too. We are angry at Satanta, and I came here to tell you we will go after the Kiowas and get your stock back."

"You know where he is?"

"I sent wolves out scouting for him right now. I promise you I can find him. Please, let me talk to Parmetar."

Hardy took his hat off and dabbed the sweat from his brow. "I don't know, Chief. Shit rolls downhill, ya know. The captain's been on a two-day bender, and he's corned but good. This just ain't too good a time for any Indian to be around here."

"Will you ask him? He knows me, and we are friends."

"Right," Hardy huffed. "Him and Satanta was pretty chummy the other night, too – right up to the time the Kioways put an arrow through the heart of one of our sentries."

"Lieutenant, I promise you we are not here to do the same. You know me! You know we will never fight you!"

"Yeah, yeah, I know that. Hell, I believe you, Left Hand."

"How about this," Left Hand said. "I send my men back to our village right now. I will come in with you by myself."

Hardy tossed a frustrated look at his boys. He would never tell them *or* Left Hand this, but his fear was more of Parmetar than the Indians. "You really reckon you can get those horses and mules back?"

"I am trying to keep peace with you and all the whites. Satanta threatened the safety of my people with his arrogance. I will bring his damn head to Parmetar if he wants it!"

Hardy spit some chaw and put his hat back on. "He'd probably settle for about 240 head of stock right now. Okay, tell you what - you and your boys stay put and don't make a move. Don't do no singin' or make them noises you fellows do, cause even if you're just being friendly, everybody in camp's walking a thin line and streaked as hell."

"Do you want me to send my men away?"

"Naw, don't do that. I'm thinking maybe if Parmetar agrees, I can round up some troops to go huntin' Satanta with ya right now."

"That is good," Left Hand said. "We could fight together."

"Yeah," Hardy said, "I wouldn't mind riding with you boys myself. Stay quiet now." He turned his horse and the sentries galloped back to the fort.

Left Hand and Neva watched. Neva knew enough English to follow the council. "This would be a first," he mumbled in his native tongue. "If anyone saw us riding with soldiers, they would think we were drinking Parmetar's firewater."

Left Hand threw a tense sigh. "I could use some right now..."

Hardy and his men rode past the breastworks. He threw caution to the soldiers perched at the dirt mounds with their rifles. Two were stationed at the howitzer.

"They're alright," Hardy said. "Keep an eye skinned on that white flag, and don't nobody fire unless you hear an order. Clear?"

The men acknowledged and warily watched the Arapahos.

Hardy dismounted and approached Captain Parmetar's hut. He banged on the creaky wooden door. "Captain! It's Hardy."

Parmetar's leaky voice boomed from within. "Piss off!"

"Captain! Can I come in?"

Hardy waited for a turn, and then carefully pushed the door open, meeting Parmetar, face-to-face.

"What the hell do you want?" Parmetar mumbled.

"Captain," Hardy said, "Left Hand is here. He wants to talk."

Parmetar, bottle in hand, squinted into the sunlight. "Shoot him." He wandered back inside.

Hardy followed. The heat of day made the hovel stifling. It smelled of liquor and urine. Parmetar, his trousers damp, stumbled and half-fell in his chair. He took a drink and swallowed hard. "You still here, boy?"

"Captain, Left Hand wants a parley. He knows where Satanta is, and he offered to go after him and get our stock back."

"Taste of some old orchard?" Parmetar said, offering the bottle.

"Sir, if we can retrieve that stock, it'll get Curtis off your back."

"Do tell?" Parmetar said. "Then listen. I have a great idea. Why don't you and old Left Hand go fuck yourself." He pulled a cigar from his pocket and missed his mouth twice before finding it. He struck a match several times, but the cigar fell from his mouth when he tried to light it.

"Captain. Just give me the order. I'll take my company out with Left Hand, and we'll find Satanta."

"What the hell are you talking about?" Parmetar said.

"Left Hand, sir. He's here."

"Who's here?"

"Left Hand! A band of Arapahos are with him. They want to help us get the stock back!"

"Arapahos? Jesus goddamit, don't that just cap the climax! Let's go greet the son of a bitch and settle his goddam hash!" Parmetar stumbled to his feet and clumsily hooked his suspenders. He grabbed his sidearm and shoved Hardy aside, blasting out the door and nearly falling into the dirt. "Indians, boys!" he hollered. "Look alive!"

The soldiers froze in their boots. Parmetar waved his weapon, and a few boys ducked for cover. "Captain!" Hardy yelled, trailing behind. "Left Hand wants to talk!"

"I'll talk to him!" Parmetar said. He wildly fired into the air as the soldiers dodged from the drunken captain's sights. Parmetar rambled toward the howitzer, still waving his gun...

Left Hand curiously looked at Neva. "Was that a gunshot?"

Neva squinted and looked toward Fort Larned. "What are they doing?" From this distance, all the Arapahos could see were soldiers running about...

"Prepare to attack!" Parmetar bellowed. He stumbled to the cannon, shoving a corporal out of the way. "Give those bummers a taste of grapeshot!"

"Godammit, Captain!" Hardy yelled.

"How far out?" Parmetar asked the bewildered corporal.

"What?"

"They want to talk!" Hardy said. "They're showing the white flag!"

"Are you crazy, man?" Parmetar said. "They're gonna attack! Fire on your own hook, boys!"

"Stand down, everyone!" Hardy ordered.

"What's that?" Parmetar tried to focus on Hardy. "I'll have you cashiered, you son of a bitch!" He fired his pistol in Left Hand's direction, but the bullet's range was far too short to reach the Arapahos...

"Now, I *know* that was a gunshot," Left Hand said.

"Who are they shooting at?" Neva asked.

The braves grew restless, looking around to see if perhaps a war party was approaching.

Left Hand and Neva continued to peer out toward the fort. "Are they shooting at us?"

"From that distance?" Neva said.

"Do you see anybody else out here?"

"They would have better luck throwing the balls at us."

"What is going on over there?"

The Arapahos continued to curiously watch. Suddenly, a puff of smoke arose from the breastworks of the fort, and a few seconds later they heard a loud boom.

"Get out of here!" Left Hand ordered.

As they turned their horses, a cannonball streaked in, exploding dangerously close and throwing grape at the Indians.

"Ride!" Left Hand yelled. The Arapahos quickly galloped away...

Lieutenant Hardy peered over a dirt mound with another soldier. As the dirt and smoke fell in the distance, they scanned to look for signs of life.

"You see anybody?" Hardy said.

"I don't think so," the soldier said.

"God dammit," Hardy puffed. He looked back at Parmetar, who reeled over the howitzer. The captain's eyes rolled as he began to list to the left. He suddenly vomited on himself and screwed into the dirt.

The soldier looked at Hardy. "If he ain't dead, can we just shoot him and say the injuns got him?"

"Shut up," Hardy growled. "Get the bastard out of here."

Hardy looked back out to where the Arapahos had been. The dust had settled, and the Indians were gone...

Word of the incident at Fort Larned passed both up and down the Arkansas like a spring flood. At Fort Lyon, Major Wynkoop, not known to take bad news with much dignity or grace, considered Captain Soule's suggestion that they go to Larned and stake Parmetar naked to the ground and feed him to the fire ants. Instead, Wynkoop relented and settled for breaking a chair against a wall. However, at Fort Leavenworth, the ensuing fit thrown by General Curtis could be heard clear to St. Louis. Captain Parmetar's latest stunt was but one of a series of displays of outrageous behavior, and this was the last straw. The general's rage swept west across Kansas and into Denver City, as well, and Colonel Chivington took the blow head-on. Curtis ordered Chivington to immediately ride to Fort Larned and dispose of Parmetar. Chivington wasted little time, taking a coach to Larned with Captain C. B. Backus, a soldier who had moved up the ranks of the Colorado First and a man Chivington implicitly trusted. He stormed into the post and arrested Parmetar on the spot, temporarily replacing the old drunk with Captain Backus until Major Anthony could fix his papers and come down from Fort Riley to assume command. Chivington informed the troops at Larned that he would play thunder with any soldier who dared to disgrace the uniform again.

After the incident at Fort Larned, Left Hand returned to his village with the enraged warriors of his party, who quickly scattered and spread the word that the soldiers attacked them under the white flag. Despite Left Hand's attempt to quiet the angry warriors, his words fell on deaf ears, and the young men went on a violent rampage...

Fort Lyon, Colorado Territory
July 26, 1864
Hon. John Evans
Governor and Superintendent Indian Affairs
SIR:
When I last wrote you I was in hopes that our Indian troubles were at an end. Colonel Chivington has just arrived from Larned, and gives the sad account of affairs at that post. They have killed some ten men from a train, and run off all the stock from the post. As near as I can learn, all the tribes were engaged in it. The colonel will give you the particulars. There is no dependence to be put on any of them.

I have done everything in my power to keep peace. I now think a little powder and lead is the best food for them.
Respectfully, your obedient servant,
S.G. Colley
United States Indian Agent

Major Wynkoop instructed Agent Colley to ride out to the Arapaho camp to get Left Hand's side of the story. Colley met with Left Hand and Little Raven. Black Kettle and White Antelope arrived shortly after hearing that Colley was there. John Smith accompanied Colley, and he interpreted for Black Kettle and White Antelope, whose command of the English language was minimal. Left Hand and Little Raven, however, had no problem voicing their opinions in language any white man could understand...

"Those cocksuckers are lucky Left Hand only had 25 braves with him!" Little Raven raged.

"It was Parmetar!" Colley said. "It was all his fault!"

"Hardy lied to my face," Left Hand said. "Stay right where you are, he said. Do not make a move; do not show hostility."

"Hardy told us everything that happened," Colley said. "It wasn't a suck-in, Left Hand."

"The hell it wasn't!" Little Raven said.

"I'm tellin' ya, Hardy didn't have nothing to do with attacking you. He said Parmetar was liquored up, and *he* ordered the howitzer fire. The soldiers had no choice but to obey his order."

Black Kettle spoke to Smith, and Smith relayed: "Is this the kind of chief you have? He commands his men when he can't even see?"

"Parmetar's a goner," Colley said. "I guarantee he ain't going nowhere but a stockade."

White Antelope chattered at Smith now. "He says, what good does it do now?" Smith said. "Says, the Arapaho warriors are all riled, and they's going to the Dogmen to smoke the war pipe."

"Aw, shit!" Colley barked. "Left Hand, can you stop 'em?"

"Stop them?" Left Hand said with an exasperated laugh. "Can you stop a whirlwind? It is done now. I lost control of them the minute that cannon fired."

"How about you, Raven?" Colley said. "Your boy's a warrior. Can you tell him to calm them down?"

Little Raven shook his head. "I already tried that. You have a son, so you know how it is to reason with one when he is angry. He did not listen to a word, and he is out looking to join the Dogmen, too."

"Shit-fire," Smith said. "Ain't we on the little end of the horn. I know for a fact some of the Dogmen are down with the Kioways right now. You side them up with Satanta and Left Hand's boys, and there's gonna be smoke risin' up the Arkansas from end to end."

Colley cursed and rubbed his face. He desperately searched for a solution. "God dammit. God *dammit!* Boys, you gotta try and stop them."

Black Kettle spoke. Smith followed up: "He wants to know why it's always up to them to stop reprisals for what *we* do. Shit, that's a damn good question."

"Left Hand approached Larned with a white flag," Little Raven said. "He made a good-faith offer to help them go after Satanta, and what did he get? A cannonball! I think it is time we tell *you* to stop *your* warriors!"

"I know... I know," Colley sighed.

"Look," Left Hand said, "I am not going to fight the whites. You can put me in your stockade, you can shoot at me, but I am not going to fight. I know what your soldiers can do, and I know we cannot win, but young men think they are invincible in battle. I was not so much mad about what happened at Larned as I was confused. Hardy reassured me and I trusted him. You say it was Parmetar's fault, so I believe you, but my young men are not going to take this without a fight."

Black Kettle spoke to Smith again. Said Smith, "Black Kettle's still with us, but he agrees with Left Hand. He says he is committed to peace, but he says that this thing may be all to pieces war now."

Colley looked at Smith. "What the hell are we gonna do?"

Black Kettle spoke. "He wants to talk with a white chief," Smith said. "He wants a council."

Colley looked at Black Kettle. "I wish I could say yes, but it ain't in my power to arrange it."

Smith and Black Kettle conferred. Said Smith, "He wants to know who *does* have the power?"

"Maybe Chivington," Colley said.

"Aw, Christ," Smith said. "What, did you have shit in your ears when that bastard made his intentions known at Lyon? He don't want to council with nobody who ain't signed up to vote."

"Curtis and Blunt ain't gonna council. They put Chiv on his own out here."

Colley and Smith sat silently for a moment.

"Maybe Wynkoop?" Smith said.

"I just had the same idea," Colley said. "But he doesn't have the authority to negotiate."

"Yeah, but that old buffler could talk a couple of horny bull elks into kissin' one another. Maybe if he talks to Black Kettle and sees the chief means business, he'll take it back to Chivington. Him and Soule are old pards of Chiv, ya know. Maybe they could talk some sense into him."

Left Hand joined in. "I know Wynkoop. He is a good man."

"I know him, too," Little Raven said. "He was with the first of the Spider People that came for gold. He could be a prick, but he always talked straight with me."

"Shit, I don't know," Colley said.

"I know these boys, Sam," Smith said. "Warriors don't back down 'till all's said and done. Dogmen are already committed to go cross lots to kill any white they find, and now we just lost the Kiowas and the Arapahos...What do we got to lose?"

10

BENT'S RANCH
August 7, 1864.
TO: *Major Colley*

About 10 or 11 o'clock to-day four Kiowa Indians came in sight and finally came up. One of them was Satanta, or Sitting Bear, and one of them the Little Mountain, or Tohason's son. They said they were on a war party, and when they first left their camp that there was a very large party of them, and on the Cimarron they killed five whites, and the most of the party turned back from there.

The Little Mountain's son says he was sent to me by his father to see if I could not make peace with the whites and them. I told him that I could not say anything on that subject to them until I saw some of the proper authorities. I then told them that I had heard that General Curtis was at Fort Larned, and that he was a big chief, and that he was the man that they would have to talk to. They asked me about you. I told you were at the fort. The Indians are all over the hill, and I am afraid they have killed old man Rule's folks. I think I will have to move from here soon. The women are alarmed, and I don't think it safe here. We will send this down after night, as we don't think it safe to send a man in daylight. The Little Mountain's son appeared to be very anxious for peace, but it may all be a suck-in. I have no more to say. I am not in very good humor, as my old squaw ran off a few days ago, or rather went off with Joe Barraldo, as she liked him better than she did me. If I ever get sight of the young man it will go hard with him.

Yours truly,
WM. W. BENT

HEADQUARTERS
FORT LYON, COLORADO TERRITORY
August 9, 1864
TO: Colonel John Chivington
District of Colorado, Denver, Colorado Territory
SIR:

I have the honor to report for information of the colonel commanding that on the night of the 7th instant at about 10 o'clock I received intelligence that a train had been attacked about seven miles from this post by a band of Indians supposed to be Kiowas and Comanches, who immediately crossed to the south side of the river, and there joining a large party proceeded up the river.

I immediately sent word to Captain Gray, at Camp Wynkoop, to throw his command on the opposite side of the Arkansas River to cut off the retreat of the Indians, should they proceed in that direction. In the meanwhile, with eighty men and one howitzer, I crossed the river at this point for the purpose of proceeding up the other side rapidly in pursuit. My command consisted of detachments of Company D, commanded by Captain Soule, and Company K, commanded by Lieutenant Quinby, and Company G, with howitzer, commanded by Lieutenant Baldwin.

While crossing the river I received a dispatch from Bent's Ranch to the effect that a party of Indians had been there that evening, including Satanta, war chief of the Kiowas, and two more of their principal chiefs, that they had but a small party with them in sight, but the supposition was, judging from the importance of the chiefs present, that a very large war party was in the immediate neighborhood. The dispatch also stated that the Indians had proceeded down the river, and a few miles below Bent's Ranch they attacked a house occupied by a family named Rood and murdered all the inmates.

By a forced march I proceeded up in the direction of Bent's Ranch, seeing no signs of Indians until I reached the house said to have been attacked by the Indians, which was unoccupied, but which bore evidence of there having been a conflict, an attempt having been made to fire the house from the outside, which had proved unsuccessful. I afterward learned that the house had been gallantly defended by four men who had been attacked by fourteen of the red devils and had finally driven them off, killing one of them.

I then proceeded as far as Bent's Ranch, scouting the country, but finding no evidence of there having been more than fourteen Indians, and those having apparently rapidly decamped in direction of the Cimarron, after fruitless search I returned to-day to this post, my men having been in the saddle for two nights, being entirely exhausted. I am well convinced Satanta with 1,000 or more warriors of the Kiowas and Comanches is located over on the Cimarron or in that vicinity. I have also received information that four white men have been murdered by these same Indians near the Cimarron Crossing.

The available troops that I have in this garrison will not warrant me in attacking Satanta at present, not being able to take more than fifty men into the field, after leaving what would barely suffice for the absolute protection of the post. If it is possible I would respectfully recommend that I receive some re-enforcements, so that I may take a sufficient command in the field to punish this fiend Satanta and his murdering crew.

All of which is respectfully submitted.

I have the honor to remain, with much respect, your obedient servant,
E. W. WYNKOOP,
Major First Colorado Cavalry, Commanding Fort Lyon.

FORT LYON, COLORADO TERRITORY
August 12, 1864
TO: Major E. W. Wynkoop
SIR:

In pursuance to Special Orders, Numbers 169, dated at these headquarters, Fort Lyon, Colo. Ter., August 11, 1864, I started from this post at 12 p. m., proceeding down the river a distance of four or five miles and took a due north course for three miles, and there came in sight of a band of Indians who were from five to six miles in advance of us, they going in a northeast direction.

I immediately gave chase, and after a race of fifteen or twenty miles I came up with them, fourteen in number, who immediately turned and charged my command, and at the same time endeavoring to get to our rear. At the time that the fight commenced I had but six men; the rest, whose horses had failed, were to our rear, coming up as fast as possible. As soon as the rest of our men had joined us we advanced, driving them and following them four miles, in which it was a running fight, resulting in wounding four Indians and capturing one pony, with no loss on our side. I here sent back a messenger to report the facts to you, and ask for instructions. We were then twenty-five miles from the post; all of our horses given out.

After a rest of a few moments we went over on Sand Creek for water, which we found in abundance; then followed on for twenty miles farther, but were unable to get nearer than three quarters of a mile of them. Our horses all gave out but three. Went into camp on Sand Creek at an Indian crossing, where from 100 to 150 had crossed but an hour or two before we arrived, their trail leading southeast. At 10 at night there came up a very heavy rain-storm spoiling all our ammunition, thereby obliging us to start *for the post, where we arrived a little after sunrise on the 12th, traveling a distance of ninety miles.*

Allow me here to speak of the men who accompanied me, all of whom, with one exception, behaved with coolness and bravery. I would more particularly speak of Sergeant Forbes, Company D; Corporal Yakee Company D; and Sergeant Reed, of Company L, and recommend them to your notice. Had we had good arms I am satisfied we could have captured the whole band, but our carbines were useless, only two out of eleven that could be fired.

Respectfully submitted to Major Wynkoop for approval.
Very respectfully, your obedient servant,
JOSEPH A. CRAMER,
Second Lieutenant Company G, First Cavalry of Colorado.

FORT LYON, COLORADO TERRITORY,
August 13, 1864.
TO: Colonel John Chivington
District of Colorado, Denver, Colorado Territory
SIR:

I have the honor to report, for the information on the colonel commanding, that on the 11th instant while my ordnance sergeant, Kenyon, was a few miles north of this post in search of a stray horse, he was pursued by fifteen Indians, they following him to within sight of the commissary building. In ten minutes I had thirty men in the saddle, and dividing them into two squads started them immediately in pursuit. The detachments were respectively commanded by Lieutenants Cramer and Baldwin, copies of whose reports I enclose. Toward night, after hearing that Lieutenant Cramer was fighting the Indians, and receiving a message from him to the effect that he believed there to be a very large body in his neighborhood on Sand Creek, I hurriedly dispatched Lieutenant Quinby with thirty men to re-enforce Lieutenant Cramer. In the meanwhile Company E, Captain Gray, having arrived from Camp Wynkoop, I left them to garrison the post and followed in person with a section of the battery, Lieutenant Hardin, and a small detachment of cavalry, Captain Soule.

I was accompanied by Captain Robbins, chief of cavalry. It was very dark when I left the post, and I had gone but a few miles when a thundershower arose, making it impossible to know with any certainty what direction I was proceeding. I still kept on, and after a march of over six hours succeeded in finding Sand Creek; there halting the command I sent out scouts and remained until daybreak. On account of having been thrown considerably out of my course by the storm, I was unable to find either Lieutenant Cramer or the whereabouts of the Indians. The Indians are sup-

posed to be Kiowas. There is a probability that they are Arapahos. At all events, it is my intention to kill all Indians I may come across until I receive orders to the contrary from headquarters.

Just as I was about leaving the post with the above-mentioned command, two men were driven in by the Indians who were proceeding up the river. I have received official intelligence to the effect that thirty men of Company A, First Cavalry of Colorado, have had a fight with a large body of Indians, near the crossing of the Arkansas, and lost all their horses. A few days before that two men of Company A were murdered while out alone; two men of Company E while at Camp Wynkoop are supposed also to have been murdered.

I desire also to report the fact that the carbines with which our regiment is armed are absolutely worthless, it being impossible to discharge over two-thirds of them. I am obliged to depend almost altogether on the pistol and saber, and you are aware that a large number of the men are without pistols. I have no doubt that the post was surrounded by Indians for the purpose of endeavoring to run off my herds, but so far I have entirely baffled, not having lost a single head. I will continue to remain as vigilant as possible.

All of which is respectfully submitted.

I am, sir, very respectfully, your obedient servant,

E. W. WYNKOOP,

Major First Cavalry of Colorado, Commanding Fort Lyon

FORT LYON, COLORADO TERRITORY
August 12, 1864
TO: Hon. JOHN EVANS
Governor and Superintendent of Indian Affairs
SIR

The Indians are very troublesome. Yesterday a party of fifteen chased a soldier within three miles of the post. Lieutenant Cramer with fifteen men pursued them. After a chase of fifteen miles the Indians halted and gave fight. We killed 2, wounded 2 more, and captured 2 horses. They then retreated toward Sand Creek. Our horses were so much exhausted that our men were unable to pursue farther. Last evening an expressman was driven back by four Indians. There is no doubt but large parties, since the re-enforcement of Larned, have come up the river and are now in this vicinity. I fear the work at the agency will have to be abandoned if troops cannot be obtained to protect it. I have made application to Major Wynkoop for troops. He will do all he can, but the fact is we have no troops to spare from here. We cannot ascertain what Indians they were, but I fear that all the tribes are engaged. The Arapahoes that I have been feeding have not been in

for some time. It looks at present as though we shall have to fight them all.
S. G. COLLEY,
U. S. Indian Agent, Upper Arkansas.

No one ever claimed a desire for it. No one took responsibility for it. Despite the peace overtures made by many whites and Indians alike, the war that no one wanted just swallowed three territories whole, and both sides quickly pointed the finger of blame at each other. The skirmishes that began on the northernmost boundaries of the South Platte in Nebraska last April now bled down to the Arkansas, and no one, white or red, was safe.

Fort Lyon's small detachment barely held its own with worn animals and worthless weapons, while reinforcements from Fort Leavenworth and Fort Riley were inadequately small. General Curtis, although preoccupied with the war in the States, was forced to turn his attention to the Indians, an enemy he neither understood nor desired to confront. Curtis and General Blunt, under Curtis' command in the Upper Arkansas Military District, rarely saw eye-to-eye on matters, having butted heads over policy on numerous occasions. Curtis, who only now took an active role in the Indian war, was irritated by Major Wynkoop's dedication to Chivington, despite the fact that he himself had given Chivington authority to attack Indians without regard to district lines. Wynkoop was clearing all orders from headquarters through Chivington, often delaying procedures until Chivington gave his blessing. In the meantime, the Indians committed more raids and murders in the Larned area, for which Wynkoop and Chivington were blamed.

Curtis sent a scathing dispatch to Chivington stating, "I fear your attention is too much attracted by other matters than your command," alluding not-so subtly to Chivington's political aspirations. To this, Chivington angrily responded, "I have not spent an hour nor gone a mile to attend to other matters than my command... "

Curtis immediately joined patrols in search of warriors along the eastern forks of the Smoky Hill and Republican Rivers, but he had no success engaging in a battle with them. The major general's inexperience with the cunning Indians was tantamount to a little boy chasing fireflies at dusk. The Indians would appear and disappear as quickly as Curtis could find them, and he frustrated his troops with the naïve assumption that they were scaring the warriors out of the territory. After but a few marches, Curtis was convinced the problem was not as serious as the Coloradoans had portrayed it, and he informed General Blunt that the 600 men and a few howitzers allotted was more than a sufficient force to defeat the Indians. At that time, the combined forces of the Cheyenne, Arapaho, Sioux, Kiowa and Comanches numbered in the thousands. Despite the general's haughty conclusion, the warrior bands were neither frightened, nor interested in retreat...

11

Laura Roper was a petite 16-year-old with lovely brown hair and a smile of an angel. Born in Pennsylvania, Laura's father moved his wife Pauline and five children to the Nebraska Territory in 1860, homesteading at Oak Grove on the Little Blue River near the Kansas border. With partner Marshall Kelley, Joseph Roper opened a store and sold goods to emigrants. In early August 1864, Dogmen and Sioux war parties attacked and killed 15 whites along the Little Blue River in Kansas, and committed a half-dozen other like attacks in Kansas and Nebraska around the Little Blue and Plum Creek. Joe Roper himself was a victim of one raid, but he was fortunate to lose only horses with no one injured. He organized the men in the area to fortify their ranches and businesses, warning Laura and her sisters to never go outside alone.

On a sunny Sunday afternoon, Laura hitched a ride with Kelley and hired hand J. H. Butler, who headed for Nebraska City to pick up supplies. The road took them past the farm of Roper's neighbor, William Eubank, who had invited Laura to a family gathering after church. The large Eubank family included several children with whom Laura kept frequent company.

Laura hopped from the wagon and waved to Butler and Kelley.

"Thanks for the buggy ride!" Laura called.

The boys gave her a wave and hailed their team. They pushed on, sharing chewing tobacco and off-color jokes reserved exclusively for boys on the road. A mile or two rolled between them and the Eubank farm as they turned northeast, up the Little Blue for a half-mile. The rugged road along this portion of the trail could loosen a man's teeth and shock the spine. Butler let out a mighty wind from his bowels that sounded like the steam horn of a sternwheeler.

"Lordy mighty!" Kelley laughed. "You musta popped a button with that one!"

Butler broke wind again, bouncing and laughing with his boss.

"God dang, keep her on the road, will ya?" Kelley said.

"Whoosh!" Butler disgustedly waved the foul air.

The boys couldn't help but laugh. It was naturally accepted among young men that farts were funny, no matter how bad they smelled. Kelley raised a cheek to fire one in Butler's direction, but his eyes suddenly widened in utter horror. For a spell, he couldn't believe what he saw. An arrow whizzed through Butler's neck and pierced out of his throat. Butler lurched forward and drunkenly flailed as a river of blood spewed into Kelley's face.

"God almighty!" Kelley cried as Butler fell into him and dropped over the buckboard.

Cheyenne Dogman Big Crow jumped aboard, giving Kelley but a moment to react. Big Crow split Kelley's forehead with his tomahawk and counted coup with his bow before slowing the team. White Bird jumped on from the other side and stabbed Kelley several times. The Dogmen brought the wagon to a halt, and ten more warriors rode in, led by Chief Tall Bull. Big Crow scalped Butler, and White Bird took Kelley's hair. They whooped as they held the bloody scalps for all to cheer...

Laura passed the lazy afternoon away with the Eubank children, unaware of the horrible fate that Kelley and Butler had suffered just a few miles away. Lucinda Eubank fed the children fresh baked cookies, while they played games with Laura and Bill Eubank's teenage sister, Dora. Bill played cards and drank beer with his brothers, Joe, Fred, Henry, Jim, and their father, William Sr.

"Would you like to stay for supper?" Lucy asked Laura.

"No, thank you," Laura said. "I better be heading back home. It's getting on to four o'clock, and Mama's expecting me to help cook our supper."

Laura said goodbye to the children.

Bill Eubank left the boys at the card table. "I'll walk you home, honey."

"Oh, it's not too far," Laura said.

"I don't care if it's three steps away," Bill said. "You shouldn't be out walking by yourself. Lucy, you wanna stretch your legs?"

"That sounds good. I think I will." Lucy left her sister-in-law in charge of the kitchen and walked to the door with Laura and Bill.

"I wanna go, too!" cried three-year-old Isabel, pulling on Lucy's skirt.

"Let's just make a family outing of it," Lucy smiled. She pulled her infant son from his crib, for he had just awakened from a nap and was wide-eyed and grinning.

Laura and the Eubank family strolled out to the porch, followed by Grandpa Will Eubank, who was headed home with his nine-year-old grandson, Ambrose Asher.

"See ya Wednesday, Pop," Bill said.

Grandpa gave a wave and lifted Ambrose into his wagon. They rode off in the opposite direction.

Laura and little "Belle" walked hand-in-hand and sang a nurs-ery rhyme, while Bill and Lucy strolled close to the river. Bill handed baby Willie to Lucy and grabbed a handful of stones to toss into the water. Bill pulled his shoes off and waded into the banks of the stream, kicking water at the girls. Belle squealed and hid behind Laura, and Lucy turned to keep the water off the baby.

"Stop it!" Lucy laughed. "I swear you're worse than the chil-dren!"

"Come on and dip your feet!" Bill said. Indeed, for a 28-year-old man, Bill still had the heart of a four-year-old.

He carried on for another minute as Laura and Belle walked fur-ther up the road toward the 'Narrows,' where the road allowed a tight passage along the water.

"Dang!" Bill yelped. He limped from the creek and two-hopped in pain from a cocklebur lodged between his toes.

"Ha!" Lucy said. "Serves you right!" She continued toward Laura and Belle, while Bill perched on a rock and dug out the bur.

Laura and Belle laughed and stopped to wait. Down the road, Bill managed to get back on his feet. Suddenly, he stopped and cocked his head back toward the house. Laura curiously looked back, hearing a woman's scream from that direction. They saw a dozen Dogmen descending on the house, one chasing Dora Eubank, and the others tearing into Bill's brothers.

"Oh no!" Lucy cried. She ran to Laura and Belle, and they hun-kered down in the brush. Bill stood frozen for a moment, watching the Dogman shoot his brothers and viciously pounce on Dora. Torn between his two families, Bill made the decision to run for his wife and children. He shuffled them down the narrows to a buffalo wal-low, where they took cover in deep timber.

Belle began to cry, and Laura snatched her up to quiet her. Lucy trembled and clutched Willie to her breast as Bill pulled them close. In the distance, they heard the hideous war cries of the Dogmen.

"What should we do?" Lucy said.

"Be quiet," Bill whispered. "Laura, honey, try to keep Belle quiet."

Too terrified to speak, Laura buried Belle's head in her bosom.

Bill's body trembled with fear and rage. He cursed himself for not bringing a weapon. They listened to the Indians for a minute or two, and then Bill warily crawled to a small rise to peer out. He quickly dropped back down, his eyes wet and wide.

"What?" Lucy whispered.

"They're coming," Bill said.

They dug themselves into the grass and brush, Laura struggling with Belle, who squirmed in terror. Bill snatched his handkerchief and stuffed it in Belle's mouth. "Be quiet honey, be quiet. We'll be alright."

In a moment, they heard the ominous sound of horse hooves clopping along the road. The Dogmen continued to whoop and excitedly chatter. The family hunkered down when the Dogmen passed, not more than thirty feet away. Bill nearly crushed Laura and Belle, and the little girl began to suffocate under the weight. Bill clenched his eyes without letting up, praying to God that he wouldn't smother his own daughter. Belle suddenly broke free and spat out the kerchief. She threw a mighty yowl, and the warriors abruptly stopped.

Tall Bull spun his horse around. "What was that?" he said.

Big Crow peered off towards the trees. Belle screamed again. "Little rabbits!" Big Crow cried, and the Dogmen quickly pushed into the trees.

Bill jumped up and defiantly stood in front of his family. "Get out of here!" he screamed. He desperately grappled at the loose timber and pulled a dead branch out. The Dogmen formed a circle and rode around the terrified family. Bill wildly swung the branch, much to the amusement of the warriors.

"Swing your stick!" White Bird railed in Cheyenne. "You cannot touch me!"

"Try to touch me!" Big Crow taunted.

"Get back!" Bill cried, valiantly swinging his stick.

Lucy screamed in terror, still clutching her baby. Laura simply dropped atop Belle and prayed.

"Do you like your own medicine?" Tall Bull growled. "Do you want to kill us?"

The Dogmen continued to circle the family.

"You are a sick coyote!" Big Crow laughed. "You do not have any medicine from the Long Knives now, do you!"

Bill's eyes were wet with rage. He gasped for breath. "Leave us be! These are children, for God's sake! Leave us be!"

"He cries like his baby!" White Bird railed. "Stand up and fight like a man!"

The Dogmen stopped circling, and Tall Bull dismounted. He walked up to Bill and glared at him. Exhausted, Bill tried to raise his stick. "He wants to count coup," Tall Bull said to his men.

The Indians let out their war cries. Bill looked at Tall Bull, and for a moment, he thought he might be able to reason with the chief. "In God's name, please leave us alone."

Tall Bull cocked his head, still staring at Bill. He reached across his chest and grabbed the dog rope tied to his shoulder, gently stroking it. "I am a man," he growled. He let go of the dog rope and slowly reached for Bill, who cautiously watched. Tall Bull put his hand on Bill's shoulder, and the Dogmen screamed their approval of the chief's coup. Tall Bull then smiled and backed away. Bill tried to smile and nod back, but the Dogman chief suddenly raised a pistol and shot Bill in the head.

The girls hysterically screamed as Bill's body dropped to the ground, his head spurting blood like a geyser. The Dogmen screamed with the women as Tall Bull dropped on Bill and unsheathed his knife. He put his knee in Bill's back and wrenched his bloody head back. Lucy violently shook, and Laura could scream no more as they watched Tall Bull slice a long swath across Bill's skull. Tall Bull ripped Bill's scalp off and raised it to the sun. He gave a hideous war cry, and Lucy's knees buckled. She dropped down, her screaming infant gasping at her breast. Laura cried and covered Belle's eyes...

The Dogmen celebrated Tall Bull's coup for several minutes, and then Big Crow approached Laura, who would not let go of Belle. Big Crow curiously looked at Laura's sun hat and ripped it off her head. He examined it for a minute and then put it on his head. He shoved Laura to the ground and took her slippers, and stole a ring from her finger. He reached for Laura's gold necklace and tried to yank it from her neck, but it didn't break. She cried out as Big Crow tried to dislodge the chain a few more times before giving up. The other Dogmen gathered around Lucy, stealing similar souvenirs and then dragging the girls out to the road. They swept them onto two ponies and rode back to the Eubank house.

As they approached, Laura and Lucy saw Dora Eubank lying in the dirt. She appeared dead until they rode closer and saw her still breathing, her hands clutching a hideous gash in her neck. A red-brown pool of blood spread beneath her, and Lucy tried to speak to her through her sobs. They continued past the dying girl and came upon the scalped bodies of Bill's brothers. Laura desperately gasped for breath at the sight of the dead men. The Dogmen dragged the women off their ponies and roughly led them into the house.

Tall Bull kicked a table over, and Big Crow and White Bird commenced to destroy everything inside. The women circled around the children and trembled in a corner, but now it appeared the Dogmen had no interest in them. The women heard the war cry of another warrior, who walked in with Dora's bloody scalp dangling from a stick. After the Indians ransacked the house, Tall Bull approached the women and spoke in broken English.

"We go," he said. The terrified women looked at him, unable to comprehend. Tall Bull quickly rummaged around the house and found a blanket. He brought it back and shoved it at Lucy, gesturing at the baby. "We go!" he said.

Lucy wrapped the infant in the blanket, and Tall Bull shoved her toward the door. He looked back at Laura, who quickly looked around for something to wrap around Belle.

"My daughter needs clothes," Lucy whimpered. She looked at Tall Bull and pointed at Belle's room. "I need to get her clothes."

Tall Bull nodded and shoved her. In a moment, Lucy came back with a few of Belle's dresses, which she wrapped in her arms with the baby. She put on a sunbonnet, and the Dogmen took the women and children back outside, loading them all on a single horse. They gathered food and weapons taken from the house and pushed the horses south, traveling a mile before coming upon a burning wagon on the road. Two more Dogmen stood by the wreck, holding a trembling boy by his hair.

"Oh, dear God," Lucy cried. "Grandpa..."

The old man's charred corpse lay in the burning rubble. The Dogmen took young Ambrose and slung him up on a horse. One climbed aboard with the boy, and the party set out for the long ride back down to the Smoky Hill River...

The war party and their captives rode throughout the moonlit night. Laura and Lucy, still numb with shock, desperately clung to the children, their bodies aching from the relentless pounding of their horse. The children were entirely spent, and they slept in the ladies' arms. The warriors, accustomed to long rides over the prairie, showed little mercy and made threatening gestures whenever the women cried out. It was well past midnight when one Indian, a man the women had not seen until now, rode up by Laura. In the darkness, she could barely make out his features, but he spoke English clearly.

"Just keep your mouths shut, ladies," he softly said. "You'll get out of this alive if you don't give these bucks no trouble."

Ravaged by exhaustion, Lucy was too tired to speak, but Laura couldn't help her curiosity. "Who...who are you?"

"Keep your voice low, girl. My name's Joe," he said. "Joe Beralda."

"Are you an Indian?" Laura whispered.

"Shit, no...s'cuse the language. Leastwise, I ain't but half Indian on my mama's side."

"Where did you come from?"

"I caught up with you 'bout two miles back. I was camped and seen you all a-comin,' so I thought I'd talk to these boys and try to make sense outta what they done."

"You know them?"

"They's Cheyenne Dogmen, and a couple of 'em are Arapaho warriors. I know these parts, and they sometimes trade with me for information as to where the soldiers are. I tried to see if they'd sell ya to me, but I ain't got nothin' worth exchangin' for all four."

Lucy gave a breathy whimper and let her head hang down.

"You best keep as quiet as you can, lady," Beralda said. "You go makin' a loud fuss, and they'll kill you sure as hell. They don't want no noise to draw attention to them."

"Where are they taking us?" Laura said.

"There's a big injun camp about two days ride from here."

"They killed Mrs. Eubank's husband," Laura said. "They killed his whole family."

Beralda shrugged. "You best try to forget 'bout that now. Ain't nothin' you can do but try to keep yourself alive."

"But my mama and daddy," Laura said, trying not to cry. "They're just a mile away from the Eubank's farm."

"Ain't nothin' you can do about it, girl. I cain't say for sure, but I didn't hear them say nothin' bout killin' anybody but the ones at the lodge you came from."

"Can you help us, Mr. Beralda?"

"Cain't say I can. Like I told ya, I ain't got enough to trade."

"Oh no." Laura closed her eyes and prayed.

"You afraid they gonna kill you, too?"

Laura sucked back her tears. "I guess, if that's what they wanted, they'd have done it by now."

"I'm thinkin' the same thing," Beralda said. "I got a suspicion you're worth more to 'em alive than dead."

"What do you mean?"

"They take captives usually for slaves, but sometimes for barter."

"Barter?"

"That's right. And right now, white women and children are the best barter for getting what they want from the soldiers. I reckon they may give you up soon, if you're lucky. You just have to buck up and be brave. Don't show no weakness, 'cause an injun respects a strong woman. Don't cry none, 'cause that's the worst thing you can do 'round 'em."

"Please help us."

"Girl, I cain't take you. They'd kill me if I tried. All I can do is go and tell the soldiers they got you. The injuns want them to know, anyways."

"Can you find out if my mama and papa are alive?"

"I told you – you best forget about them."

"Please. My name is Laura Roper, and they live on the Little Blue. Please find them and tell them I'm alive."

Beralda puffed a sigh. "Cain't make no promises, girl. I'll see what I can do." He turned his horse and rode into the darkness...

By sunup, the party reached a small creek, where they dismounted and pulled the women and children from their horse. Lucy dropped to the ground, her arms now frozen around her baby. Laura's legs and back were painfully stiff, but she managed to sit Belle down in the shade of the pony before collapsing. Belle whimpered and Laura quickly tried to quiet her when Tall Bull approached them.

"Go," Tall Bull said, pointing at the creek, where the Dogmen gathered to drink and rest. Laura and Lucy took the children to the water, and they tried to quench their thirst and relieve themselves. Tall Bull came to them soon and offered strands of dried buffalo meat for them to eat, which they gratefully accepted.

They stayed there for an hour before the air was pierced by a distant war cry. The Dogmen looked up and returned the greeting of five Arapahos riding in from the west. This second war party, loaded with stolen horses and bounty from a raid on Plum Creek, joined Tall Bull's men. Despite the extraordinary horror of her predicament, Laura felt a small amount of relief to be able to ride on her own horse now. She was an experienced rider, and she offered to carry Belle with her. Tall Bull approved, for Belle screamed when the Indians tried to separate her from her mother or Laura. Lucy, a bit stronger from the brief rest, was able to mount a horse and carry her baby.

The party ventured south again, and rode for the entire day until darkness again swallowed the prairie. By now, Laura and Lucy were delirious from lack of sleep, but the Indians appeared impervious to fatigue. The children slept for the most part, and the women fell into light slumber when a warrior would lead their horses from time to time. They finally reached a deep ravine, and in the darkness, the women were left on their own to guide their horses through. Laura fared well, but her saddle suddenly slipped, and she instinctively lurched forward to catch herself. Startled, her pony bolted and stumbled in the wet grass. In an instant, the horse went down, tossing Laura and Belle headlong into the water. Laura tried to protect Belle, twisting to take the fall on her shoulder. They hit hard, and Belle gave a loud cry. Laura tried to scramble to her feet, pushing Belle away from the lunging pony, but the horse's left leg swung around and struck Laura in the face. Everything went black as Laura crumpled to the ground.

She lay there for a moment, trying to collect her thoughts and clear the swirling stars from her head. The Indians stopped, and Big Crow jumped from his horse. He pulled Laura away from the struggling pony, and with unexpected sympathy, he gently put her down and held her steady. Laura put her hand to her face and tried not to cry out, but her broken nose was bleeding badly. The other warriors gathered around her, and Tall Bull brought a sheet stolen from the Eubank's house and roughly wiped the blood from Laura's face. Although the gesture exacerbated Laura's pain, she gritted her teeth and gave not a single cry.

"We should call her 'Crooked Nose' now," Big Crow said, and the Dogmen laughed.

Laura defiantly took the sheet and cocked her head back to control the bleeding.

"Are you okay?" Lucy whimpered.

Laura simply nodded and spat blood.

Big Crow pulled her to her feet and thrust her back on her horse. He then grabbed Belle, who was too spent to cry, and handed her to Laura.

"Are you okay, honey?" Laura asked Belle. The little girl whimpered for a moment and then put her head down to sleep.

The journey resumed...

The party rode into the next dawn, and the hot summer sun then traced across the sky until it was high overhead. Mid day passed, and Tall Bull finally chose a spot to stop. At last, the warriors' stamina waned, and they were ready to rest. They camped near a small creek by a grove of trees for protection from the heat. White Bird and Big Crow shouldered their bows and crept down the stream in search of wild game. The others laid out buffalo robes on the soft ground and allowed the women and children to lie down. There, they ate more dried buffalo until Big Crow and White Bird soon returned with a turkey they had killed. The bird was gutted and cooked over a fire, and Laura tried to eat, although her face was terribly swollen. She struggled, but her hunger overcame the pain, and she managed to swallow a few bites. The warriors eagerly tore into their sparse meal, chattering and laughing. A few of them lit cigars – trophies of their recent raids – and they enjoyed fresh coffee and whiskey.

When the meal was over, everyone laid back to rest, and Lucy and the children fell into a deep slumber. Laura tried to sleep, but she struggled in agony, her right eye now locked shut. For some time, the warriors paid little attention to her, but an Arapaho medicine man suddenly approached her with a sticky red poultice in his hands. He dipped his finger in it and reached for Laura's face. She fought her impulse to pull away, for he gave her a smile and gestured as if to say he would not hurt her. She relented, and the medicine man gently smudged her face with the herbal mixture. He only stayed for a moment, and he then returned to the fire. Before long, sleep overtook Laura, and she was able to rest for a short time...

"Go!"

Laura's eyes fluttered. For a moment, she was asleep in her warm featherbed. But now, as her eyes broke to the prairie, there was no sunshine of early dawn. It was dark. Reality returned in short order, and Laura looked at the burning embers of the fire, while the Dogmen busily packed their horses. It was time to travel again.

"Go!" Tall Bull ordered again, and Laura quickly pulled herself to her knees. The familiar pain around her eyes crept into her consciousness, but it had grown merciful in her sleep. She gingerly touched her broken nose, which was still swollen, but only half as large as before. Her right eye could now focus, and she looked for Lucy and Belle, who scrambled to their feet nearby. Belle was cranky at the unkind awakening, and she began to cry and fuss. Baby Willie wailed for food as well, and the warriors grew angry at the noise. They barked at Lucy, and Laura moved in to stand her ground, recalling the advice given to her by the stranger she'd met along the road. She took Belle in her arms, while Lucy turned and allowed the baby to suckle. Belle would not be pacified, however, and she screamed her displeasure to Laura and the Indians - and to the Great Spirit, if it was interested.

Big Crow stepped in and reached for the little girl, but Laura wouldn't let him take her.

"Stop it!" Laura ordered. "I'll quiet her! Just let me have a minute!"

The other warriors laughed at Laura's defiance, which infuriated Big Crow. The big warrior grabbed Belle by her curly locks and ripped her from Laura's arms.

"No!" Laura cried. "Let her go!"

Big Crow shoved Laura to the ground and unsheathed his knife, while Belle bawled at the moon. He put the knife to Belle's throat.

Laura leapt to her feet and lunged at Big Crow. "No!" she screamed. She gave him a mighty swing, grabbing at the knife and struggling to pull it away from the little girl's throat. Big Crow grappled with Laura, while the warriors whooped their approval. Laura forced the Dogman to back off as Lucy snatched her daughter away.

Laura huffed and puffed, defiantly glaring at Big Crow. "You keep your filthy hands off of her!"

The Dogmen whooped and cheered.

"Brave Squaw!" Big Crow said in English, laughing with the boys.

Tall Bull stomped up, irritated. "Stop wasting time! Get your horses and we go!"

Big Crow obeyed, still chuckling with his friends. He opened his hands to Laura, gesturing that he was finished playing. He led her to a mule. "Brave Squaw – you like Screaming Bird? You keep her quiet now."

Laura looked at the beast disapprovingly. "It's too small for us. I want a horse." Big Crow didn't understand, until Laura carried Belle over to a sturdy pony. "I want *this* horse."

Big Crow caught more chiding laughter from the warriors. "You will be sorry you took *that* one," White Bird cackled. "Looks like you met your match!"

Now more frustrated than angry, Big Crow tried to lead the mule to Laura again.

"*You* ride that mule, you bully!" Laura said. "I'm tired of you! You hear?" She swung herself on the pony and pulled Belle up.

"Let her ride the damned pony!" Tall Bull ordered. "We have to go!"

Big Crow shook his head and mounted his horse. "Brave Squaw," he muttered...

Another brutal ride through the night and the following day delivered unrelenting aches and pain to the captives, while the warriors rode with strength and determination. From time to time, the children would fuss, but they had little strength to persevere for long. Lucy and Laura summoned strength from every fiber without complaint, and little Ambrose bravely obeyed the warriors without a tear. The new day ushered in more heat than the previous, and everyone lustily suckled at the few creeks and streams they found along the way.

By noon, the party neared the Smoky Hill, but before reaching the river, they caught sight of a large band of warriors heading in from the west. The rendezvous was joyous, as the braves proudly displayed their plunder and joined in a scalp dance. The new band examined Tall Bull's live bounty, admiring the women and children like precious jewels. Laura and Lucy were so beaten down by now that they had little fright left in them. When they were first captured, they were terrified of being sexually violated, but at no time since had any warrior made any overture of the kind. The new band was equally cautious, for none of them dared to touch the prized possession of the fearsome Dogman, Chief Tall Bull.

The warriors now readied themselves for something of which the captives were unsure. It appeared they were preparing to fight, for they painted their faces and put feathers in their hair. They took on a similar countenance of the uniformed Union soldiers that Laura had seen along the Little Blue. When the warriors were finally prepared, the combined forces headed for the Smoky Hill, showing military reverence to Tall Bull and the two chiefs of the other bands. Laura and Lucy rode well behind the main body, their horses led by a young warrior boy who appeared frustrated by the minimal duty assigned to him. They rode for over an hour, as several wolves - Indian scouts - would ride ahead and circle back to report their findings.

Finally, one wolf came back, excitedly gesturing to Tall Bull. The chief stopped and briefly spoke with the boy. He then turned and gave a hand signal that spurred a wild celebration. The band erupted and galloped to a hill, whooping and cheering. Lucy and Laura held on for dear life as their escort pulled the horses hard to keep up.

When they reached the top of the rise, Laura heard herself gasp as the sight of a vast Indian camp sprawled before her. Thousands of Indians dotted the prairie, many mounting their horses and riding out to greet them. The war party rode in to a reception fit for royalty. Laura and Lucy were driven away from the main party and accosted by a pack of whooping squaws, who ripped the women from their horses and knocked them to the ground. The children were taken away, and the squaws kicked and beat Laura and Lucy for several minutes. Laura covered herself, trying her best to protect her injured nose, and for the first time since she watched the Dogmen murder Bill Eubank, she was certain that *her* time to die was near. The beating persisted for another minute or two, but then subsided as quickly as it had begun. Laura peered up and saw the squaws back off, now warbling over their bounty.

Lucy was taken away by one squaw, and another led Laura

across the village to a teepee. Inside, the squaw pushed Laura down on a buffalo robe. Laura scrambled to her haunches, her nose bleeding, and prepared for another attack. The squaw simply smiled and pointed to the buffalo robe. Laura wiped the blood from her face, and the squaw offered her a white man's handkerchief. Confusion scarcely described Laura's emotion right now, but she accepted the squaw's offer to clean her face. The Indian woman, who just moments ago ripped Laura's hair and beat her, now treated her as if she were comforting a child. She spoke a few gentle words and helped her lie down on the robe. Laura suddenly felt as if her very life had just drained from her body. Lying on the soft robe in the cool stillness of the Indian lodge, she turned her eyes to darkness, and sweet sleep washed over her like gentle rain...

After several hours of dreamless sleep, Laura awoke. She could barely move for a moment, her stiff back and legs protesting, but her senses were salved by an inviting smell. The squaw knelt beside Laura, holding a piece of tree bark piled high with strands of freshly cooked buffalo.

The squaw gently touched Laura's nose. "Hurt," she softly said.

Laura sat up. "It's not too bad. Do you speak English?"

"Ing-lish," the squaw curiously said. "Eat?" She pushed the buffalo to Laura.

"Thank you," Laura said. Ladylike manners were all but forgotten now, as Laura ripped into the meat. When the buffalo found her tongue, she gave a satisfied moan. Never before had any food tasted this good, and she made the fare disappear in an instant. The squaw gave her water and fresh strawberries, and before long Laura's body responded to the nourishment. While she ate, the squaw fussed over Laura's hair, combing and twirling it into braids. Laura didn't know why the woman's disposition had turned so, but she was too grateful for the food to care. When she finished, the squaw smiled.

"More?" she asked.

"Oh, no," Laura said. She rubbed her tummy. "I'm full. Thank you."

"Than-kyoo," the squaw said.

Laura smiled back, and she pointed at her chest. "I am Laura."

The squaw cocked her head. "Laa?"

"Laura. My name is Laura."

"Larr-ahh."

"What is your name?"

"Namm."

"I'm Laura. You?"

The squaw looked at Laura, but she didn't comprehend. Before she tried to speak, the lodge suddenly shook, and the tent flap drew back. Laura and the squaw jumped as a large warrior entered, his eyes red with anger.

Terrified, Laura reared back. The Indian looked like a giant bear, glaring at Laura with a terrible scowl.

"No!" Laura cried.

The warrior turned to the squaw and spoke Arapaho. "What did you do to her?"

"Nothing!" the squaw said, sharing Laura's fear. "I fed her! I let her sleep!"

The warrior, still enraged, knelt down before Laura. He saw her trembling hands and looked into her terrified eyes. He then reached for Laura's crooked nose.

"Please! Don't hurt me!" Laura screamed.

The warrior suddenly pulled back. "I am sorry," he said.

Laura froze, utterly astonished. After two days and nights with murderous warriors that cackled and crowed in a tongue she couldn't begin to understand, she suddenly found herself in front of the meanest-looking Indian she ever saw – and he spoke English as well as any white man she ever knew.

"I did not mean to frighten you," he said. "You are safe, and no one is going to hurt you."

"Dear me," Laura said.

"Who did this?" he said, pointing to Laura's face. He looked at the squaw. "Did you break her nose?"

The squaw reared back, still frightened and unable to understand white man words.

"No!" Laura said. "It was an accident! I fell off my horse!"

The warrior relented with a sigh and spoke to the squaw. "I am sorry," he said in Arapaho. "I am not mad at you."

"Then why are you yelling at me?" the indignant squaw said. "I was nice to her, and she was nice to me – until you came in and started growling like a wolf!"

"I *said* I am sorry."

The squaw swatted him on the back and rolled her eyes at Laura. "Men," she said. "Do you want me to go?"

"No," he said. "She is frightened, and I am not helping matters."

"Shuhh," the squaw huffed. "Try acting like a lamb instead of a jackass."

"Enough," he said. "Sit down here and help me comfort her."

Laura watched the squaw come to her and gently rub her arm.

The warrior spoke English again. "We will help fix your nose. We have good medicine for you."

Laura sucked back her fear. Don't be weak, she told herself. "Sir, why did you do this to me and my friends? Where is Lucy and her children - and the little boy they kidnapped?"

"I will see that your daughter is brought to you."

"My daughter?"

The warrior gestured as if Laura just said something stupid. "Your little girl."

"Belle? She's not my daughter. She's Lucy's girl."

"Awww!" The warrior put his face in his hands and rubbed. "The little girl you carried is not yours?"

"No! She's Lucy's daughter!"

He looked at the squaw. "This just gets worse," he muttered in Arapaho.

"What?" the squaw asked.

He waved her off and turned back to Laura. "What is your name, child?"

"Laura Roper." She politely put her hand out. "What is your name?"

The warrior smiled. "You go through all this, and you are still a lady. I am Niwot." He extended his left hand.

"Naa - what?"

He looked at his extended hand. "Your people call me Left Hand."

Laura took his hand. "How do you do."

"I am sorry that this happened to you," Left Hand said. "I am told your people were rubbed out."

"They were my friends, not relatives. I was visiting them when your men killed Lucy's family."

"I know you will not feel any better about me, but the men who attacked you are not my people. They are Dogmen and two warriors of another band of my tribe."

"You're right, it doesn't make me feel any better. It was cold-blooded murder. Mr. Eubank and his brothers and sister didn't do anything to those savages, and they shot them and scalped them. They made me and Lucy and her children watch."

Left Hand shook his head. "I am sorry, Laura Roper. That is all I can say about it."

"If you're sorry, then let us go."

"I cannot."

"Why?"

Left Hand stood and paced the lodge. "I know you have been

through a terrible thing, and I do not want to make it worse for you, but I have bad news."

Laura felt her heart drop. "How could anything be worse?"

Left Hand sighed. "Your friend, the one you call 'Lucy.' While you were asleep, the Dogmen sold her and her baby to the Lakota."

"The what?"

"Lakota. You call them Sioux. A warrior named Two Face traded for them. His band then rode away."

"What about Belle?"

"The little girl is still here. They thought she was your child."

"No, no."

"They said you carried her all the time. They thought she was yours."

"What about the little boy – Ambrose?"

"He is still with the Dogmen."

"Why do you people behave like this?" Laura wanted to cry, but she held back. "How can you be so heartless to kill people and take a child from her mother?"

"I told you, it was not me!"

"What does that matter? You act like you are in charge. Are you a chief?"

"Yes. I am a chief of Cloud People. You call us Arapaho."

"Sir, if you are a chief, then why did you let those savages take Lucy?"

"I lead my people. I have no say what the Dogmen do with their slaves. And this all took place before I arrived. Believe me, if I could have talked them out of it, I would."

"Slaves? Is that what I am?"

"No. I have seen to that."

"What do you mean?"

"I paid the Dogmen for you and Belle. You will go with us."

Laura sat back and closed her eyes, unsure how to take this news.

"You will not be mistreated, I promise."

"So... so am I *your* slave now?"

"No. I promise I will try to return you to your people, but you must know it may take time."

"How long?"

"I do not know – that is the truth. I will see to it that you and the little girl are fed and kept warm, but we must travel all the time to avoid the soldiers."

"Why can't you just give us to the soldiers?"

"It is not that easy," Left Hand sadly said. "We are at war with them. We cannot approach them without getting into a fight."

"Oh, dear God help us."

"I will keep you safe," Left Hand said. "My people are good Indians, and the Cheyennes we travel with are good Indians. Come, I want you to meet their chief."

Left Hand led Laura out, and they walked across the large village, approaching the main lodge of the Cheyenne encampment.

"You will meet the Cheyenne chief – he is a bigger chief than me, and he is my good friend. You will show him respect, for he is a good man and will protect you."

Laura waited as Left Hand entered the big lodge. Her heart raced while many new Indian faces curiously passed by and looked her over. In a moment, Left Hand came out, followed by a man whose very countenance struck Laura with a sense of awe. The chief's magnificent features were ground in granite, and he moved with deliberate grace. He was an older man, and when he stepped out, the Indians respectfully acknowledged his presence.

His deep voice resonated in the Cheyenne tongue. "Is this our little Brave Squaw?" he asked.

"Her name is Laura Roper," Left Hand said.

"Laa-raa Roop – Rope-her," said the chief. He looked at Left Hand. "She knows that her friend is gone?"

"Yes," Left Hand said. "She *is* brave."

"Tell her she is safe with us. Tell her I will try to help her."

"He says he will help you," Left Hand said.

"Tell him I'm obliged."

Left Hand spoke, and the big chief gave her a reassuring smile. "Laa-raa Rope-her," he said.

"What is his name?" Laura asked.

"Moke-tav-a-to," Left Hand said. "Your people call him Black Kettle..."

12

The South Platte route was cut off by the middle of August, leaving Denver entirely isolated. The relentless sacking of supply trains, settlements and stagecoaches by Indian war parties whittled Denver's food supply down to scraps, and prices for the most basic necessities tripled. The locust blight of July destroyed virtually all of the crops along the river, and those farmers who managed to cultivate some product were pinned down and unable to deliver. White settlers on the Nebraska and Kansas prairies abandoned their homes and fled to the east in droves, encountering the scalped bodies of neighbors along the way. But the Colorado citizens along the Front Range had nowhere to run. They were surrounded by Indians to the north, east and south, and blocked by a majestic but treacherous 14,000-foot mountain range to the west. With little armed military protection along the river routes, any attempt to flee was an invitation to disaster.

The time to act was now. Governor Evans could wait no longer. His pleas to General Curtis for more military support as yet unfulfilled, he went directly over Curtis' head to Secretary of War Edwin Stanton in Washington. In no uncertain terms Evans informed Stanton that he had unimpeachable evidence that proved the five Indian nations of the plains were now united in war against the whites, and a large military force of at least 10,000 troops was immediately required to put down the Indian uprising. He urgently requested that the Colorado Second Regiment, fighting Confederates on the Kansas-Missouri border, be immediately called home. Otherwise, Evans warned, Denver would surely be destroyed.

The wily governor's gamble paid off. The powers in Washington finally realized the consequences of losing the linchpin of commerce in the gold-laden Rocky Mountains, and Stanton lit a fire under General Curtis to respond to Evans' admonition. Both Curtis and the War Department immediately replied. Evans was informed that the Colorado Second was engaged in defending against a Confederate move on Kansas City and could not return to Denver. As an alternative, the War Department authorized Evans to raise the volunteer regiment he had vehemently requested all summer. The home militia would be commissioned as the new Colorado Third Volunteer Regiment, and volunteers would be guaranteed pay for a maximum of 100 days.

Evans wasted little time. Colonel Chivington declared martial law and immediately began a recruitment campaign, dragging storekeepers, gamblers, miners, drunks, and even jailed prisoners to Camp Weld, and Governor Evans took his case to the public:

BY ORDER OF HON. JOHN EVANS
GOVERNOR, TERRITORY OF COLORADO
AUGUST 11, 1864
PROCLAMATION

Having sent special messengers to the Indians of the plains, directing the friendly to rendezvous at Fort Lyon, Fort Larned, Fort Laramie, and Camp Collins for safety and protection, warning them that all hostile Indians would be pursued and destroyed, and the last of said messengers having now returned, and the evidence being conclusive that most of the Indian tribes of the plains are at war and hostile to the whites, and having to the utmost of my ability endeavored to induce all Indians of the plains to come to said places of rendezvous, promising them subsistence and protection, which, with few exceptions, they have refused to do.

Now, therefore, I, John Evans, governor of Colorado Territory, do issue this my proclamation, authorizing all citizens of Colorado, either individually or in such parties as they may organize, to go in pursuit of all hostile Indians on the plains, scrupulously avoiding those who have responded to my said call to rendezvous at the points indicated; also, to kill and destroy, as enemies of the country, wherever they may be found, all such hostile Indians. And further, as the only reward I am authorized to offer for such services, I hereby empower such citizens, or parties of citizens, to take captive, and hold to their own private use and benefit, all the property of said hostile Indians that they may capture, and to receive for all stolen property recovered from said Indians such reward as may be deemed proper and just therefor.

I further offer to all such parties as will organize under the militia law of the Territory for the purpose to furnish them arms and ammunition, and to present their accounts for pay as regular soldiers for themselves, their horses, their subsistence, and transportation, to Congress, under the assurance of the department commander that they will be paid.

The conflict is upon us, and all good citizens are called upon to do their duty for the defense of their homes and families...

William Byers printed Governor Evans' newest proclamation in the *Rocky Mountain News*, and for the first time since April, the citizens of Denver could entertain a glimmer of hope. Rumors of an Indian invasion of Colorado ran rampant, and now the governor had licensed any able-bodied man with a rifle and an ounce of courage to forego conventional law and take matters into his own hands. In essence, those who reasoned that killing an Indian in self-defense was justifiable could now reconcile with the notion of hunting down and killing one for sport...

The dark smoke of war now clearly loomed on Colorado's eastern horizon. From the open expanses of the Wyoming prairie, to the banks of the Upper Arkansas, Colorado settlers organized small militias to protect their families, farms, ranches and mining camps. Many initiated Indian hunting expeditions along the Front Range, and some turned their attention to the mountains, where Ute tribes were targeted. A few skirmishes broke out, claiming several white and Indian lives, but most self-appointed white vigilantes lacked the experience or tenacity to track and kill seasoned Indian warriors. While Chivington and Evans pressed to fill the Colorado Third Cavalry with volunteers, soldiers of the First Regiment increased patrols on the protected routes. At last, the white citizens of the Colorado Territory believed Evans was doing something to protect them.

Colonel Chivington used the institution of martial law to inflate his power, and many Denverites suddenly found themselves under his thumb. He vehemently enforced curfews, shut down stores and services, rationed supplies and trade, and forbade travel out of the city – all measures to corral volunteers for the Third Cavalry. The colonel took a hard stance on the subject of patriotism and duty, admonishing citizens to either join his militia, or donate to its cause. A feeding frenzy broke out among Denver businessmen to outfit the new regiment, and Chivington wielded his influence to sway the lucrative government contracts to those who toed the party line. His political campaign strategy was well defined, for it was proven throughout the United States that military heroes could virtually write their own ticket to Congress...

Ninety miles south of Denver at Pueblo, where Indians were now scarce, the citizens had another old nemesis with which to contend. Jim Reynolds was back. The crafty thief and his gang of Confederate misfits were sniffing around the Colorado gold mines like ravenous coyotes on a blood trail. The last anyone had seen of Reynolds was down by the Red River in Texas last spring, where Major Wynkoop's boys lost his scent. More serious problems with Indians made a further search for the Reynolds Gang inappropriate, and Wynkoop turned his men on the scent of larger game. But now, nine of Reynolds boys had slithered undetected up the Arkansas and into the foothills above Cañon City, robbing several coaches and collecting a mighty bounty of money, jewelry and gold dust. Although they had left several people beaten and penniless, they hadn't killed anyone – yet.

Reynolds picked a bad time to wander into the Colorado mountains. Because the eastern region of Colorado was consumed by Indian problems, Reynolds thought a few armed robberies on his way to the gold fields wouldn't draw much resistance. Common sense had never been Jim Reynolds' strongest suit. Notwithstanding the fact that miners rarely lived under *any* civil code of honor when it came to gold thieves, the governor himself had just given his blessing for Coloradoans to dispense justice any way they saw fit. Adding to the mix, the Colorado First Regiment was slowly drifting back in from Kansas to fortify the river routes. Now that a new regiment was forming in Denver, soldiers of the First were springing up in places they'd never been seen before. The Reynolds boys figured they'd walk into a gold mine, but instead, they stepped into a bear trap.

The gang held up a few unsuspecting miners around Fairplay, but the fun ended when a miner militia spotted their campfire near Kenosha Pass. The militia ambushed the gang, but the gunfight didn't last long in the dark, and both sides hunkered down for the rest of the night. By sunup, the Reynolds boys had scrambled into the forest, leaving all their supplies and Owen Singleterry behind. Singleterry, wearing a Union soldier's coat, lay dead of a gunshot through the heart. The miners were among the first to take advantage of Governor Evans' order to kill an 'enemy of the territory' and keep any bounty they found. They divided up the stolen gold, money and jewelry, and they cut off Singleterry's head and displayed it in Fairplay as a warning to other prospective outlaws.

The Reynolds Gang, now on the run, split up and tried to disappear back down the mountain along the Arkansas. Tom Holliman didn't get too far before he was captured and beaten by a Fairplay posse near South Park. The miners put Holliman in chains and forced him at gunpoint to help search for the other gang members. Word of the discovery of the Reynolds Gang reached Camp Fillmore, and Colonel Chivington immediately sent orders for Lieutenant George L. Shoup to go up the Arkansas and head Reynolds off. Shoup picked up a scent in Cañon City, and dispersed his command both up and down the river. Two of the Reynolds boys were soon spotted in a makeshift raft on the Arkansas, which was still running high from the summer runoff. Shoup and his troops laughingly followed, watching the bandits flip over the wicked rapids until their raft disintegrated. The boys pounded down the river, slamming into the rocks and desperately swimming for their lives. They both miraculously managed to find the shore, where Shoup took them into custody. Reynolds and another partner were later spotted and captured by civilians down river. Lieutenant Shoup shackled the ragged band of Texans and delivered them to the U. S. Marshal in Denver...

Colonel Chivington stood by the corral at Camp Weld, keeping a wary eye on the early recruits of the Colorado Third Cavalry. Many well-intentioned Denver civilians gallantly volunteered to risk their lives to protect their homes and families from the brutal Indian attacks that raged all summer, but a dangerously large portion of them were thieves, drunkards and murderers who'd ventured into the western territories to hide from the law. As a result, the militia was devoid of military discipline or protocol. Due to time constraints of their 100-days commission, the new volunteer 'soldiers' would receive very little military training before Chivington pressed them into service.

Today, they were put on their own hook to claim a horse among the hastily rounded-up mounts donated to the cause. Although the War Department had promised a supply of army horses, the blocked trails leading to Denver prevented delivery. The local stock readily available to Chivington were old knotheads, croppies and other outcasts suited better to hauling freight or pulling plows, and the recruits, many of whom were inexperienced riders, had turned this simple exercise into a full-blown comedy show. The volunteers were mostly out-of-work miners, trappers, prisoners, and drifters desperate for money and grub, and military regulations regarding the prohibition of alcohol consumption was of little consequence. A few of the more inebriated 'Hundred-Daysers' wobbled and flailed as they tried to catch and mount a horse or stubborn mule. One fellow slung a leg over his mount and rolled over the other side, planting himself into the dust. Another whelped and hooted as his horse bolted and bucked him into a fence rail.

Chivington breathed a deep sigh and shook his head. He leaned against the fence and watched a hapless corporal from the First Regiment try to train the volunteers, barking orders and inventing new ways of cussing. Chivington suddenly perked when he saw Lieutenant Shoup approach.

Shoup watched the circus in the corral as he walked up. "Colonel, if you're trying to kill yourself, there are better ways to put yourself out of misery."

Chivington chuckled. "If I shoot them first, I'll at least die a happy man."

Shoup leaned on the fence with Chivington. "Major Downing said you wanted to see me?"

"Indeed. As you can see, we have a new regiment."

"Do you think you can whip these idiots into shape?"

"Most of them will never be true soldiers," Chivington said, "but an Indian dies just as fast if he's shot by Kit Carson or a measly drunk."

Shoup nodded. "Kit's a real Indian fighter, though. You're not gonna know what kind of heart you got here until you lead them under fire."

"I'm not going to lead them all by myself," Chivington said with a wry smile.

"Uh-oh. I don't like that look in your eye."

"You look like you could use a change of scenery."

"Change?" Shoup said. "I assume that entails my teaching these bummers how to mount a horse without breaking his neck?"

"You get the idea," Chivington said. "Welcome to Denver, Lieutenant, and congratulations, the Third Regiment is all yours."

Shoup watched the show for another minute. "Are you punishing me for some reason?"

Chivington belted a laugh and slapped Shoup on the back. "By the way, I don't plan to call you 'Lieutenant' much longer. You're long overdue for a promotion. Your fine work in catching the Reynolds scoundrels clearly proves that."

"A captaincy?" Shoup said, now a little more interested.

"At least," Chivington said. "I'm impressed with the decisions you made down on the Arkansas. Even old Ned Wynkoop couldn't track down those greasy rascals, and you went and grabbed them easy as you please."

"I wouldn't call it easy. I had mighty strong help from my command and some plucky civilians down there."

"Give yourself, credit, George. You did good work."

"Thank you, sir."

"Governor Evans expects me to make my recommendation for the commanding officer of the Third. There's a political tussle going on for that position right now, but no one will dictate the selection to me. I will assign the command to whoever I please, and I believe you are the man for the job. How does Lieutenant Colonel Shoup sound?"

Shoup was taken back. "It sounds – a bit daunting. I'm a first lieutenant, sir. Isn't Major Downing a more appropriate choice?"

"Downing's been fighting Indians all summer and is better suited to field command. He's a superb warrior, and I want him to concentrate on what he does best. Your strength is obviously your tactical skills. I have no reservations about my decision to put you in command, and I don't expect any from you, either."

"Thank you, sir. I'll try not to let you down."

Chivington looked back at the corral, where another dayser was just catapulted from his bucking mule. "I don't see how you could."

Shoup laughed. "Is this the best stock we can expect?"

"With the limited resources we have, be glad they're not riding billy goats. We're just going to have to do our best."

"Where do we go from here?"

"Well," Chivington said, "I agree with you that these boys need some experience under fire before we take them to face down a savage. There's nothing like a little taste of blood to whet the appetite. We need to initiate a few small forays, and let them overcome the shakes at the sight of a dying man. It's one thing to have the heart to kill, but it's an entirely different proposition for the stomach."

"From the looks of these boys, I think their stomachs are pickled."

"Granted," Chivington said. "Under better circumstances, I'd play thunder with a drunken soldier, but we mustn't fool ourselves into regarding them as true military stock."

"I'll tell you now, Chiv, I'm not comfortable with the prospect of commanding a pack of old sots."

"Just hear me out, George. Liquor is the blight on mankind, but it does have a peculiar power to muster courage in a man who might otherwise be a coward. We've managed to recruit over 200 men already, some who want nothing more than to exact a pound of flesh from the red rebels. A little Old Orchard here and there just might bolster the nerve."

"But that's contrary to what we're taught, Colonel. We're trained to rely on judgement and not emotion. There's nothing more dangerous than a drunkard bent on vengeance."

"Lieutenant, we don't have time to school these men in the art of military warfare. I'm assembling the finest officers available from the First Cavalry to lead them, and it's your sound judgement on which I'll rely. I don't care if these boys find their courage in a bottle, because the raw emotion of vengeance may be the only thing that will keep them from running in battle."

Shoup tossed a heavy sigh. "You're sure you won't let me go back to Fillmore?"

"I said I'm assembling the best, Lieutenant...pardon me, I mean Lieutenant *Colonel*."

"Alright," Shoup said. "What's our plan?"

"Walk with me," Chivington said.

Chivington and Shoup walked across the compound.

"The red rebels' horses are still fat, and the heathens are equally strong right now," Chivington said. "They've owned the territory this summer because we haven't had adequate numbers to kill them. General Curtis is unaccustomed to fighting Indians. He doesn't know how they think, and he's woefully short on knowledge of their strengths and weaknesses. Now that we're mounting a stronger force, we're going to take this war to the savages' underbelly."

"A winter campaign," Shoup said.

"Precisely. The timing of the Third's 100-day enlistment couldn't have come at a better time. The Indians, in their usual treacherous way, will begin to sue for peace when the weather turns. I have no doubt that they'll begin to make overtures about treaties when their horses can't forage, and they can't rely on government annuities. We'll encourage them to lower their guard, and then we'll strike them hard, regardless of age or gender. To mold them into proper Christians, you have to put the fear of God in them first."

"That means marching deep into Kansas and Nebraska. The elements won't be any kinder to us."

"We'll survive," Chivington said.

They entered Chivington's office, where Major Jacob Downing and Captain Theodore Cree waited. They stood and saluted.

"Gentlemen," Chivington said. "Have a seat. I've apprised Lieutenant Shoup of our situation, and after we go through proper channels, he will take command of the Third Regiment."

"Congratulations, George," Cree said. Downing, a bit less satisfied, nodded and shook Shoup's hand. Shoup was just twenty-eight, and although an experienced soldier, his sudden jump from lieutenant to colonel was unprecedented and transparent. Shoup had cast his political lot with the pro-statehood movement in Colorado, having sidled up to Chivington and Evans at the Colorado constitutional convention a year earlier. Downing, an older and more experienced officer with a formal legal education, was clearly a formidable in-party rival of Chivington, and he knew the Fighting Parson would never allow him to steal his thunder.

"We're going to spend this next month whipping the troops into shape, and by all indications we'll have mustered in perhaps four or five hundred more recruits by the end of September. I estimate a division of at least 12 companies by then, so I want you all to submit names of worthy officer candidates. Captain Cree, I have a job for you."

"Yes sir," Cree said.

"Those boys out there need time in the saddle. Company A is

yours. We have official business to tend to regarding our old friend, Jim Reynolds."

The five Reynolds Gang members were turned over to the custody of United States Marshal A. C. Hunt when Shoup brought them into Denver. In light of Governor Evans' recent proclamation declaring Colorado under martial law, Colonel Chivington persuaded Marshal Hunt to return the prisoners to the military for trial. Chivington sent a dispatch to General Curtis, requesting permission to try Reynolds by a military commission. If found guilty, Chivington asked Curtis for permission to execute the guerillas. Although the Reynolds Gang had committed robbery and assault, they had taken no lives in their most recent raids within the Colorado Territory and were therefore not liable to be executed if found guilty in a trial. Curtis, wary of Chivington's apparent zeal to kill Reynolds, claimed he had no authority to grant permission, and he passed the buck to the Department Commander. Undaunted, Chivington sought a more expedient resolution to enforce his word as law in Colorado.

"I don't believe Mr. Reynolds and his boys can receive a fair trial way up here in Denver," Chivington said. "Their crimes were committed on the Arkansas, so you will take them there."

"To Fort Lyon?" Cree said.

"You will draw rations for your company and depart in the morning," Chivington continued. "Rations for *only* your company. Is that clear?"

Cree hesitated for a moment.

"Do you understand your orders, Captain?"

"I believe I do, sir."

"That's not an adequate response," Chivington said.

"Yes, sir, I understand. I am to take the prisoners to Fort Lyon for trial."

"I didn't say anything about Fort Lyon, Captain. You will draw rations for Company A only, and proceed in the direction of the Arkansas route with the express intent of delivering the Reynolds Gang for trial. If at any time the Reynolds Gang attempts to escape, you will leave them on the prairie. Do you understand your orders, Captain?"

Cree looked at Downing, who had the hint of a smile on his face. "Absolutely, sir," Cree said...

The newly formed Company A of the Colorado Third Regiment departed for the Arkansas River the next morning with the five members of the Reynolds Gang in chains. The nine-day excursion to

Fort Lyon normally followed the Cherokee Trail south, through Castle Rock, over the Palmer Divide, and down to Pueblo, but Captain Cree's party moved slowly. After four days, they had only made it as far as Castle Rock, stopping frequently to take target practice, perform military drills, and drink. The recruits took their rations and taunted the Reynolds boys, who remained shackled in a wagon and denied exercise or food. The bandits were sick with agony in the hot sun, and they vainly begged Captain Cree for mercy.

Cree halted the party near the small outpost of Russellville and ordered his company to dismount and take water. Many of the boys opted for whiskey.

Captain Cree wandered back to the prisoner wagon, where Sergeant Abe Williamson had just climbed down and made a show of taking a long, healthy drink of water from his canteen.

Reynolds could barely speak above a whisper. "Captain, in God's name please let us get down and have some water."

"God's name?" Cree asked. "That's rich! Since when did God join up with *you*?"

"Since these sorry bastards got bagged!" Sergeant Williamson laughed. "I reckon God must hang around jail cells!"

Cree stalked the wagon. The five prisoners, chained back-to-back, were crumpled in the tight quarters, their legs and arms swollen, and their faces and hands severely sunburned. "I guess this ain't what you boys had in mind when you came to Colorado in search of gold, is it?"

"Please," Reynolds cried.

"Shut your mouth, rebel!" Cree said.

Tom Holliman managed to grunt. "You bastard sonofabitch."

"What did you call me?" Cree said. He jumped on the wagon and pistol-whipped Holliman, drawing the attention of the other soldiers. They gathered, many whooping and cheering, while others simply stood and watched the beating in shock. "Did you hear that, gentlemen? This rebel thief just called *me* a bastard!"

"I want a piece of that Texas prick!" Williamson hollered. He joined Cree and kicked Reynolds in the groin.

"Have a taste of Colorado justice!" Cree said. He and Williamson wrestled Reynolds down from the wagon, dragging the other four shackled boys with them. The gang landed hard in the weeds, their arms and legs twisting around one another. Holliman gave a cry as his shoulder dislocated under the weight of the others. Captain Cree backed off, while Williamson kicked the prisoners, now joined by other soldiers of the Colorado Third Regiment. The beating lasted for several minutes before Cree called the boys off.

"Alright, gentlemen," Cree said, pushing through. "Get 'em on their feet."

The prisoners were yanked up, still tangled together. Holliman's shoulder dangled from the socket, but he received no sympathy.

"Gentlemen," Cree said, "Colonel Chivington has ordered a military tribunal to be convened for the purpose of trying these men on the charges of sedition. I hereby appoint you all to hear their testimony."

"Wait a minute," Reynolds choked. "You can't try us out here in the middle of nowhere."

"You're in the Colorado Territory, sir. Texas may be nowhere, but I assure you that right now you're standing in the middle of somewhere."

"That's right!" Williamson shouted along with a pack of other soldiers.

"This ain't no court," Reynolds said. "Ain't no judge – no witnesses. We got a right to a lawyer."

"Sergeant Shaw!" Cree barked.

A bearded little dog of a man stepped forward. "Yes, sir!"

"You are appointed as council for the prisoners," Cree said. "They are accused of armed robbery, assault, and crimes against the Territory of Colorado. You got any witnesses?"

Sergeant Williamson raised a hand. "Yeah, I'm a witness."

"Sergeant Abe Williamson, of the Colorado Third Cavalry," Cree said. "Do you have information pertinent to this trial?"

Williamson approached Reynolds and looked him in the eye. Reynolds, his face beaten and bloody, could barely make out the craggy old freighter.

"You remember me, boy?" Williamson said.

Reynolds wavered. "I don't know you, old man."

Williamson blew hot breath into Reynolds' face. "Hell, we met just a few months ago up in the hills. I was drivin' a stage, and you and your pards here saw fit to put a gun in my face."

"Aw, Jesus," Reynolds said.

"Cap'n, I was drivin' a coach from Buckskin Joe with my boss, Billy McClellen. These here boys held us up – took Billy's gold watch, his gun, and $400 cash. They stole over $3,000 in gold dust from the company and took my personal sack, too."

"Sergeant Shaw," Cree said. "How do your clients plead?"

"Guilty," Shaw growled.

"To the sedition charges, what's your plea?"

"Hell, we're guilty all around!" Shaw laughed.

"Well, I guess that wraps it up then," Captain Cree said.

"This ain't no trial!" Reynolds said.

"Boys, I find you all guilty as charged," Cree said. "Colonel Chivington has authorized me to carry out punishment, which is death by firing squad."

"Hold on!" Reynolds said. "You cain't do that!"

"Watch me," Cree said. "Sergeant Williamson, carry out the sentence. I gotta go take a crap."

"My pleasure, sir!" Williamson said. "Shaw, round up some volunteers!"

Sergeant Shaw obeyed and found eight willing soldiers to accompany them. The party unshackled the prisoners' hands and turned them around, cuffing them again with their hands in front of them. With their leg irons still attached, the Reynolds boys were forced to march almost two miles west into a wooded area. By the time they arrived, the prisoners were half dead from hunger and exhaustion.

"Okay, boys, this is far enough," Williamson said. "Line 'em up!"

Sergeant Shaw and several soldiers forced the gang to their knees.

"Don't do this!" Reynolds cried. "Sir, I'm sorry! We didn't hurt ya! Cain't you show me the same mercy?"

"Ten paces back boys," Williamson ordered.

The soldiers complied and then turned to face the prisoners.

"Fire on my order!" Williamson said.

"I beg ya!" Reynolds cried.

"Ready!"

The soldiers raised their rifles, but the sudden realization of what these former miners, store clerks and barkeeps were about to do slowly wafted over the firing squad. Two of the eight executioners, however, indeed were ready.

"Aim!"

Four executioners didn't obey, two aimed above the heads of their targets, and two drew a deadly bead.

"Fire!"

The rifle shots echoed over the trees and were heard back at Captain Cree's train. Cree, who'd settled into the shade and took a draw from his cigar, looked westward with sudden apprehension. He blew a hard breath...

"What the hell kinda shootin' is that!" Sergeant Williamson bellowed. He stomped up to the prisoners and found just Jim Reynolds dead, a rifle ball blown cleanly through his chest. The four others, still quivering and crying on their knees, were uninjured. "You call yourself soldiers? You couldn't hit my fat momma! Reload!"

"The hell with that!" hollered one of the boys. He hightailed into the woods, and three others followed him.

"Godammit! Get back here, soldiers!" Williamson ran back to the firing squad.

Sergeant Shaw, a bit confused by what just happened, drew on the fifth of whiskey he'd been nursing along the way. "Let's give her another go, boys. Hell, I'll do it." He drew his pistol.

"Load your weapons!" Williamson ordered.

"This ain't right," said another executioner. "I ain't shooting no unarmed shackled man!"

"I gave you an order, you sumbitch!" Williamson hollered.

"Fuck your order!" The boy lighted into the woods, followed by two more shooters.

"Jesus goddam Christ!" Williamson said. "What the hell they gonna do when they face a goddam bloodthirsty injun?"

"I'll shoot the bastards!" Sergeant Shaw said.

Williamson stared down his last executioner. "Well, what about you, boy? You gonna turn into a whimpering whore, too?"

The soldier looked at Reynolds lying dead by his partners. He knew his bullet had found the bandit. He swallowed hard, threw his rifle on the ground, and disappeared into the forest.

"Sumbitch!" Williamson screamed. He drew his pistol and walked up to Tom Holliman. Sergeant Shaw followed with his revolver and aimed at a third prisoner. "Give my regards to the devil, boy," Williamson growled. He put the barrel to Holliman's head and fired. Shaw fired simultaneously, and a spray of blood and skull fragments peppered them.

"Holy fuck!" Shaw said, staggering back. The bandit that he shot lay on the ground, squirming for a moment before exhaling a mouthful of blood.

"What you think now, boys?" Williamson said to the two remaining prisoners.

"Mercy!" one cried. "Mercy!"

"I'm fresh out!" Williamson said. He fired point-blank into the boy's face. "Finish this, Shaw!" He looked over his shoulder and caught just a glimpse of Sergeant Shaw making a beeline into the woods.

"Aw, for Christ's sake," Williamson grumbled. He looked at the final prisoner, who gave up and fell into the dirt without a whimper. Williamson stood over the boy, who asked God for forgiveness.

"Sorry, boy," Williamson said, "but where you're headed – God ain't got no say in the matter."

He fired a single shot into the back of the boy's head...

The Colorado Third Regiment had its first taste of blood, and Chivington scored his first victory as its supreme commander. Of course, no United States or Army tribunal code called for capital punishment in the case of thievery, but somewhere along the road back to Denver, Captain Cree's actions at Russellville were reported by the *Rocky Mountain News* as a necessary response when the Reynolds Gang attempted to escape. Many Colorado citizens celebrated the disposal of the nefarious highwaymen, and they credited Chivington for bringing their reign of Texas terror to a fitting end. Others, however, openly wondered how five shackled prisoners could escape from an armed military escort that then returned home without the bodies. Among the skeptics was Colorado's U.S. Attorney, S. E. Browne, who had a vested political interest in making headlines by prosecuting Jim Reynolds. Angry that Chivington had snatched the Texas rebels from under his nose, Browne, who had eagerly enlisted and was commissioned as a captain in the Colorado Third Regiment, sent a dispatch to General Curtis, claiming that Reynolds suffered a much more sinister fate than what was reported.

"The whole five were butchered, and their bodies, with shackles on their legs, were left unburied on the plains, and yet remain there unless devoured by the beasts of prey that don't wear shoulder straps," reported Browne.

He claimed Chivington boasted to his supporters that he sanctioned the execution, and warned his new recruits of dire consequences if they didn't obey his order. Browne concluded, "Our people had no sympathy with these thieves, as they have none with other thieves, but they feel that our common manhood has been outraged, and demand that this foul murder shall not be sloughed over in quiet...There is no doubt in the minds of our people that a most foul murder has been committed, and that, too, by the express order of old Chivington."

General Curtis, still haplessly wandering the Kansas prairie and hunting down more buffalo than Indians, was losing his patience with Chivington, but his role in the Reynolds affair was a matter of record. If he were to investigate this latest stunt, his ambivalent attitude towards Chivington's request to execute the gang would surely implicate him.

The Colorado Third Regiment was now successfully forming, but to any attentive observer, it was off to a rather precarious start...

13

Throughout August of 1864, the white settlers of Kansas and Nebraska paid a dear price for the army's killing of Dog Soldier Chief Lean Bear. August concluded as the bloodiest month of the Indian war to date, for in that month alone, Indian war parties had killed 50 whites, stolen several hundred wagons, horses, oxen and mules, and taken four women and six children hostage, among them Laura Roper and Lucy Eubank. Army attacks on Indian encampments during the previous months paled in comparison, but Chivington was determined to even the score now that he had a larger force to press a winter campaign...

Two thousand Cheyennes and Arapahos were now camped on the south fork of the Smoky Hill River. Among them were many Southern Cheyenne chiefs of the Council of Forty-four, Arapaho chiefs, and leaders of the Dog Soldiers, Bowstrings and Elkhorn Scrapers. Another large camp of Lakota Sioux were nearby, many of whom were closely allied with the Dog Soldiers.

Although rumors of the existence of Governor Evans' first proclamation issued on June 27th had passed from camp to camp, Black Kettle had not seen it until now. William Bent searched for Black Kettle for a month in order to deliver it personally, and he finally caught up with the chief just days earlier. Although Governor Evans had since rescinded his overtures of peace with the Indians by issuing a second proclamation that authorized all citizens to go to war, no one in this wilderness, including Bent, heard about it. He told Black Kettle that the first proclamation's guarantee to treat fairly all peaceably inclined Indians who surrendered to Fort Lyon was a good faith offer, and he advised the chief to come in.

Black Kettle received Bent's advice with cautious optimism, and he called for a general council to discuss it with several of the more influential peace chiefs of the Cheyennes and Arapahos. Bent had to return to his ranch, but he instructed his son George to attend the council and offer any assistance he could. George Bent was not a chief, but Black Kettle trusted the young man and welcomed him to the council, along with interpreter Edmund Guerrier. Bent and Guerrier were both intimately familiar with the whites and Indians, and could speak both languages fluently. They would prove to be valuable assets in Black Kettle's attempt to communicate with the soldiers and propose a truce.

Cheyenne chiefs Black Kettle, War Bonnet and White Antelope sat in the council lodge, carefully surveying the consortium of chiefs that had just smoked and prayed for guidance within the sacred circle. Left Hand and Little Raven, of the Arapahos, sat to Black Kettle's right. Beside them were Dogmen leaders Bull Bear and Tall Bull, flanked by Eagle Head, a Bowstrings sub-Chief. George Bent, known to the Cheyennes as 'Beaver,' sat with Guerrier outside the circle with One Eye, a Cheyenne, Neva (Left Hand's brother), and a half-dozen Dogmen warriors...

"You all heard the words on this paper that Little White Man delivered," Black Kettle said. "I believe we have a valuable opportunity here."

"Opportunity?" Tall Bull said. "What do they offer? When have they ever shown any interest in peace?"

"When have *you* shown any?" Black Kettle angrily asked. "You attack innocent men and women in their lodges – you take children from their mothers. What do you have to gain from this?"

"Respect," Tall Bull said. "The Long Knives thought they were superior – that they could push us and make us bow to them, but we have taught them a lesson they will never forget."

"A white man never forgets," Left Hand said. "And I promise you that *they* are going to be the teachers now."

"We will see about that," Tall Bull said. "This paper from their big chief – what does it say? Surrender? His soldiers cannot catch us, so he says come to their forts and surrender. What it really says is show yourself so we can kill you."

"That is not what it says," replied War Bonnet. "Beaver can read the white words, and he tells us the soldiers will allow us a place to camp without fear of attack."

"Beaver," Tall Bull growled. "Little White Man's son. Do you believe his Indian half, or his white half?"

"Can I speak?" Bent said.

"You may," Black Kettle said.

"I am a Cheyenne. I live with Cheyennes. I hunt with my people, and I defend my people. I am just as liable to be killed with them, so do not accuse me of trying to suck them into an ambush."

Little Raven spoke. "It does not make sense that Little White Man would betray us, knowing his relatives would be killed."

"I am not convinced," Bull Bear said. "What about the soldiers who attacked Left Hand when he showed them the white flag? According to the time this paper was written, they knew some Indians would surrender."

"I admit I was mad at them," Left Hand said, "but since then I learned that it was a mistake. Two of the white men had the courage to come and face me, and they admitted it. I am satisfied with what they told me."

"I do not care what they told you," Tall Bull said. "Whites are natural-born liars."

"No," Bull Bear said. "That is not true about all of them."

"Listen to you," Tall Bull said. "Lean Bear believed the same thing, and what did it get him? I think you are all crazy, and I turn my ears away from any bargain with those coyotes."

The Dogmen from Tall Bull's band voiced their agreement.

"Be quiet!" Black Kettle ordered.

Left Hand confronted Tall Bull. "You think this country is nothing more than one river to the other, but it is much bigger than that. There are thousands of white soldiers from rivers you never imagined, and the war you made on those lodges is going to draw them on all of us."

"Tell them to come!" Tall Bull said. "I need more scalps for my lodge!"

"You fool," War Bonnet growled.

"*You* are a fool!"

"Enough!" Black Kettle said. "I am tired of this! We cannot have this division among us. Left Hand speaks the truth. The Long Knives are too large to fight, and they do not rely on this land to survive. We have to hunt for the winter. If you continue to kill the whites and steal from their lodges, they will bring a war on us unlike anything we have ever known. Our people will starve. We must propose a peace *now*."

"I agree," War Bonnet said.

White Antelope and Left Hand also concurred.

"Bull Bear," Black Kettle said, "I have waited for you long enough. I want to know where you stand."

Bull Bear looked at Tall Bull, who glared back. "I have tried for peace, but my people want war. They would rather die than surrender."

"What about you?" Black Kettle asked.

Bull Bear contemplated the question for a moment. "I would rather live."

"That is not a choice the white man gives you," Tall Bull said.

"If they try to kill me, I will fight them," Bull Bear said. "But if Black Kettle still believes he can make peace with the soldiers, I will support him."

"I am with Black Kettle, too," Little Raven said.

"Eagle Head?" Black Kettle said.

The Bowstring leader, a strong but quiet young man, simply nodded.

"Then it is done," Black Kettle said.

"It may be done for you," Tall Bull said. "It will not be done for me until I kill every white in the country. If they kill me first, I will laugh at you from the spirit world when you die while eating from their hands." Tall Bull abruptly stood and departed with his warriors.

The others in the council lodge watched, insulted by the show of disrespect, but not overly surprised.

"I suggest we reply to Evans' proposal," Black Kettle said.

"Should we ride to Little White Man's lodge and show ourselves to the soldiers?" Left Hand said.

Black Kettle smiled. "You must like to give the soldiers target practice, my friend."

The Indians all laughed. Embarrassed, Left Hand simply shrugged.

"Holding Brave Squaw and the little child here in our camp would not please the soldiers very much. They say that they will allow friendly Indians to their forts, but these children in our possession would not give them reason to believe we are friendly."

"I agree," George Bent said. "Just think of how we would feel if they held an Indian child hostage."

"They are not hostages," Bull Bear said. "Left Hand has treated them like his own children."

White Antelope chuckled. "Would you like to yell that to the soldiers before, or *after* they shoot their cannons at you?"

The chiefs pondered the problem. The council lodge grew desperately quiet.

"We are screwed," Little Raven finally said in English.

Black Kettle looked at his cantankerous old friend. "I know enough of the white man's words to understand that."

"Perhaps we should keep the children here," White Antelope suggested, "and Beaver could accompany a small party to the fort. He could explain our situation to his father and the soldiers."

"What do you think?" Left Hand asked Bent.

"I don't know," Bent said. "They trust my father, but I don't know if they trust me. I fought on the side of the southern whites for a time, and many of them have not forgiven me for that."

"No," Black Kettle said. "We cannot afford to give them any reason to doubt us. And if we send Beaver to speak for us, it would look like we are hiding behind him. I must take responsibility and show them that we are sincere. They must hear from me, so they will know that I speak for all."

"It is not wise for you to go there," Bull Bear said. "I mean no disrespect to Beaver and Little White Man, but if this paper *is* a trick to draw us in, they will kill you. If that happens, this whole country will be on fire. Every Cheyenne and Arapaho will go to war."

"I agree," War Bonnet said. "It is far too dangerous for you to go."

"I am not afraid of them," Black Kettle said.

"No one thinks that," War Bonnet said. "But you are the Principal Chief. To our people, it would appear as if you are groveling to the whites if you go, and it would be a disaster if you were killed."

Black Kettle nodded. "My wife would not be pleased, that is for certain."

Good laughter filled the air.

"I would not want to be the one to tell her," White Antelope said.

They laughed again, and the tension of this council eased. "Alright," Black Kettle finally said. "Here is what we will do. Beaver, I want you to help me write a letter to them. We will state our intention to make peace and offer to return the children as a show of our good faith. Bull Bear, the Lakota still hold Brave Squaw's friend and her baby. Can you buy them back?"

"I do not know. I do not get along with them as well as Tall Bull does. In fact, I do not like them at all."

"Tall Bull is not with us, is he?" Black Kettle growled. "It is up to you."

"The girl's mother is with Two Face," Bull Bear said. "He is a coyote. I do not think he will trade with me."

"Whatever he wants, give it to him," Black Kettle said. "I have many horses. You can use them for barter."

"Alright," Bull Bear said. "There are others with the Lakota or Dogmen clans, too. Two little boys and two women."

"Get them," Black Kettle said. "The more prisoners we can offer to the soldiers, the more we can show them we mean business."

"What else do you want me to write in this letter?" Bent asked.

"We will talk it over. Who is the chief at the camp?"

"His name is Wynkoop," Bent said.

"Yes," Black Kettle said. "He is the white chief we heard about before. Do you think he will listen?"

"Yes. My father trusts him, and he has treated me with respect. But be warned, he is a fierce warrior, and he talks very hard about the Indians."

"I know him," Left Hand said. "Long ago I called him my friend when we lived by the Denver camp."

"Then we will write the letter to him," Black Kettle said.

"I think it would be wise to write two letters," Bent said. "We should give one to the agent – Sam Colley. He speaks for the Great Father Lincoln and does not answer directly to the soldiers. This way, your proposal will be known to those who have authority over the soldiers."

"Very well, it will be done this way," Black Kettle said.

"What shall we propose?" Little Raven said.

"A peace council," Black Kettle said. "I will offer to meet this Wynkoop and tell him I will give him the prisoners."

"I will take the letter to Wynkoop," Left Hand said.

"No," Little Raven said. "That presents the same problem as before. If they kill a chief, we will never have peace."

"If they kill anyone, it will be a problem," Bull Bear said. "But I agree, we must send someone who is not a big chief. Someone who can speak their language and earn their respect - someone who will keep his head if the talk gets hard."

"I will go," Eagle Head said.

Everyone turned to the Bowstring leader, almost surprised.

"The dead speaks," Bull Bear said.

"I am not as big a chief as the rest of you," Eagle Head said. "I am expendable."

"Can you talk the white man's words?" Black Kettle asked.

"I can talk some of them," Eagle Head said.

"You are taking a great risk," Left Hand said.

"I have looked in the white soldiers' eyes," Eagle Head said. "They are strong warriors, and we cannot fight them forever. I do not want my children to die."

"I will go with him."

The chiefs turned and looked at a familiar friend.

"I can speak all of the white man's words," old One Eye said. "My daughter is the wife of a white man who owns a lodge near Fort Lyon. The chief they call Chivington once gave me his approval as a friendly Indian."

"It is true," George Bent said. "One Eye saved my father from the Kiowas once. He will vouch for him."

"Besides," One Eye said, "I am expendable, too."

Black Kettle smiled with admiration. "No one of our people is expendable. Eagle Head, One Eye - we are grateful for what you offer us. What I call both of you - is brave..."

14

As the early September winds turned cool, Major Wynkoop prepared Fort Lyon for the upcoming winter months. The barracks were fortified, timber was cut for wood stoves, and the sutler took inventory of rations and warm clothing. Between patrol shifts and supervising the construction details, Captain Soule corresponded with Hersa whenever mail could be sent. In her letters to Soule, Hersa made frequent overtures to coming down to Fort Lyon. She offered to cook for the troops, or become a laundress – anything just to be with him, but Soule insisted she stay with her family and the safer and more comfortable confines of the Coberly ranch. He knew his forays into Indian country would increase this winter, and the fort was no place for her. It was a decision of the mind rather than the heart, for Soule ached to be with the love of his life, and Hersa desperately missed her Silie, especially now that her father's death left such a void in her heart. Hersa and her sister and brothers helped their mother run Halfway House through the summer, but they now talked of moving her to the nearby settlement of Huntsville, where she had friends and neighbors to look out for her...

Sergeant Charles Cooley took his patrol down the Arkansas a mile east of Fort Lyon near a grove of cottonwood trees. It was a routine patrol, if one could ever be called that, for the sight of an Indian was no rarity in these parts. But lately, few warriors had been spotted, and Cooley and the two privates riding with him found time for small chatter and good chew. They moved slowly, scanning every horizon now and again.

Cooley suddenly reared his pony. "Son of a bitch!" he hollered.

Privates Byrd and Conrad quickly brought their horses around.

Atop a hill, about a half-mile to the south, three Indians sat astride their ponies. The soldiers scurried for their weapons and quickly leveled their sights.

"Got one, Sarge," Byrd said. "I can pick him off right now."

"Hold it," Cooley said.

"But he ain't moving!" The young soldier was clearly scared.

"I said wait!" Cooley peered ahead, shading the sun from his eyes. "They're showing a white flag. Is that a squaw with them?"

"We may not have another chance, sir!" Byrd excitedly said.

"And I said wait a goddam minute! You want to shoot a woman, for Christ's sake?"

"What the hell are they up to?" Conrad said.

The three Indians stoically sat on their horses. The leader cautiously waved his white flag.

"What are they doing?" Byrd said.

"What do ya think?" Conrad said. "They're surrendering, knucklehead."

Cooley carefully watched. "I don't know for sure, but that old boy looks a lot like One Eye."

"You know him?" Byrd asked.

"I saw him once up at Bent's ranch – long time ago. He's a Cheyenne."

"We got orders to shoot anything that moves out here, Cap'n," Byrd said, still taking deadly aim.

"Do they look like they're moving?" Cooley said. "You don't never shoot at a white flag. Lower your rifle and don't be so damn skittish, son."

"Are we gonna take 'em prisoner?"

"I sure as Christ don't want killing an unarmed woman on *my* conscience," Cooley said. "Keep your weapons ready, but don't fire unless they give you a reason."

"What if there's a goddam pack of braves on the other side of that hill?" Byrd asked.

"Cheyenne warriors don't hide behind their squaws," Cooley said. "Think with your head, son."

"I don't like this, Sarge," Byrd said.

"Just follow my lead, and you'll be alright."

"It's okay, pard," Conrad said to Byrd. "Sarge knows what he's doing."

Cooley gently nudged his horse forward. "Let's just move up slow and see what they want..."

Ned Wynkoop propped his chair back and swung his dusty boots on the desk. He heaved a great sigh, weary from a day's work of constructing new breastworks on the southern perimeter of the fort. He pulled a bag of tobacco and rolled a much-needed smoke.

Two sturdy knocks shook the door. Outside, Captain Soule gave a holler. "Yo, Major!"

Wynkoop wanted to hide. Just ten goddam minutes by myself, he thought, that's all I ask. "Come!" he said.

Soule pushed the door open and peered in, that ever-present cocky grin on his dirty and sunburned face. "Hey, Ned, how ya doin'?"

"How do I look?" Wynkoop grumbled. "My back's twisted, and I got blisters on both hands."

Soule walked in. "Ya sure look comfy there, Major."

"I'm not moving till grub."

"Wanna bet?"

Wynkoop warily looked at Soule. That damned Irishman's smile wouldn't go away, even if the entire Cheyenne Nation were looking to turn him into Swiss cheese. "Before you say anything else," Wynkoop said, "I want to know – is this going to pucker me up?"

"Oh, yeah," Soule said. "You can't even imagine the level of puckered you're gonna be."

"Just a minute," Wynkoop said. He lit his cigarette, threw his head back, and blew enough smoke to set his office aflame. "Okay. Give me both barrels."

"We got visitors."

"Shit." Wynkoop quickly sat up. "Chiv?"

"Oh no, not *that* bad," Soule said. He enjoyed this, and he wasn't about to let Wynkoop off the hook too quickly.

"Are you going to tell me?"

Soule smiled. "Cooley's patrol just came in. You know those orders that District issued about not allowing Indians near the post?"

"Oh, no," Wynkoop said. "God damn it, Sile, if this is a joke, I'm not remotely near the proper spirit for it."

"It ain't a joke, Ned."

"How many?"

"Three."

"How far out?"

Soule cleared his throat. "I'd estimate about fifty feet."

Wynkoop bolted from his chair. "What?"

"They're right outside."

"Son of a *goddam bitch!*" Wynkoop snatched his sidearm and belted up.

"Take it easy, Ned," Soule said. "They're unarmed."

"Easy my ass!" Wynkoop said.

"One of 'em is a squaw. Don't worry, she ain't big - I think I can take her."

"Get the hell outta my way!"

Wynkoop pushed Soule aside and ran out to the balcony. He looked down on the compound where Sergeant Cooley was dismounting. The three Cheyennes sat on their ponies, bound at the hands. A large crowd of soldiers surrounded the party.

"I'll kill him," Wynkoop calmly said. He looked at Soule. "I'm gonna kill him and serve him for grub!" He pounded down the stairway, Soule on his heels.

Cooley knew this was going to require some fast talk. He saluted. "Sir!"

"Cooley! What the hell is this?"

"Prisoners, sir!"

"No shit! What the hell are they doing here?"

Cooley stuttered and missed his second opportunity. "Well, ya see, we was-"

"Let me ask you a question, Sergeant! Did you forget that we are surrounded by five hostile Indian tribes that want our hair?"

"No sir."

"Let me ask you another question! Did you forget my orders to chase away any Indian who sets foot near this fort?"

"No, sir, but-"

"A final question before I throw your sorry ass into the stockade, Sergeant! Have you taken leave of your goddam senses?"

"Sir! Permission to explain?"

Soule quickly stepped in front of Wynkoop. "Major, maybe you ought to have a word with the sergeant in private." He winked and motioned to the crowd of soldiers, whispering, "It ain't good to do this in front of the boys, Ned."

Wynkoop relented with a nod. "Cooley! In my office - now!"

"Yes, sir!" Cooley threw a final glance at Byrd and Conrad before scampering up the stairway.

"Gentlemen, I want sentries at all points. Don't forget what happened at Fort Larned. This may be a trick, so keep your eyes skinned!" The soldiers broke and ran to their posts.

Conrad stepped forward. "Major, permission to accompany Sergeant Cooley?"

"Sir, I'd like to come, too," Byrd said.

"Denied!" Wynkoop said. "He can speak for himself. You two take these prisoners to the stockade. Keep those shackles on them."

The troopers obeyed.

"I'll give them a hand," Soule said.

"Not so fast, Captain!" Wynkoop said. "You're coming with me..."

Cooley stood at attention in Wynkoop's office, warily watching the major pace in front of him.

"I'm looking for a reason not to court-martial you, Sergeant!"

"If I may," Cooley said. "We was out-"

"I'm looking for a reason not to *shoot* you, Sergeant!"

"Can I explain?"

"I'm looking for a reason not to drown you in the goddam river!" Wynkoop suddenly turned on Soule. "And *you*, Captain!"

Soule stopped lighting his pipe. "Me? What'd I do?"

"You let this dumb son of a bitch bring those Indians in here!"

"Wait a minute! I'm just the fiddle player here!"

"Didn't you see them coming? Didn't *anybody* see them coming? Is there any fucking reason why we have sentries posted? Let me give you a hint! *General order - no goddam Indians near the fort!*"

"Sir," Cooley said, "if I could just explain..."

"Do either of you have any idea what General Curtis is gonna do to me when he finds out I let three Indians into this post?"

"My lips are sealed," Soule said. "How 'bout you, Sarge?"

Cooley closed his eyes and waited for the gunshot.

"Shut up, Captain!" Wynkoop paced the room. He angrily snatched his tobacco pouch and rolled a cigarette. "I don't goddam believe this..."

Soule lit his pipe and sat on Wynkoop's desk. "Alright, Charley, why don't you stand at ease and tell us what happened."

"Major Wynkoop, Captain Soule," Cooley said, "I'm sorry I disobeyed orders, but I got a good reason."

Soule looked at Wynkoop, who drew a few smoky breaths to calm down. "What do you say, Major?" Soule said. "Sure beats the hell out of killin' him."

Wynkoop walked back to his desk and sat. He drew another long smoke and looked at Cooley. "Explain away, Sergeant."

"Me and my boys was on the river about a mile or two out. We seen those three up on a rise, just sitting on their horses. I recognized one of 'em, - name of One Eye - and I know he's one of the good Cheyenne elders. Honest to God, sirs, they had no weapons, and the old man was waving a white flag."

"Sergeant," Wynkoop said, now under control, "do you have any idea how dangerous that was?"

"Well, sir, *we* was the one with guns. I'd say they were in more danger than us."

"Good point," Soule said. "But all considered, I'd say you're in more danger right here, right now."

"Captain, when I want your opinion, I'll ask for it."

"Yes, sir," Soule said.

Wynkoop looked back at Cooley. "Sergeant, did it occur to you that you might be walking into an ambush?"

"Well, yeah, but then I got to thinkin' about it, sir. We've had to mix it up with our share of Cheyennes this summer, and there ain't a one I ever seen go to battle with a woman in front of him."

Soule chuckled, but he was stopped short by Wynkoop's glare. "Hey," Soule said, "you gotta admit he's right."

"Did I ask, Captain?"

"No," Soule said, "but I couldn't help myself."

Cooley pulled two pieces of paper from his tunic. "The old man gave me these. It's two letters written the same – both from Black Kettle. He said to give one to you – he called you Chief Wynkoop - and the other one is for Agent Colley."

Wynkoop took one letter, and Soule took the other. They both read for a moment.

"Well, I'll be damned," Soule said when he finished.

Wynkoop read the letter twice, puffing his cigarette down to a stubble. He stood and walked to the door, peering out into the sunset. He read the letter again before he finally spoke. "Well, Sergeant," Wynkoop said, "I really went and did it this time."

"Sir?" Cooley said.

Wynkoop turned back and faced Cooley. "I guess I won't drown you."

Cooley tried to smile. "My children will be obliged, sir. I'm sorry I disobeyed orders."

"Under the circumstances, your actions were entirely appropriate. In fact, what you did was courageous and damned decent. On the other hand, my behavior was less than military, and for that I offer you my sincere apology."

"Hell, sir, I knew you'd blow your stack, but I figured you'd understand once I told you what happened."

"Nevertheless," Wynkoop said, "I will address the men of my mistake."

"Aw, that ain't necessary, sir. Them boys would walk across fire for you, and so would I."

Wynkoop shook Cooley's hand. "Go get yourself some grub, Charley."

Cooley blew a huge sigh. "Damned if I couldn't eat a horse now!"

"We can't spare any," Soule said. "That was fine work, Sergeant."

"Thank you, sir." Cooley saluted and walked out. "Jesus and God thank you!" he bellowed.

Soule laughed and pointed a scolding finger at Wynkoop. "You trained them yourself, Neddy! You gotta trust your boys!"

"Jesus," Wynkoop growled, dropping into his chair. "Why the hell didn't you stop me?"

"I need my fingers!" Soule puffed his pipe and sat on the desk. He looked over the letter. "Well, ain't this a pip?"

Wynkoop rolled another smoke. "I have to say this is a first for me. Of all the mail I've received down here, I never expected to get a letter from Black Kettle."

"This is pretty danged amazing, Ned. This ain't written by no ignorant savage."

Wynkoop nodded. "I reckon taking an early sleep just went out the window tonight. Go down and give the Indians some grub. We need an interpreter, so round up John Smith..."

The three Cheyennes took a good supper in the stockade, and they were then taken to the council room, where they met Wynkoop, Soule and Smith. Three armed guards stood by, but the Indians were polite and docile. They sat together in the soft lantern light with blankets draped over their shoulders. Wynkoop poured a glass of whiskey and offered it to One Eye, who gave a grateful nod and drank. Eagle Head waved off the offer to drink.

"Mr. Smith," Wynkoop began. "What is this man's name?"

One Eye spoke. "Nah-ku-uki-yu-us. I am Lone Bear."

"He speaks English pretty good," Smith said, "but don't talk at him too fast. He can understand ya for the most part. He's Lone Bear, but he mostly goes by One Eye. Guess you can see why – got it poked out in a fight with the Kioways."

"One Eye," the old man said with a smile.

Wynkoop nodded. "My name is Wynkoop. I'm in command of this post."

"I know of you," One Eye said. "It is good to meet with you. Little Raven and Left Hand speak with good words for you."

"Little Raven? He and Left Hand are Arapahos. I'm told you're Cheyenne."

"I am to speak for Black Kettle and the Arapaho chiefs. We hold hands in the words I brought to you."

"And this gentleman?" Wynkoop said, looking at Eagle Head.

"I am Min-im-mie."

"We call him Eagle Head," Smith said. "He's one of the leaders in the Cheyenne military – the Bowstrings. He's pretty good with English."

"My squaw," One Eye said, pointing to his wife.

"Ma'am," Wynkoop said.

"Their daughter is John Prowers' wife," Smith said. "He owns a ranch not far from here."

Wynkoop pointed to Soule. "This is Captain Soule. He is my second-in-command."

Smith interpreted and told the Indians that Soule was a sub-chief. They nodded to him.

"Howdy," Soule said with a friendly wave. The Indians liked Soule's smile.

"Gentlemen," Wynkoop began, "it's apparent that you speak some English, but I've asked Mr. Smith to be here, so that you will clearly understand me. I received this letter, and the other one will be delivered to Mr. Colley. I want Mr. Smith to read it now, so you will know that there is no misunderstanding."

One Eye and Eagle Head agreed.

"Mr. Smith," Wynkoop said. "You may read the letter now."

Smith squinted in the candlelight and read Black Kettle's letter:

Cheyenne Village
August 29, 1864.
TO: Major Wynkoop, Major Colley
Sir:

We received a letter from Bent wishing us to make peace. We held a council in regard to it; all came to the conclusion to make peace with you providing you make peace with the Kiowas, Comanches, Arapahoes, Apaches and Sioux.

We are going to send a messenger to the Kiowas camp and other nations about our going to make peace with you. We heard that you have some prisoners in Denver. We have seven prisoners of yours which we are willing to give up providing you give up yours.

There are three war parties out yet, and two of Arapahoes; they have been out some time and expected in soon.

When we held this council there were a few Arapahoes and Sioux present. We want true news from you in return. This is a letter.

Black Kettle & other Chiefs

"Gentlemen," Wynkoop said, "I have read this, and I understand. Do you verify that this letter was indeed written by Black Kettle?"

"Yes," One Eye said. "I was present with him when it was written. The words were written down for him by George Bent and Edmund Guerrier."

"Where is Black Kettle now?"

One Eye looked at Eagle Head, who nodded. "Smoky Hill River."

"How many Cheyennes are camped there?"

One Eye looked to Smith for clarification. Smith asked him in the Cheyenne language.

"He says there's about two thousand Cheyennes and Arapahos, and maybe two or three hundred Sioux," Smith said.

"It says here you got a letter from Mr. Bent," Wynkoop said.

"Little White Man," One Eye said. "He delivered the paper from your big white chief."

"I think he means that proclamation from Evans," Smith said.

"That was sent in June," Wynkoop said. "Are you telling me you didn't see it until now?"

One Eye spoke to Smith. "He says that the tribes have been scattered all over the country until now. Black Kettle just saw the proclamation a few days ago."

"Tell me more about the prisoners Black Kettle mentions in this letter. Who are they?"

"Women and children taken by Dogmen, Sioux and Arapaho warriors."

"Are these the people kidnapped around the Republican last month?"

One Eye listened to Smith interpret. "Yes," One Eye said.

Wynkoop sternly confronted the Indians. "Am I to understand that you kidnapped these people, and now you want to trade them on the condition that we talk peace?"

"We did not kidnap them," One Eye said. "They were taken by warriors. Black Kettle and Left Hand are trading to get them into our camp, so they can be returned to you."

"That's not what this letter implies, sir," Wynkoop said. "Black Kettle clearly calls them prisoners."

"Prisoners, yes," One Eye said. "They were prisoners of other warriors. We have some in our camp now, and they are not prisoners. They are treated well until they can be given up."

"Who are they? I want names."

"A woman they call Brave Squaw. Black Kettle says her name sometimes. Rope-her? A name something like that."

"Rope-her?" Wynkoop said.

"Roper," Captain Soule chimed in. "I've heard that name. She's one of the children reported lost up around the Little Blue towards Nebraska."

"She is with Left Hand in Black Kettle's camp."

"Left Hand has her?" Wynkoop said.

"He did not take her from her lodge," One Eye said. "He bought her from the Dogmen who did, and he treats her well."

"I know Left Hand," Wynkoop said. "I knew both him and Little Raven up in Denver."

"Black Kettle wants to give her and her little girl back."

"Her little girl? How old is she?"

"A little one," One Eye said. "Almost a baby."

"God almighty, a baby?" Wynkoop said. "It says here that you have seven of these children?"

"In our camp we have Brave Squaw, her little girl and a small boy – I do not know their names. The Sioux and Dogmen have other women and children. Black Kettle is trying to trade for them now."

"In this letter, Black Kettle says he wants to trade them for Indian prisoners in Denver. I don't know of any Indians being held up there. In fact, if any Indian showed up there, he would surely be killed."

"I do not know. Black Kettle did not tell me of Indian prisoners in Denver."

"I want those children now, One Eye. We won't consider a peace council with Black Kettle until he surrenders and those children are safely returned. If I have to, I will take them by force."

One Eye raised his hands defensively. "We do not want any more fighting. Black Kettle wants to return them in peace."

"This letter sounds like an ultimatum to me," Wynkoop angrily said.

One Eye looked at Smith.

"Give me a minute to explain that one," Smith said. He talked with One Eye and Eagle Head. They argued, and then Smith spoke to Wynkoop. "One Eye says that Black Kettle wants to return the prisoners and hold council at the same time – it's a show of good faith. Major, I know these people, and I think Black Kettle's bein' truthful."

"With due respect, One Eye," Wynkoop said, "it sounds like he's ransoming those children for annuities now that winter's coming. You declared war on us, sir!"

"We have not made war!" One Eye said.

"No?" Wynkoop said. "How do you explain the peck of dead white people strewn across Kansas?"

"We!" One Eye said. "I mean *our* people – the bands with Black Kettle and Left Hand and other chiefs. We have not made war with you."

"I know what's he's trying to say," Smith said. "Let me try and sort it out. The Cheyennes and Arapahos is divided into many bands, Major. They all act independent of one another."

"Some clans have declared war," One Eye said, "but others want to make peace. Black Kettle and other peace chiefs are trying to make the warrior bands stop fighting."

Wynkoop contemplated One Eye. The old chief's sincerity leaked from his eyes. He then looked at young Eagle Head. "What about you, sir? Mr. Smith says that you are a warrior. Do you want peace?"

"Yes," Eagle Head said. "I do not want this war with the soldiers. Nothing good will come of it – for either side."

"I want to talk straight with you," One Eye said. "There was a time when we called whites our brothers. We traded with you; we sought advice from you. Bent is my friend, and I was almost killed once, trying to protect him. Back then, we could leave our lodges to hunt buffalo and know our women and children were safe. Now, we return to find our camps desolate, our families scattered across the prairie in fear of the soldiers. Because of this, many of our young warriors strike back as hard as you strike us."

"Governor Evans made many attempts to council with you, One Eye. He fed you, and gave you land-"

"But your chiefs took it away just as fast as they gave it," One Eye said.

"We tried to get along with you," Eagle Head said. "But your soldiers rubbed out Lean Bear when he tried to make friends and talk peace."

Wynkoop warily looked at Soule, who returned a knowing glance. "I don't know exactly what happened there," Wynkoop said, "but I regret that Lean Bear was killed."

"Bad things have happened to both Indians and whites," One Eye said. "One thing has led to another thing, and each time it gets bigger and more people die. Black Kettle speaks for many Cheyennes and Arapahos. We want to turn around and make things better between us."

"I'm curious," Wynkoop said. "It's obvious that you took a great risk by coming here. Surely you knew that you were in great danger when you approached my men today."

"I am not afraid of dying," One Eye said. "I was not afraid when I was a young warrior, so why should I be now?"

"We all agreed that something must be done to make peace with you," Eagle Head said. "If I have to, I will die for my people to make it so."

One Eye put his hands out. "George Bent, the Little White Man's son, and Left Hand told us you are a good white man – that you would take us by the hand and listen to us. I prayed on it, and the Great Spirit whispered to me – you must try to save your people. Even if the soldiers kill you, they will find Black Kettle's letter on your body, and your death may bring peace to The People."

Wynkoop lit a smoke. He sat back and looked at these three Indians with reluctant admiration. "I'm not authorized to conduct a peace council. I would have to ask permission from my chief, and I don't think he would allow it." He then read over Black Kettle's letter once again. "But I want those hostages turned over."

"I don't reckon you're gonna get them without at least talking to Black Kettle, Major," Smith said.

"Oh, I'm going to get them, Smith. I assure you, one way or another – you can tell these gentlemen that."

Smith made Wynkoop's intentions clear to One Eye, and the old warrior nodded. "We can make this the right way – without a fight. Black Kettle wants to talk to you because Left Hand told him you will listen."

"One Eye, if I agree to talk, how does Black Kettle propose to meet?"

"We will take you to our camp."

"Two thousand Cheyennes on the Smoky Hill, and he expects me to ride out there for a little chat?"

"We are afraid for Black Kettle's safety if he comes here," One Eye said. "He is the biggest of all chiefs, and he must be protected. If he comes here, our strongest warriors would insist on coming with him, and we all decided that was a bad idea. We were afraid you would think we wanted to fight, and there would be very little talk."

"You're asking for a heap of trust from me, One Eye," Wynkoop said.

"We came here, and the Great Spirit protected *us*," One Eye said. A smile suddenly curled his lips.

"How do I know this isn't a trap?" Wynkoop said.

"I give you my word."

"And mine," Eagle Head said.

Wynkoop smoked and paced the council room. He looked at Soule. "What do you think, Sile?"

"Do you even have to ask?"

"No," Wynkoop said. He returned to the Indians. "If I agree to go out there, let me make this clear to you. I won't go out there alone. I'll bring soldiers with me, and we will be prepared for a fight at the first sign of treachery from your people. And you, sir, will be the first to die."

"I told you that you have my word," One Eye defiantly said. "And I will promise you this – if any warrior attacks, I will fight alongside your men and kill them."

"I will fight them, too," Eagle Head said.

"Alright," Wynkoop said, "I'll take the rest of tonight to think it over. You will sleep in the stockade, and I'll see to it that you are comfortable. Tomorrow, I will give you my answer."

"Agreed," One Eye said. "But I have to tell you - you have to move quickly. Our clans must move all the time to avoid the soldiers. I cannot say how long Black Kettle will stay where he is."

"Understood," Wynkoop said.

The Indians stood, and One Eye faced Wynkoop. They shook hands, and Eagle Head followed, offering his hand. The guards then escorted the Indians out, followed by John Smith. Wynkoop sat down and rubbed his eyes. Soule stoked his pipe.

"Well, I'll ask again, and I want a complete answer this time. What do you think?"

"I'm a captain," Soule said, "I ain't paid to think."

"Alright," Wynkoop said. "I just promoted you to general. Give me some advice, sir."

"Oh, well, in that case, let me tell you exactly what to do. They got seven women and children out there, living in tepees and counting the minutes until they die. Just give the order, and I'll leave tonight."

"Spoken like a true Jayhawker."

Soule wasn't smiling now. "Look, Ned, my daddy and me didn't run slaves to freedom for glory or profit, because there are easier ways to get to heaven – if there is one. We did it because Daddy always said that a man's got to take stock of himself sooner or later. Let's just say, if there *is* a heaven, I don't want to bump into Daddy someday and have to explain why I didn't try to save those children."

"Do you think Black Kettle is sincere?"

"I ain't seen a Cheyenne yet who bluffs, that's for sure. If Black Kettle's wise enough to trust that you wouldn't kill One Eye and Eagle Head, then I'll bet a dollar he'll extend us the same courtesy."

Wynkoop drew a hard breath. "You know something, Sile, until now, I thought the Indians were some kind of two-legged creatures that without exception were cruel and had no feeling for friend or kindred."

"Until you shook hands with one of them," Soule said.

"God as my witness," Wynkoop said, "tonight I felt as if I were in the presence of something quite superior here."

Soule agreed. "We all drop from the same kinda womb. You know - some tenderfoot takes a buffalo hide, and he leaves the rest to rot; yet, he watches the Indians turn the beast into food, clothing and shelter, leaving not a single bone on the prairie, and he calls *them* uncivilized."

Wynkoop nodded. "Makes a body think, doesn't it?"

"A God-fearing abolitionist feels right good freeing a slave, so long as that old boy gets on his knees and starts praying to the Almighty in English. But an Indian? He has no master but that Great Spirit of his. The government must reckon it's easier to slaughter the whole lot and leave their emancipation to God himself. It's a hell of a lot simpler than parading him to church with scalps hanging from his belt."

Wynkoop measured his old friend. "You can tell me I'm wrong, but I get the idea that you and God have a little rift going."

Soule blew a smoke ring. "Well, if he really *is* my maker, then he knew what he was getting into."

Wynkoop laughed. "Bit off more than he could chew, if you ask me."

"I'll give him this," Soule said, "he packs a pretty good wallop now and again."

The boys smoked and contemplated. The room was drearily dark, but the security was a comfort. "I'm in a tight spot here, Sile," Wynkoop finally said.

"That's an understatement. You know what Chiv will say if you ask to go out there."

"Yeah, and Curtis will say no."

"I don't know," Soule said. "Considering we just might be able to get Black Kettle on our side, the general might be interested in talking."

"Time's not on our side right now. One Eye said Black Kettle may move at any time. It could take weeks for a messenger to track down Curtis, and more for him to send a message back. In the meantime, all hell could break loose."

"And those children might be killed."

"Shit," Wynkoop growled. "I just have to go and take my chances with Curtis and Chiv later."

"Well, you ain't gonna go it alone, pard."

Wynkoop smiled. "I guess I don't have to ask you to go with me?"

"I'm going, whether you ask or not."

"You love this, don't you..."

"With every breath I take."

"Alright, then. Let's think this out. We have to decide how many men can go without leaving the post shorthanded."

Soule chuckled. "Hell, if there really *are* two thousand Indians at that camp, ain't gonna matter how many we take. I sure hope those warriors are in good spirits when we come a-calling."

"Amen. I want at least 100 – maybe three companies."

"We just got a new company in from New Mexico. I'd say we could afford about 125 men, give or take."

"I don't want to order anybody to go. The minute we leave, we'll be in violation of direct orders. We need men who are acting on their own volition, since any sane man would consider this suicide."

"You just had to go and say that, didn't you?"

"The mission will be strictly voluntary," Wynkoop said.

"Let's call the boys together and explain the situation. I'll wager we'll get more than we need."

"I hope you're right. I'd like to think we have more than just two fools at this post."

"Oh, Neddy, we're gonna get drawn and quartered for this."

"I know," Wynkoop said. "But we have to try to save those women and children. And look at the bright side: if we talk Black Kettle into calling off this war, we'll be the first drawn-and-quartered heroes this army's ever seen."

"Either that, or I'll be meeting Daddy sooner than I expected..."

Fort Lyon, Colorado Territory
September 6, 1864

Dear Hersa,

I'm still here, my love; still here, and yet still there with you. It's how much I love you that keeps me breathing, and my belief that I'll see you again someday that makes my heart beat.

I have something to do, and it won't be easy. In fact, unless I have much to say about it, I might not return. Me and Ned have to try to do something good for a lot of people, which is going to send us to Indian country. Where we're going is a spiritual ground on which few Christians ever stepped, trying to accomplish a deed that so far the government has not. We have to try to stop the Indians from doing all the things that hurt you and your family, and I know that you would give your blessing because that's what's in your heart. What's more – there's some innocent children and women that the Indians say they'll give up. We just can't turn our backs on that. I know that you can pray good, so ask God, if he's listening, to keep an eye on me even if he don't want to.

What we're going to do seems sound outright, but maybe somebody smarter than us would think otherwise. If what happens when we get there means I have to take my last breath, I want you to know that I'll be thinking of you. But try not to worry about me, because I don't have any intention of going just yet. We have too much life together ahead of us, so just pray and always be thinking of me so I can come back.

I love you always and in all ways.

Your everlovin' Silie

15

Major Wynkoop and Captain Soule called a general meeting of officers and presented their case. A lively debate ensued, and Wynkoop dropped ranks to allow the men to speak freely, and in some cases, quite boldly. Many officers argued against Wynkoop's proposal to venture to the Smoky Hill, calling it foolhardy and reckless, but Wynkoop stood his ground, arguing that the lives of the captives in Black Kettle's possession were at stake. In the end, Wynkoop simply declared the matter settled, and he expected his men to support his decision, to which they unanimously agreed.

A call for volunteers followed, and Wynkoop organized a detachment of 130 soldiers for the extremely hazardous mission. Captain Soule and Lieutenants Joe Cramer, George Hardin and Charles Phillips offered their service, and John Smith volunteered to interpret for the Indians. The detachment was mounted with two howitzers and four supply wagons. One Eye, his squaw, and Eagle Head were brought along to serve as scouts and act as liaisons...

SEPTEMBER 10, 1864

The Fort Lyon party rode for two days and nights until they reached the headwaters of the Smoky Hill River. There, they followed the river in a northeasterly direction, penetrating the depths of the Kansas prairie occupied by the fierce Cheyennes. Along the route, the vigilant soldiers maintained a wary lookout for any sign of trouble, but the prairie was eerily quiet. One Eye assured the soldiers of their safety time and again, but out there a man trusted no one. He might see a shadowy movement in the distance, or hear the cry of a hawk that sounded all too human - all signs of an invisible enemy with the power to attack in a fleeting moment.

Eagle Head circled back from his scouting rounds and approached Wynkoop's command, raising his hand.

"Hold up," Wynkoop said, and the troops stopped.

"Not far now," Eagle Head said. He then excitedly spoke to Smith in Cheyenne.

"He says the camp is about five miles ahead," Smith said. "Says we need to put down here for a time, and he's supposed to ride on ahead and make smoke to let Black Kettle know we're here."

"Very well," Wynkoop said. "Tell him to go ahead. One Eye and his wife will remain here with us." Wynkoop looked at Eagle Head. "Your friends are my prisoners. You keep that in mind when you're calling Black Kettle out. When you find him, you be sure to tell him we're not here to fight, but we are prepared to defend ourselves."

"I will tell him," Eagle Head said. "You can trust me."

Wynkoop and his command watched Eagle Head ride north.

"Gentlemen, we'll take rations and water here. You know the situation, so keep an eye skinned."

The troops nervously dismounted and led their horses to the stream.

Captain Soule walked to a shady spot, aware that a few of the boys were beginning to rattle. He took off his hat, stoked his pipe, and began to sing:

> *"Far away in the East was a dashing young blade,*
> *And the song he was singing so gaily;*
> *'Twas honest Pat Murphy of the Irish Brigade,*
> *and the song of the splintered Shillelagh..."*

Black Kettle and Medicine Woman Later emerged from their lodge when they heard the commotion. A young wolf had just ridden in, excitedly hollering at the villagers. The young boy rode directly to Black Kettle.

"Soldiers! Soldiers!"

"Where?" Black Kettle said. "How far?"

"Still a long distance on the river!" the wolf said.

"How many?"

"I counted more than one hundred!"

"Just soldiers?"

"No! One Eye and Eagle Head ride with them!"

"Are you sure?" Black Kettle said.

"Yes! And they ride freely! They were not tied up, and they carried their own rifles!"

Black Kettle felt a sudden exhilaration. He looked at Medicine Woman Later, who shared his excitement. "Do you think it worked?"

"Why would One Eye ride with the soldiers if it did not?" she said.

Black Kettle turned back to the scout. "Ride to Left Hand's camp and tell him they are coming! Tell everyone you see that the soldiers may be coming to us in peace!"

The boy let out a whoop and steered his pony toward the Arapaho camp.

"Everyone prepare!" Black Kettle said to the villagers. "Squaws take the children to your lodges, and spread the word to the men to dress and mount their ponies."

The other Cheyenne chiefs quickly assembled and held a brief council to organize their warriors...

The Arapaho village erupted in a similar fashion when the young scout announced the news. Left Hand and Little Raven immediately dispatched other chiefs to organize and prepare to ride to the Cheyenne camp. He scurried about, barking orders and directing the women to take shelter. The villagers excitedly prepared. Three squaws ran in with Laura Roper and little Belle Eubank, their arms full of berries picked from a creek nearby. Left Hand ran up to Laura.

"What's happening?" she said.

Left Hand knelt beside her. "I did not want to fill you with empty words before, but I have news of something that may be good for you. There are soldiers approaching."

"Oh, my goodness!" Laura said.

"We do not know what their intentions are yet, but we may be able to talk to them without a fight."

Laura desperately fought to hide her tears. "Do you think Belle and I can go with them?"

"I cannot promise that, but I will try. We want to give you to them, if they are not coming to fight us."

The squaws sang and hugged Laura and Belle.

"Go to your lodge," Left Hand ordered. He saw Neva approaching.

"They are coming!" Neva said. "Look!" He pointed to the western horizon.

A black plume of smoke wafted above the trees.

"Hurry!" Left Hand said to the women. "Neva, go with Brave Squaw and Little Screaming Bird. Do not let them out of your sight!"

Neva complied and shuffled the girls and squaws to their lodge...

"Smoke signal!" Lieutenant Hardin hollered. He pointed to the east, where a second ball of smoke rolled into the air.

The soldiers gathered to look at the signal.

Wynkoop walked up next to Soule and peered at the horizon. "Well, I don't think our presence here was a secret anyway, but it looks like we've just been formally announced."

"Mount up, boys!" Soule ordered. "Watch your butts!"

The troops organized, and within an hour they began the last leg of their journey. One Eye rode at point with Wynkoop and Soule. They took their time, not wanting to appear aggressive as they approached. After covering three miles, Eagle Head suddenly came over a rise, riding at a steady gait. Wynkoop stopped his men and watched Eagle Head come in.

"The people are coming!" Eagle Head said.

"Is Black Kettle with them?" Wynkoop asked.

"Yes! He is waiting just ahead over that hill!"

"Alright, gentlemen," Wynkoop said. "This is it. Stay tight and follow my orders."

"Wynkoop," Eagle Head said, "you must know this – there are Dogmen with Black Kettle."

"How many?"

"Enough," Eagle Head said. "They insisted on coming to protect Black Kettle."

"Who leads them?" One Eye asked.

"Bull Bear."

Wynkoop snapped at One Eye. "What's the meaning of this?"

"It is not a trick!" One Eye said. He turned back to Eagle Head. "Is just Bull Bear waiting? Or is Tall Bull there, too?"

"I did not see Tall Bull," Eagle Head said.

"This is good," One Eye said. "Bull Bear supports Black Kettle. He is the one who has tried to buy the Sioux prisoners."

"You better not be lying, sir," Wynkoop said.

"I promise you."

"What about these other Dogmen with him? Are they going to behave themselves?"

"They will obey Bull Bear."

Wynkoop took a moment to confer with Soule. "What's your best guess?" he asked.

Soule watched Eagle Head and One Eye for a beat. "Well, we trusted them so far, and they've come through. But let's not go into this with our heads up our ass."

"Move forward!" Wynkoop ordered. "Form a line and circle the train!"

The soldiers proceeded, with Wynkoop and Soule on point. One Eye's wife was directed behind the main force, and Eagle Head and One Eye rode with Wynkoop. Although drawn into battle forma-tion, the detachment continued to ride slowly up the hill, keeping a wary eye on the perimeter. As they reached the crest of the hill, the Cheyenne and Arapaho warriors came into full view – well over a thousand strong, mounted and drawn into a line of battle. The Dogmen, guarding both flanks, blurted war cries, but the Indians did not make a move.

"Halt!" Wynkoop ordered. His heart raced at this awesome display of warrior strength.

"Oh, lordy," Soule said. "Whose bright idea was this?"

Lieutenant Cramer clutched his rifle. "What do we do, Major?"

"Just don't move," Wynkoop coolly said.

"I think I just stained my britches," Soule said. "Does that count?"

Wynkoop's eyes never left the war party ahead. "Talk to me, One Eye."

"They are prepared to fight only if you attack," One Eye said. "Black Kettle is at the center."

Wynkoop peered out and looked at the principal chief. Even at this distance, Black Kettle's countenance was magnificent. He sat astride his pony in full regalia, holding a multi-feathered coup stick in his right hand. Beside him were Little Raven and Left Hand, whom Wynkoop recognized as old friends from his Denver days. He also recognized George Bent, who sat with White Antelope, War Bonnet and several other Cheyenne chiefs. On Black Kettle's left was a beefy, war-painted young chief, sporting a long dog rope on his shoulder...

Black Kettle gazed at the soldiers without a word.

"Look at them," Bull Bear said. "Either they have a thousand soldiers hiding behind them, or they are crazy."

"The wolf told us that this is all they have," Left Hand said.

"Then they *are* crazy," Bull Bear said.

"No," Black Kettle said.

"Are you looking at the same thing I see?" Bull Bear said.

"With my eyes, perhaps," Black Kettle said.

"They have cannons!" Bull Bear said. "Drawn in a line to fight us! If you do not see a few fools wanting to be rubbed out, what do you see?"

Black Kettle contemplated the question, still looking at the tall soldier chief, who bravely stared back. "Courage," he said.

The Dogmen let out more whoops.

"Bull Bear, I warn you. Keep your men quiet."

"Respect Black Kettle's words!" Bull Bear ordered. "You will not move unless I say so!"

Black Kettle summoned George Bent. "Tell me who you see."

"The tall one in front is Wynkoop," Bent said. "The one beside him is Soule. He is a good soldier."

"Do you trust them?" Black Kettle asked.

"Yes. They would not come with so few men if they intended to attack. Wynkoop is not a fool."

"For his sake," Black Kettle said, "I hope you are right..."

"Alright," Wynkoop said. "One Eye – Eagle Head - it's time for you boys to do some talking. Go down there and tell Black Kettle that I'm here to talk about the letter he sent me. You make it clear that I do not want a fight. Your wife will stay here with us, One Eye."

One Eye glanced back at his woman and gave her a gentle nod. He then rode to the warriors with Eagle Head. The soldiers pensively watched One Eye converse with Black Kettle.

"I sure hope old Black Kettle's feelin' chirky today," Soule said.

Wynkoop looked back at his detachment. The boys, although clearly scared, were resolved to take whatever was thrown their way.

"Keep a cool head, boys," Wynkoop said.

"Christ," Soule whispered. "If they got a mind to, they could gobble us up."

"Keep your Irish up, Sile."

"Don't worry. They may try to eat me, but I'll make 'em spit me out."

The conversation with Black Kettle concluded, and One Eye rode back to the soldiers alone.

"Black Kettle says he wants to talk!" One Eye said.

"Where?" Wynkoop said.

"The Dogmen are restless, and Black Kettle and Bull Bear want to control them. Black Kettle asks that you return in the direction you came for a few miles and camp there. He will take his party back and make the warriors be quiet. He said he will come to your camp in the morning with the other chiefs."

"Very well," Wynkoop said. "Give him my word that my men will not fight, so long as he controls his."

One Eye rode back down to Black Kettle and briefly spoke with him. As Wynkoop watched, the chief rode forward a few paces and looked up to him. He raised his coup stick. Wynkoop raised his hand. Black Kettle then gave an order, and the warriors turned and rode away from the soldiers.

Wynkoop's men gave a hardy cheer.

"Well, shit!" Soule said. "Now that wasn't so hard, was it!"

Wynkoop felt a huge sigh of relief blow from his lungs. "Damn, Sile," he said. "I think we just may live at least one more day."

"Fall back!" Soule ordered, and the troops turned.

One Eye and Eagle Head returned and joined the soldiers. They were followed by a few of the younger Cheyennes and Arapahos, who broke from the main body of warriors that went back to their village. They clearly showed no signs of animosity, keeping a healthy distance from the soldiers. Occasionally, they called out to the men.

"Who are those boys?" Wynkoop asked One Eye.

"Don't let them scare you," One Eye said. "They are not Dogmen. They're singing because they're happy. They want to be friends with you."

"They probably want to get in the grub line," Soule said. "They may not be so friendly if they get a taste..."

Wynkoop's command spent a chilly night under the Cheyenne stars. The Indians had pointed out a good place to camp, directing them to a spring where they could take water. One Eye then sent them back to their own camp for the night, so the soldiers could take their rest without fear of them. The soldiers huddled in the fire-light, some taking whiskey for warmth, although none were anxious to dull the senses too much. In the cavernous darkness of the Kansas prairie, they heard distant sounds coming from the direction of the Cheyenne camp. A steady rhythmic beat of drums pounded the air, and when the breeze was right, the soldiers heard singing and an occasional gunshot. One Eye reassured them that these were the sounds of celebration for the prospect of making peace with the whites. The singing carried well up to midnight before slowly dying out. The soldiers tried to sleep, but few managed. It was a long, arduous journey to the dawn...

At first light, the soldiers prepared for the council, mounting several patrols and taking grub early. Around nine o'clock, Wynkoop and Soule walked out and watched the Indian party approach. Black Kettle rode in front, followed by Left Hand, Neva, Little Raven, Big Mouth, Bull Bear, White Antelope, Big Wolf, and George Bent. A party of warriors followed, whom One Eye identified as friendly Cheyennes from Black Kettle's band. The warriors kept their distance as Black Kettle rode into Wynkoop's camp, keeping a wary eye on the equally vigilant white soldiers who watched them.

The chiefs dismounted, and Wynkoop and Soule approached with John Smith standing by. Wynkoop and Black Kettle stood face-to-face.

"Chief Moke-tav-a-to," Wynkoop said.

Black Kettle was slightly taken back by Wynkoop's ability to speak his name. He almost smiled. "Wine-koop."

"I'm honored to meet you, sir."

Smith interpreted, and Black Kettle nodded and spoke Cheyenne. "He says, 'likewise,'" Smith said.

Wynkoop and Black Kettle shook hands. Wynkoop then looked at Left Hand. "It's been a long time, old friend."

Left Hand shook Wynkoop's hand. "Too long. I am glad to see you."

Wynkoop greeted Little Raven, and was introduced to White Antelope. He then faced Bull Bear, who was less than cordial.

"Sir," Wynkoop said, extending his hand.

Bull Bear looked at Wynkoop, and then begrudgingly shook his hand without a word.

Wynkoop introduced Captain Soule to the chiefs, and the group retired to a large tent, where the proceedings began...

"It was a soldier's nightmare," Soule would later tell Hersa. "There we sat, eye-to-eye with the main chiefs of the Cheyennes and Arapahos – by all accounts the devil's eldest sons. The way the council began, I thought we were gonna end up stuck with arrows and scalped before it was over. They yelled at us about starting the war, we yelled at them for starting it. Both sides didn't really care to take credit for the mess we were in, and a few times it looked like the whole thing was gonna turn into an old-fashioned donnybrook. Bull Bear had a mean look in his eyes when he started throwing accusations, but Ned stood up to him, and I think that big Dogman couldn't help but respect him. After awhile, once everybody vented spleen and couldn't think of no more insults, things started to settle and get more civil. Old Black Kettle had been sitting there, listening to the fight and not saying a single word. Sometimes he looked irritated, but sometimes, particularly when Ned had the floor, the old chief seemed to show admiration for the way my old pard could reason out his position. Once or twice, I caught old Black Kettle in a smile. He reminded me of my daddy. I guess, by virtue of being on this earth longer than most, an old man has reason to be amused by young fools with hot heads..."

Wynkoop sat back and contemplated the Indian leaders. Soule sat beside him, and John Smith and George Bent sat in the middle, weary now from interpreting this rapid-fire argument. Lieutenants Cramer and Phillips sat behind the military contingent, and One Eye and several older Cheyennes sat behind the chiefs.

"Gentlemen," Wynkoop said, "I think we've aired our grievances, and it's clear that we both have legitimate complaints. But let me get to the bottom line. If you expect me or my chiefs to take a peace treaty seriously, I demand that you turn over the white captives immediately."

Wynkoop waited for John Smith to interpret, and the chiefs briefly spoke to one another in Cheyenne.

"They're saying that they want some assurance that you'll talk about peace after they give them up," Smith said.

"I told you before, gentlemen – I will not accept that as a condition! These are separate matters."

"Then what assurance do we have that you will accept them as a show of our good intentions?" Left Hand asked.

"I won't lie to you," Wynkoop said. "I am not authorized to negotiate a treaty here and now. Give them up, and I promise I will report your good-faith gesture to General Curtis."

Smith relayed Wynkoop's words to the chiefs.

Bull Bear, who spoke some English, looked at Wynkoop. "Why you come here – risk lives of your men, just to say you cannot make peace?"

"Because I am not the big chief," Wynkoop said. "The big chief is General Curtis, the man who is my superior officer."

"Then why did he not come here?" Bull Bear asked.

"I could not get Black Kettle's letter to him fast enough. I'm not even sure where he is right now. One Eye told me that you all might move at any time, and my main reason for coming here was to get those white prisoners. Now that we're here and have talked to you, what I can promise is that I will go to my big chief and tell him that Left Hand rescued those children and you all agreed to turn them over as proof of your peaceable intentions; that your actions clearly warrant his consideration to discuss a peace arrangement for your bands."

"How do we know you will not leave here with the children, and then continue to attack our people?" Left Hand asked.

"I won't stand for you forcing a peace treaty in exchange for your releasing those people," Wynkoop said. "I believe you when you say that none of you approved of your warriors killing their families and kidnapping them, but if we acquiesce to this condition, what will prevent those warriors from kidnapping more whites to get what they want?"

"What will prevent you from pushing the war farther?" Little Raven said.

"I want those children!" Wynkoop said. "No conditions! When they are given up to me, I promise I will do everything in my power to persuade General Curtis to meet with you and discuss a peace treaty."

Lieutenant Hardin suddenly entered the tent, quite agitated. "Major Wynkoop, we got trouble out here!"

"What!" Wynkoop angrily said, annoyed by the interruption.

"Some of them injuns been moving closer to the camp!"

"Are they looking for a fight?"

"Well, not rightly, but they're snoopin' around."

"What are they doing, Lieutenant?"

"Well, shit, they came up and started diggin' at my drawers for some tobacco."

"Aw, Jesus," Captain Soule said. "Give 'em a goddam smoke, for Christ's sake!"

"But they're snoopin' around the cannon, too!" Hardin said.

"What? Are you worried they'll fire it?" Wynkoop said. "They don't even know how the goddam thing works!"

Smith jumped in. "They's just curious, Major. Ain't no way any warrior's gonna attack with Black Kettle sitting here in a council with us."

"Handle the goddam problem, Hardin," Wynkoop barked. "Make friends with them, let them have a smoke – goddam dance with them, but don't stir up a fight!"

"Tall Chief?" Black Kettle said. "Trouble?"

"Uncle John," Wynkoop said. "Explain it to the chief."

"Your boys are wandering in and scaring the soldiers," Smith said to Black Kettle.

Black Kettle angrily turned to one of the elders behind him. "Go tell them to back away!"

The elder scurried out of the tent.

"I am sorry, Tall Chief," Black Kettle said through Smith. "Some of my young men have never seen a white man up close."

"That's okay, Chief," Soule said. "Maybe they'll see that we don't have tails."

George Bent told Black Kettle what Soule said, and the chiefs all chuckled.

Bull Bear suddenly stood. "Face me, Tall Chief," he said. Wynkoop stood and looked Bull Bear in the eye. "We have talked hard with you. You scold me as if I am a child or a woman! I am a Dogman – a chief! Talk to me like a man! Black Kettle has traded many horses and buffalo robes to save those women and children. He offers to save them so you will make peace with us, but you say give them up for nothing but an empty promise!"

"He's right," Little Raven said. "We always got along with you whites. Little White Man was my friend before you soldiers came to our country and attacked our villages. Left Hand comes to a fort with a white flag, and you shoot at him! Lean Bear offers to talk to soldiers, and he is shot from his horse! Why should we trust you? Just because you come here and act friendly? You are just talking peace because you know we could rub you out right now!"

One Eye could stay quiet no longer. He jumped up and confronted Bull Bear and Little Raven, speaking in Cheyenne. "Stop hollering at Tall Chief!"

"Go away!" Bull Bear said. "You are not a big enough chief to talk here!"

"I will be heard, Dogman!"

"I am tired of talking to these coyotes!" Bull Bear growled. "We should just shoot them and leave them for the birds to eat!"

Wynkoop turned to Smith. "What are they saying?"

"Wah, they's just bickerin' again," Smith grumbled. "Give 'em a minute and they'll work it out."

"If you shoot them, you have to shoot me!" One Eye said.

"Stop!" Black Kettle stood, and the argument instantly subsided. The old chief glared at Bull Bear. "That is enough from you! Sit down!"

Bull Bear turned in frustration and complied with Black Kettle's order. Little Raven also relented.

"I want to hear One Eye," Black Kettle said.

One Eye calmed down. "Bull Bear, you have two ears and one mouth. Try to listen twice as much as you talk."

Smith quickly interpreted One Eye's words to Wynkoop.

"I know we have hard differences between us, Bull Bear," Wynkoop said. "But rest assured, I do not think of you as a child. If I treated you that way, I apologize. I know you are a chief, just as I am a chief. All I can do is give you my word and my respect."

Bull Bear still seethed, but he nodded at Wynkoop, somewhat pacified by the apology.

One Eye then spoke in Cheyenne. "Maybe I am not a big Dogman chief, who measure his bravery by the number of white women and children he kills..."

"I have never killed a white woman or child!" Bull Bear roared. "That was the act of others!"

"You are a Dogman Chief!" One Eye said. "It is up to you to control them! And if you want to fight these soldiers, you will have to fight me, too! Just remember, I have many friends out there."

Bull Bear tossed a hard sigh and spoke in Cheyenne. "Just stop, One Eye. My heart is mad. I want to yell at them, but I do not want to fight."

"Then do not make threats at a peace council," One Eye said.

"You make noise for what? A few horses and buffalo robes traded for the lives of those poor women and children? How about I give you one of my best ponies if you just shut up?"

Bull Bear couldn't help but smile at this brave old man. "The swift black one?" he said.

"Any one you want," One Eye said.

"Done."

Wynkoop and Soule listened to Smith explain the conversation. Soule leaned toward Bull Bear. "I got a bag of good pipe tobacco. What do ya say? I'd like to live, too."

Bull Bear hadn't been able to read Soule all day, but that Irish grin was good. "The pipe, too?"

"Naw, that's my daddy's pipe. It's got my spit in it, anyways."

Bull Bear gave a disgusted grunt, and everyone laughed.

Little Raven spoke up. "I apologize for this. We are all angry over this war, and we lash out sometimes."

"I think we all respect a man who speaks his mind," Soule said. "It's better we're here hollering at each other instead of wasting powder and arrows."

The chiefs all agreed, and Left Hand offered this: "I want this understood, Wynkoop and Soule. Most of my people want to be friends with the whites. Many more than those who want to fight, but I cannot abide being shot at when we try to approach you to make peace."

"I'm very sorry for what happened at Fort Larned," Wynkoop said. "Captain Parmetar wasn't fit to command, and it was our mistake to let him remain there. My chiefs were warned about him before the day he shot at you, but the war in the States kept General Curtis from acting in time. But I promise you, when he heard about what happened, he sent Colonel Chivington to arrest him."

"I am glad that you are sorry now," Left Hand said, "but I could not control some of my warriors after that. That letter from Governor Evans was sent before Parmetar shot at us. Evans said that friendly Indians should not be attacked. Parmetar must have known about those orders."

"He did," Wynkoop said. "I make no excuses for him. He was a drunkard, and he went on a bender after Satanta tricked him."

"And what about this letter from Evans?" Little Raven asked. "Many of the soldiers from Denver have attacked us, despite his orders to consider who is friendly and who is not. If you ask me, Evans speaks out of both sides of his mouth."

"I can understand why you think that," Wynkoop said, "but you must admit that many of your chiefs are getting their orders mixed up, too. You say you control your warriors, but many of them have continued to attack our settlements."

"They attack because *you* attack!" Bull Bear said.

"You said you would shut up," One Eye said.

"Enough," Black Kettle said. George Bent interpreted: "I have listened, and now I have decided. It is time we stop bickering over old events, because we only end up where we began this council – mad at each other without any solution to our problem. I am confident that Tall Chief did not come here to scold or ridicule us like children. He knew he came here with too few soldiers to fight us. It was like walking through fire, and he is brave to sit here and talk to us. We must admit that there are some bad Indians who have killed whites, just as there are some bad whites who have provoked and attacked us. I believe the soldiers are to blame for the worst of it, but I am willing to hear your big chief tell his side. I will always be for peace between us, and I do not believe we have gone so far that we cannot resolve our differences. It is time for good men on both sides to stand up and put a stop to this war so we can take the white soldiers by the hand and call them our brothers."

"I want that, too, sir," Wynkoop said. He blew hard and tried to calm down. "We're making progress here, and we don't need any more animosity between us."

"Ani-?" Black Kettle said.

"Major, try to keep it simple," Smith said.

For the first time, Wynkoop couldn't help but smile. "I don't want us to be mad at each other any more, sir."

Black Kettle understood. He returned the smile. "We wish to talk to your chiefs. Where can we meet them?"

Wynkoop drew a long breath. "I have an idea. Sir, what would you say to going with me back to Fort Lyon? From there, we can obtain supplies and then go up to Denver and talk to Governor Evans."

"Not Curtis?" Black Kettle asked.

"General Curtis is somewhere between here and Missouri. With all the trouble going on out there, it's too dangerous to set out across Kansas looking for him. This way we could get the children to safety at Fort Lyon, and then travel a protected route up to Denver where you could discuss a peace agreement with Evans. He has the authority to hold council with you. You both might find it easier to reach an understanding if you looked each other in the eye."

"I do not like it," Bull Bear said. "What protection would he have?"

"Come with us, Bull Bear. In fact, bring any chiefs you wish."

Bull Bear contemplated Wynkoop. He then looked at Black Kettle, who gave him a reassuring nod.

"S'cuse me for sayin'" Soule interrupted, "but, Neddy, do you think that's smart? You got any idea what Evans would do if you waltz into Denver with these boys in tow? Besides shittin' his drawers, that is?"

"You got any better ideas?" Wynkoop said. "We don't have any time to waste here. This may be our only chance to sit Black Kettle down with somebody in authority to treat with the Cheyennes. We may not be able to stop this war, but we might have a chance here to at least slow it down."

Soule shrugged. "No argument, but if we do this, we best keep our heads tucked in when Evans gets a load of what we brung him; the whole town, for that matter."

Wynkoop tossed a sigh. Soule was right. "Sir," he said to Black Kettle, "I hope you understand that what I'm proposing is not exactly in obeyance to the orders of my chiefs. I must ask, when we get near Denver, that you allow me to treat you as prisoners under the white flag. This means that you will not be permitted to carry weapons into town, but I promise that my men will protect you. I also promise, if we cannot reach an accord with Evans, you will be guaranteed safe passage back here to your camp."

Black Kettle asked for a moment to confer with the other chiefs. They spoke in their language, and Wynkoop told Smith to allow them privacy by not interpreting their conversation.

"I propose this," Black Kettle finally said through Bent. "You will break your camp here and ride back toward your fort for half a day. Camp there for the night, and I will come to you with the women and children when the sun rises. When we meet I will tell you if we agree to go with you. If I choose to stay, you may still leave with them."

"Agreed," Wynkoop said. "I trust you, sir. But I have to tell you, if you don't bring those children, we will come for them."

"I understand," Black Kettle said. "You have my word. I will bring them to you."

"Thank you, Moke-tav-a-to. I know we can make peace."

"Wine-koop," Black Kettle said. "Peace is only road I travel with you." He offered his hand, and they shook on it.

Black Kettle exited the tent. Each chief shook hands with Wynkoop and Soule, and they followed Black Kettle outside. Bull Bear was the last to leave. The Dogman didn't smile, and he hesitated when he faced Wynkoop. The major offered his hand, and Bull Bear reluctantly shook it. He then turned to Soule.

Soule gave a wink, and handed Bull Bear a pouch of tobacco.

"I have nothing to offer you in return," Bull Bear said.

"I ain't worried," Soule said. "We'll see each other again."

Bull Bear nodded and accepted the pouch. He then shook Soule's hand...

Wynkoop led the detachment back along the Smoky Hill River, stopping when the sun touched the western horizon. They camped there for another chilly, sleepless night. Wynkoop apprised the men of what had transpired during the council with Black Kettle. After facing down the large warrior regiment the day before, some of the boys thought they had pushed their luck far enough. They came to Wynkoop and voiced their concerns, suggesting they continue the march and make a healthy run for Fort Lyon. The men implored Wynkoop to make this retreat, for they believed the Indians were sucking them in for a night attack. Wynkoop wouldn't budge, however. He told them that they were on the verge of rescuing the white captives without firing a shot, and he wasn't going to stop now.

"Hell, boys," Soule told them, "as deep in the well as we are, we might as well enjoy the swim..."

Daylight finally arrived, and the sun moved to noon before a sentry gave the excited call. Indians were approaching the camp. The soldiers remained in a defensive posture, but it was quickly apparent that the Indians would not attack. Left Hand led the small party that surrounded Laura Roper, who rode her own pony with Belle Eubank. A young boy rode with a warrior, and another boy rode alone behind them.

"Lordy God," Soule said. "Look at this, Ned."

"Come on!" Wynkoop said. He rode out to meet the party with Soule, Lieutenant Cramer and two corporals. Soule quickly dismounted and ran to Laura.

Laura could barely believe her eyes when she saw her handsome rescuer.

Soule took the reins of her pony. "I'm Captain Soule, ma'am. We're gonna take you home."

During her long ordeal, Laura often cried when the squaws in her lodge were asleep, but now she couldn't hold back. "Thank you," she wept. "Oh, thank you."

"Where are the others?" Wynkoop said. "Where's Black Kettle?"

"He will come," Left Hand said. "He is still trying to trade for the others. Brave Squaw was with me, and I bring her and these boys now to prove we are trying to do our best."

"Left Hand," Wynkoop said, "you said you have seven people to give up."

"The Sioux were angry, and they moved away from our camp when we came to council with you," Left Hand said. "I do not know what happened, but our scouts came and told us of a bad thing. One of the women they held got frightened and hanged herself. She is dead."

Wynkoop tried to control his ire in front of the children. "When is Black Kettle coming?"

"He will come at the next sunrise with more captives, if he can find them. He has decided to ride with you to Denver with some of the other chiefs."

"Will you go with us?"

"No," Left Hand said. "I have a sickness, and I cannot ride that far. I will send Neva in my place. He is my family."

Wynkoop conceded, and he pushed his horse to the young boys. He looked at the young fellow who rode with a warrior. "Hello, young man, what's your name?"

The boy was reluctant to answer, but the warrior reassured him. "Ambrose," he barely whispered.

"Lieutenant Cramer," Wynkoop said, "why don't you let this young fellow ride with you."

Cramer rode up. "Howdy, pal. Come on over."

Ambrose threw his arms around the Indian.

"It's alright, son," Wynkoop said, a bit surprised.

"You go," the warrior said.

Clearly in shock, and incoherent from his experience in captivity, young Ambrose clumsily burrowed into the warrior.

"No. You go." The warrior handed him to Cramer.

Wynkoop sadly watched the pitiful child surrender to Cramer's gentle arms, and then looked at the second, older boy. "And who are you?"

"Daniel. Are you gonna take me home?"

"I sure am. Corporal, take Daniel to the camp and see if you can find some candy for him."

"Can I keep my horse?" he asked.

"No. But I bet we can find you one just as good."

"Okay." He hopped off the Indian's pony and ran to the soldier. Cramer then led them away.

Wynkoop approached Laura. "Hello, ma'am. What's your name?"

"Laura Roper, sir."

"Are you alright?"

"I am, but I'd give anything for a proper bath."

"Well, that will have to wait for another day or two."

Laura looked at Left Hand. "I'm obliged to you for saving my life."

"It is good that you go home to your people, Brave Squaw."

Wynkoop looked at little Belle. "Who do we have here?"

"Her name is Isabelle Eubank," Laura said.

"Eubank? She's not your child?" Wynkoop asked.

"Wynkoop," Left Hand said. He rode up and spoke softly so Belle couldn't hear. "Her mother and another baby are with the Sioux. We do not know where they are."

"Dear God," Wynkoop whispered. He looked at the child. "Miss Roper, Captain Soule will take you to the camp. Let me take Belle."

Laura handed Belle over, and the little girl whimpered. "I want my mama. Where is mama?"

Wynkoop cradled her in his arms. "It's alright, little one. I'll take you home."

Left Hand said goodbye to Laura, and he turned his party back.

"Thank you, Left Hand," Wynkoop said.

"I hope we meet again in better days – Ned," Left Hand said.

The Indians rode away, and Soule led Laura toward the camp. He just couldn't help himself, and in a minute, Laura was laughing at his silly remarks – the first laugh she'd had in over two months.

Wynkoop touched Belle's face as the little girl cried. "Be still, my little darling. I'll take you home."

Belle softly wept in his arms, and Wynkoop's emotions suddenly crept upon him. Deprived of sleep for several nights, and worn by the intense danger that still surrounded him, Wynkoop's throat tightened at the woeful cry of this poor motherless child. A tear streaked Wynkoop's cheek, and he slowed his horse to gather himself before returning to camp.

As the former captives rode in, the soldiers erupted in a joyous celebration. Even the most war-hardened of them could not help but shed a few tears at the sight of the children...

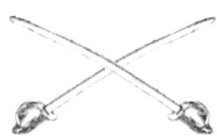

16

Black Kettle arrived the following morning, as promised, accompanied by Cheyenne chiefs White Antelope and Bull Bear. Little Raven stayed behind with Left Hand, but they sent four of Left Hand's relatives to represent the Arapahos in Denver: Neva, Bosse, Heap of Buffalo, and Knock Knee. The chiefs informed Wynkoop that they had no more white captives to give up, and Wynkoop had little choice but to accept this troubling news. The chiefs simply had no further information as to the whereabouts of Lucy Eubank, her infant son, Willie, and two other women who were captured in the August raids. The Sioux were nowhere to be found, and Wynkoop refused to risk the lives of the rescued children searching for them. There was no alternative but to turn back for Fort Lyon...

Rations were in short supply on the long trail back to the Arkansas, but the soldiers made certain to feed their precious cargo well. Laura became the center of attention along the way, but the curious soldiers did not wish to press her for information regarding her captivity. Until the final leg of their trip, the weary young girl was reticent, obviously overwhelmed by her experience and reluctant to talk about it. She wasn't, however, so reserved that she didn't appreciate the polite concern displayed by so many brave and dashing young men. One of them, in particular, caught her fancy.

Captain Soule slowly rode up beside her. "We're not far from freedom now, ma'am."

"I don't know what it will feel like to sleep in a soft bed again," Laura said.

"If you have a mind to, would you tell me how you got the name Brave Squaw?"

Laura giggled. "I hit one of the warriors who was mean to me."

"You hit a Dog Soldier?"

"Well, it really was quite frightening. He threatened to cut Belle's throat because she was fussing, and I made my mind up right then to stand up to him. He's the one who named me Brave Squaw."

"I'd say he was right," Soule laughed.

"Captain, do you know anything about my mother and father up on the Little Blue River? We lived near the Eubank place – called the Liberty Farm – I was visiting them when the Indians attacked us."

"I'm sorry, but I don't. I remember reading your name in a dispatch detailing the raids in your country, but it only stated that you were among those missing."

"When I was in the Arapaho camp, I saw an Indian wearing a coat. I'm sure it was my father's coat, because the Indian also had one of my dresses that he cut up to make a sunshade. Neva was looking out for me then, and I asked him if he knew if that Indian had killed the people where he got the clothes. Neva asked the Indian, and he said the people at the ranch were gone, but they burned our place down."

"I reckon you just have to keep up hopes that your family is safe," Soule said. "When we get you to Denver, we'll try to get some information about them. Any sisters or brothers?"

"Yes, three sisters and a brother," Laura said. "I'm so worried about them. And if they're alive, I know they're worrying about me."

"Well, it won't be long before we get you back to your people."

"You all have been so kind to me. I can't rightly think of the words to thank you."

"It's our pleasure, ma'am. I just hope the Indians accorded you the same."

Laura shrugged. "At first, it was so frightening. The warriors killed poor Mrs. Eubank's entire family right before our eyes. I don't know if I'll ever push that from my thoughts as long as I live. I'm afraid for Lucy and her baby. They're probably killed by now. Belle and I were so fortunate to be taken in by Left Hand and Neva."

"How did you come into their possession?"

"They arrived at the Indian camp right after we were brought in, and they traded five ponies for me and Belle. If they hadn't done that, I don't know what might have happened to us. But poor Lucy got sold to the Sioux, and they took her and her baby away from Belle."

Soule sadly shook his head. "It must have been terrible for you all."

"We can only thank our lucky stars that we're safe now here with you."

"What about these young fellows with you?"

"Ambrose is Mr. Eubank's nephew. He was visiting their farm when the Indians attacked us. He was riding in a wagon up the road with Mr. Eubank's father. The Indians killed Mr. Eubank's father, but they spared Ambrose. I'd never seen the other boy, Danny, until the other day when Left Hand brought us to you. He told me the Indians killed his mama and daddy at their farm up on Plum Creek."

"But you say that Left Hand and Neva treated you well?"

"They never hurt me, but I wasn't accustomed to the harsh life they live. They kept me with the squaws, who were good to me – that is – they didn't like me at first and hit me, but then after Left Hand scolded them, they always were good after that."

"What did they give you to eat?"

"Mostly buffalo, when they could kill one - that, and antelope or other game. A lot of them love dog and roasted turtle, but they didn't make me eat those things. I think I would have just asked them to kill me first."

Soule laughed. "Indian fare is just a bit too strong for you, is it?"

"Oh, yes! But the buffalo meat was good."

"So, did you stay in one place for long?"

"No. We moved about almost every day, so the soldiers couldn't attack us. One time, the Indians brought a warrior in that was killed by soldiers. I never heard such wailing and moaning in my life. The women all cried, and they cut terrible gashes in their arms and legs. The men built a scaffold in the trees and laid the dead warrior in it. Neva told me that's how they bury their dead. They carried on and cried and moaned for the longest time."

"Did they ever get into a fight while you were with them?"

"No, but one time a scout came in and told us that there were Comanches coming to fight, and all the women and children packed and traveled away from the camp. It turned out to be a false alarm, but I was pretty scared."

"Rightly so," Soule said. He looked ahead. "Well, lookie yonder!"

The troops suddenly broke into a cheer as a small mounted patrol from Fort Lyon approached. The patrol greeted Wynkoop's party, stunned at the sight of both the white children and Indian chiefs who rode with them.

"Dang, Major," Sergeant Cooley said, "you're a sight for sore eyes!"

"The feeling's mutual, Sarge," Wynkoop said.

"These sore eyes may just be seeing things! Holy jeez! That ain't Black Kettle, is it?"

"Indeed it is," Wynkoop said.

"We been sayin' prayers to get you boys home safe, but we didn't count on God sending *him* with ya! What in the world?"

"I want you to ride ahead to the post and inform the officer of the day that we are coming. Find Mr. Bent, and tell him to arrange quarters for the children. Remind the troops that these chiefs are prisoners, and they come with peaceful intentions. Everyone is to stay in line."

"Yes sir!" Cooley and his patrol swung around and galloped ahead...

A raucous celebration ensued when Wynkoop's party arrived at the fort, despite the wary eyes thrown toward the chiefs. The Fort Lyon troops cheered and whooped at the sight of Laura Roper and the other three children, and the rescue party was embraced with hardy handshakes and congratulations.

Soule helped Laura down from her horse. "Welcome to Fort Lyon, ma'am. It's a bit dusty and rude, but I guarantee happier days from here on out."

Laura couldn't hold back the tears. "You've been so kind, Captain. Thank you." She threw her arms around him and wept.

"At your service," Soule said. "Now dry your eyes, and somebody will take you to that soft bed you're looking for."

"Hey, Captain!" Joe Cramer said. The dusty lieutenant walked up to Soule and leaned on his shoulder. "I have two things to say, you old Jayhawker."

"Tell me one at a time, Joe. My ears are full of dirt."

"Okay. First thing is, I don't reckon two officers have ever stuck their necks out so far without getting hatched. What you and Ned did out there was the gol-dangdest show of guts I ever seen. You made old Chiv's march on Glorieta look like a square dance!"

Soule tossed the Irish brogue. "Why, thank you, laddy. But I seem to recollect you bein' there with your neck out, too, m'boy."

"Yeah! That *was* me, wasn't it!"

The boys embraced and slapped large plumes of prairie off their backs. "Sure is good to be alive, ain't it?" Soule said.

"Well, it's gonna get even better for you, old pard! That's the second thing I wanna tell ya."

"What's that?" Soule asked.

"Well, I just saw old Bent ride in. In fact, his wagon is right behind you, and you ain't gonna believe who's with him."

Soule cocked his head at Cramer. He then turned and looked at the wagon. "Oh, lordy God..."

Hersa Coberly stood next to Bent, her tearful smile lighting up Soule's aching heart. She ran up, and he swept her into his arms. The kiss that followed set the troopers into a frenzy of wild cheers and applause. Laura Roper watched with a melancholy smile. It was a distant dream anyway, she reckoned, and she sadly clapped with the boys.

"Silie!" Hersa cried.

Soule buried her head in his shoulder. "I ain't gonna cry...I ain't gonna cry..."

Hersa laughed. "I'll cry for both of us!"

"I can't believe you're here."

"The supply train came by the ranch, and I talked the driver into taking me with him."

"Well, if I wasn't so happy, I'd be mad. Did you get my letter?"

"We met the mail on the way down, and they said they had a letter for me. Oh, Silie, I've been frantic with worry. When I got here, Mr. Bent told me all about what happened. I prayed to God. I knew he'd bring you back."

Soule held Hersa tightly and looked skyward. "Okay, pard, you win this round."

"What?"

"Nothing, darlin'. Nothing..."

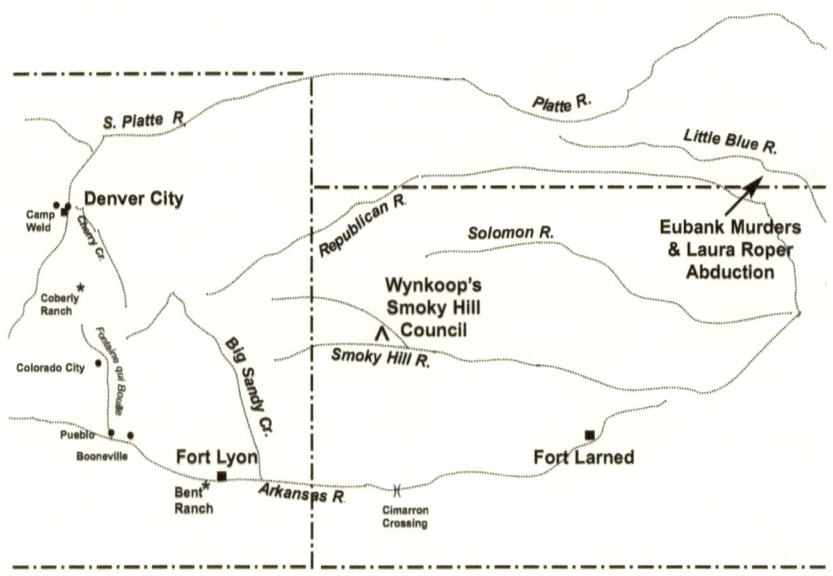

17

It was done. Wynkoop's gamble at the Smoky Hill paid enormous dividends, but the fact remained that his unauthorized mission was a serious breach of command. Had he just rescued the captives, the army might have overlooked the impropriety and yielded to the end result, but Wynkoop opened a can of unsavory worms by bringing the Indian chiefs to Fort Lyon without the approval of General Curtis. When word reached Denver of his daring rescue, Wynkoop was heralded a hero, but his star quickly tarnished when further details of the expedition trickled in. According to rumors, Wynkoop was harboring and feeding Cheyenne and Arapaho renegades at Fort Lyon. What's worse, there was talk that he planned to bring them to Denver and drop them in Governor Evans' lap – the same governor who had declared martial law and authorized anyone with a gun to kill Indians on sight.

On September 18, the rumors were confirmed through a letter from Wynkoop to Governor Evans that provided full details of the Smoky Hill expedition. The lengthy dispatch described the affair from the moment One Eye approached Fort Lyon, to the contentious council that resulted in Black Kettle's surrender of the captive white children.

The letter concluded:

The released captives that I have with me now at this post consist of one female named Laura Roper, aged sixteen, and three children (two boys and one girl), named Isabella Eubanks, Ambrose Asher, and Daniel Marble; the three first mentioned all being taken on the Blue River, in the neighborhood of what is known as the Liberty Farm, and the latter captured somewhere on the South Platte with a train of which all the men were murdered.

I have the principal chiefs of the two tribes with me, and propose starting immediately to Denver City, Colorado Territory, to put into effect the proposition made aforementioned by me to them. They agreed to give up the balance of the prisoners as soon as it is possible to procure them, which can be better done from Denver City than it can from this point.

I have the honor to remain, very respectfully, your obedient servant,
E. W. WYNKOOP,
Maj. 1st Colorado Cavalry
Commanding Fort Lyon

It wasn't a request. It was a bold statement of intention, and Governor Evans blew his stack. In Evans' mind, Wynkoop's brazen defiance of military protocol could very well undermine his long-suffering plan to arm a militia for the purpose of waging a full-blown campaign of Indian extermination. Colonel Chivington, on the other hand, viewed Wynkoop's proposed peace council as an opportunity to gather information that would help the Third Regiment's upcoming winter campaign. A healthy portion of Evans supporters shared the governor's rage, while an equally boisterous contingency of political opponents applauded Wynkoop, declaring that the chickens were about to come home to roost...

Denver, Colorado Territory
September 26, 1864
TO: Major General S. R. Curtis
Fort Leavenworth
Department of Kansas
Sir:
I have been informed by E. W. Wynkoop, commanding Fort Lyon, that he is on his way here with Cheyenne and Arapaho chiefs and four white prisoners they gave up. Winter approaches. Third Regiment is full and they know they will be chastised for their outrages and now want peace. I hope that the major-general will direct that they make full restitution and then go on their reserve and stay there.
J. M. CHIVINGTON,
Commanding District

TO: Colonel J. M. Chivington
Denver, Colorado territory
September 28, 1864
...I shall require the bad Indians delivered up, restoration of equal numbers of stock; also hostages to secure. I want no peace till the Indians suffer more. Left Hand is said to be a good chief of the Arapahoes, but Big Mouth is a rascal. I fear agent of Interior Department will be ready to make presents too soon. It is better to chastise before giving anything but a little tobacco to talk over. No peace must be made without my directions...
Major General S. R. Curtis
Fort Leavenworth
Department of Kansas

Wynkoop sent Agent Colley to deliver annuities to the Cheyennes and Arapahos on the Smoky Hill as a show of good faith and assurance of Black Kettle's safe arrival at Fort Lyon. He then mounted a regiment of 40 soldiers to take the chiefs and former captives to Denver. The winds of Governor Evans' anger had reached the troops by the time they reached Pueblo, and Wynkoop ordered his men to remain vigilant on the journey north. The Indian chiefs were huddled in a wagon surrounded by the troops for protection, but they encountered little resistance from the white settlers by the time they reached the Coberly ranch.

Wynkoop left his troops to camp at Coberly's, and he rode ahead to assess the general disposition of Denver City and its irritated governor. He took residence at the Planters House, for he had sent his wife and children back to Leavenworth with an armed military train in the summer. Upon his arrival, he indeed found himself among a snarling pack of wolves not unlike the Dogmen he'd faced down on the Smoky Hill, but he was not without his own supporters as well. Undaunted, Wynkoop requested a meeting with Evans, but the governor refused to see him, his emissary claiming that Evans was ill in bed. Wynkoop then sought out Chivington, but the colonel was away from Camp Weld, due back in a few days.

He returned to the governor's office and informed his emissary that he would come back tomorrow to see if Evans was well enough to talk. If not, he would come back the day after that, and the day after that...

The night spent in Denver was a surrealistic dream to Wynkoop, who was hardened by the rigorous lifestyle at the fort and on the plains. He paid for a hot bath and a shave before looking up old friends at a local saloon. There, he felt safe among fellow soldiers and old Jayhawkers, who hung on every word he uttered about his trip to the heart of Cheyenne country. Although some questioned his sanity, no one challenged the enormous courage Wynkoop and his men had showed. The boys warned Wynkoop about the animosity of many Evans supporters in town, but they vowed to stand by him when he brought Black Kettle in. Wynkoop and Silas Soule were nothing short of royalty in the eyes of the Jayhawkers, and they assured him that anyone with a mind to make trouble would answer to them.

The boys bid a fond goodnight, and Wynkoop returned to the Planters just a bit more secure in his intentions. He took a long and deep sleep unlike anything he had enjoyed for some time, and the next morning he quickly dressed and planned to dog the good governor again. Just as he prepared to leave, a harsh knock rattled his door. Wynkoop warily strapped on his sidearm and inched the door open.

"Major," John Evans said.

"Governor!" Wynkoop opened the door.

"Can I have a word with you?"

"I was just about to call on you. Shall we go downstairs?"

"I'd prefer meeting right here. More privacy."

"By all means." Wynkoop welcomed Evans in. He curiously looked out into the hallway.

"I'm alone," Evans said. "I want to speak with you, man-to-man – no politics, no bullshit."

Wynkoop closed the door. "Sounds fine to me, sir. Have a chair."

"I'll stand," Evans said. He hitched his holster, obviously trying to draw Wynkoop's attention. "I'm not comfortable sitting down any more in this town. It's much harder to shoot a moving target."

Wynkoop tried to laugh. "You're not planning to use that sidearm in here, are you?"

"Oh, I see," Evans growled. "Another taste of the renowned First Cavalry humor. I guess Chivington raised an entire *pack* of comedians. Let's set the record straight, Major, this isn't a social call. I'm just not in the mood."

"Very well, sir. By the way, I hope you're feeling better."

"Better?"

"I was told you're ill."

"You were told a lie. Truth is, I have no interest in seeing you, but from what I understand, this meeting was inevitable, so let's get on with it."

"Alright."

Evans walked to the window and kept his back to Wynkoop. "That's Denver City out there, Major. I don't suppose I have to remind *you* of that. Seven months ago, this town was full of dreams. Those streets were busy and teeming with commerce. Hell, when Cherry Creek leveled the place, the citizens reacted as if it were nothing more than a spring shower. They pulled themselves out of the mud and put their faith in God to rebuild it, stick by stick." He peered out on the late September morning. "But look at it now. Hardly a soul out there. The banks can barely breathe, the stores are empty – hell, for all we know, Denver may die before the first snowfall. And it's all courtesy of those red rebels you want to bring here."

The governor turned from the window and glared at Wynkoop. "So, in light of this, I have one simple question for you."

"Yes sir?"

"Who in the hell do you think you are?"

"Governor, I understand why you're angry."

"Angry? That highfalutin education of yours should provide

you with a far better description of how I feel right now. What in the hell gives you the right to send me a letter, declaring your intention to march a pack of wild renegades into this city and demand a council with me?"

"They didn't demand anything, Governor. The council was my idea. Black Kettle gave up the captives as an act of good faith. In return, I promised to bring him here to discuss a peace treaty with you."

"On whose authority did you make this promise, Major? It wasn't mine, and I sure as hell know Curtis and Chivington didn't approve!"

"I did what I had to do to save those children, sir, and I'll answer to the general for my actions. I wasn't in a position to send a dispatch and wait for a reply – not with the welfare of those children at stake."

"I'll give you this, Major - it was courageous of you to rescue them, but bringing those savages here was not only a clear violation of orders, it was damned reckless. You should have attacked those Indians when you had the chance."

"I could only spare 130 men from the fort, Governor. There were upwards around two thousand Indians out there! Besides, Black Kettle wanted to talk, not fight, and he willingly gave up those children after we parleyed."

"You could have sent the captives back here, and held the chiefs prisoner at Fort Lyon until you received instructions from General Curtis."

"Governor, the line of communication between Lyon and headquarters is virtually non-existent. If I send a dispatch, it has to be taken by messenger across Kansas, which is dangerous and time consuming. Besides, our council at Smoky Hill all came about due to the proclamation that you sent them. I told Black Kettle and the others that I would bring them here to discuss it with you."

"Well, bringing them to me was certainly a bad choice," Evans said. "We're at war, Major. I have no authority to make a treaty with them."

"Sir, you're Superintendent of Indian Affairs. What more authority do you need?"

"It's out of my hands, Wynkoop! We're under martial law here! Do you think Denver is some godforsaken prairie outpost where you can parade murdering savages in and out? You had absolutely no authority to propose a peace council with me, or anyone for that matter!"

"This is Black Kettle, Governor! He's the Principal Chief of the

Cheyennes. He wants to end this war, and he came over four hundred miles with me to prove his sincerity!"

"What – so he can take annuities for the winter? When spring comes, he'll just start this war all over again!"

"I don't believe that," Wynkoop said.

"I tell you what I believe. That child-murderer sucked you in! He slaughters men and women, takes their children hostage, and then ransoms them for blankets and food!"

"Governor, I'm convinced Black Kettle is not behind the depredations committed this summer. He told me that the Dog Soldiers and Sioux warriors are responsible, and the elder council chiefs are trying to put a stop to it."

"What balderdash! Black Kettle is a murdering liar!"

"Due respect, sir, but you don't have a goddam inkling who Black Kettle is!"

"You watch your mouth, son. You're talking to the governor of this territory."

"And *you're* talking to an army officer! I put my damned life on the line for this territory more times than I can count. In twenty days, my men rescued four children and talked the biggest chiefs of the Cheyennes and Arapahos into calling a truce – something *you* haven't managed to accomplish in *three years* as governor."

"Why, you arrogant son of a bitch!"

"If that's what it takes to get you to talk to Black Kettle, then I'll take it as a compliment. Those chiefs risked their lives coming here to try to end this war!"

Evans angrily pondered Wynkoop. "What about this Dog Soldier chief you have with you? Do you expect me to believe *he* has any interest in peace?"

"Yes sir, I do. I'm told Bull Bear has influence with the other Dog Soldiers chiefs, and he is willing to negotiate with us."

"Negotiate? Those red bastards don't negotiate! Look, Major, you've been down on the Arkansas a long time. Things have drastically changed up here. It took me all summer to convince Washington to let me raise the Third Regiment for the sole purpose of taking this war to the Indians. I put my career on the line, begging those bastards to outfit that regiment. No, sir, I'm through talking. The only negotiation those Indians will get is the Third Regiment charging down their lying throats."

"Governor, if the Cheyennes and Arapahos align with us, there isn't another hostile tribe within five hundred miles of here that could defeat us."

"No," Evans flatly said. "If we accept peace terms with them without sufficient punishment for their depredations, the government would be acknowledging it was whipped. Besides, if I make peace now, what am I going to do with the Third Regiment?"

"Send them with the Cheyennes to fight the hostile bands!"

"Indians are Indians, Major," Evans said. "They're treacherous liars, and I would never trust them to watch a soldier's back. The Third Regiment was raised to kill Indians, not cavort with them. A peace before conquest, in this case, would be the most cruel kindness, and the most barbarous humanity."

"What?" Wynkoop said. "What the hell does that mean?"

"It's not in my hands, Major. What's done is done. I've raised the Third, and they will serve out their hundred days in pursuit of Indians. I will not negotiate a peace with your chum, Black Kettle, is that clear?"

"I made a solemn promise to him," Wynkoop said. "He made one to me. Like it or not, they will be here tomorrow."

"Oh, no," Evans said. "Don't you even dare try. You will take them back where you found them, and if you're any kind of soldier, you'll kill them."

"I don't take my orders from you, Governor. Right now, word is spreading all over Denver that you are going to council with Black Kettle. I'd say, if you have any hope of saving your political career, the citizens will be interested in how hard you try to put a stop to this Indian war."

"You better take a caution, Major," Evans said. "You don't have the clout to blackmail me."

"That's your word, not mine, Governor. But you might want to take a look out that window again. A lot of people make jokes about that sidearm you carry. They think it's just a fancy decoration, but there are some hard-as-stone boys from Kansas around here who say you have good reason to carry a pistol."

Evans glared at Wynkoop, but the son of a bitch glared right back. He took a long pause before he spoke. "Okay, Major. I'll play your little game. Bring your renegade pals in, and I'll hear them out. But you best consider every move from now on, because you just made a serious mistake."

Wynkoop opened the door. "They'll be here in the morning."

Evans angrily walked out, and Wynkoop slammed the door behind him. He blew a titanic sigh and sat on the bed, slapping himself in the head. "Jesus Christ, Ned," he whispered. "What the hell are you doing?" He stood and wandered to the window. His heart raced as he gazed out on the deserted streets of Denver...

Wynkoop's party arrived in Denver at first light. For the first time in weeks, Denver was alive with men, some armed and optimistic, some armed and dangerous. No matter the disposition of those who dared approach the military entourage, the First Regiment was clearly prepared for business. Black Kettle and the chiefs huddled in their wagon, boldly displaying an American flag on a pole and peering out at the Denver citizenry with wide-eyed apprehension. Behind them was a smaller wagon carrying Laura Roper and the three rescued children, who were wildly cheered by onlookers. The parade moved along Lawrence Street, where the children were intercepted by a contingency of citizens in carriages and taken away to a large reception in town. Wynkoop and Soule led the chiefs on to Camp Weld, where the Hundred-Daysers gathered and watched like a pack of hungry wolves.

"They're lookin' at us like we got war bonnets on," Soule said.

Wynkoop shook his head. "So these are the governor's vaunted Indian fighters. We should have brought some raw meat with us."

Inside the gates, Evans stood watching with Colonel Chivington and Bill Byers.

"You should court-martial that son of a bitch," Evans growled.

"I'm not going to court-martial that sly fox," Chivington said. "Don't you see what old Ned is doing? He just delivered a strategic advantage right at our feet. That is, if you don't panic."

"Panic?" Evans said. "I'm supposed to greet this Black Kettle monster with an olive branch in one hand and orders to blow him to hell in the other! What if this is a trap? What if those chiefs have a thousand warriors surrounding Denver as we speak?"

"Governor," Chivington calmly said, "that's pure humbug. Do you think we're sitting here without armed patrols guarding the roads? Give Wynkoop credit. He wouldn't have brought those children in here without considering all the risks. I raised good officers."

"This is on your head, Chiv," Evans said. "You better be right."

"I'm always right." Chivington gave Wynkoop and Soule a hardy wave. "Besides, what are you worried about? The Governor of Colorado just rescued four children from the devil's grasp. Your friend from the *Rocky Mountain News* here is about to make you a national hero."

Byers smiled. "You'd think I'd get a little more respect around here, no?"

"You just make sure you don't mention the fact that I may be committing political suicide," Evans said.

"Allowing the Third Regiment's 100-days commission to expire without taking a Cheyenne scalp would be suicide," Chivington said. "We're going to invite these little flies into our web and find out where their friends are hiding."

"You think you can find out in this council?" Byers asked.

"I'll just let the governor do the talking. In the meantime, those red rebels will tell me everything I need to know."

"If you ask me," Byers said, "those double-face villains are just looking for food. That's the matter here."

Wynkoop's party halted at the gates, and the stiff and weary chiefs slowly crawled out of the wagon. The soldiers escorted them into the camp under heavy guard.

Wynkoop and Soule dismounted and saluted Chivington.

"Major! Captain! Welcome!"

"Thank you, sir," Wynkoop said.

"What, are you trying to put the old colonel out of business here?"

"Maybe just trying to make our jobs a little easier," Wynkoop said.

"You rascals," Chivington laughed. "I knew the minute you two got together there'd be mischief."

Wynkoop warily evaluated the colonel. "So, should we turn ourselves in to the stockade?"

Arrival of chiefs in Denver, September 28, 1864.
Wynkoop & Soule far right corner.

Chivington laughed. "Nonsense, Ned! I want to hear all about your adventure at the Smoky Hill."

Soule stretched. "My butt's about to fall off."

"Well, I'll see if I can find you a good pillow!" Chivington led his officers to the mess, leaving Evans to his own stew...

The Camp Weld Council commenced in the afternoon. Present with Governor Evans were Colonel Chivington, Lieutenant Colonel Shoup, Wynkoop, Soule, Cramer and several other First Regiment soldiers. John Smith served as interpreter, and a Ute Indian Agent, Simeon Whiteley, volunteered to record a transcript of the proceedings. Whiteley entered the following names of the chiefs representing the Cheyennes and Arapahos:

> Black Kettle, leading Cheyenne Chief
> White Antelope, Chief central Cheyenne band
> Bull Bear, leader of Dog Soldiers, (Cheyenne)
> Neva, sub-Arapaho Chief
> Bosse, Arapaho Chief
> Heap of Buffalo, Arapaho Chief
> Na-ta-nee (Knock Knee)

"Alright, gentlemen," Evans began, "Major Wynkoop tells me you have something to say."

Black Kettle spoke first through John Smith. He explained that he received Governor Evans' proclamation and accepted his demand that all friendly Indians were to turn themselves in at Fort Lyon. He told Evans the particulars of his meeting with Major Wynkoop on the Smoky Hill River, and how he returned Laura Roper and the other three captive children. He stated that two women, Mrs. Eubank and her baby, and a Mrs. Morton, taken by warriors on the South Platte, were still captive, and he would deliver them as soon as he could locate them.

"I followed Major Wynkoop to Fort Lyon," Black Kettle continued, "and he proposed that we come up to see you. We have come with our eyes shut, following his handful of men like coming through the fire. All we ask is that we have peace with the whites. We want to hold you by the hand. You are our father. We have been traveling through a cloud. The sky has been dark ever since the war began. These braves who are with me are all willing to do what I say.

"We want to take good tidings home to our people - that they may sleep in peace. I want you to give all the chiefs of these soldiers to understand that we are for peace, and that we have made peace -

that we may not be mistaken by them for enemies. I have not come here with a little wolf bark, but have come to talk plain with you. We must live near the buffalo or starve. When we came here, we came free, without any apprehension to see you. When I go home and tell my people that I have taken your hand, and the hand of all the chiefs here in Denver, they will feel well, and so will all the different tribes of Indians on the Plains, after we have eaten and drank with them."

"I am sorry you did not respond to my appeal at once," Evans said. "You have gone into an alliance with the Sioux, who were at war with us. You've done a great deal of damage - stolen stock, and now have possession of it. However much a few individuals may have tried to keep the peace, as a nation you have gone to war. While we've been spending thousands of dollars in opening farms for you, and making preparations to feed, protect, and make you comfortable, you have joined our enemies and gone to war. Hearing, last fall, that they were dissatisfied, the Great Father at Washington sent me out on the plains to talk with you and make it all right. I sent messengers out to tell you that I had presents, and would make you a feast, but you sent word to me that you did not want to have anything to do with me, and to the Great Father at Washington that you could get along without him. Bull Bear wanted to come in to see me at the head of the Republican, but his people held a council and would not let him come."

"Yes," Black Kettle responded, "this is true."

"After all the expense I was at, I had to return home without seeing you. Instead of meeting me, you went away and smoked the war pipe with our enemies."

Black Kettle shook his head. "I don't know who could have told you this."

"It doesn't matter who told me. Your conduct has proved to my satisfaction that this is the case."

"This is a mistake," White Antelope said. "We have made no alliance with the Sioux or anyone else."

"Well," Evans continued, "as far as a peace treaty is concerned, we will not do it. Your young men are on the warpath, and my soldiers are ready to fight. You've had the advantage all summer, but my time is coming. You think just because we are at war in the East that you can drive the whites from this country. But I assure you that the war in the States is almost finished, and soon this prairie will be swarming with United States soldiers. My proposition to the friendly Indians has gone out. They may come in under it, but I have no new propositions to make. I will not make a peace treaty, because the war has begun, and any treaty you want to make now must be made with our great war chief."

"I am trying to do everything in my power to make peace with you," Black Kettle said.

"My advice to you," Evans said, "is to turn on the side of the government, and show, by your acts, that friendly disposition you profess to me. It is utterly out of the question for you to be at peace with us while living with our enemies and being on friendly terms with them."

"What do you mean when you say 'turn on the side of the government?'" Bull Bear asked.

"First," Evans said, "you must make arrangements with the soldiers to help them. Join in their fight against hostile Indians. Obey our laws, provide information, act as scouts. I assure you, those who don't help them will be treated as enemies."

Black Kettle agreed. "We will return with Major Wynkoop to Fort Lyon; we will then proceed to our village and take back word to our young men, every word you say. I cannot answer for all of them, but think there will be but little difficulty in getting them to assent to helping the soldiers."

"Did not the Dog Soldiers agree, when I had my council with you, to do whatever you said, after you had been here?" Wynkoop asked.

"Yes," Black Kettle said.

White Antelope spoke: "I understand every word you have said, and will hold on to it. The Cheyennes, all of them, have their eyes open this way, and they will hear what you say. Ever since I went to meet the Great Father, I have called all white men as my brothers. But other Indians have since been to see him, and got medals, and now the soldiers do not shake hands, but seek to kill them. What do you mean by us fighting your enemies? Who are they?"

"All Indians who are fighting us," Evans said.

"How can we be protected from the soldiers?"

"You must make arrangements with the military chief."

"I fear that these new soldiers here may kill some of my people."

"Oh, yes," Evans said, "there is great danger of it. Look, it's out of my hands now. Whatever peace you wish to make must be with the soldiers, not me."

The chiefs looked at each other in frustration over Evans' curt answers. "How may we help you?" White Antelope said.

"You can start with a little honesty," Evans said. "Are the Apaches at war with the whites?"

"Yes, and the Comanches and Kiowas as well; also a tribe of Indians from Texas, whose names we do not know. There are thirteen different bands of Sioux who have crossed the Platte and are in alliance with the others named."

"How many warriors with the Apaches, Kiowas and Comanches?"

"Don't know," White Antelope said, "but many more than of the southern tribes."

"Who committed the depredations on the trains near the Junction, about the first of August?"

"I did not know any were committed. I have taken you by the hand and will tell the truth - keeping back nothing."

"Who committed the murder of the Hungate family on Running Creek?"

"The Arapahos," Neva said. He spoke English well. "A party of the northern band who were passing north. It was Medicine Man, or Roman Nose, and three others. I am satisfied from the time he left a certain camp for the north, that it was this party of four persons."

Agent Whiteley chimed in. "That cannot be true."

"Where is Roman Nose?" Evans asked.

"You ought to know better than me," Neva said. "You have been nearer to him."

"Who killed the man and boy at the head of Cherry Creek?"

Neva took a moment to speak with Bosse and Knock Knee. "Kiowas and Comanches," he finally said.

Evans perused his notes. "Who stole soldiers horses and mules from Jimmy's Camp, twenty-seven days ago?"

"Fourteen Cheyennes and Arapahos together," Neva said.

"What were their names?"

"Powder Face and Whirlwind, who are now in our camp."

"I counted twenty Indians on that occasion," Colonel Shoup said.

"Who stole Charley Autobee's horses?" Evans asked.

"Raven's son," Neva said.

Governor Evans continued his laundry list. "Who took the stock from Fremont's Orchard, and had the first fight with the soldiers this spring north of there?"

White Antelope grew agitated. "Before answering this question, I would like for you to know that this was the beginning of war, and I should like to know what it was for, as a soldier fired first."

"Oh, no," Evans said. "The Indians had stolen about forty horses. The soldiers went to recover them, and the Indians fired a volley into their ranks."

"This is all a mistake!" White Antelope said. "They were coming down the Bijou, and found one horse and one mule. They returned one horse to a man there, then went to Geary's ranch, expecting to turn the other one over to someone. They then heard that the soldiers and Indians were fighting somewhere down the Platte; then they took fright, and all fled."

"Who were the Indians who had the fright?" Evans asked.

"They were headed by the Fool Badger's son, one of the greatest of the Cheyenne warriors, who was wounded. Although still alive, he will never recover."

"I want to say something," Neva interrupted. "It makes me feel bad to be talking about these things and opening old sores. Mr. Smith has known me ever since I was a child. Has he ever known me commit depredations on the whites? I went to Washington last year - received good council. I hold on to it. I determined to always keep peace with the whites. Now, when I shake hands with them they seem to pull away. I came here to seek peace and nothing else."

"Your stealing and murdering has done us great damage," Evans said. "You come here and say you will tell me all, and that is what I am trying to get."

"The Comanches, Kiowas and Sioux have done much more injury than we have," Neva said. "We will tell what we know, but cannot speak for others."

"I suppose you acknowledge the depredations on the Little Blue, since you have the prisoners then taken in your possession," Evans sarcastically said.

"We Cheyennes took two prisoners west of Fort Kearney and destroyed the trains," White Antelope said. "We will answer to that."

"Who committed depredations at Cottonwood?" Evans asked.

"The Sioux," White Antelope said. "What band, we do not know."

"What are the Sioux going to do next?"

Bull Bear spoke through John Smith. "Their plan is to clean out all this country. They are angry and will do all the damage to the whites they can." Bull Bear looked Evans squarely in the eye. "I am with you and the troops, to fight all those who have no care to listen to what you say. Who are they? Show them to me! I am not yet old - I am young. I have never hurt a white man. I am pushing for something good, and I am always going to be friends with the whites. They can do me good."

"Where are the Sioux?"

"Down on the Republican, where it opens out."

"Do you know that they intend to attack the trains this week?"

"Yes," Bull Bear said. "About one half of all the Missouri River Sioux and Yanktons, who were driven from Minnesota, are those who have crossed the Platte. I am young and can fight. I have given my word to fight with the whites. My brother died in trying to keep peace with the whites. I am willing to die in the same way, and expect to do so."

The council had not gone to the chiefs' satisfaction, for it was apparent that Governor Evans would stand firm on his refusal to discuss a treaty.

"I know the value of the presents which we receive from Washington," Neva finally said. "We cannot live without them. That is why I try so hard to keep peace with the whites."

"Well," Evans said, "I cannot say anything about those things, now. In fact, I have nothing more to say. Colonel Chivington, before we adjourn, do you have anything you wish to add?"

Chivington stood and stalked the chiefs, towering over them and glaring at each one. "I am not a big war chief," he said, "but all the soldiers in this country are at my command. My rule of fighting white men or Indians is to fight them until they lay down their arms and submit to military authority. You all are nearer Major Wynkoop than anyone else, so you can go to him when you are ready to do that."

With that, he boldly walked out of the council room. Evans sorted his papers and followed Chivington, leaving the chiefs in a quandary...

Black Kettle and his party spent a cold night in the Camp Weld stockade. They listened to the hoots and hollers of the Hundred-Daysers outside, who were determined to send a clear message to their unwelcome guests. Wynkoop stationed a guard from his regiment to protect the chiefs, cutting a deep chasm between the disciplined soldiers of the Colorado First and the wild and dangerous militiaman of the Third. Many of the drunken dragoons of Chivington's new regiment chided Wynkoop's men, keeping a healthy distance while calling them Indian lovers and traitors, but none had the courage to stand and confront the true soldiers of the First.

Inside the stockade, the chiefs did not discuss the council, for it was apparent that their efforts to secure a true peace with Evans had gone for naught. Bull Bear seethed with anger, but he kept his opinions to himself for now. The Arapahos were angry, too, but they were under strict orders from Left Hand to behave themselves.

Black Kettle and White Antelope, the elders of this party, were simply disappointed, but their resolve was true. Black Kettle was already planning his next move, for he knew he had reason to be optimistic. The big chief Evans clearly stated that Black Kettle had a simple option – to surrender to the soldiers at Fort Lyon. Had there been any other commander of that post, Black Kettle might not have any reason for hope, but he believed the Great Spirit had given him one last chance to save his people. It was a gift in the form of the Tall Chief...

Colonel Chivington walked outside the Camp Weld gates with Major Wynkoop and Captain Soule. Wynkoop's regiment was mounted and circled around the Indian chiefs' wagon.

"It's been interesting, boys," Chivington said. "But do me a favor. From now on, if you have a mind to go calling on Indians out in the wild again, let me know so I can slap some sense into you."

Wynkoop puffed a final smoke and then ground it into the dirt. "To be frank, sir, I don't think we accomplished much."

"On the contrary," Chivington said, "you did more than you might think. We put the fear of God in those savages, for one thing. You just might be able to keep some of those devils quiet this winter."

"Evans didn't give them a damned thing," Wynkoop said. "Just a lot of spit and fire."

"He's a politician, Ned," Chivington said. "Don't give him any undeserved credit. Now, take these chiefs back down to the Arkansas and keep them in line. If they come in and submit, put them to their old reservation and watch them like a hawk."

"Can we give them annuities?" Captain Soule asked.

"I want them to give up their arms and any stolen stock in trade for food. They may keep a few bows for hunting, but use your good judgement as to how many. I want frequent reports as to their location and numbers. I want to hear from both of you all winter, savvy?"

"What about Curtis?" Wynkoop asked. "He's been pretty quiet. Do you think he'll want my hide for this?"

"He may," Chivington chuckled. "But you leave Curtis to me, son. Just do your duty from here out, and I'll square things with the general."

Wynkoop and Soule saluted and mounted their horses. "Good luck with your new regiment," Soule said. "From the looks of it, you'll need it."

Chivington laughed. "Don't underestimate the Colorado Third,

Silas! I could whip a pack of heathen Chinamen into a proud fighting regiment. In fact, I do believe I could run an entire empire! Godspeed, gentlemen!"

Wynkoop's regiment turned and rode out of camp. Wynkoop and Soule rode together at point.

Soule sighed. "It's a rich man's war, but a poor man's fight, Neddy."

Wynkoop sadly shook his head. "I just wonder where you and I fit into his empire."

"Well, I for one intend to hide out somewhere in a dark corner of it..."

Indian party attending the Weld Council in Denver, Sept. 28, 1864

Front row (kneeling) L-R - Maj. Edward Wynkoop, Capt. Silas Soule

Middle row (seated) L-R - White Antelope, Bull Bear, Black Kettle, Neva, Knock Knee.

Back row (standing) L-R - Unidentified soldier, Jack Smith (son of Indian Agent John Smith), John Smith, Heap of Buffalo, Bosse, trader Dexter Colley, unidentified soldier.

18

Wynkoop's party bivouacked at Coberly's for the night, surrounding the ranch with campfires and tents. As they had throughout their journey, the Indian chiefs used military tents pitched within the encampment for protection. They held a private council in which they prayed and smoked before discussing the events of the last few days. Wynkoop and his soldiers respectfully gave Black Kettle and his fellow chiefs a good distance, where they could speak freely among themselves.

Wynkoop and Lieutenant Cramer sat in the light of a small campfire, away from the rest of the boys tonight. They passed a bottle and smoked cigarettes, able to relax a bit for the first time since leaving Fort Lyon. The late September air had a bite to it, and the cheap whiskey felt good in the belly. They suddenly perked to the sounds of rustling in the nearby brush.

"Did you hear that?" Cramer said.

Wynkoop sat up and warily peered into the darkness. He drew his pistol.

The brush swayed again, and Captain Soule sprang out with a blood-chilling scream.

"Jesus Christ!" Cramer yelled.

"Sile! Goddamit!"

"Hey, boys!" Soule laughed. "Oh! Whiskey!" He sauntered in and grabbed the bottle.

"You scared the bejesus outta me," Cramer said.

Wynkoop holstered his pistol and leaned back with a sigh. "Knucklehead..."

Soule started to drink, but relented. "Wait a minute! What the hell am I doing?" He handed the bottle to Wynkoop. "I'm up the pole right now. I bet the sutler sixty bucks against a new winter coat that I wouldn't take a belt 'till Christmas."

"Fine with me," Wynkoop said. "More for us."

"My little angel don't want me drinkin,' anywho," Soule said. He slapped his hands together, still spilling over. "Whoo-we! Chilly tonight! Winter's a-coming!"

Cramer shook his head. "You're a pain in the ass when you're in love."

Soule threw that cocky laugh. "Can't blame a man for being happy, Joe! You oughta try it sometime."

"If you're so dad-blamed happy, why are you sitting here with us instead of inside with Hersa?"

"She kicked me out," Soule said. "Ain't exactly proper to steal into my gal's bedroom when her Mama and little sis are sleeping next door. Besides, old Bill just came in from Leadville, and he got himself a shiny new shotgun. That old boy sure is protective of his little sister." Soule winked. "She did give me a little sugar, though."

"I don't want to hear about it," Wynkoop said.

"Sorry, old buddy," Soule said. "I'll change the subject. So, Joe, you got any lately?"

"Shuddap!" Cramer said. "Jeez..."

The laughter died when Black Kettle suddenly appeared out of the darkness. Startled, the boys stood up.

"Moke-tav-a-to!" Wynkoop said. "Good evening."

Black Kettle nodded. Bull Bear, White Antelope and Neva walked up behind him. "Wine-koop. May we come?"

"Certainly," Wynkoop said.

The chiefs carried blankets, which they offered to Wynkoop and the boys.

"We give you these presents," Black Kettle said.

"Thank you," Wynkoop said, and the boys responded in kind. "Please, sit down with us."

Everyone gathered around the fire.

"I want to talk as friends," Black Kettle said.

Wynkoop smiled. "That suits me. Joe, get Uncle John over here to help."

Cramer jumped up and wandered into the darkness. "John Smith! Where are ya?"

A craggy voice came back. "Wraa!"

"Front and center, Uncle John!" Cramer hollered.

"Up yours! I'm sleeping!"

"We got some Taos Lightning here!"

In a flash, Smith stumbled toward the firelight. "Why didn't ya say so!" His eyes popped when he saw the chiefs. "What's this? A council?"

"Come and join us," Wynkoop said.

Smith eagerly sat and grabbed the bottle. "Whoo! That warms the innards."

"Moke-tav-a-to? Would you like a drink?" Wynkoop said.

Black Kettle took the bottle and sniffed. He took a drink of the Lightning and coughed hard.

Smith laughed. "He says, 'you drink this? No wonder Cheyennes think white men are crazy.'"

"Drink a toast boys," Soule said.

"You ain't drinking," Cramer said.

"I know, but here's a toast anyway. Here's success to port, for it warms the heart for sport. Here's success to whiskey, for it makes the spirits frisky. Here's success to cider, for it makes the frame grow wider. And here's success to sherry, for it makes the heart be merry."

Soule proudly smiled, but he received empty stares.

"Didn't like that one?" Soule said. "Try this: Here's to the ships of our navy, and here's to the women of our land. May your ships be well masted, and your women well manned..."

More silence.

"There was a young girl from Nantucket-"

"Shut up, Sile," Wynkoop said.

Black Kettle chuckled as he passed the bottle to White Antelope, who warily refused and passed it on. Neva drank, and then passed the bottle to Bull Bear. The Dogman took a hardy drink and almost choked.

"Ain't no Irish in this lot!" Soule laughed.

"Irish?" Black Kettle said.

"It's another word for loudmouth," Cramer said.

"Irish Loudmouth," Black Kettle said, pointing to Soule.

"At your service," Soule said.

Black Kettle smiled at Soule. "Captain – always with a happy heart. It is good." He then spoke to Smith.

"The chief says he wants to smoke with you and the boys, Ned. That's an honor – like he's offering to be friends. In Indian ways, smokin' together means that everyone will tell the truth."

"Tell him I would be proud to smoke with him," Wynkoop said.

Black Kettle lit the Cheyenne sacred pipe. He pointed it to the sky and to the earth. He then pointed it to the east, west, north and south. He then smoked and passed the pipe to Wynkoop.

"It's proper to take four puffs," Smith said.

Wynkoop smoked, and Black Kettle then offered the pipe to Soule, who drew hard and belched out the tarry smoke.

"Smoo-thh!" Soule coughed as he handed the pipe to Black Kettle. The old chief smiled, and the pipe was then passed all around.

Soule pulled out his briarwood pipe, and he offered it to Black Kettle. "I'd like you to have this," he said. "It was my daddy's pipe."

As Smith interpreted, Black Kettle nodded to Soule. "Thank you, Irish Loudmouth."

Soule meekly looked at the boys. "Looks like I ain't gonna get rid of that name."

Wynkoop turned to Bull Bear. "Sir, I want to bury the tomahawk with you. I want to call you my friend."

Bull Bear measured Wynkoop, still wary. He finally relented. "If I do not have to drink again?"

"Agreed!" Wynkoop said. They shook hands.

"Sometimes my head is angry with whites," Bull Bear said. "I talked hard with you before because I did not trust any white soldier. I learn now that I was wrong about you and *your* soldiers. Sometimes my mouth makes words before my heart can stop them."

"I'm told I have the same problem," Soule said.

"I think we all had to prove ourselves," Wynkoop said.

"Do you have family, Tall Chief?" Bull Bear asked Wynkoop.

"Yes," Wynkoop said. "My wife is Louisa, and I have two children. I also have seven brothers and sisters."

"I had a brother," Bull Bear said.

"I know," Wynkoop said. "I am truly sorry that you lost him."

"I hope you do not watch a brother die," Bull Bear said. "A part of you dies with him."

"This makes me sad," White Antelope said. "Let us talk of better things. Let us talk of making peace, so no one will die anymore."

"Tall Chief," Black Kettle said, "your big chief at Denver – talk plain?"

"Yes, sir," Wynkoop said. "He's determined to punish the bad Indians who've made war this summer. I'm afraid there will still be much fighting if your warriors continue to attack my people."

"But we will not fight," Black Kettle said. "We want to be quiet. We need you to help."

"I will, sir," Wynkoop said. "But I need your help, too. You must control your warriors."

"Will your big chief Evans control *his* soldiers and not attack the Indians who want peace?"

"That's a more difficult proposition," Wynkoop said. "I will talk plain with you. The soldiers from Denver consider every Indian to be at war with them. This is a very dangerous time for the friendly Indians. Unlike you, my big chief doesn't always have the final word with the soldiers."

Black Kettle spoke to Smith. "He wants to know why that ain't like him?"

"Well," Wynkoop said, "you are the main chief. Your word is final."

The chiefs all chuckled.

"Major," Smith said, "the Cheyenne's got forty-four chiefs.

Black Kettle is chief of the Wotap band. Bull Bear's chief of a Dogman band called Masikora. White Antelope is Isiometannui. There's more chiefs than you can shake a stick at. Black Kettle right now is pretty much considered the Principal Chief, but they's all equal in Council, and sometimes they can't agree on a damn thing. They fight just as much as white boys in Congress – sometime worse."

"What are the Dogmen?" Soule asked. "Are they Cheyennes?"

"They're Northern Cheyenne blood," Smith said, "but for years they been outcasts in the eyes of the whole Cheyenne Nation. The warrior clans ain't much different from our military. Young Indian bucks serve as soldiers, just like you boys, and they have their own leaders, who answer to the Council of Forty-four. Before the war broke out, a lot of Cheyennes didn't approve of the way the Dogmen always shot first and asked questions afterwards. But once the whites started moving in on Cheyenne and Arapaho hunting ground, the Dogmen gained a lot of respect for the way they fought back."

"Bull Bear," Soule said, "can you control the Dogmen and convince them to stop fighting?"

Bull Bear listened to Smith interpret. "If you have the medicine to quiet a young man's anger, I will offer you all my ponies for it," Bull Bear replied. "Many of them are determined to fight whites to the death."

"Why did *you* offer to make peace with us?" Soule asked.

Smith continued to interpret for Bull Bear: "When my brother came back from meeting the Great Father in Washington, he told me about the wonders he saw there. He said it was like he had new eyes. He told me the whites could offer us better ways for our children to live. He told me that he was willing to die for this, and he asked me to help him. When he was killed, it is our way to smoke the war pipe and go for the ones who killed him, but I could not – because of the promise I made to him. I still see with his eyes, and I know that killing all white men just to avenge what one soldier did can only hurt us."

"I hope you can talk this wisdom to the young warriors," Wynkoop said.

"It is hard to say," Bull Bear said. "They came up in a different world than Black Kettle and White Antelope. They never knew the time when the People were friends with the whites. Many of them do not open their eyes and ears to learn what the whites can do for us. They only know the white man who takes and never gives."

"That's not fair," Wynkoop said. "It's not true of all white men."

Bull Bear shrugged and spoke English. "Not all Dogmen are killers, too."

"Tell me, Tall Chief," Neva said, "what would you do if you lived on a land for a long time, and then an invader attacks you and pushes you away? They chase you and try to kill you – taking the land that feeds your wife and children. Would you not fight them?"

"Brothers," Black Kettle said through Smith, "we could complain to Tall Chief about injustice all night, and tomorrow we would still have the same problem. We must find a way to stop the troubles between us."

"I agree," Wynkoop said.

"Bull Bear wants to know about Chivington," Smith said. "He says the colonel tells them he is not a big chief, but he acts like no one tells him what to do. He says he was very near to hard talk with Chiv."

"Colonel Chivington's mouth sometimes makes words before his brain works," Soule said. "But he is *not* a big chief, and he can't act without orders."

Wynkoop agreed. "Chivington and Evans gave me authority to treat with you and end the trouble between my soldiers and you. The soldiers in Denver will go to fight the bad Indians up north on the Platte and Republican this winter. We are very far away from those troubles down on the Arkansas, so if you control your warriors and keep them quiet, I know we can begin a lasting peace between us. What I ask is that you go to your people and urge those who want peace to come to Fort Lyon and surrender."

"Can I tell them that they will not be shot at?" Black Kettle asked.

"You have my word," Wynkoop said. "Anyone of your people who surrender and follow my advice will not be harmed. Bull Bear, I worry about the Dogmen. Will you convince them to stop making war and submit to us?"

"It will take time," Bull Bear said. "Many of my young men are in trouble with you for what they have done, and I do not think I will be able to convince them. As for others who want to stop fighting, I must round them up and talk to them. I fear attacks by soldiers who do not care which boy is good, and which is bad."

"You just bring the good boys to me," Wynkoop said. "If they behave, I will protect them. I will always honor the white flag."

"May we camp at your fort?" Black Kettle asked.

"That's not a good idea," Wynkoop said. "You may come in and surrender to me, but if you camp too close to the fort it will frighten the white families who live by us. Something bad could happen.

Until I can get some word from General Curtis regarding a true peace agreement between us, you will have to keep your distance."

"But the other soldiers from Larned and Riley might not be in favor of protecting us," Neva said. "We do not feel safe if we camp too far away from you. We must find a place nearby, where we can hunt and find food."

"I will give you some annuities," Wynkoop said, "but there is a limit to what I can provide. You can find some buffalo and game on Sand Creek. It's not far from the fort, and we can protect you there."

"Then it is done," Black Kettle said. "We will go back to our people and tell them this. I will also do my best to return the other white prisoners to you."

"Agreed," Wynkoop said. "If you do what you say, I know we can reach a peaceful accord."

"I will take your advice in my heart, Tall Chief."

"Bull Bear?" Wynkoop asked.

"I will do my best," Bull Bear said.

"That's good enough for me," Wynkoop said. Everyone shook hands, and the chiefs started to leave.

"Why don't you stay a bit longer," Wynkoop said. "Perhaps you'd like another drink, and we can talk more."

Black Kettle smiled. "I would like that."

"Let me try more of your white poison," Bull Bear said. The chiefs huddled in their blankets by the fire, and the bottle was passed.

"Moke-tav-a-to," Wynkoop said, "do you have a wife?"

"Yes. Medicine Woman Later. She has a smile like sunshine."

"The chief lost his first wife in a fight with the Utes a long time ago," Smith said.

"Black Kettle was a great warrior," Neva said.

"I fought and won – sometimes I lost," Black Kettle modestly said.

"Were you a Dogman?" Soule asked.

"No. Elkhorn Scrapers," Black Kettle said. "Most young men dream of being a warrior. Much like you, many become warriors to protect the People."

"Black Kettle was a Bowstring first," Smith explained. "Later, he joined the Elkhorn Scrapers. Warriors have a better chance to become a chief someday. They move up in ranks by proving themselves in battle. They sacrifice themselves in sacred rituals to seek wisdom and strength, so someday they can lead their clans."

"What kind of rituals?" Wynkoop asked.

"One is called the Sun Dance," Smith said. "That ain't nothing you'd wanna do for sport, I tell ya. A warrior takes two ropes and hooks them into his chest. They throw the ropes up on a pole and hang there sometimes for hours. If the lances don't rip outta their chest first, the medicine man cuts them out at the end of the dance."

Soule winced and rubbed his chest. "That must smart."

Black Kettle smiled at Irish Loudmouth. He opened his blanket and exposed two hideous scars on his chest.

"Only the strongest can cope," Smith said.

"What's the purpose of it?" Cramer asked.

"It shows a warrior will sacrifice and take pain for his people. It's a sacrifice to *Maheo* – what they call the Great Spirit – and it brings them luck. They do the Sun Dance for all kinds of reason – the hunt, for war, or when there's sickness in their people. When all the bands get together for the summer hunt, they do the Sun Dance to renew the spirit of the earth."

"I'd say the Great Spirit ain't much different from the white man's God," Soule mused. "Wonder if the old Fighting Parson ever considered that."

"How did you lose your first wife?" Wynkoop asked Black Kettle.

Black Kettle sighed. "I was in a war party to kill Mexicans – they attacked my band and killed two warriors. Little Sage and two other squaws traveled with us to cook and keep the horses. On our return near the Cimarron, we were attacked by the Black People – what you call Utes – and Apaches. We were surprised by them and got into a fight. They were too many for us, and they took our women. I wanted to go for them, but I was wounded, and the others were too beaten by the fight to come back for them. We had to give up. I never saw Little Sage again, and it made great pain in my heart."

"I'm sorry," Wynkoop said. "My duty keeps me away from my wife and children for long periods. It makes pain in my heart, too. So, you then married Medicine Woman Later?"

"She was Wotap," Black Kettle said. "I met her at a time when I was in great sorrow. We mourned together for Little Sage, and long after that we married."

"It's Cheyenne tradition for the man to join his wife's band," Smith said. "Although he was born in the Suhtai, he was so respected by the Wotapio that he by-and-by became their chief."

"But, too much talk of me," Black Kettle said. "What of you and Irish Loudmouth? How did you become chiefs?"

"These boys are great warriors, too," Smith explained in Cheyenne. "Tall Chief was with the first whites to open Denver. Captain Soule was a strong fighter to help set the black white man free from their captors in the south."

Bull Bear was feeling a bit woozy now from the Taos Lightning. "What is it about you whites that you hate people with prettier skin?"

Soule laughed. "Well, Bull Bear, that's something I ain't figured out myself. I think it's something called Christianity that puts some white men to thinking they're better than others. Don't ask me why, cause other God-fearing white men think just the opposite."

"That white woman in the lodge here," White Antelope said. "Is she your wife?"

"She ain't yet," Soule said, "but once we set things straight this winter, I intend to marry her."

"Pretty Squaw," Bull Bear said. "Irish Loudmouth better be good to her."

"She don't have any idea how good this old lucky loudmouth is gonna be to her," Soule said.

"How did you fight for the black white man?" Black Kettle asked.

Cramer jumped in. "Old Silas here has gonads of steel! The southern whites arrested another white man who was trying to help some slaves run to freedom. The captain took some of his boys to the calaboose and tried to bust that boy out."

"Did you take them?" Neva asked.

"Well, no," Soule said with a laugh. "We sure had a mind to, but things didn't work out like we planned. I gave it my best, though. I got myself all liquored up, and got arrested and put in the same jail as old John Brown and his boys. I sang some Irish songs and told the jailer a few tall tales, just to soften him up. I talked him into putting me in the cell with Mr. Brown, where I let him in on our plan to spring him. But, damned if he didn't flat-out refuse to go."

"Why not?" Black Kettle asked.

"I've spent a lot of time pondering that," Soule said. "His reason was that he was happy to die for his cause. At the time, I was madder than a cat with his tail tied in a knot. After all the trouble I was at to set him free, I couldn't see why a man was happier with a rope tied round his neck than to run for freedom. But, all of a sudden, I sit here and listen to Bull Bear tell me about his brother giving his life for his people, and it makes me feel a tad ashamed. My daddy always said, you don't have to stand tall, but you goddam better stand up."

Wynkoop chuckled at his old friend. "Seems your daddy was *always* saying something."

"Couldn't get a word in edgewise with the old man around,"

Soule said. "Reckon that's why I make up for it now."

The boys laughed and passed the bottle again. Cramer pulled out his harmonica and played softly.

The chiefs were pleased, for they had never heard such a sound.

"I do not think we are so different," Black Kettle finally said.

"We can make a peace between us, sir," Wynkoop said. "It makes no sense for us to fight for this land, when it's surely big enough for all of us."

Black Kettle smiled. "Makes no sense to fight and kill when we can be friends instead, unless you are one of the Wolf People."

"Who?" Wynkoop said.

"Pawnees," Smith laughed. "I don't reckon you'll ever get the Cheyennes to like them."

"They are skunks," Bull Bear said. "Wolf People pat you on the back and smile, but too late you find out he has a knife in his hand."

"We have some whites who are like that," Soule said. "We call 'em 'Texans.'"

When Smith explained, the chiefs laughed with the boys.

Cramer began to play a tune, and Soule sang along. A chorus of coyotes suddenly howled in the distance.

"The coyotes sing better than Irish Loudmouth," Neva chuckled.

"I beg your pardon," Soule said. "They just know a sweet Irish tenor when they hear one. Let me teach you this song." Soule sang again, prompting the Indians to join him. Black Kettle laughed and waved him off, but old White Antelope and Neva gave it a whirl. In a moment, old Taos Lightning persuaded Bull Bear to give it a try. Around the camp, the soldiers of the First Cavalry turned a curious ear. In the distance, the coyotes accompanied this peculiar choir.

> *"There was a Sergeant John McCaffery,*
> *and Captain Donohue;*
> *They'd make us march and toe the mark,*
> *in gallant Company 'Q';*
> *Oh, the drums would roll upon my soul,*
> *this is the style we'd go;*
> *Forty miles a day on beans and hay,*
> *in the Regular Army-O..."*

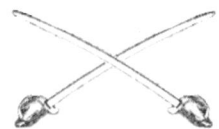

19

When Wynkoop's party arrived at Fort Lyon, Black Kettle and the chiefs immediately departed for the Smoky Hill. They set out to locate their people and convince them to surrender under the informal terms of their agreement. Skeptical of Colonel Chivington's boastful reassurances, Wynkoop determined his interest was better served by writing a full report to General Curtis, detailing the events at the Smoky Hill and in Denver, and taking full responsibility for his actions.

In his report, Wynkoop concluded:

I think that if some terms are made with these Indians, I can arrange matters so, by bringing their villages under my direct control, that I can answer for their fidelity. We are at war with the Sioux, and the Kiowas, and Comanches; these Indians, the Arapahos and Cheyennes, tell me they are willing to lend me their assistance in fighting the Kiowas and Comanches. It is the universal desire of the settlers of this part of the country for peace.

I enclose a copy of a communication received from the settlers to prove that such is the case, and if I may be pardoned for the suggestion, I deem it the best policy to adopt at present, in consequence of the necessity of the services of our troops elsewhere, and in consequence of having had considerable experience in this country. I know that in a general Indian war it will take more soldiers than we can possibly spare to keep open the two lines of communication, protect the settlements, and make an effective war upon them.

Deeming these matters to be of the utmost importance, and dispatch required to bring the same before the major general commanding, I have taken the liberty of ordering an officer to carry this communication, and return with instructions as soon as possible.

Hoping that I have not been too bold in the responsibility I have assumed, which may lay me liable to the censure of the commanding general, I have the honor to remain your obedient servant,

E. W. WYNKOOP,
Major First Cavalry of Colorado,
Commanding Fort Lyon, C. T.

OCTOBER 10, 1864

The sun kissed the horizon overlooking Summit Springs, a few miles south of the Platte in the northeast corner of the Colorado

Territory. Two lodges stood by a small creek. Young Red Hair, just fourteen, wandered the sleeping camp as two squaws emerged from one lodge and walked out to collect water and berries. Red Hair approached his father's lodge and stood outside.

"Father," he called.

Big Wolf, a Dogman warrior, hollered from his lodge. "Go away!"

"The sun is coming. It is time to pack," Red Hair said.

"Later!"

"But it is almost daylight!"

"Go away, Red Hair!"

The young boy curiously stood by his father's lodge. Five other Dogmen were already up and packing their horses. From inside the lodge, Red Hair heard soft laughter. It was his mother. Red Hair cocked his head when she suddenly gave a passionate moan. The young boy shrugged and returned to the horses...

Duncan Kerr had a face that would scare Satan himself. The grisly scout peered over an outcrop of rocks on the bluff above Summit Springs. He quickly rolled back down the hill, where forty 'daysers' of the Third Regiment's D Company were mounted, under the command of Captain David Nichols.

"They're just rousing, Cap'n," Kerr whispered.

"How many?" Nichols asked.

"Maybe no more than a dozen. I seen five warriors, two squaws and a young buck."

"Alright, boys, remember what you learned," Nichols said to the troops. "Stay tight and move directly. Don't give them any slack, and take the fight directly to the warriors. It's time we start collecting a debt."

The company charged over the rise, guns blazing.

Red Hair gave a shout and tried to run, but three rifle balls instantly cut him down. The daysers overwhelmed the village, some firing into the teepees, while others struggled with their rifles. Three daysers fell from their mounts, their horses spooked in terror. The five Dogmen, taken by surprise, had little time to run for their weapons. They quickly fell in the barrage of fire. Big Wolf scampered from his lodge, but he was shot before he could run. His naked wife emerged, carrying an infant in her arms.

Kerr gave a wild howl and chased the woman, shooting her in the back. He leapt from his horse and pulled a hunting knife. Big Wolf, mortally wounded, tried to crawl to his wife, but Kerr pounced on him and insanely screamed as he scalped the Dogman alive. Big Wolf dropped to the dirt, his head spewing blood. The day-sers rounded the village, whooping with garish joy as they shot into the dead Indians. Several dismounted and entered the two lodges, searching for booty. Several troopers, who had a thirst for revenge when they first charged, now slowed and stopped the attack.

"Whoa!" Kerr growled. "Look at this!" He slowly walked up to Big Wolf's naked wife, who sucked for her few remaining breaths. Although shot in the back, she desperately tried to protect her baby. Kerr tossed a wicked laugh as he kicked her in the ribs. She cried out and fell atop the infant. Kerr stomped on her head.

Private Morse Coffin quickly rode up. "Stop it!" he hollered. "She's dead!"

"The hell she is! This Indian whore's still looking to fight!" Kerr kicked her again and jammed his knife into her throat. "Let's see if this'll do it!"

Coffin jumped from his horse and tried to grab Kerr, but the wily mountain man shoved him back.

"What's the matter with you?" Kerr bellowed.

"That's enough!"

"The bitch is protecting a goddam warrior!" Kerr rolled the squaw over and grabbed at the screaming infant.

"God damn you bastard! Leave it alone!" Coffin yelled.

"What? You lost your nerve already?" Kerr said.

"It's a baby, for Christ's sake!" Coffin pleaded.

"It's a fuckin' animal!" Kerr backed up and shot the baby twice as it still lay in its mother's dead arms. He gave another whoop and ran toward the Dogmen lodges.

Coffin shuddered and backed away from the bodies, his eyes never leaving the dead infant.

"Sweet revenge, boys!" Captain Nichols crowed as he rode around the dead Indians. "Those sons-a-bitches in Denver ain't gonna call us the Bloodless Third anymore!"

The scavenging daysers gave a cheer. Private Coffin quietly watched with a few other militiamen who'd taken similar stock of the attack. The lodges now burned, throwing smoke into the new dawn...

Colonel Chivington's new regiment had finally drawn Indian blood in Colorado, after more than half of their 100-days commission had passed without a single Indian encounter. Captain Nichols' raid on Big Wolf's camp near Summit Springs reportedly yielded seven dead warriors and three squaws, but nothing was mentioned of the baby that Private Morse Coffin would later write about in his personal memoirs. Nichols turned over ten captured ponies and one mule to Chivington, along with bills of lading and a white woman's scalp that the soldiers found in Big Wolf's lodge. A Third Regiment soldier also claimed to have found a certificate of "good character" in Big Wolf's name, adding fuel to Chivington's declaration that all Indians were murderous liars, and none should be spared.

The raid at Summit Springs did little to impress Chivington's and Evans' political opponents in Denver, however. Many believed that Wynkoop's efforts to bring the Cheyennes to the bargaining table in September appeared to be working, for the number of Indian attacks on the South Platte had diminished over the following month. Although a few skirmishes had broken out on the fringes of the Colorado Territory, the fierce war party presence along the Platte and Republican receded toward Kansas and Nebraska. The Colorado Third Regiment, laughingly dubbed the "Bloodless Third" by cynical Denverites, was on the hook, for the minimal raid on Big Wolf's family only provided fodder for Union Democrats to accuse Evans of exaggerating the "Great Indian Confederation" against the Colorado Territory. The cynics were closing in and claiming the governor's emergency commission of a volunteer militia was nothing more than political grandstanding.

With the contentious issue of Colorado statehood under hot debate in Congress, the coveted congressional seats were up for grabs if the bill passed. Due to the mounting dissatisfaction with Governor Evans' mishandling of the Indian problems, things were looking bleak for statehood promoters. Under mounting pressure from his party, Evans reluctantly withdrew from the November senatorial race, as he had become a liability to the statehood issue. The Fighting Parson, however, still had a chance to be elected as a delegate to Congress, providing he could resuscitate the sagging reputation of the Colorado Third Regiment. Time was running out on Chivington and the Hundred-Daysers, however. In fact, Chivington's enlistment in the army had expired in September, and he was due to muster out of the service, providing anyone at the War Department might notice that Colorado's military commander had technically been a civilian for more than a month. This was a minor technicality, however, for Evans' second proclamation had authorized all Colorado citizens to independently organize militias to exterminate Indians. Chivington simply had his own army equipped and mounted on the government's nickel. If a large band of Indians could be vanquished inside the new congressional district, Chivington believed his military heroics would revive his chances for Congress. The Indians, however, presented a slight problem. Within the boundaries of the vast Colorado Territory, there were few to be found...

By mid October, Chivington gave up on the Platte and ordered Colonel Shoup to move the Third Regiment south toward the Bijou Basin in the central portion of the territory. Just weeks ago, when Black Kettle and his party met with Evans in Denver, General Blunt and Major Scott Anthony mounted a party from Fort Riley and marched southwest toward Cimarron Crossing on the Arkansas. There, they discovered an unidentified Indian camp believed to be Cheyennes and Arapahos associated with Black Kettle and Left Hand. Blunt quickly ordered his troops to attack in the middle of the night, but the wily Indians outmaneuvered the soldiers after a brief fight. Blunt and Anthony pursued the Indians toward the Smoky Hill for two days until they ran out of supplies and exhausted their horses. They were forced to return to Fort Riley, having killed but few Indians, with one soldier dead and seven wounded.

Again, the Indians had disappeared into the depths of Kansas, and it was growing quite apparent that the army, although fiercely adept at fighting confederate soldiers, was inept at waging war with the cagey Indians, thus adding fuel to political fires in Denver. The resulting backlash of discontent swept the issue of Colorado statehood to a resounding defeat in the November election, and Chivington, too, was mauled at the polls. New pressure mounted on Evans and Chivington from the west, where Brigadier General Patrick E. Connor, commanding the District of Utah, smelled political blood running in the streets of Denver. Connor was mounting a defense of the stage line between Salt Lake City and Fort Kearney, Nebraska, hoping to score a large Indian victory for his own political résumé. To further weaken Chivington and his impotent Indian-fighter militia, Connor requested troops from the Third Regiment to support his flank.

Chivington was enraged by Connor's ploy, which would essentially reduce him to the role of Connor's subordinate until the Third Regiment's commission expired at the end of November. Due to be mustered out at any time, Chivington, humiliated by defeat in his first political foray, had no intention of limping into his new political career with nothing more than Big Wolf's scalp hanging on his belt. He urgently wired General Curtis, questioning Connor's authority to commandeer troops from the district, but he received no reply before Connor arrived in Denver on November 14 to round up the daysers.

Chivington refused to meet Connor, for coincidentally, he arose early that morning and ordered three companies of the Colorado First Regiment to leave Denver and join the Colorado Third Regiment on the Bijou. Their departure would leave Denver virtually defenseless in the event of an Indian attack, but Chivington was willing to take that gamble. The Third Regiment had only a few weeks left to find an Indian fight in Colorado, and Chivington held an ace in his hand – by the name of Wynkoop. Before his detachment marched for a rendezvous with the daysers, however, General Connor accosted him at the gates of Camp Weld. The discussion was heated, but Connor, with no authority to stop Chivington, lost the duel.

"Respectfully, General," Chivington said, "it's obvious you have no other purpose here but to check up on me. If that indeed is the case, you may report back to the War Secretary that the Colorado Third Regiment was not raised to carry supplies for you."

"From what I've heard," Connor replied, "that might be too arduous a task for your boys."

"Indeed?" Chivington said. "Well, I promise you will hear otherwise in the very near future."

"Colonel, I have no doubt your men might have a good go at the Indians if you were up in the mountains, where you might trap them in a canyon and have a turkey-shoot. But on the plains, you don't stand a chance of finding them, much less mounting a sufficient attack."

"Maybe," Chivington said. "Maybe not."

"Curtis and Blunt have been chasing them for eight months!" Connor said. "What makes you think you can do better?"

"That's the trick that wins the game, General," Chivington smirked. "You don't have to chase them if you know where they are."

"Oh, and I suppose you hold this coveted secret?"

"There are only two officers in the territory who know where to find them – myself and Colonel Shoup." Chivington turned his men away as he called over his shoulder. "Have a safe trip back to Salt Lake, General..."

In the middle of October, Governor John Evans sent a telegram to Secretary of State William H. Seward, urgently requesting a leave of absence from Colorado, to begin on the first of November. Evans stated that his purpose for the furlough was to go to Washington to formally protest a grassroots movement by anti-statehood opponents to remove him from office. To date, his request was unanswered. On November 16, two days after Chivington departed for a rendezvous with the Third Regiment on Bijou Creek, Evans simply packed up his family and left for Washington without permission...

20

Left Hand and Little Raven's band, numbering over 600 Indians, were the first to come to Fort Lyon and submit to Wynkoop's authority. Per his agreement with Wynkoop, Black Kettle took his band directly to Sand Creek and camped near a large bluff for protection against the elements. The Cheyenne chief sent messengers to the fort to inform Wynkoop of his arrival, and Wynkoop sent John Prowers, the son-in-law of One Eye, to deliver annuities and confirm the conditions of Black Kettle's surrender.

The weather had dramatically turned throughout late October, and many of the Arapahos were sick with fever and desperately hungry. Wynkoop was sympathetic to their destitution and immediately issued rations and annuities for ten days. He allowed them to erect over 100 lodges a few miles from the fort, so they could come in and trade buffalo robes for provisions offered by traders and locals. Wynkoop cautioned Left Hand and Little Raven that they would soon have to move to Sand Creek when their people were stronger, but while the Arapahos freely moved in and out of the fort, a few of Wynkoop's troops grew uneasy. A general dissention emerged from this small group, and rumors began to leave the area accusing Wynkoop of giving Left Hand and Little Raven free reign at the post.

The news traveled quickly, and when it reached General Curtis at Leavenworth, this was decidedly the final straw. Whether the rumors were true or not, Curtis was fed up with the continual controversy surrounding his brassy officer. It was time to reign him in. Curtis immediately ordered the District Commander to relieve Wynkoop of his command at Fort Lyon and send him to headquarters, where Curtis planned to give Wynkoop a good dressing down. When Chivington got wind of Wynkoop's removal, he at last spotted the opportunity to play his ace in the hole. Taking the motley, undisciplined Third Regiment into a battle with the fierce Dogmen in the depths of a Kansas winter was not only a politically unsound decision – it was virtual suicide. But now that Wynkoop was leaving Fort Lyon, Chivington believed that no one could stand in the way of the Third Regiment attacking a far less formidable Indian band well within the boundary of the Colorado Territory...

Bull Bear sat in council far out on the Republican River with fellow Dogmen Tall Bull, Big Crow, and White Horse. They huddled around a fire in the lodge, sniping and growling at each other like wild dogs.

"It is the price of peace, brothers!" Bull Bear said.

"A price paid with Big Wolf's life!" Tall Bull said.

"Big Wolf ran raids and killed anything with white skin!" Bull Bear said. "He all but asked for trouble when he camped so close to Denver!"

Big Crow waved Bull Bear off. "What kind of medicine did the whites trick you with? Since you went to them, you talk like a white coyote!"

"The sun lighting the darkness is no trick," Bull Bear said. "There are many good whites like the Tall Chief."

"Eh, this Tall Chief," White Horse angrily said. "He is no better than any other pale liar!"

"No!" Bull Bear said. "Tall Chief and Irish Loudmouth are my friends. You do not even know them, so how can you say?"

"If they are your friends, then I am sorry for you," Tall Bull said.

"And I am sorry for *you*," Bull Bear said. "If you will not listen and take the advice of Tall Chief, you will die. We cannot fight them forever."

"I will," Tall Bull said. "Go ahead - surrender to them and see how long you live."

"You can go to Sand Creek," White Horse said, "but I will not."

"Nor I," Big Crow agreed.

"Then you dishonor Black Kettle," Bull Bear said.

"Black Kettle is an old fool," Tall Bull said. "He fears the Long Knives, so he crawls to them and goes back to Sand Creek, where the whites have always wanted us to starve to death. There is little water and nothing to hunt there."

"And in the winter, he camps there?" Big Crow said. "He will do nothing but give the Long Knives good target practice."

Bull Bear sat back in frustration. "Is there no compromise in any of you?"

"No," Tall Bull said. "I will not bargain with those liars, and if you have any sense, you will stay here with us. We will *not* camp with those old men and women at Sand Creek. The whites lied to you. Giving in to them will only get you killed."

"And what if they did not lie?" Bull Bear asked. "What if Black Kettle and the Arapahos align with the soldiers? The Dogmen will truly be alone then."

Tall Bull looked at his brothers. "No bargains now. The whites have to prove themselves. I know you are wise, Bull Bear, so I will give you that. We will winter from here to the Solomon. If we spend the winter without being attacked, and those bands on Sand Creek are still there when the grasses turn green, we will again take up council and talk of what you propose."

Bull Bear considered his brethren. "Is this what you all want?"

The other Dogmen agreed. "You have a choice," Tall Bull said. "If you go, then it is *you* who will be alone."

"You leave me no choice but to stay," Bull Bear said. "I will send word to Black Kettle that, no matter what the rest of you decide after the winter, I will join him in the spring..."

SPECIAL ORDERS,
HEADQUARTERS
DISTRICT OF THE UPPER ARKANSAS,
FORT RILEY, KANSAS

I. Major E. W. Wynkoop, First Cavalry of Colorado, is hereby relieved from the command of Fort Lyon, Colorado Territory, and is ordered to report without delay to headquarters District of the Upper Arkansas, for orders.

II. Major Scott J. Anthony, First Cavalry of Colorado, will proceed to Fort Lyon, Colorado Territory, and assume command of that post, and report in regard to matters as stated in Special Orders...

In a dispatch to Major Henning, Wynkoop's immediate superior at Fort Riley, General Curtis stated:

...The treaty operations at Lyon greatly embarrass matters, and I hope you have disposed of Major Wynkoop and directed a change for the better. Indians must be kept at arm's length. Even if they come in as prisoners of war we are not obliged to receive them, or feed them, or allow them inside the forts. The old and infirm and lazy will come in, while the wicked are allowed to go on with their devilment. I suppose Left Hand and some of the Indians who have been in may be sincere, but they must evince their fidelity by strong proofs, such as turning over the culprits, arms, horses, etc., and becoming the foes of hostile bands, ready and willing to fight them. I am going to send troops forward with a view of further operations at the proper time, but do not desire the public to know my purposes, and therefore will not dilate upon them...

NOVEMBER 5, 1864

Wynkoop slammed the orders on his desk and advanced on Major Scott Anthony. "What the hell is this?" he shouted.

Anthony, a wormy, scurvy-ridden man much smaller than Wynkoop, backed away. "Orders from Henning," he said, blinking his watery, red eyes. "I'm taking over here, and you're ordered to go to Fort Riley."

Captain Soule took his hat off and angrily slapped the dust from his trousers. "Well, ain't that just goddam perfect! What's the reason for it?"

"I think you both know that," Anthony said.

"What the hell's that supposed to mean?" Wynkoop said.

"Hey," Anthony said, "maybe you boys ain't heard, but we're in a goddam war with the redskins! You're in direct violation of orders letting those Arapahos camp so close to the fort. From the looks of things around here, you seem to be running a hotel for the bastards."

"What?" Wynkoop said.

"Maybe if you acted more like an officer, you wouldn't have been demoted!"

Wynkoop grabbed Anthony's collar. "You little son of a bitch!"

"Back off, Wynkoop!" Anthony hollered.

Soule stepped between the two, pulling Wynkoop away. "Take it easy, Ned." He suddenly turned and drove Anthony into a wall. "What do you mean, if he acted more like an officer!"

Stunned, Anthony whined and covered his face. "Let me go!"

Wynkoop pounced on Soule and pulled him away. "Sile!"

"I'll whip your ass!" Soule said.

"And I'll court-martial you, Captain!" Anthony wheezed.

"You'll have to do it with a broken arm!"

"Alright!" Wynkoop said. "That's enough! Sile – go sit down!"

"I'll sit on his fucking head," Soule mumbled as he backed to Wynkoop's desk. "What the hell do you mean, act more like an officer? You ain't half the officer Ned is on your *best* goddam day."

"Sile?" Wynkoop said. "Are ya done?"

"Son of a bitch. I'll tell that rat bastard when I'm done."

"Sile!"

"Okay," Soule said. "Now I'm done."

"Oh, you're more than done, Captain!" Anthony said.

Soule came back. "You think so?"

"Stop!" Wynkoop said.

"Jesus Christ, don't you keep a muzzle on this Jayhawker?"

Soule relented and returned to Wynkoop's desk, still mumbling. "I'll muzzle you."

Wynkoop looked at Anthony. "Scott, do me a favor – don't keep lighting his fuse, because you can't win here."

Anthony measured Soule. "Look, I'm just following orders. You got a beef, then take it up with Curtis."

"Don't hand me that," Wynkoop said. "You've been at Riley. What the hell's going on?"

"Henning told me to take command here and evaluate the Indian situation."

"What situation?"

"He told me there's a problem here," Anthony said. "Says Left Hand's got the run of the fort."

"Who told him that?"

"How would I know? I can't say I like what I see. That goddam Arapaho camp isn't more than a mile away. That's a clear violation of orders to take prisoners and corral them far away from the fort."

"They're camped there temporarily," Wynkoop said. "They surrendered to me, and I've allowed them to trade for supplies and medicine. Hell, half of them are dying of cholera and pneumonia. They're going to move to Sand Creek just as soon as they can."

"No order has been violated," Soule added.

"Well, that's not what I heard," Anthony said. "Word is the Indians are coming directly into the post, taking government rations, getting drunk..."

Major Scott J. Anthony

"Who said that?" Wynkoop asked.

"I told you – I don't know. My guess is it came from here."

"What – do you think we're having a goddam party down here?" Soule said. "We been bustin' our backs trying to get these Indians to settle down. Ned's got a good rapport with both Left Hand and Black Kettle. He's the only man in the whole regiment who made any headway with these people, so how's it gonna look to them if the army pulls him out of here?"

"My interest doesn't include any concern for the Indians," Anthony said. "I have my orders to push them away from the fort. Ned, you got no choice here. You're ordered to report to Fort Riley."

"God damn," Wynkoop whispered.

"I need you here for a few weeks to help me get familiar with the situation. Look, gentlemen, don't make me the bastard here. I'm just following orders. I'll make a fair report to Curtis based on what I see. If things aren't as bad as the rumors say, I won't hesitate to pass it along... "

TO: *Major Henning*
District of Upper Arkansas, Fort Riley, Kansas
SIR:

I have the honor to report that I arrived at this post and assumed command...Major E. W. Wynkoop, 1st cavalry of Colorado, was in command of the post. One hundred and thirteen lodges of Arapaho Indians, under their chiefs Little Raven, Left Hand, Neva, Storms, and Knock Knee, and numbering, in men, women and children, 652 persons, were encamped in a body about two miles from the post, and were daily visiting the post, and receiving supplies from the commissary department, the supplies being issued by Lieutenant C. H. Copett, assistant commissary of supplies, under orders from Major E. W. Wynkoop, commanding post.

I immediately gave instructions to arrest all Indians coming within the post, until I could learn something more about them. Went down and met their head chiefs, half way between the post and their camp, and demanded of them by what authority and for what purpose they were encamped here. They replied that they had always been on peaceable terms with the whites, had never desired any other than peace, and could not be induced to fight. That other tribes were at war, and, therefore, they had come into the vicinity of a post, in order to show that they desired peace, and to be where the travelling public would not be frightened by them, or the Indians be harmed by travelers or soldiers on the road.

I informed them that I could not permit any body of armed men to camp in the vicinity of the post, nor Indians visit the post, except as prisoners of war. They replied that they had but very few arms and but few horses, but were here to accept any terms that I proposed. I then told them that I should demand their arms and all the stock they had in their possession which had ever belonged to white men; they at once accepted these terms. I then proceeded with a company of cavalry to the vicinity of their camp, leaving my men secreted, and crossed to their camp, received their arms from them, and sent out men to look through their herd for United States or citizens' stock, and to take all stock except Indian ponies; found ten mules and four horses, which have been turned over to the acting assistant quartermaster.

Their arms are in very poor condition, and but few, with little ammu-

nition. Their horses far below the average grade of Indian horses. In fact, these that are here could make but a feeble fight if they desired war. I have permitted them to remain encamped near the post, unarmed, as prisoners, until your wishes can be heard in the matter. In the interval, if I can learn that any of their warriors have been engaged in any depredations that have been committed, shall arrest them, and place all such in close confinement.

I am of opinion that the warriors of the Arapahos, who have been engaged in war, are all now on the Smoky Hill, or with the Sioux Indians, and have all the serviceable arms and horses belonging to the tribe, while these here are too poor to fight, even though they desired war.

Nine Cheyenne Indians today sent in, wishing to see me. They state that 600 of that tribe are now 35 miles north of here, coming towards the post, and 2,000 about 75 miles away, waiting for better weather to enable them to come in. I shall not permit them to come in, even as prisoners, for the reason that if I do, I shall have to subsist them upon a prisoner's rations. I shall, however, demand their arms, all stolen stock, and the perpetrators of all depredations. I am of the opinion that they will not accept this proposition, but that they will return to the Smoky Hill. They pretend that they want peace, and I think they do now, as they cannot fight during the winter, except where a small band of them can find an unprotected train or frontier settlement. I do not think it is policy to make peace with them now, until all perpetrators of depredations are surrendered up to be dealt with as we may propose.

The force effective for the field at the post is only about 100, and one company, (K, New Mexico Volunteers) sent here by order of General Carlton, commanding department of New Mexico, were sent with orders to remain sixty days, and then report back to Fort Union. Their sixty days will expire on the 10th of November (instant.) Shall I keep them here for a longer period, or permit them to return?

The Kiowas and Comanches, who have all the stock stolen upon the Arkansas route, are reported south of the Arkansas River and towards the Red River. The Cheyennes are between here and the Smoky Hill. Part of the Arapahos are near this post. The remainder north of the Platte. With the bands divided in this way, one thousand cavalry could now overtake them and punish some of them severely, I think, but with the force here it can only be made available to protect the fort. I shall not permit the Cheyennes to camp here, but will permit the Arapahos now here to remain in their present camp as prisoners until your action is had in the matter.

I have the honor to be, very respectfully, your obedient servant,
SCOTT J. ANTHONY,
Major 1st Cavalry of Colorado
Commanding Post

Wynkoop remained at Fort Lyon for three weeks, but Major Anthony severely limited Wynkoop's accessibility to the Indians. Anthony's treatment of Left Hand and Little Raven was curt and unfriendly, although after learning through the majority of Fort Lyon soldiers that Wynkoop indeed had not been derelict in his duty, he agreed to follow Wynkoop's original course of allowing some prisoner rations to be delivered to the Indians. When Black Kettle heard that Wynkoop was no longer in charge at Fort Lyon, he was alarmed and immediately requested a council with the new commander. With Anthony's permission, Black Kettle and One Eye came to the fort with a small Cheyenne party to reiterate their peaceful intentions. John Smith and John Prowers attended the council to interpret for Black Kettle...

"The chief says he's concerned about Major Wynkoop leaving," Smith said.

"Tell him nothing will change," Anthony said. "I'm aware of the arrangements he made with Major Wynkoop. If his band stays quiet and remains at Sand Creek this winter, they have nothing to fear from my soldiers."

Smith spoke to Black Kettle, and then looked at Wynkoop. "He wants to know if you heard anything from Curtis about a peace agreement?"

"I'm sorry, no," Wynkoop said. "The war in the States has kept him preoccupied with fighting rebels. I am going to Fort Riley, and I promise I will do my best to contact him."

Black Kettle suspiciously looked at Anthony. "You will know if Curtis grants a true peace?"

Anthony blinked and dabbed his watering eyes with a handkerchief. "Of course."

"Major Anthony is a good chief," Wynkoop said. "I've told him about our efforts to bring about peace."

"That's true," Anthony said. "I'll admit, I heard a lot of bad things about you and your people, but now that I'm here, I don't see any problems. As long as your people behave themselves and continue to submit to my authority, I will support Major Wynkoop's efforts with General Curtis."

"May we trade for food?" Black Kettle asked.

"I can't offer government annuities without authorization," Anthony said. "There's some buffalo and wild game at Sand Creek, and I'll consider allowing the local traders to come out and do business. When Major Wynkoop speaks with General Curtis, he will send us word of the decision that is made, good or bad. If the general grants permission to give you rations, I'll see to it immediately."

"What if Curtis makes the decision not to make peace?" Black Kettle asked.

"Major Anthony," Wynkoop said, "because Black Kettle's village is presently under our protection, I think we are obliged to send word to him if General Curtis won't treat with him. Under those circumstances, we could no longer guarantee their safety. It's the only decent thing for us to do."

"Agreed," Anthony said.

"This war has been long," Black Kettle said through Smith. "You will forgive me if I cannot go back to my people with full confidence of our safety. How may we give any soldier who comes close a sign that we will not fight them?"

"A white flag?" Wynkoop said to Anthony, who agreed. "Moke-tav-a-to, you should fly a white flag high over your village. I think it proper to give you an American flag to fly as well. This should let any soldier know that you will submit to him without a fight."

Black Kettle nodded. "I am satisfied," he said. He spoke to Smith, who laughed.

"Old Black Kettle says he'd like to have this all in writing..."

November 26, 1864

After his council with the chiefs, Major Anthony granted Black Kettle and One Eye permission to stay at John Prowers' ranch for the night. The next morning, Prowers gave the chiefs a wagonload of sugar, flour, coffee, and tobacco to take back to Sand Creek. One Eye held his daughter and told her goodbye, for he would undoubtedly not see her again until the spring. Along the trail back down the Arkansas, Black Kettle stopped near Left Hand and Little Raven's camp, where Major Wynkoop was visiting before he continued on to Fort Riley. Captain Soule had accompanied his old friend this far, but he would send a small detachment to guard Wynkoop's coach for the rest of the trip.

Wynkoop tossed a smile at the old chief and shook his hand. "Moke-tav-a-to, I won't see you for awhile."

Left Hand interpreted for Black Kettle. "He says not to worry. He hopes to see you before the grasses turn green."

"If you have any problems, go to Major Anthony," Wynkoop said.

Black Kettle huffed a sigh. "Red-eyed chief... I spit farther than I trust him."

Soule couldn't help but laugh. "You're a wise man, sir."

"Well," Wynkoop said, "you can always go to Captain Soule or Lieutenant Cramer."

Black Kettle smiled at Soule. "Visit me, Irish Loudmouth. We smoke and sing with the coyotes."

Soule simply smiled and shook hands with Black Kettle. "Be well, Moke-tav-a-to."

"I hope I did not make you in trouble with your big chief," Black Kettle said to Wynkoop.

"If we end the trouble between your people and mine, it will be worth it," Wynkoop said.

"Wynkoop," Left Hand said. "We hear there are Sioux war parties near Fort Riley."

"I worry for you," Black Kettle said. "I send a party with you?"

"No, that's alright," Wynkoop said. "I have a good escort of soldiers here. You need to go to Sand Creek. It's important that you do exactly what Major Anthony tells you to do."

"Very well," Black Kettle said. He offered his hand. "Your friendship is in my heart, Tall Chief."

Wynkoop felt a tug at his throat. "I never knew my father, sir, but I'd like to think he was very much like you." He hesitated, and then embraced the Cheyenne Chief.

Black Kettle smiled at Wynkoop and Soule. "You could be my good sons."

The Indians mounted. The large Arapaho band, already mounted and packed to leave, slowly turned and rode east with Black Kettle, Left Hand and Little Raven.

Wynkoop and Soule watched the Indians ride over the horizon.

"Well, pard," Wynkoop said, "I guess this is so-long for now."

Soule kicked at the weeds. "I was just getting accustomed to riling you."

"I wasn't," Wynkoop said. He put his hand on Soule's shoulder. "Can I trust you to refrain from killing Anthony?"

"Nope."

"I can't tell you how bad I'd feel if you ended up in front of a firing squad."

"Well, in that case..."

"Good luck down here," Wynkoop said.

"Ain't staying," Soule mumbled.

"How's that?"

"I've had it, Neddy. I requested a 30-day leave. Shit, Anthony and I ain't gonna get along. He nearly broke his hand approving my request. I want to take Hersa back to Bangor to meet my mother.

When I get back, I'm gonna ask Chiv to transfer me to Camp Weld. I don't want to stay here with that little weasel."

"Well, after three years of service without a day off, I'd say you've earned a furlough," Wynkoop said.

"I got a hunch, though, that I may end up stopping at Leavenworth to spring you out of the stockade."

Wynkoop laughed. "I promise I'll go if you do. Wouldn't look good for Kansas' most notorious Jayhawker to fail again. But don't lock me up just yet. Curtis isn't going to take me down without a fight."

"Shit, Neddy, you and I both know we didn't accomplish a goddam thing down here. Anthony is just blowing smoke. The minute Curtis gets hold of you, what we did's gonna get filed away in some dusty old ledger book."

"Not if I can help it, pard," Wynkoop said. "Give Hersa a big kiss for me."

Soule and Wynkoop embraced. "Keep your head down."

"You do the same."

Wynkoop climbed in the coach and gave Soule a wave as he departed...

The Cheyennes and Arapahos rode for ten miles, stopping where the Big Sandy dumped into the Arkansas. Little Raven rode up to Black Kettle and Left Hand.

"Moke-tav-a-to," Raven said. "You will always have my respect."

"But?" Black Kettle said.

"I do not trust them."

"You are not going with us..."

"I wish my heart could be open like yours. I am sorry."

"There is nothing wrong with your heart, Raven," Black Kettle said.

"I feel I am letting you down, but I have a bad feeling about Sand Creek. I smoked on it, and the spirits told me to stay away. Please go with us to Big Timbers. We will be safer there, and we can escape if the soldiers' words are not true."

"I cannot do that," Black Kettle said. "I made a promise to Tall Chief. If Curtis grants his proposal for peace, what would he think if I am not at Sand Creek?"

"Tall Chief has no say anymore," Little Raven pleaded. "That red-eyed chief knows just where to find you."

"Raven, I cannot say I will go to Sand Creek and then not go. I gave my word."

"I just do not know..."

"We will be safe," Black Kettle said. "Do not worry. I have a way of handling these white chiefs."

"Damn," Little Raven said. "How is it that we have become so old?"

"Just lucky," Black Kettle said. "Left Hand, where will you go?"

Left Hand, weary from a fever, shook his head. "Sand Creek. So many of my people are still hurt with the sickness. I hope for the best – that the soldiers will bring us medicine. Good luck, Raven."

Little Raven informed his people, and the Cheyennes and Arapahos took a moment to embrace and bid each other farewell. Little Raven's band then continued on down the Arkansas, and Black Kettle and Left Hand took their people north along the winding creek they called the *Ponoeohe*...

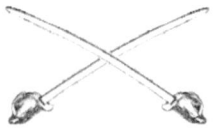

21

FORT LYON, COLORADO
November 25, 1864
TO: MAJOR E. W. WYNKOOP
DEAR SIR:

Having learned with regret that you have been relieved and ordered to Fort Leavenworth to report your official proceedings in regard to Indians while in command of this post, I cannot let the opportunity pass without bearing testimony to the fact that the course adopted and carried out by you was the only proper one to pursue, and has been the means of saving the lives of hundreds of men, women, and children, as well as thousands of dollars' worth of property.

No one can doubt that the lively aid rendered by you (at the risk of your own life as well as the lives of your small command) to the captives among the Arapahos and Cheyenne Indians, was also the means of saving their lives. For this act alone (even if you had not done more) you should receive the warmest thanks of all men, whether in military or civil life.

Your visit to Denver with some of the principal chiefs of the Arapaho and Cheyenne tribes was productive of more good to the Indians, and did more to allay the fears of the inhabitants in the Arkansas valley, than all that has been done by all other persons in this portion of the department.

Since that time, no depredations have been committed by these tribes, and the people have returned to their houses and farms, and are now living as quietly and peaceably as if the bloody scenes of the past summer had never been enacted.

Hoping that in all things your course will be approved by the commander of this department, and that you will soon be restored to your command in this district, I remain your obedient servant,

JOSEPH A. CRAMER, Second Lieut. First Cavalry of Colorado, Commanding Co. K.

We the undersigned, being conversant with all the facts set forth in the foregoing letter, heartily concur in the same:
R. A. HILL, Captain First New Mexico Vols.
JAMES D. CANNON, First Lieut. First New Mexico Vols.
WILLIAM P. MINTON, Second Lieut. First New Mexico Vols.
C. M. COGSIL, First Lieut. First Cavalry of Colorado.

S. G. COLLEY, United States Indian Agent.
HORACE W. BALDWIN, Lieut. Ind. Battery C. V. A.
SILAS S. SOULE, Captain First Cavalry of Colorado.
G. H. HARDIN, First Lieut. First Cavalry of Colorado.

HEADQUARTERS FORT LYON, C. T.
November 26, 1864
Respectfully forwarded to headquarters district, with the remarks: That it is the general opinion here by officers, soldiers, and citizens, that had it not been for the course pursued by Major Wynkoop towards the Cheyenne and Arapaho Indians, the travel upon the public road must have entirely stopped and the settlers upon the ranches all through the country must have abandoned them or been murdered, as no force of troops sufficient to protect the road and settlements could be got together in this locality.

I think Major Wynkoop acted for the best in the matter.
SCOTT J. ANTHONY,
Major First Cavalry of Colorado, Commanding Post

Major Wynkoop's party arrived at Fort Riley without incident, and Wynkoop immediately reported to Major Henning. He carried with him the letters written by Lieutenant Cramer and endorsed by Anthony and other officers of Fort Lyon, and another letter written and endorsed by 27 civilians in the Fort Lyon area:

We, the undersigned, citizens of the Arkansas Valley, of Colorado Territory, in view of your recent action in taking certain chiefs of the Arapaho and Cheyenne tribes of Indians to Denver to have a consultation with the governor of this Territory, and your efforts thereby to effect a treaty of peace and restore pacific relations between us and those tribes who have threatened our peace and safety as settlers of this country, desire to express to you our hearty sympathy in your laudable efforts to prevent further danger and bloodshed, and sincerely congratulate you in your noble efforts to do what we consider right, politic, and just, whether those efforts on your part prove successful or not, sincerely hoping they may prove successful, and peace instead of war reign throughout our land.

In consideration of the danger and risks you have incurred in achieving the rescue of prisoners from those tribes, the hazard to your own life and the lives of the men under your command, we desire to further express our appreciation of your bravery, as well as your sense of right, and earnestly express the hope that the merit which is justly your due may not go unrewarded in official preferment as well as the gratitude of private citizens...

These letters, however, were not the only communications flowing from Fort Lyon to the Kansas high command. General Curtis received a preceding dispatch from Major Anthony, which contained a decidedly different inference than what the "Red-Eyed Chief" had endorsed in the letter from his men:

> ...*I have been trying to let the Indians that I have talked with think that I have no desire for trouble with them, but that I could not agree upon a permanent peace until I was authorized by you, thus keeping matters quiet for the present, and until troops enough are sent out to enforce any demand we may choose to make.*
>
> *It would be easy for us to fight the few Indian warriors that have come into the post, but as soon as we assume a hostile attitude, the travel upon the road would be cut off, and the settlements above and upon the different streams will be completely broken up, as we are not strong enough to follow them and fight them upon their own ground. Some of the Cheyenne and Arapaho Indians can be made useful to us...My intention, however, is to let matters remain dormant until troops can be sent out to take the field against all the tribes...*

On November 26, John Smith received permission from Major Anthony to take a wagon loaded with trade goods to Black Kettle's village at Sand Creek. Smith took Private David Louderback and Watson Clark, a teamster employed by Sam Colley's adult son, Dexter. Smith's party arrived in a light snowfall and was greeted by Black Kettle, One Eye and White Antelope. The Cheyennes and Arapahos cheered Smith's arrival, gathering around the team and gratefully perusing the bounty of goods available for trade.

Among the Indians were George Bent and his teen-aged brother, Charley, who had lived with the Cheyennes for most of his adolescence. Charley was a wild buck, often to the embarrassment of his brothers and father, for he was infatuated with the warrior culture. Young Charley Bent aspired to become a Dogman, and with little knowledge or respect for his father's honorable history with the Indians, he ignorantly adopted the radical political position of Tall Bull and the other renegade warrior chiefs. Also in the camp was John Smith's son, Jack, another teen-ager who lived with his mother in the Cheyenne camp. John Smith's duties to the army kept him far from his family for many months at a time, but whenever he could steal a moment to be with his boy, a happy reunion ensued.

At last, if perhaps only for a short time, Black Kettle's Cheyennes and Left Hand's Arapahos were united in a place where they believed they could safely hunt, perform the renewal of the Sacred Arrows, and pay homage to *Maheo*...

* * *

My Sweet Hersa,

I'm still here, my love. I reckon you know that. First, a summer hot as blazes and full of mosquitoes in the habit of biting, and now the wind blows, and it is so cold that I can hardly see the lines on the paper. How I wish, beyond the sadness of this wilderness, that you and I were rooted on our Kansas farm - without feathers and arrows, gray coats or blue, hatred and death. I reckon all we can do is hope someday, maybe after we are in our graves, that humans will have learned to get along better.

Every day I look for your letters, but we haven't seen mail or supplies in weeks. I requested a leave and am waiting for approval from headquarters before I can come up to Denver to see you. I want to take you home to Maine to meet my mother and my sisters. When the good news arrives and I can come to you, I hope your satchel is packed!

I adore you, Hersa, and I can't fathom my life without you. I want to raise a brood of little Hersas and Silies, and teach them how to make a better world than the one we got. When I next cast my eyes upon you, please take me in your arms and tell me you will be my wife. I promise to love you beyond forever and then again. I end this letter with hope.

Your ever lovin'
Silie

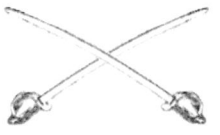

22

Captain Soule and Lieutenant William Minton slowly led a patrol along the western route between Bent's ranch and Fort Lyon. The cold sun had long ago dropped below the western horizon, and the air turned the soldiers' breaths to steam. They suddenly pulled up and peered into the distance. Earlier in the evening, the patrol spotted what appeared to be campfires to the west. Soule went back to Fort Lyon and reported to Major Anthony, who ordered him to go back with more men to investigate...

"They're still there, Cap," Minton said.
Soule nodded. "God damn, that's a big camp."
Minton squinted. "Jesus, you think it could be Kioways?"
"That don't make sense. There's gotta be five or six hundred down there. There ain't that many Indians in that direction. It's too damn dark, but I don't think I see any lodges."
"Maybe this is why we ain't seen a mail train in weeks," Minton said.
"Well, those are campfires for sure," Soule said. "Boys, we'll put down here for the night and keep an eye on this. At first light, we'll move in and have a look-see..."

Soule's patrol pitched in and kept a wary eye on the distant camp until dawn. When the sun peeked over their shoulders, they picked up and cautiously moved west, using rocky bluffs and groves for cover. After traveling for a mile or two, a large mule train creaked over the road and into view.
"Son of a bitch," Minton said with relief. "That's a military train!"
The soldiers came out of hiding and approached the wagon.
"Halloo!" Soule called.
The lead teamster gave a wave. "Yo, Captain!"
"You heading for Fort Lyon?"
"Sure am."
"You didn't run into any Indians back on the road, did you?"
"Injuns? Hell, no! Ain't no injun gonna follow us!"
"Are you with that large camp we spotted?"
"You betcha!"

"Who's back there?"

"Redemption, Cap'n! You got more soldiers comin' your way than my belly's got worms!"

"What soldiers?"

"The daysers! Old Chivington's riding point with five hunnert boys loaded for serious injun' hunting! We're finally gonna get some payback!"

The driver pushed his team onward, and Soule looked west at a sea of troops rolling over the rise.

"Shit," Soule whispered. "Come on, boys!"

Chivington, Colonel Shoup, and Major Downing led the entourage. Beside them, William Bent's son, Robert, and the old mulatto scout, Jim Beckwith, sat on their horses with their hands shackled.

"Captain Soule!" Chivington hollered as the patrol rode up. "Good morning to you!"

Soule pulled up. "Colonel. This is a surprise."

"That's the idea," Chivington said. "No rumors and innuendoes leak when you cut off the source!"

"What are you doing here?" Soule asked. "I thought you were going to campaign on the Platte."

"So did the Indians," Chivington laughed. "Tell me, Captain, I hear you have some bad savages yearning to die around here."

"Colonel, you know our situation. Major Wynkoop and I sent you dispatches about the Indian prisoners camped below the fort."

"Captain Soule," Robert Bent said, "I been trying to tell him that!"

"Shut your mouth, half-breed!" Chivington barked.

"What are you doing?" Soule said. "That's Mr. Bent's son!"

"I know who he is," Chivington said. "We stopped by Bent's ranch and honored him with recruitment to scout for the Third Cavalry, just in case old Beckwith here dies in the snow."

"Colonel, there are no hostile Indians here," Soule said. "Major Wynkoop secured an agreement with Black Kettle."

"Major Wynkoop isn't in charge of Fort Lyon," Chivington said. "He's undoubtedly in irons for his gross insubordination. I told you two to keep the Indians in line, not invite them to a party. From what I've heard, Left Hand's been running things down here."

"Chiv, what the hell-"

"Captain Soule, you will address me properly!"

"Colonel Chivington," Soule said, "may I ask then why you are clearly out of your district with this regiment?"

"No you may not!" Chivington said. His hot eyes locked with

Soule's. "Wynkoop already betrayed me, Silas, so don't you even think about it."

"The Indians below Fort Lyon submitted to military authority! They're camped as prisoners!"

Duncan Kerr bellowed from behind Chivington. "They ain't gonna be prisoners when we get there!" The boys around him let out a cheer.

"Fall in with us, Captain," Chivington ordered.

"My orders are to patrol this area and report any suspicious activity to my commander," Soule said. "That's what I intend to do!"

"I said, fall in!"

"You are *not* my commander!" Soule said. "I remind you that you have no military authority in this district!"

"Major Downing, provide an escort for Captain Soule and his men."

Downing ordered the daysers to surround Soule's patrol.

"Colorado belongs to me, Captain," Chivington said. "You'd better remind yourself of that, or I swear to God almighty I will play thunder with you..."

Fort Lyon suddenly erupted in panic when sentries spotted the ocean of soldiers rolling in. A bugler sounded the alarm, and the Colorado First soldiers scurried to defend the fort. Major Anthony rushed up to the turret and looked out.

"What's this, Corporal?"

"Look out there! Jesus Christ, are those rebs?"

"Coming in from the west?" Anthony said. He took the sentry's binoculars and steadied for a closer look. "Well, I'll be...those aren't rebels." He let out a whoop. "Those boys are in blue!" He turned and yelled over the compound. "Chivington's coming!"

Instead of the joyous celebration that Anthony expected, the soldiers simply stood in confusion.

"Stand easy, men!" Anthony hollered. "We got reinforcements!"

The Third Regiment rolled in and surrounded Fort Lyon. Chivington rode into the gates with Shoup and Downing as Major Anthony ran up to greet them.

"Colonel Chivington!" Anthony saluted.

"Major Anthony, give me a moment." He turned to Downing. "Major, picket this fort. No one leaves. If anyone tries, shoot him!"

Anthony stopped short. "What?"

"Just a minute, Scott. Downing – round up that rascal Soule and bring him in here. I want to keep an eye on him."

"Yes, sir!" Downing said.

"Sorry, Major Anthony," Chivington said. "Greetings to you, sir."

"Colonel," Anthony said. "What's the meaning of this? Shoot anyone who tries to leave?"

"Precisely, Major. I'm here on a mission of utmost secrecy. Let's go to your office, and I'll fill you in."

Major Downing exited the gates and found Captain Soule, who quickly dismounted and headed for the gates.

"Soule!" Downing ordered. "Report to Colonel Chivington!"

"In your ear," Soule said, brushing past Downing's horse.

Downing jumped off and confronted Soule. "That's an order, Captain!"

"You want to give it a whirl, Jake?" Soule said. "They ever teach you to go fists in law school?"

Downing swallowed hard and backed away. "You have your orders!"

"Order this." Soule gave Downing the universal gesture of defiance known to man since the beginning of time itself. "Step in my way again, and I'll eat your fucking heart." Soule blew by the lawyer-turned-soldier and ran into the fort.

Cramer spotted him. "Sile, what the hell's going on?"

"Mutiny," Soule growled. "Is Colonel Tappan still here?"

"Yeah, but he's in the infirmary."

"What?"

"His horse tossed him last night, and his foot's busted bad."

Sam Tappan, a fellow Glorieta veteran and crony of Soule and Wynkoop, had stopped at Lyon on his way to Fort Garland. It never much mattered to Soule before, but Tappan harbored a hatred for Chivington since the Fighting Parson muscled his way to District Commander.

"What kind of shape is he in?" Soule asked.

"Loopy. He's been taking whiskey and morphine for the pain ever since."

"Perfect," Soule said.

"Sile, what the hell is Chivington doing here?"

"What do you think? His goddam dragoons couldn't step on a spider, much less fight a Dogman!"

Outside, the Hundred-Daysers milled about, laughing, drinking, and taking an occasional shot at the clouds. "Oh, shit," Cramer whispered. He looked up at Anthony's office, where Chivington and the major walked in just moments ago. "That little red-eyed fucker's gonna give him Black Kettle."

"He's gonna have to go through me first," Soule said.

"I'm with ya, pard."

"Joey, round up the officers and tell them to meet me in the council room, pronto..."

Chivington stalked Anthony's office like a caged tiger. Anthony sat at his desk, eagerly hanging on Chivington's every word.

"I trust everything is in order down here, now that Wynkoop's been disposed," Chivington said.

"Well, sir, things weren't quite as bad as the rumors."

"He was feeding those red animals and allowing them to come to the post, wasn't he?"

"Yes, sir, but-"

"And I trust you are not the Indian-lover that Wynkoop is?"

"Of course not." Anthony wiped his eyes.

"Good lord, what's wrong with you?"

"Scurvy, sir."

"Well, keep your distance, son, you're disgusting," Chivington said.

"Yes, sir. May I ask why you are here?"

"Why do you think, Scott? You requested a proper force to hunt and kill Indians, didn't you? Here I am."

"Thank God!" Anthony said. "Curtis finally took action! I've been champing at the bit to wade into those bastards. When did he give the order?"

"Never mind that. Where are the Indians camped?"

"Black Kettle and Left Hand are on Sand Creek, about 40 miles northeast of here."

"How many?"

"Six, maybe seven hundred Cheyennes and Arapahos."

"Warrior strength?"

"There are a few young bucks there, but the village is mostly mid-aged and elderly. The Smoky Hill is our best bet to start after the Dog Soldiers."

"Is Little Raven at Sand Creek?"

"No, sir. My scouts watched them split at the Arkansas just yesterday. Little Raven's band went east. We'd waste time and rations going after him."

Chivington rubbed his thick red beard. "You don't suppose, if we paid Black Kettle a little visit, that we just might find a few wolves in the fold?"

"Well, I'm sure a few hostiles might be camped there, sir, but that village isn't worth our time. Black Kettle and Left Hand submitted to my authority. Those people are settled in and ready to hunt buffalo. There's no taste for a fight there. With the force you brought, we can go after the Dog Soldiers and Sioux."

"Oh, Major," Chivington said, "you don't know how I've longed to wade in gore. Those heathens seek some word of God – some light in the darkness of failure to understand the almighty. We're going to give them that light."

"It'll be glorious," Anthony said. "God knows I've been waiting for a chance to pitch into them!"

"How many men can you spare?"

"Colonel, every last man here will be eager to go!"

"Well, we'll leave some to protect this post, and we'll ride for Sand Creek tonight."

"Sand Creek?" Anthony said. He curiously looked at Chivington.

"Did I stutter?"

"Don't you mean the Smoky Hill?"

"No."

"Excuse me, sir, but I don't understand."

"What's the matter? You have scurvy of the ears, too? We'll push to Sand Creek tonight and attack at sunrise."

"Attack?" Anthony said. "Sir, the Sand Creek village is camped under our protection."

"Not any more," Chivington said.

"But I agreed to honor Wynkoop's arrangement with Black Kettle. They're waiting to hear from General Curtis regarding a peace treaty."

"Wynkoop?" Chivington said. "That traitor's finished. We have no agreement with any Indian."

"But, sir - respectfully, may I suggest we not waste powder on those Indians at Sand Creek. There aren't any Dog Soldiers or Sioux warriors there."

"You just said there might be warriors hiding out with Black Kettle."

"Well, perhaps. We might root out the few hostiles there, but the best fight is out on the Smoky Hill."

"You're not going soft on me, are you, Scott?"

"Of course not. But we'll be wading into Kansas for most of the winter. I respectfully suggest we use our resources sparingly until we find the Dog Soldiers."

"So noted, Major. Prepare your men. We'll leave this evening."

"One thing, sir," Anthony said. "When we get to Sand Creek, I think it wise to spare Black Kettle, Left Hand and White Antelope. They have acted in good faith. I wouldn't be surprised if they give up the hostiles in their camp without any trouble."

"Indeed?" Chivington said. "Alright, we'll see..."

Chivington strutted across the Fort Lyon compound, barking orders to the soldiers of the First Regiment. Anthony nipped at his heels like a hungry puppy. The post boiled with activity, as preparations were made for the evening march. Chivington sent Anthony to round up his officers, while he went out to organize the daysers.

Captain Soule and Lieutenant Cramer quickly approached Anthony, followed by Agent Colley and a group of Lyon officers.

"Major!" Soule said. "What's this? We're going with Chivington?"

"That's right," Anthony said.

"We're gonna attack Black Kettle?" Cramer asked.

"No no! We're going to demand he give up any hostiles there, and then we'll push on to hunt down the Dog Soldiers."

"Dogmen?" Soule laughed. "You know damned well that Chivington has no intention of going any farther than Sand Creek! Those bastards will level that village and high-tail back to Denver, leaving us with a pack of wild dogs bearing down on this post!"

"Wrong!" Anthony said. "Chivington's taking us right to the Republican if necessary!"

"Black Kettle is under our protection!" Cramer said.

"I told you, we're not going to attack him!" Anthony said.

"You believe that?" Cramer said. "Wynkoop pledged our support. Hell, Louderback and Smith are out there right now!"

"To hell with Wynkoop!" Anthony said. "I'm in charge here!"

"That man-eating Methodist is in charge, Major!" Soule said. "We're not under his command!"

"I've had about enough of you, Soule!"

"Chivington has no authority over you," Soule said. "I respectfully recommend that you try to find out if anyone at headquarters knows Chivington is here."

"Come on, Captain," Anthony said. "Colonel Chivington wouldn't be here without orders!"

"He's running for God!" Soule said. "He takes orders from no one! Please, Major, you got a responsibility to confirm this before you commit us to that pack of mongrels!" The officers behind Soule and Cramer all agreed.

"No! We're leaving tonight!" Anthony said. "As I said, we're stopping at Sand Creek to make Black Kettle deliver up hostiles. Then, we're pushing on to Kansas!"

"Just ride into that village and demand a handful of them to step forward for execution?" Soule said. "That doesn't make any sense! That sonofabitch parson ain't gonna risk a fight with the Dogmen with those drunk fools! He's gonna take scalps at Sand Creek and tell the world he's a God-fearing Indian killer!"

"What's going on here?" Chivington bellowed. He pushed through the mob, followed by Downing and Shoup. "Major Anthony, why aren't your officers preparing for the march?"

"They are!" Anthony said. "Come on, men, let's go!"

Soule and his officers stood firm. "Colonel, Black Kettle and Left Hand obeyed every demand we've made of them! Wynkoop pledged to protect them!"

Chivington glared at Soule. "Under whose authority did Wynkoop pledge this to murderers?"

Soule stepped up to the gigantic Chivington. "Under whose authority did you march out of your district with this mob of civilians bent on revenge?"

"The authority of almighty God, that's who!"

"I didn't know God mustered in!" Soule said. "Whose god are we talking about - yours, or Black Kettle's?"

"How dare you defame the almighty!" Chivington bellowed.

"Gentlemen!" Anthony squeaked.

"Easy boys!" Cramer stepped between Chivington and Soule.

"Don't push me, Silas," Chivington said. "You have no idea what I could unleash upon you."

"Yeah?" Soule said. "Well, you got a pretty good idea of how I'll respond! You want to go after Dog Soldiers, I'll fight every last one of 'em; but I won't be a part of attacking those Indians at Sand Creek, and anyone who does ain't nothing but a cowardly son of a bitch!"

Chivington shook with rage, but Soule stood firmly without the slightest fear of the Fighting Parson. It was the first time that Chivington ever encountered such defiance, and the wicked little Jayhawker sent a chill down his spine.

Cramer gently moved Soule back. "Sile, easy, old boy," he whispered. "The sumbitch will shoot you."

"He better pray he don't miss," Soule said.

"Back off, pard," Cramer said. "We gotta take a better route than this."

Soule patted Cramer. "You're right." He looked over Cramer's shoulder at Chivington. "We'll see about this, Chiv."

He angrily spun around and walked away, his back protected by the bevy of First Cavalry officers who followed him. Cramer and Agent Colley stayed behind.

Chivington still rattled with anger. "I swear by all that's right-eous, that little Dutchman just put one foot in the grave. If I had a rope right now I'd string him up myself!"

"Sir," Cramer said. "You gotta understand that we been under a hell of a strain down here. Wynkoop and Soule's laid their careers – hell, their *lives* on the line to stop the war."

"They're *both* insubordinate rodents," Chivington said. "I'll see them both to hell."

"Please, sir, just hear me out," Cramer said. "Major Wynkoop made a pledge as an officer and a man that Black Kettle would be protected as long as he stays at Sand Creek and waits for word from General Curtis regarding a true peace agreement. We all stood there in front of Black Kettle and supported it."

Colley agreed. "It's true, Colonel. I heard it, and I reported this to Evans. John Smith and Private Louderback are out there right now with a civilian driver."

"Ah, Colley," Chivington chuckled. "*You* reported to the gover-nor, did you? As I recall, you also reported that these savages were unbending and in need of a little powder and lead!"

"The Dogmen are the ones that want a fight! Not Black Kettle!"

"I'm beginning to understand," Chivington said. "Your freight-ing partner Smith is out there right now, making a nice little profit, isn't he? You don't want to kill anyone who lines your pockets!"

"Colonel, the Indians that raided the Platte this summer ain't in Black Kettle's camp!" Colley protested.

"That's right, sir," Cramer added. "They're the people we met on the Smoky Hill. We were outnumbered five-to-one, and if it weren't for Black Kettle and One Eye, they would have killed all of us. You told them in Denver to surrender to Wynkoop, and they did just that. How can we go and attack them?"

"What web of deceit did Wynkoop spin down here?" Chivington said. "Gentlemen, I am at war with *every* Indian on the plains. They've killed and tortured white women and children, but their reign of terror ends now! I will not rest until I have killed every one of them! It is righteous and just!"

Major Downing chimed in. "Cramer, if you believe anything to the contrary, maybe you and Wynkoop ought to get out of the army."

"I will gladly fight the warriors who killed those white people," Cramer said, "but the Indians camped at Sand Creek are peaceful. Attacking them ain't nothing but murder, pure and simple!"

"Damn *any* man who is in sympathy with an Indian!" Chivington screamed. "And God help any man here who dares stand in my way! Major Anthony! We will march for Sand Creek at eight o'clock!" He stormed away.

"Yes, sir!" Anthony said. "Let's move! Daylight's burning!"...

Captain Soule sat by Colonel Sam Tappan's bunk, a half-full glass of whiskey in his hand. Tappan lay with an arm draped over his forehead, wigged-out on morphine and whiskey. The fractured bone in his ankle still screamed at him through the drunken haze. The soft candlelight threw ghostly images against the wall.

Tappan pulled his arm down, wincing in pain as he reached for his bottle. He raised it up to Soule. "To Glorieta, Sile. You and the old Fightin' Parson are off to glory again. God's goddam-speed."

"God's got no hand in what I'm about to do," Soule said. He threw down the whiskey. "Shit, I was gonna win that bet, but that's down the drain, too."

"Wha?"

"Nothing."

"Well, I got a solution for ya, if ya got a mind to it," Tappan mumbled.

"What's that?"

"Blow Chivington's fuckin' head off right now."

"Thanks, Sam," Soule said. "I knew I could count on you."

"I'd do it, but I'd probably miss – even though old Chiv's head makes for a mighty easy target."

"Well, no offense, but I don't think I'll take your advice, Colonel."

"*Lieutenant* Colonel," Tappan said. "Pushed aside and condemned to that sorry-ass dump Fort Garland, after the one and only military battle in Chivington's pathetic career."

"Pardon me if I ain't in the spirit to feel sorry for you, Sam."

"Well, what the hell ya want me to do?"

"Stop him. There are plenty of officers here that would back you."

"I can't even see right now, Sile – much less walk."

"Yeah, I know," Soule sighed.

"You know as good as me that Chivington can't be stopped anyway. What you say he's got – 500 troops out there to lick his boots? You Lyon boys ain't got but maybe a couple hundred here. They may be real soldiers, but they couldn't stop that many daysers."

"I know...I know."

"Take my advice, Sile. Don't put yourself in the ground. You can't lick him here, cause he's a master at eliminating his enemies when he's got the advantage."

"Word is, I ain't even gonna make it to that village tonight," Soule said. "Cramer heard that Chiv's got snipers ready to take me out."

"Jesus Christ," Tappan sighed. "I'm sorry, palley. I swear, if I could, I'd go after that bastard. Get your boys together, have 'em surround you."

"Joe's got that covered," Soule said.

"Chivington's a prick, but he ain't stupid, Sile. You keep your friends around you, and he won't take a chance on you. He can't kill the whole goddam First Cav."

"Just do me one favor, Sam," Soule said.

"Anything, pal."

"Keep your head clear. I want you to know that, whatever happens out there, I ain't taking part in it. Don't wake up tomorrow without remembering this conversation."

"Don't you worry about that," Tappan said. "You just stay alive. Once this is finished, I'm gonna stick Chivington on a spit and cook him alive."

Soule leaned over and handed Tappan a sealed letter. "I want you to hold this letter for me, Sam. If I don't make it back, please deliver it to Hersa." Soule choked back a tear. "Tell her that I love her."

The booze twisted Tappan's throat. He took the letter and watched Soule walk out the door...

John Milton Chivington's 450-man civilian militia, under the colors of the Colorado Third Cavalry, took the trail at 8:30 on Monday night, November 28, 1864, accompanied by 250 soldiers of the combined detachments of the First Regiment from Fort Lyon and Camp Weld.

Captain Soule led Company D, accompanied by Cramer's K Company, and C Company, under Lieutenant Horace Baldwin. The First Regiment was under the command of Major Anthony and Lieutenant Luther Wilson. The Third Regiment, under Chivington, Shoup and Downing respectively, was divided into three large companies, led by Lieutenant Colonel Leavitt Bowen, Major Hal Sayr, and Captain Theodore Cree. The military party moved through the dark, moonless night in cavalry style, walk, trot, gallop, and dismount. Someone was overheard to say, "Ain't this a queer way to surprise Indians?"...

The village at Sand Creek was alive that night with happy singing and dancing. A good feast of several buffaloes caught that day helped ease the hunger crying from the Indians' bellies. John Smith, Watson Clark and Private David Louderback watched the happy powwow, taking time to converse with their Cheyenne and Arapaho hosts.

Black Kettle sat with Medicine Woman Later near a big fire. White Antelope, One Eye, old Yellow Wolf, and their squaws completed the circle. White Antelope passed a bottle to One Eye.

White Antelope's wife stopped him. "Enough for you," she said. "I do not want to carry you."

White Antelope gave her a stupid grin. "You carry my heart, can you not carry the rest of me?"

"Oh, pssh!" Buffalo Woman looked at the others, who laughed.

"Look," White Antelope said, pointing at young Charley Bent, who followed a pretty young squaw across the village, flexing his muscles and turning a cartwheel or two.

The wives cooed. "Little White Man's son is going to wear himself out over Fleet Bird," Medicine Woman Later said.

Buffalo Woman nudged her husband. "Why do you not turn flips for me anymore?"

"I would break my neck," White Antelope said. "I will play my flute. Where is it?"

"You are sitting on it."

Everyone laughed as the old man rolled around in the dirt. "Here it is." He started to put the flute to his mouth, but he suddenly reconsidered and sniffed it. "How about I just sing to you?"

The old friends chuckled as White Antelope began to caterwaul.

Medicine Woman Later looked at Black Kettle, who managed but a thin smile. "You do not talk much tonight," she said.

"Tired."

"Do you not feel well?"

Black Kettle shrugged. "Just tired."

She touched his face. "Something is bothering you."

Black Kettle was a bit annoyed. "You never let anything go by, do you?"

"I am the wife of a chief," she said, smiling. "Now, tell me what is wrong."

"I had a vision early this morning when I was waking. It bothered me all day."

"Tell me."

Black Kettle was uneasy. "A wolf. It growled at me, and I could not run from it. There was blood on its teeth. When I woke, it was like the wolf was still there, but I could not see it."

Medicine Woman Later pulled a blanket over her shoulders

and snuggled close to her husband...

The Cheyenne wolves wandered the perimeter of the Sand Creek village. Two sat on the bluffs surrounding the western bowl. They curiously watched tiny pinpoints of light dancing in and out of view in the distance.

"Campfires?" young Snow Bird said.

"They move like fireflies," Wolf said.

"Spirits?"

Wolf laughed. "You are stupid. It is soldiers moving. We see their torches."

"Should we tell?"

"No," Wolf said. "I have seen this before. The soldiers move back and forth all the time."

They watched the flickering lights.

"Pretty," Snow Bird said...

"What's going on up there?" Chivington hollered.

The troops stopped, and Chivington peered ahead into the darkness. Behind him, a soused dayser flipped off his horse and landed unconscious in the dirt.

Chivington looked back. "Somebody pick that idiot up!" Ahead, his attention was drawn to the sounds of water splashing and a symphony of cursing. "Up there! What's happening?"

Duncan Kerr and Lieutenant Rennock finally stumbled back through the brush, leading their horses. Their trousers were soaked in mud. "That goddam redskin led us right into a pond!" Kerr said.

Chivington glared at Robert Bent, who sat on his pony next to Major Downing. "You think you can drown us, half-breed?"

Bent stared ahead without emotion. "Only a white man could drown in three feet of water."

"It's enough to soak our ammunition," Chivington said. He pulled his pistol and pointed it directly at Bent's head.

"Colonel!" Downing said. "We need him!"

"I don't *need* any half-breed. Mr. Bent, I will warn you but once. Your kind no longer rule this prairie. It's been too long since I've had the pleasure of killing an Indian. You will properly lead us to our destination, or I will eat you for breakfast. Savvy?"

The troops slowly maneuvered around the dark pond and continued their northeasterly course...

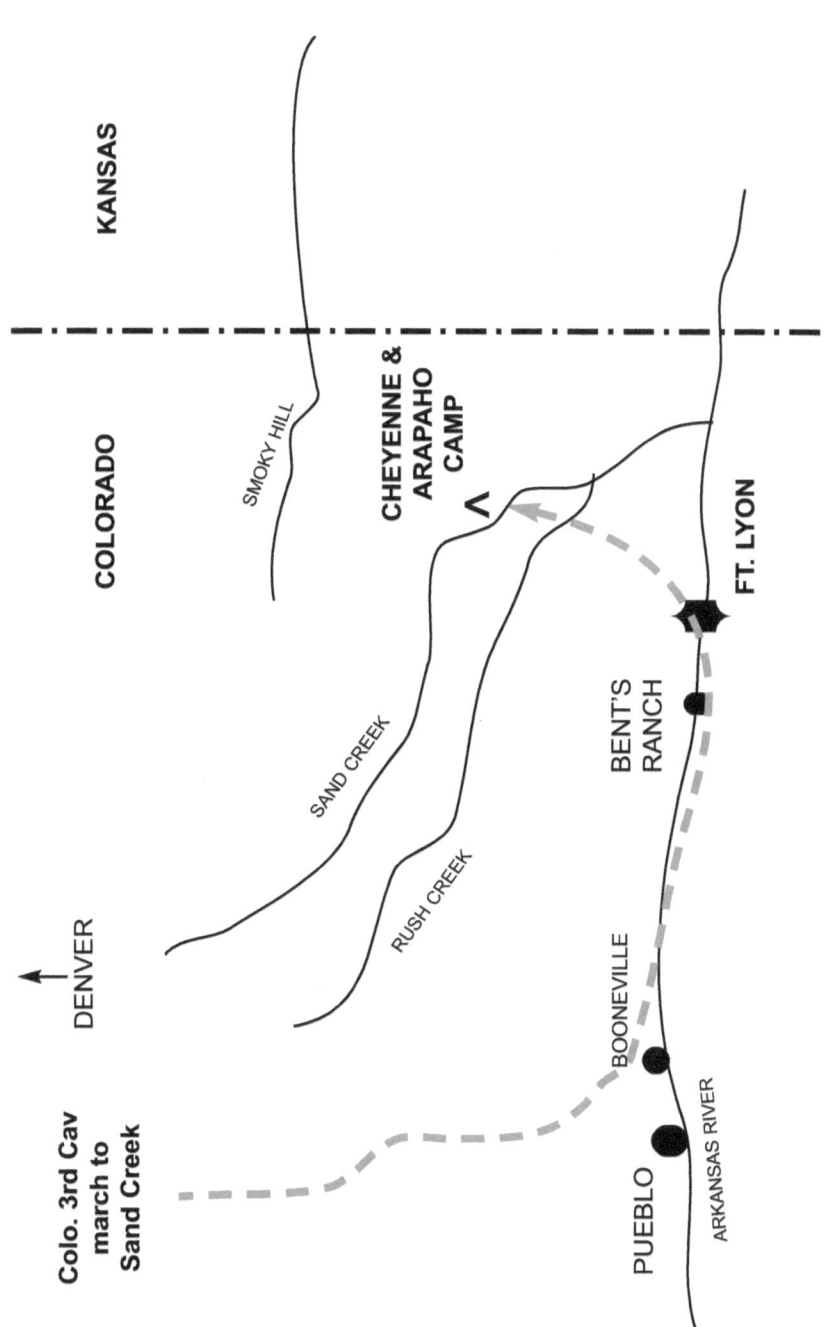

KANSAS

COLORADO

SMOKY HILL

CHEYENNE & ARAPAHO CAMP

SAND CREEK

RUSH CREEK

FT. LYON

BENT'S RANCH

BOONEVILLE

PUEBLO

ARKANSAS RIVER

DENVER

Colo. 3rd Cav march to Sand Creek

NOVEMBER 29, 1864

The cold morning sky gave first hint of light, and the earth began to reveal a long, desolate prairie ahead. Chivington sat astride his horse, two miles from the Sand Creek village, the combined forces of the First and Third Cavalry drawn in a battle line. Chivington moved his horse back and forth.

"Gentlemen, I don't have to remind you of the horror and fear that your women and children have suffered since that black day in Denver, when Nathan Ward Hungate and his family were brought to us in bloody pieces. Since then, countless innocent white men, women and children have been molested, tortured, and cut to ribbons by the godless creatures who happily sleep over that rise. They have committed unthinkable crimes against God and humanity, and it is the righteous duty of every man here to now hold them accountable. Yea, their day of reckoning is at hand, and God has appointed you to dispense justice of the Almighty. Today, the evil tide of their treachery will turn and swallow them whole!"

"Colonel!" Major Anthony said.

"Excuse *me*, Major Anthony. I am addressing these brave soldiers!"

"Wait a minute!" Anthony said.

"Shut up!" Colonel Shoup ordered.

Chivington continued. "Gentlemen, we will leave no heathen savage alive! Take no prisoners!"

"Sir!" Anthony said. "There are hundreds of squaws and old people there!"

"I told you to shut your goddam mouth!" Shoup said.

The Fort Lyon soldiers sadly looked at one another with resignation. "Stupid bastard," Cramer breathed. "Old red eyes finally figured it out."

"I will not tell you what you are to kill, gentlemen," Chivington said. "That is between you and God."

Anthony pleaded. "Colonel, please! Respectfully, may I request that we approach the village and demand that Black Kettle give up the hostiles – as we discussed yesterday?"

"Request denied!" Chivington said.

"At least spare the children!" Anthony said.

"Nits make lice, Major!" Chivington said. "No prisoners, gentlemen! Make a clean thing of it!"

Colonel Shoup gave the order, and the Third Regiment charged in an explosion of hooves and howitzer carriages. The First Regiment soldiers had no choice but to follow...

The Sand Creek village lay serenely quiet in the frigid dawn. Gentle smoke rose from 115 Cheyenne teepees along the bend of the creek. Eight Arapaho lodges threw smoke to the southeast, below a grove of bare cottonwoods that stretched from patches of clean, white snow. The bluffs, thirty feet high, stood between the village and the charging militia that could not yet be heard.

A dozen young braves, among them Charley Bent, arose early and ran to the outskirts of the village, shoving each other and happily chatting. The boys were off to hunt game, mounting their ponies and riding north along Sand Creek. They never looked back. If they had, perhaps they might have seen a strange dark cloud above the southern horizon. High on the village bluffs, Snow Bird and Wolf lay sleeping in their blankets. The young wolves should have been watching the southern perimeter.

A few squaws stirred now. They emerged from their lodges and began to light fires and prepare food. Several nervous dogs wandered the camp, scrounging for scraps and sniffing the air. A squaw's attention was drawn to one dog in particular. The mutt stood rigidly, like a tree, staring southward and letting a low growl. The woman cocked her head and looked to see what made the dog act so peculiarly, but it seemed he was staring at nothing. She slowly walked toward the animal, passing War Bonnet's teepee. Inside, the enormous snores of John Smith made her giggle. Old Smith's wife had come out earlier, and now the tent was consumed by Smith's sleep growl, which drowned the formidable snores of War Bonnet and his other guests, Private Louderback and Watson Clark.

Suddenly, the dog barked, and the squaw curiously looked at him. He barked again, and several other dogs joined him. She stopped and remained very still, cocking her ear to a strange noise - a rumble? She looked toward the bluffs as a few sleepy heads peeked from a lodge here and there. The rumble from the bluffs increased, and the squaw became alarmed. Thunder in winter? It couldn't be. Buffalo?...

The young hunters rode several miles north now. The laughing chatter suddenly died when Charley Bent halted them.

"Do you hear something?" one said.

Charley spun his horse back to the south. "Look over the hills!" he said.

"What is that?"

"I do not know..."

The Third Regiment's approach now awakened many villagers. The squaw ran to War Bonnet's teepee and called for the men to wake up. In a moment, John Smith crawled out, groggy but concerned.

"What in hell?" he mumbled, turning his eyes to the sound over the bluffs.

Louderback and Clark emerged.

"What's going on?" Louderback asked.

"Damned if I know..."

The young braves suddenly cried out. From their position, they could see what the villagers could not. An ocean of soldiers and howitzer carriages rolled toward the Sand Creek village in full charge.

"Come on!" Charley Bent cried. The young hunters whipped their ponies west toward the corral, hoping to prevent the soldiers from capturing the herd. They rode hard, but Lieutenant Baldwin's company charged over a rise and chased them away from the Indian horses...

"That sounds like a goddam regiment on the charge," Louderback said.

Smith felt a sudden ball of acid burn his belly. "Oh, Jesus. You don't think General Blunt's coming this way?"

"I don't know," Louderback said, "but if he is, we better get mounted and head him off. Quick, we gotta get us a white flag!"

"Jack!" John Smith called to his son. "Go round up some horses!" Young Jack Smith quickly scampered across the village and pushed up the hill.

Louderback and Smith returned to War Bonnet's teepee to gather their clothes, but they suddenly stopped at the frantic screams of the women in the village bowl. Smith turned and looked. As if evil spirits were descending, the bluffs grew wickedly alive with Colorado militiamen.

Rifles leveled, and cannons rolled up...

The Sand Creek village suddenly exploded in a terrific plume of smoke, and the Indians scattered in terror. Smith and Clark scampered into War Bonnet's teepee and buried themselves flat. Rifle balls pierced the lodge as War Bonnet gathered his weapons and ran out. Louderback, still outside, frantically waved a pitifully small white handkerchief at the soldiers, desperately trying to stop them from firing. The daysers simply used Louderback's kerchief as a target. He dove into the dirt and crawled to the teepee.

Terror consumed the village, as squaws and children fell dead or wounded to the soldiers' bullets. A cannonball exploded in the center of the bowl, throwing several Indians high in the air. Young braves and old men rolled out of their lodges, firing back at the soldiers.

High atop the bluffs, Colonel Chivington barked orders and tried to direct the daysers to strategic battle positions, but the enraged militiamen broke in many directions, wildly firing into the bowl and across the creek.

"Wilson!" Chivington bellowed. "Bring those fools back! They're shooting the wrong way!"

Lieutenant Wilson spurred his horse around the bluffs and desperately shouted orders, but the daysers ignored him and continued to fire at will. Lieutenant Baldwin's company suddenly found themselves in a dangerous crossfire, forced to retreat back toward the pony herd.

John Smith crawled out of the lodge and scurried for cover. Louderback followed, but was quickly pinned down by a barrage of dayser fire. Smith desperately waved a buffalo robe at Lieutenant Wilson.

Lieutenant George Pierce, riding near Wilson, saw Smith.

"Wilse!" he hollered. "They're firing on Louderback and Smith!"

Wilson couldn't hear Pierce over the din as he tried to quell the rabid daysers.

"Hold your fire!" Pierce yelled. The daysers ignored him and screamed with garish joy as they wildly shot down into the bowl. "Godammit! There's friendlies down there!"

Duncan Kerr yowled as he took aim at Smith. "Kill that old sonofabitch!"

Lieutenant Pierce suddenly whipped his pony down the hill, praying the daysers would cease firing when they saw him. He barely reached the bottom of the bowl before multiple rifle balls cut him down. Pierce died before he hit the ground.

"Jesus Christ!" Smith cried.

Louderback hollered at the soldiers on the bluffs, but he could scarcely hear his own voice.

A few of the daysers stopped shooting when Pierce fell, but others took a few random shots at the lieutenant's body...

Cheyenne warrior Little Bear quickly scampered across the village bowl. He leveled his rifle and shot a dayser from his horse, and then ran west toward the creek, trying to herd several screaming women and children to safety under the bluffs. Chief Black Kettle searched for Medicine Woman Later as he, too, directed the women toward the bluffs. He desperately pulled the white flag that stood by his lodge and tried to wave it at the soldiers, but a barrage of rifle fire forced him to drop and scurry for cover.

Nearby, White Antelope knelt by his lodge, away from the sight of the soldiers. He held Buffalo Woman as she took her final breath. He looked over at old Yellow Wolf, who lay dead in a growing pool of thick blood. In a moment, White Antelope laid his wife down and slowly walked into the line of fire...

Captain Soule rode up to the ridge on the northeastern edge of the bluffs, having crossed the creek by order of Major Anthony to avoid the daysers wild and random crossfire. The soldiers of Company D surrounded Soule, blocking him from the sight of the frothy daysers. Soule's heart raced as he watched the carnage in the village below. His eyes suddenly met the eyes of White Antelope, who defiantly stood in the middle of the bowl with his arms crossed over his chest. The old Cheyenne chief stared at Soule, as he angrily chanted a Cheyenne death song. The top of White Antelope's head suddenly exploded, and he screwed into the ground.

Soule dropped his head and closed his eyes. "God...*dammit!*" he hollered.

Although surrounded by his loyal company, Soule stood virtually alone now.

"Captain!" Major Anthony hollered from across the bluffs. "They're making a run north! Go after them!"

Soule looked at Anthony and didn't move.

"What do we do, Captain?" a private asked.

"Soule!" Anthony hollered.

"Stay put!" Soule ordered.

A few random shots and arrows zipped past D Company.

"Back away!" Soule said. "Take cover. Defend yourselves if you have to, but do not fire on that village!"

His men swung around into the cottonwoods, and they watched the battle from there. To a man, the soldiers of D Company did not question Soule's order...

Anthony rode over to Chivington. "Colonel! Captain Soule is retreating!"

Chivington looked at Soule's company in the trees. "Order him to re-engage!"

Anthony considered the route he would have to take and relented. "Colonel, your men are out of control! There's a crossfire between me and him!"

"Major, you will go and order Soule to re-engage the enemy! Do it now!"

Anthony cursed and rode the gauntlet, ducking the daysers' bullets and frantically spurring into the trees.

"Soule! What the hell are you doing? Move your company out and shoot those bastards before they escape up the creek!"

"I will not!" Soule said.

"That's an order, Captain!" Anthony yelled.

"We're soldiers, Major, not murderers!"

"Godammit! Chivington will kill you!"

A corporal rode in front of Anthony. "You tell Chivington – if Captain Soule dies today, *he* dies today! We'll blow that son of a bitch parson to kingdom come!"

The boys of Company D fiercely agreed.

"Back off," another yelled, "or you'll go down, too!"

"What the hell!" Anthony squealed. "You better think twice about this!"

"We're not under Chivington's command," Soule said. "And neither are you, Major! Only a goddam coward would take part in this!"

Exasperated, Anthony looked back across the bluffs, where the daysers continued to range wildly out of control. "It's fuckin' mayhem! Those bastards are shooting at *my* men!"

"Cramer's company just backed off, too," Soule said. "Others are gonna follow. You're running out of friends, Major."

Anthony looked across at Chivington, who rode along the ridge, helplessly watching his Third Regiment run amok.

"Fuck!" Anthony screamed. He turned and rode back through a volley of wild shots.

Soule and his men turned back and watched the Cheyenne village die. Left Hand's Arapaho camp on the eastern perimeter was entirely decimated, and there were but a few Indians alive at the foot of the bluffs. The remainder of the fight quickly moved north, up the creek, as hundreds of Indians made a run for it. A few First and Third Regiment soldiers pursued them in a running battle that would continue into the afternoon. Many of Chivington's Third Regiment soldiers, however, stayed firmly in place, circling the bluffs and shooting at mostly dead bodies now. Occasionally, a squaw or child would peer out from the brush below, attracting a hail of rifle fire.

One dayser, slugging whiskey for courage, slid down the hill, where a very old and infirm Cheyenne squaw lay in a pool of her own blood. As the drunken dayser approached her, she cried out and struggled to her knees. She backed away, pleading for mercy as the dayser pulled his knife and cut her scalp away. Screaming in agony, the old squaw fell as the dayser turned and held the tuft of gray hair, much to the amusement of his cronies. The old woman crawled several feet and then dropped in the dirt, the remainder of her bloody scalp flapping over her eyes.

Soule and the boys of Company D watched the entire affair. A young boy behind Soule bent over and vomited on his boots.

"Jesus, Cap," a corporal whispered, "this is the shits..."

Soule looked across the bluffs at Chivington, who watched the daysers celebrate and take potshots at several scampering children. One by one, the militiamen began to slide down the hill and move into the village. Fifty to sixty Indians, mostly women, children and elderly lay dead in the bowl. The daysers rooted out the remaining survivors in the brush, shooting them as they begged for their lives. Knives were now brandished, and the militiamen set out for trophies. Every Indian corpse was scalped, and some were decapitated. The boys danced with the severed heads held high, while others were not yet satisfied. They harvested women's breasts, and cut off hands, arms, legs and sex organs.

One dayser gave a sudden yowl, and the boys turned his way. He stood over a dead squaw, swinging a bloody fetus he had just cut from her belly...

Captain Soule's eyes finally met Chivington's. The Fighting Parson had finally scored the Indian victory that could very well vault him to any political office he wanted – perhaps the presidency, if he so desired. He had but a few loose ends to tie, however. He glared at Soule, considering his next move.

In the devastated village on Sand Creek, once occupied by a Cheyenne peace chief called Black Kettle, the bloody harvest would continue for hours...

Headquarters, District of Colorado
In the field, on Big Bend of Sandy Creek
Colorado Territory, November 29, 1864
TO: Mr. William Byers
Editor, Rocky Mountain News
Denver, Colorado Territory
Sir:

I have not the time to give you a detailed history of our engagement of today, or to mention those officers and men who distinguished themselves in one of the most bloody Indian battles ever fought on these plains. You will find enclosed the report of my surgeon in charge, which will bring to many anxious friends the sad fate of loved ones who are and have been risking everything to avenge the horrid deeds of those savages we have so severely handled.

We made a forced march of forty miles, and surprised, at break of day, one of the most powerful villages of the Cheyenne nation, and captured over five hundred animals, killing the celebrated chiefs One Eye, White Antelope, Knock Knee, Black Kettle and Little Robe, with about five hundred of their people, destroying all their lodges and equipage, making almost an annihilation of the entire tribe.

I shall leave here, as soon as I can see our wounded safely on the way to the hospital at Fort Lyon, for the villages of the hostiles, which are reported about eighty miles from here, on the Smoky Hill, and three thousand strong; so look out for more fighting.

I will state, for the consideration of gentlemen who are opposed to fighting these red scoundrels, that I was shown, by my chief surgeon, the scalp of a white man taken from the lodge of one of the chiefs, which could not have been more than two or three days taken; and I could mention many more things to show how these Indians, who have been drawing government rations at Fort Lyon, are and have been acting.

Very respectfully, your obedient servant,
J. M. Chivington
Colonel, Commanding Colorado Expedition against Indians on Plains

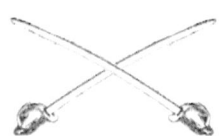

23

Cries of anguish pierced the night, as hundreds of Cheyennes and Arapahos wandered east through the shadowy darkness of the Kansas prairie. Many of the wounded were carried in makeshift travois, while others simply dragged themselves, or were carried by the uninjured. Small twig fires were lit to guide the wolves to the Smoky Hill River.

George Bent wandered back and forth, limping from a rifle shot to his hip. He searched until he finally found the man he was looking for.

Black Kettle emerged from the darkness.

"Come with me," Bent said. "I found her."

Black Kettle and George Bent walked for an hour, back toward the Sand Creek village, where the light of the soldiers' campfires could be seen in the distance. A small group of Cheyennes knelt beside Medicine Woman Later, who lay near the icy creek.

Black Kettle, nearly dead from exhaustion, ran to his wife and fell to his knees. He wept as he pulled her body into his arms. Suddenly, he felt her cold hand squeeze him. Astonished, Black Kettle looked into her glazed eyes. He tearfully gave thanks to Maheo for sparing his wife. The Cheyennes hastily built a travois and placed her in it, and Black Kettle helped them pull her toward the Smoky Hill...

Colonel Chivington sat in his tent, composing the first draft of the dispatch he intended to send to General Curtis. Before sunset, he sent a small party of soldiers and an ambulance with wounded soldiers to Fort Lyon, along with a letter to the *Rocky Mountain News*, given to a messenger with orders to ride with haste and deliver.

"Colonel Chivington?"

Chivington looked at the tent flap. "Come!"

Private Louderback entered and saluted. "Sir, may I have a word with you?"

"Louderback!" Chivington said. "Of course! Come have a seat." Louderback was caked with mud and scars. "Well, son, you look little worse for wear. You had quite an adventure today!"

"It ain't every day you get shot at by your own soldiers," Louderback said.

Chivington laughed. "Under fire you must keep your wits. You behaved well, son, and I'm glad you weren't killed."

"I didn't come here to talk about that, Colonel," Louderback said.

"Very well, what can I do for you?"

"Sir, I spent the better part of the day with John and Jack Smith, trying to keep from getting killed by that ratpack regiment from Denver."

"Go easy on them, Private," Chivington gently scolded. "Look, I know you had a harrowing experience. Your heroism will not go unrewarded, I assure you."

"Heroism? You think I'm looking for a commendation?"

"Alright, Private," Chivington said, "then what *do* you want to talk about?"

"It's Jack Smith. You got him and Uncle John under guard."

"We can't take any chances right now," Chivington said.

"But I heard talk that some of those daysers want to kill Jack because he's an Indian."

"Indeed? I wouldn't want to be in his moccasins, that's for sure."

"He's just a boy, Colonel. Besides, he's John Smith's son."

"Private, I'm very busy tonight."

"Colonel, that boy ain't gonna live out the night if you don't call off that pack of dogs."

"Thank you, Louderback. Your concerns are noted, but the Third Regiment is under strict orders to take no prisoners. I have no say in the matter."

"Sir!"

"Dismissed, Private!"

Louderback considered another protest, but he knew he was over his head. He angrily exited, and Chivington returned to his dispatch...

John Smith sat with his son in the pale light of a lantern. They huddled, filthy and beaten, in an army tent with two Indian children and young Charley Bent. Old Jim Beckwith cowered in a corner with his head dropped on his knees. A dayser guard stood over them, chewing beef jerky and washing it down with whiskey.

Lieutenant James Cannon, of the New Mexico First Volunteers, entered the tent with Lieutenant Mariano Autobee, of the Third Regiment and a friend of William Bent. He pointed at Charley Bent. "Charley, come with me."

"Hold it," the dayser said. "Ain't nobody leavin' this tent. Chivington's orders."

Autobee grabbed the dayser and twisted his arms back. Cannon put a knife to his throat.

"This artery under your ear will bleed out in less than two minutes," Cannon said. "You won't feel much when I cut it, but if you give me any more shit, I'll just cut little pieces off and let you die slow."

The dayser shuddered in terror. "Now, just hold it!"

"You got a third choice," Cannon sneered. "Sit your ass down and go on eatin' that jerky, and this young buck walks out of here with us."

"Go! I don't care what ya do!"

Cannon shoved the dayser on the ground. "Let's go, boy."

Autobee pulled the wounded boy up. Charley, spewing venom, tried to fight, but his rescuers dragged him out.

"Get your filthy white hands off of me!" Charley yelled in Cheyenne.

"Ain't got a clue what you're saying, boy," Cannon said as they walked him through the thick brush. "I know you speak English, so if you know what's good for ya, just shut up and come with us."

Cannon led Charley on a long ride to a small grove covered with army tents. A sentry stood guard on the perimeter and passed the party through. They walked Charley into the heavily guarded camp, and took him into Captain Soule's tent. Soule stood and looked at the boy.

Charley hollered at Soule with contempt. "Go ahead, brave soldier! Shoot me! I am not afraid!"

"Son, if you're cussing me out," Soule said, "you have to do it in English."

Charley complied. "I will kill every one of you!"

"I think there's been enough killing for one day," Soule sadly said. "We're gonna take you home to your father."

"I do not want to go!" Charley said. "He is a white man! I will kill him, too!"

Cannon gave Charley a good shove. "You just back off, boy! Captain Soule's gonna get you out alive. We're the only friends you got around here."

"No white man is my friend!" Charley spat in Soule's face.

"You little prick!" Cannon said, raising his hand.

"Jim - don't!" Soule said. He pulled a handkerchief and wiped his face. "Go easy on the boy. Don't you reckon you'd want to spit on the whole world after what's been done here?"

Cannon relented. "What do you want me to do with him?"

"Give him some grub. Did you find Smith's boy?"

"Who?"

"Jack Smith – shit, you don't know him, do ya?"

"Sorry, Captain. There was a couple of old men in that tent. There was a young buck, too."

"Damn," Soule said. "It's probably the kid."

"Want me to go back and get him?"

"I don't reckon you made much of an impression on the guard when you took Charley."

Cannon chuckled. "Made a little impression on his neck. He's probably got a pack of daysers around that tent now."

Soule sighed. "Shit, it's all we need to get in a skirmish with those bastards tonight. We best lay low and try for him at dawn..."

At early light, Colonel Chivington rode up to Major Downing, who sat on his horse, watching a group of daysers whoop and laugh as they dragged the lifeless body of Jack Smith around the Sand Creek village. Uncle John Smith sat atop the bluffs in the distance, his head buried in his hands.

"Jacob!" Chivington said. "What are those fools doing?"

"Just having a little fun," Downing laughed.

"Well, put a stop to it. We have work to do."

Downing rode down the hill and intervened.

Major Anthony walked up, his eyes riveted on the drunken daysers. "Those bastards shot that boy in cold blood."

"Not so, Major," Chivington said. "I understand the little savage took ill overnight and quietly passed away in his sleep. These red creatures breed infections, you know."

"Colonel," Anthony said, "these so-called soldiers of yours are nothing but a pack of bloodthirsty goons."

"You're picking a peculiar time to grow a conscience, Major. Now tell me, have all the wounded been secured and sent home?"

Anthony sighed. "Everyone's on their way back to Lyon."

"Where is Captain Soule? The little bleeding-heart crawled up to me yesterday and begged to take Bent's son back to Lyon. I didn't see the harm in it."

Anthony smirked. "Soule beg? Don't insult my intelligence, Colonel."

"Where is that old Dutch coward?" Chivington said.

"I sent him back to guard the train. Just in case your so-called 'soldiers' might have an infection in mind for him, too."

"Anthony, just what the hell is your problem?"

"You want to know, Colonel? The plain fact is – I have no taste for your method of command!"

"You have a right to your opinion," Chivington said. "You have a choice. You may obey my commands, like it or not, or you may face a court-martial."

"Yes, sir," Anthony sighed.

"That's what I thought," Chivington said. "Now, prepare your men. We're heading for the Arkansas."

"What? The Arkansas?"

"That's right. Old Little Raven is next in line for a whipping."

"Colonel, you said we were going to the Smoky Hill!"

"I said nothing of the kind! We just ripped the heart out of the Cheyennes. They're finished! The Arapahos are next on the menu!"

"What about the Dog Soldiers? Little Raven's band is no different than the village you just attacked! Or, is it that you know these idiots wouldn't last a half day in battle with Tall Bull?"

Chivington boiled with rage. "Look, you little red-eyed cockroach, I've had a bellyful of your insubordination! You are one more word away from leg irons! Now, torch this stinking Indian graveyard, and prepare your troops to march to the Arkansas! Savvy?" The Fighting Parson violently pulled his horse away and bellowed orders to his officers.

Anthony cursed and furiously mounted up. He rode down into the decimated Indian village and found Lieutenant Cramer, who was completing the ugly chore of counting the dead.

"Cramer!" Anthony hollered. "You got a report for me yet?"

Cramer, his face ashen from wading through the carnage, sadly walked up to Anthony. "Yeah. We counted sixty-nine up and down the creek."

"What's the number here in the village?"

"Well, can't rightly tell, Major. We first thought about counting up the number of arms and legs and dividing by four ..."

"Are you trying to be funny?"

Cramer blew a sigh. "I'm hip deep in guts, Major. I ain't laughed all morning."

"Just give me a count!" Anthony barked.

"With, or without gonads?"

"Goddamit, Cramer!"

"Alright! Ain't nothing but women, children and old folks in the village." He walked up to Black Kettle's burned-out lodge. He picked up an American flag and tried to brush off the blood-caked mud. "Counting the dead here, with the bodies on the creek, looks like around 170 maybe 180 all told."

"Get your company packed and mounted," Anthony said.

"Where we headed next?" Cramer said. "Back up on the bluffs to open fire again?"

Anthony simply shook his head. "We're going...back to the Arkansas."

"Oh, well, ain't that just *fucking perfect!*" Cramer said. "I reckon, since there's gonna be about two thousand fire-breathing Dogmen heading this way pretty soon, old Chiv's gonna hightail for Denver and leave our sorry asses twisting in the wind out here!"

"He says we're gonna hunt for Little Raven," Anthony said. "Burn the village, and get your men mounted." He angrily rode away.

Cramer threw the flag back into the mud. "You're never gonna learn, are ya, Major..."

The Sand Creek survivors continued their trek across the Kansas prairie for two days, following the Smoky Hill River until their young scouts finally found Dogmen wolves on the prowl for buffalo. The Dogmen quickly returned to their camps and alerted other warriors, who dispatched rescue parties with enough ponies to bring in the hundreds of refugees. Word of the attack on Black Kettle's village spread quickly to the Solomon River, igniting a firestorm of anger among the Cheyenne, Arapaho and Sioux warriors. The war pipe was immediately passed to every soldier society, and offered and accepted by the Kiowas, Apaches and Comanches. At long last, the united declaration of war on the Kansas and Colorado territories that Governor Evans had feared was about to materialize...

Within their heavily guarded encampment, the Dogmen prepared for war, holding councils and welcoming the arrival of soldier bands from other Plains Indians tribes. The Sand Creek survivors mourned their dead and prayed for the wounded, the women crying and slashing themselves for the loss of their families and friends. Black Kettle remained in his lodge, under the protection of his dwindling supporters. Cheyenne law was strictly intolerant of anyone that dared to threaten or kill a chief, but emotions ran high and Black Kettle's people took no chances. Medicine Woman Later had suffered several gunshot wounds and was treated by the medicine man and several squaws under Black Kettle's watchful eye. She fought for life with remarkable strength and courage.

Black Kettle sadly emerged from his lodge and watched the war parties dance and paint themselves and their ponies. Bull Bear saw the old chief and approached him.

"How is she?" Bull Bear asked.

"She is full of holes. Are you here to crow?"

"No," Bull Bear said. "I give you my respect, and I pray for your wife. I am sorry for what happened."

Black Kettle swallowed his anger. "I must look like an old fool to you."

"Never. You trusted the white man. I trusted them. If that makes you a fool, then you are not alone. I promise you, I will hunt down Tall Chief and kill him myself."

"No!" Black Kettle said. "I will never believe that Tall Chief was behind this."

"Who else could it be?" Bull Bear angrily said. "He lied to all of us, and he put you in that death trap for his men to rub you out."

"Tall Chief did not do this, Bull Bear! He was called away to talk to his chief in the east. I can see now that the others set both him and our people up. It was that red-eyed coyote and the big chief from Denver who led the attack. Tall Chief was betrayed as much as we were."

"It makes no difference anymore," Bull Bear said. "I will kill every white soldier I see. They want to fight like this? They will get everything they want, and more."

Black Kettle sadly shook his head.

"You know it is true, Black Kettle. You know in your heart that we have no choice but to fight now."

"I fear the war parties here are all dead," Black Kettle said. "They just do not know it yet."

"They know," Bull Bear said. "But they are not ready to join their people in the Spirit World just yet. The soldiers will kill most of us – someday perhaps *all* of us - but in the end they will have to take account for what they did to you. They will answer for all the whites who will die because of it."

"My shame is as big as the earth," Black Kettle whispered. "I once thought I was the only man who tried to be friends with them. But they clean out our lodges and kill our children – everything. It is hard for me to believe the white man anymore..."

Ned Wynkoop sat in the dim firelight of his quarters at Fort Riley. An empty whiskey bottle had just seen its last duty and now lay shattered on the floor. Wynkoop's quarters were wrecked, chairs turned to splinters, broken glass scattered, and a small table torn to pieces. Wynkoop, blind drunk and utterly devastated, looked with crossed eyes at the dispatch that was delivered two hours ago. He cursed and tore the paper to shreds. Black Kettle's old eyes danced in his head. Wynkoop could not hold his tears any longer...

24

Headquarters, District of Colorado
December 16, 1864
General:

I have the honor to transmit the following report of operations of the Indian expedition under my command, of which a brief notice was given you by telegram of November 29, 1864. Having ascertained that the hostile Indians had proceeded south from the Platte, and were almost within striking distance of Fort Lyon, I ordered Colonel George L. Shoup, 3rd Regiment Colorado Volunteer Cavalry (100-day service), to proceed with the mounted men of his regiment in that direction.

On the 20th of November I left Denver, and at Booneville, C.T., on the 24th of November joined and took command in person of the expedition which had been increased by a battalion of the 1st Cavalry of Colorado, consisting of detachments of companies C, E, and H. I proceeded with the utmost caution down the Arkansas River, and on the 28th instant arrived at Fort Lyon, to the surprise of the garrison of that post. On the same day I resumed my march, being joined by Major Scott J. Anthony, 1st Cavalry of Colorado, with 125 men of said regiment, consisting of detachments of Companies D, G, and F, with two howitzers. The command then proceeded in a northeasterly direction, traveling all night, and at daylight of the 29th November striking Sand Creek about 40 miles from Fort Lyon.

Here was discovered an Indian village of 130 lodges, composed of Black Kettle's band of Cheyennes, and 8 lodges of Arapahos, with Left Hand. My line of battle was formed with Lieutenant Wilson's battalion of the 1st Regiment, numbering about 125 men, on the right; Colonel Shoup's 3rd Regiment, numbering about 450 men, in the center; and Major Anthony's battalion, numbering 125 men, 1st Regiment, on the left.

The attack was immediately made upon the Indian's camp by Lieutenant Wilson, who dashed forward, cutting the enemy off from their herd, and driving them out of their camp, which was subsequently destroyed. The Indians numbering from 900 to 1,000, though taken by surprise, speedily rallied and formed a line of battle across the creek, about three-fourths of a mile above the village, stubbornly contesting every inch of ground.

The commands of Colonel Shoup and Major Anthony pressed rapidly forward and attacked the enemy sharply, and the engagement became general, we constantly driving the Indians, who fell back from one position to another for five miles, and finally abandoned resistance and dispersed in all directions and were pursued by my troops until nightfall.

It may, perhaps, be unnecessary for me to state that I captured no prisoners. Between 500 and 600 Indians were left dead upon the field. About 550 ponies, mules and horses were captured, and all their lodges were destroyed, the contents of which has served to supply the command with an abundance of trophies, comprising the paraphernalia of Indian warfare and life. My loss was 8 killed on the field and 40 wounded, of which 2 have since died.

Of the conduct of the 3rd Regiment (100-day service) I have to say that they well sustained the reputation of our Colorado troops for bravery and effectiveness; were well commanded by their gallant young Colonel George L. Shoup, ably assisted by Colonel L. L. Bowen, Major Hal Sayr, and Captain Theodore G. Cree, commanding 1st, 2nd and 3rd battalions of that regiment.

Of the conduct of the two battalions of the 1st Regiment I have but to remark that they sustained their reputation as second to none, and were ably handled by their commanders, Major Anthony, Lieutenant Wilson, and Lieutenant Clark Dunn, upon whom the command devolved after the disability of Lieutenant Wilson from wounds received.

Night coming on, the pursuit of the flying Indians was of necessity abandoned, and my command encamped within sight of the field.

On the first instant, having sent the wounded and dead to Fort Lyon, the first to be cared for, and the latter to be buried upon our own soil, I resumed the pursuit in the direction of Camp Wynkoop on the Arkansas River, marching all the night of the 3rd and 4th instant, in hopes of overtaking a large encampment of Arapahos and Cheyennes, under Little Raven, but the enemy had been apprised of my advance, and on the morning of the 5th instant, at 3 o'clock, precipitately broke camp and fled. My stock was exhausted. For 100 miles the snow had been two feet deep, and for the previous 15 days - excepting on November 29 and 30 - the marching had been forced and incessant.

Under these circumstances, and the fact of the time of the 3rd Regiment being nearly out, I determined for the present to relinquish the pursuit.

Of the effect of the punishment sustained by the Indians you will be the judge. Their chiefs, Black Kettle, White Antelope, One Eye, Knock Knee and Little Robe, were numbered with the killed and their bands almost annihilated. I was shown the scalp of a white man, found in one of the lodges, which could not have been taken more than two or three days previous. For full particulars and reports of the several commanders, I respectfully refer you to the following copies herewith enclosed.

If all the companies of the 1st Colorado and the 11th Ohio Volunteer Cavalry, stationed at camps and posts near here, were ordered to report to me, I could organize a campaign, which, in my judgment, would effectually *rid the country between the Platte and Arkansas Rivers of these red rebels.*

I would respectfully request to be informed, if another campaign should be authorized from here, whether I could employ one or two hundred friendly Utes, furnishing them subsistence, arms and ammunition for the campaign.

I cannot conclude this report without saying that the conduct of Captain Silas S. Soule, Company D, 1st Cavalry of Colorado, was at least ill-advised, he saying that he thanked God that he killed no Indians, and like expressions, proving him more in sympathy with the Indians than with the whites.

The evidence is most conclusive that these Indians are the worst that have infested the routes of the Platte and Arkansas Rivers during the last spring and summer. Amongst the stock captured were the horses and mules taken by them from Lieutenant Chase, 1st Cavalry of Colorado, last September; several scalps of white men and women were found in the lodges; also various articles of clothing belonging to white persons. On every hand the evidence was clear that no lick was struck amiss.

I am, General, very respectfully your obedient servant.

J. M. Chivington

Colonel, 1st Cavalry of Colorado

Commanding District of Colorado

The bodies of more than 200 Cheyenne and Arapaho Indians killed at Sand Creek were barely cold before accusations of a hideous misdeed committed by Chivington's Third Regiment drifted up the Arkansas. Had the attack yielded a larger bounty of dead warriors, Colonel Chivington might have escaped the scathing criticism emanating from the Arkansas region, but rumors of the true body count at the village simply would not go away. Fort Lyon officers and soldiers insisted that two-thirds of the Indians killed at Sand Creek were women, children and elderly. That claim alone might even have been overlooked by Chivington's superiors if not for the disturbing allegation of a savage feast of scalps and body parts taken by the daysers after the attack. Adding to Chivington's growing dilemma was the fact that a majority of the First Regiment soldiers of Fort Lyon had opposed a campaign against Black Kettle's village from the get-go. Major Wynkoop's agreement with Black Kettle, in strict accordance with the terms laid out by Governor Evans at the Camp Weld Council, was considered valid and just, not only by Wynkoop's Fort Lyon command and the residents in the region, but by Wynkoop's successor, Major Scott Anthony. The very public protestation against attacking the Sand Creek village by Captain Soule, Lieutenant Cramer, and the other officers at Lyon was a matter of record, and several eye-witnesses insisted that Chivington even made threats against Soule.

The troubling reports coming from Fort Lyon further fueled speculation that Chivington might very well have overstepped his authority by commandeering the First Regiment on an unsanctioned military operation. Not only had he attacked Indian prisoners under the protection of the United States flag, he clearly intended to ravage Little Raven's tribe, which had also submitted to Evans' demands. Throughout the entire Sand Creek debacle, the Dog Soldiers and Sioux warriors, who were most considered at war with the United States Army, remained unmolested deep in the northern regions of Kansas. It was clear that Chivington had to justify his campaign against friendly Indians camped hundreds of miles from the Dog Soldiers, and then breaking off before pushing on to search for the true perpetrators of the violent summer depredations. From a strategic military standpoint, Chivington's attack at Sand Creek was clearly a horrible blunder with potentially disastrous consequences for the citizens of Colorado and Kansas. In the eyes of God-fearing white Christians, however, the bloodthirsty evisceration of women and children at Black Kettle's village by a government-sanctioned civilian militia reduced the Methodist preacher to the depths of the most primitive of savages.

Major Wynkoop's ardently loyal military and civilian supporters would not remain quiet in the matter, and talk of a grassroots campaign to lobby Washington for an investigation into the Sand Creek attack abounded. Chivington's longtime nemesis, Colonel Samuel Tappan, was the primary suspect among those who openly spoke out against the attack, but Colley, Smith, Bent, and the officers of Fort Lyon were equally vocal in their outrage.

Chivington, however, had a strong base of support among the officers and soldiers in the Third Regiment, and he immediately implemented a damage-control strategy to justify his decision to attack the Indians at Sand Creek. He began by taking his case to the people he believed would stand behind him. His wildly exaggerated account of the Sand Creek "battle" was sent to the *Rocky Mountain News* even before he dispatched an official report to General Curtis. He then sent a message to headquarters, which oddly omitted any mention of the behavior of the Fort Lyon officers, other than to criticize Captain Soule's refusal to fire on Black Kettle's camp. Chivington's quoting Soule as "thanking God he killed no Indians" raised eyebrows of those skeptics who were intimately familiar with the emphatically agnostic Soule, but this was but a minor inconsistency compared to other claims in Chivington's report. He exaggerated the number of Indians killed, made unsubstantiated claims of finding fresh white scalps in the burned-out Cheyenne lodges, and blatantly lied that Black Kettle himself was killed in the battle. He then attempted to justify his decision to end his Indian campaign at Sand Creek without marching on to hunt the Dog Soldiers, claiming his men and horses were exhausted from the long trip down to attack and butcher several hundred Indian prisoners.

Colonel Chivington then collected reports from Third Regiment officers whose loyalty to him was unbending, and ordered only one report from a Fort Lyon officer, not surprisingly, Major Scott Anthony...

Excerpt from the reports of Colonel George L. Shoup:

...At this point Captain Talbott, of company M, fell severely wounded, while bravely leading his men in a charge on a body of Indians who had taken refuge on the banks on the north side of the creek. Here a terrible hand-to-hand encounter ensued between the Indians and Captain Talbott's men and others who had rushed forward to their aid - the Indians trying to secure the scalp of Captain Talbott. I think the hardest fighting of the day occurred at that point, some of our men fighting with club muskets; the 1st and 3d Coloradoans fighting side by side, each trying to excel in bravery, and each ambitious to kill at least one Indian. Many valuable lives of officers and men were saved by the bravery of others just as the fatal knife was raised to perform its work of death.

Early in the engagement, Captain Nichols, with his company D, pursued a band of Indians that were trying to escape to the northeast; he overtook and punished them severely, killing twenty-five or thirty and captured some ponies. Other companies of my regiment fought with zeal and bravery, but after 10 o'clock a. m., the battle became so general and covered so wide a field that it became necessary to divide my command into small detachments, sending them in all directions to pursue the flying Indians.

I am told by my officers and men that some of their comrades engaged the Indians in close combat. I am satisfied, from my own observation, that the historian will search in vain for braver deeds than were committed on that field of battle...

Second report from Shoup:

...My "officers and men" will obey orders and go to the Smoky Hill and Republican, if the colonel commanding, after due deliberation, will so order. However, they are nearly all of the opinion, (the officers) that an expedition to the above named streams at present must fail. This opinion is based upon the fact that their horses are worn out, and in an unserviceable condition; most of the animals would fail on the first forced march.

They are of the further opinion that many of these men will re-enlist to prosecute this campaign if we meet with no reverse and the men are not worn out and disheartened in a fruitless march just before the expiration of their term of enlistment.

All the above is fully indorsed by me; and while I am more than eager to duplicate the great victory of November 29, I think an expedition to the Smoky Hill and Republican, considering the worn-out condition of my horses, would prove more of a disaster than a success, at present; the failure of which would so dishearten my men, that no inducement could be held out that would cause them to re-enlist. All of which is most respectfully submitted.

GEORGE L. SHOUP, *Colonel 3d Colorado Cavalry.*

Report of Lieutenant Colonel L. L. Bowen:
SIR:

I have the honor to enclose you the reports of the company commanders of the first battalion, commanded by myself, in the action of yesterday. I fully indorse all contained in these reports; all behaved well, each vieing with the other as to who could do the enemy the most injury. This, I think, can truly be said of the whole regiment. I was in position during the action to see most of the regiment, and did not see one coward. Permit me to congratulate you upon the signal punishment meted out to the savages on yesterday, "who so ruthlessly have murdered our women and children," in the language of the colonel commanding, although I regret the loss of so many brave men. The Third Regiment cannot any longer be called the "bloodless third."

From the most reliable information, from actual count and positions occupied, I have no doubt that at least one hundred and fifty Indians were killed by my battalion.

I cannot speak in terms of too high praise of all the officers and men under my command. The war flag of this band of Cheyennes is in my possession, presented by Stephen Decatur, Commissary Sergeant of company C, who acted as my battalion adjutant.

Very respectfully,

LEAVITT L. BOWEN, *Lieut. Col. 3d Colorado Cavalry, Commanding 1st Battalion*

Report of Major Hal Sayr, Commanding, 2d Battalion, 3d Colorado Cavalry:
...Companies B, G, and K, moved across the creek and went into the action on the north side of the creek, and west of the Indian town, where they remained for several hours, doing good service, while under a heavy fire from the enemy, who were concealed in rifle-pits in the bed of the creek.

The action became general, and lasted from 6.30 a. m. until 1 p. m., when the companies divided into small squads and went in pursuit of the Indians, who were now flying in every direction across the plains, and were pursued until dark.

Both officers and men conducted themselves bravely. The number of Indians killed by the battalion, as estimated by company commanders, is about 175 to 200...

Report of Captain Theodore G. Cree:
SIR:

I have the honor to report to you the part taken by the third battalion in the fight of the 29th of November. They first formed on the left of the regiment, in the rear of the village, then removed upon the right bank of the creek, near one-half mile; there dismounted and fought the red-skins about an hour, where the boys behaved like veterans.

After finding that we had done all the good that we could do there, removed companies D and E, (company F having gone with Colonel Bowen's battalion,) and moved to the right, across the hill, for the purpose of killing Indians that were making their escape to the right of the command, in which movement we succeeded in killing many. I then made a detail from company D, of fifteen men, and sent them to capture some twenty ponies, which I could see some four miles to the right of the village; but before they reached the ponies some twenty Indians attacked them, when a fierce fight ensued, in which Private McFarland was killed in a hand-to-hand engagement; but, like true soldiers, they stood their ground, killing five Indians, and wounding several others.

The Indians, finding it rather warm to be healthy, left. The boys pursued them some eight or ten miles, and finding that they could not overtake them, returned, bringing with them the ponies they were sent for. I then returned with the command to the village to take care of their killed and wounded companions.

Company E lost one killed and one wounded; company D, two killed and one wounded.

As for the bravery displayed by any one in particular, I have no distinctions to make. All I can say for officers and men is, that they all behaved well, and won for themselves a name that will be remembered for ages to come.

The number of Indians killed by my battalion is sixty.

I am, Colonel, yours truly,

T. G. CREE, Captain Commanding 3d Battalion, 3d Colorado Cavalry.

Report of Lieutenant Clark Dunn:

...At daylight we came in sight of a large village of hostile Indians, Cheyennes and Arapahoes, numbering nine hundred or one thousand, nearly two miles north of us. We immediately proceeded to the attack by moving down a small ravine and making a charge on the village from the north side, taking the Indians completely by surprise. They rallied immediately and the engagement became general, and lasted till afternoon, when they were utterly routed and half their number left dead on the field.

We continued the pursuit till 3 o'clock p. m., when our horses being much fatigued, and our ammunition nearly exhausted, we returned to the village, which we helped to destroy, and then went into camp for the night.

I lost no men killed, and but two wounded. Sergeant Jackson had his hip broken, and Private Mull was shot through the leg.

I am, sir, very respectfully, your obedient servant,

CLARK DUNN, Second Lieut. 1st Colorado Cavalry, Commanding Co. E.

Report of Major Scott Anthony:

SIR:

I have the honor to report that I left Fort Lyon, Colorado Territory, with detachments from companies D, G, and H, 1st Colorado cavalry, numbering one hundred and twenty-five men, and two howitzers, and joined Colonel Chivington's brigade one mile below Fort Lyon, at 8 o'clock p. m., November 28, and proceeded with his command, on Indian expedition, in a northeasterly direction, striking Sand Creek at daylight of the 29th November, forty miles from Fort Lyon, when we came upon a herd of Indian horses, and I was sent forward with my battalion to capture stock. After proceeding about one mile we came in sight of an Indian camp, some two miles further.

I immediately sent word to the colonel commanding that an Indian camp was in sight, and proceeded with my command in the direction of the camp, which I reached just before sunrise. I found Lieutenant Wilson, with a detachment of 1st Colorado cavalry, upon the right and south of the camp, and Lieutenant Dunn, with a detachment of the 1st Colorado cavalry, posted upon the west bank of Sand Creek, and opposite the camp, both commands keeping up a brisk fire upon the camp.

Upon my nearing the camp upon the west side I was attacked by a small force of Indians posted behind the bank of the creek, who commenced firing upon me with arrows, and who had collected on the opposite side of camp. Colonel Chivington coming up at this time with Colonel Shoup's regiment, 3d Colorado cavalry, and two howitzers, charged through the camp, driving the Indians completely out of their camp and into the creek, in holes or rifle-pits dug in the sand. The fighting now became general. The

Indians fought desperately, apparently resolved to die upon that ground, but to injure us as much as possible before being killed. We fought them for about six hours, along the creek for five miles.

The loss to my command was one killed and three wounded. The loss to the entire command, ten killed and forty wounded. Lieutenant Baldwin, commanding the section of howitzers, attached to my battalion, had a fine private horse shot from under him. Seven horses were killed from my command.

The loss to the Indians was, about three hundred killed, some six hundred ponies, and one hundred and thirty lodges, with a large quantity of buffalo robes, and their entire camp equipage. The camp proved to be Cheyenne and Arapahoe Indians, and numbered about 1,100 persons, under the leadership of Black Kettle, head chief of the Cheyenne tribe. Black Kettle and three other chiefs were killed.

All the command fought well, and observed all orders given them. We camped upon the ground occupied by the Indians the day before, destroyed the entire camp of the Indians, and then pushed rapidly in a southeasterly direction, in pursuit of Little Raven's camp of Arapahoes, reported to be on the Arkansas river.

I am, sir, with much respect, your obedient servant,

SCOTT J. ANTHONY, Major First Colorado Cavalry, Commanding Battalion

Excerpt from the Rocky Mountain News
December 17, 1864
"The Battle of Sand Creek"
by William Byers
...Among the killed were all the Cheyenne chiefs, Black Kettle, White Antelope, Little Robe, Left Hand, Knock Knee, One Eye, and another, name unknown. Not a single prominent man of the tribe remains, and the tribe itself is almost annihilated. The Arapahoes probably suffered but little. It has been reported that the chief Left Hand, of that tribe, was killed, but Colonel Chivington is of the opinion that he was not. Among the stock captured were a number of government horses and mules, including the twenty or thirty stolen from the command of Lieutenant Chase at Jimmy's camp last summer.

The Indian camp was well supplied with defensive works. For half a mile along the creek there was an almost continuous chain of rifle-pits, and another similar line of works crowned the adjacent bluff. Pits had been dug at all the salient points for miles. After the battle, twenty-three dead Indians were taken from one of these pits and twenty-seven from another.

Whether viewed as a march or as a battle, the exploit has few, if any, parallels. A march of 260 miles in but a fraction more than five days, with *deep snow, scanty forage, and no road, is a remarkable feat, whilst the utter surprise of a large Indian village is unprecedented. In no single battle in North America, we believe, have so many Indians been slain.*

It is said that a short time before the command reached the scene of battle an old squaw partially alarmed the village by reporting that a great herd of buffalo were coming. She heard the rumbling of the artillery and tramp of the moving squadrons, but her people doubted. In a little time the doubt was dispelled, but not by buffaloes.

A thousand incidents of individual daring and the passing events of the day might be told, but space forbids. We leave the task for eye-witnesses to chronicle. All acquitted themselves well, and Colorado soldiers have again covered themselves with glory...

Whether Byers knew it or not, the summary of his glorious distortion of The Third Regiment's attack at Sand Creek was prophetic:

Among the brilliant feats of arms in Indian warfare, the recent campaign of our Colorado volunteers will stand in history with few rivals, and none to exceed it in final results...

On December 22, 1864, almost a month after attacking Black Kettle's band at Sand Creek, the Colorado Third Regiment returned to Denver in a grand parade along Larimer and Blake Streets. Colonel John Milton Chivington led the parade on his magnificent black steed, carrying a pole with a live eagle tied to it. Hundreds of Denverites turned out to greet the newly dubbed "Bloody Thirdsters," cheering wildly in the crisp, rarefied air. The boys drank and shouted, many waving Indian scalps and other more exotic souvenirs taken from the glorious Battle of Sand Creek. One soldier spotted his miner friends and rode up to them, holding what he proudly called a "titbag" – its name correctly implying what it was - a dried and hollowed-out female breast used for carrying valuables. Another showed off a dried Indian scrotum that he used as a tobacco pouch...

Amid the persistent rumors that officials in Washington were considering an investigation into the conflicting accounts of the Battle of Sand Creek, William Byers defiantly took up Chivington's defense. His newspaper criticized the "high officials" of Washington who dared to question the actions of the Third Regiment, and warned anyone who joined the investigation "to get their scalps insured before they pass Plum Creek on their way out."

The Colorado Third Regiment's 100 days of service expired on

December 28, and the volunteers officially mustered out and returned to civilian life. Colonel Chivington resigned his commission two weeks later, and his storied career in the United States Army came to an end. Major Scott Anthony resigned soon thereafter. That month of January 1865 would see the most violent Indian attacks on white settlements and trains ever before seen in Kansas or Colorado...

Fort Lyon, C.T.
December 14, 1864

Dear Ned:

Two days after you left here the 3rd Reg't with a Battalion of the 1st arrived here, having moved so secretly that we were not aware of their approach until they had Pickets around the Post, allowing no one to pass out! They arrested Capt. Bent and John Vogle and placed guards around their houses. They then declared their intention to massacre the friendly Indians camped on Sand Creek. Major Anthony gave all information, and eagerly Joined in with Chivington and Co. and ordered Lieut. Cramer with his whole Co. to join the command. As soon as I knew of their movement I was indignant as you would have been were you here and went to Cannon's room, where a number of officers of the 1st and 3rd were congregated and told them that any man who would take part in the murders, knowing the circumstances as we did, was a low lived cowardly son of a bitch. Capt. Y. J. Johnson and Lieut. Harding went to camp and reported to Chiv, Downing and the whole outfit what I had said, and you can bet hell was to pay in camp.

Chiv and all hands swore they would hang me before they moved camp, but I stuck it out, and all the officers at the Post, except Anthony backed me. I was then ordered with my whole company to Major A- with 20 days rations. I told him I would not take part in their intended murder, but if they were going after the Sioux, Kiowa's or any fighting Indians, I would go as far as any of them. They said that was what they were going for, and I joined them. We arrived at Black Kettles and Left Hand's Camp at daylight. Lieut. Wilson with Co.s "C", "E" & "G" were ordered to in advance to cut off their herd. He made a circle to the rear and formed a line 200 yds from the village, and opened fire.

Poor Old John Smith and Louderbeck ran out with white flags but they paid no attention to them, and they ran back into the tents. Anthony then rushed up with Co's "D" "K" & "G" to within one hundred yards and commenced firing. I refused to fire and swore that none but a coward would for by this time hundreds of women and children were coming toward us and getting on their knees for mercy. Anthony shouted, "kill the sons of bitches" Smith and Louderbeck came to our command, although I am confident there were 200 shots fired at them, for I heard an officer say that Old Smith and any one who sympathized with the Indians, ought to be killed and now was a good time to do it. The Battery then came up in our rear, and opened on them. I took my Comp'y across the Creek, and by this time the whole of the 3rd and the Batteries were firing into them and you can form some idea of the slaughter.

When the Indians found there was no hope for them they went for the Creek and got under the banks and some of the bucks got their Bows and a few rifles and defended themselves as well as they could. By this time there was no organization among our troops, they were a perfect mob – every man on his own hook. My Co. was the only one that kept their formation, and we did not fire a shot. The massacre lasted six or eight hours, and a good many Indians escaped. I tell you Ned it was hard to see little children on their knees have their brains beat out by men professing to be civilized. One squaw was wounded and a fellow took a hatchet to finish her, and he cut one arm off, and held the other with one hand and dashed the hatchet through her brain. One squaw with her two children, were on their knees, begging for their lives of a dozen soldiers, within ten feet of them all firing - when one succeeded in hitting the squaw in the thigh, she took a knife and cut the throats of both children and then killed herself. One Old Squaw hung herself in the lodge - there was not enough room for her to hang and she held up her knees and choked herself to death. Some tried to escape on the Prairie, but most of them were run down by horsemen. I saw two Indians hold one of anothers hands, chased until they were exhausted, when they kneeled down, and clasped each other around the neck and both were shot together. They were all scalped, and as high as half a dozen taken from one head. They were all horribly mutilated. One woman was cut open and a child taken out of her, and scalped.

White Antelope, War Bonnet and a number of others had Ears and privates cut off. Squaws snatches were cut out for trophies. You would think it impossible for white men to butcher and mutilate human beings as they did there, but every word I have told you is the truth, which they do not deny. It was almost impossible to save any of them. Charly Autobee saved John Smith and Winsers squaw. I saved little Charlie Bent. George Bent was killed. Jack Smith was taken prisoner, and murdered the next day in his tent by one of Dunn's Co. "E". I understand the man received a horse for doing the job. They were going to murder Charlie Bent, but I run him into the Fort. They were going to kill Old Uncle John Smith, but Lt. Cannon and the boys of Ft. Lyon, interfered, and saved him. They would have murdered Old Bents family, if Col. Tappan had not taken the matter in hand. Cramer went up with twenty (20) men, and they did not like to buck *against so many of the 1st. Chivington has gone to Washington to be made general, I suppose, and get authority to raise a nine months Reg't to hunt Indians. He said Downing will have me cashiered if possible. If they do I want you to help me. I think they will try the same for Cramer for he has shot his mouth off a good deal, and did not shoot his pistol off in the Massacre. Joe has behaved first rate during this whole affair. Chivington reports five or six hundred killed, but there were not more than two hundred, about 140 women and children and 60 Bucks. A good many were out hunting buffalo. Our best Indians were killed. Black Kettle, One Eye, Minnemic, and Left Hand. Geo. Pierce of Co. "F" was killed trying to save John Smith. There was one other of the 1st killed and nine of the 3rd all through their own fault. They would get up to the edge of the bank and look over, to get a shot at an Indian under them. When the women were killed the Bucks did not seem to try and get away, but fought desperately. Charly Autobee wished me to write all about it to you. He says he would have given anything if you could have been there.*

I suppose Cramer has written to you, all the particulars, so I will write half. Your family is well. Billy Wilker, Col. Tappen, Wilson (who was wounded in the arm) start for Denver in the morning. There is no news I can think of. I expect we will have a hell of a time with Indians this winter. We have (200) men at the Post – Anthony in command. I think he will be dismissed when the facts are known in Washington. Give my regards to any friends you come across, and write as soon as possible.

Yours, SS
(signed) S.S. Soule

Ft. Lyon, C. T.
December 19, 1864

Dear Major:
This is the first opportunity I have had of writing you since the great Indian Massacre, and for a start, I will acknowledge I am ashamed to own I was in it with my Co. Col. Chivington came down here with the gallant third known as Chivington Brigade, like a thief in the dark throwing his Scouts around the Post, with instructions to let no one out, without his orders, not even the Commander of the Post, and for the shame, our Commanding Officer submitted. Col. Chivington expected to find the Indians in camp below the Com but the Major Comd'g told him all about where the Indians were, and volunteered to take a Battalion from the Post and Join the Expedition.
Well Col. Chiv. got in about 10 a.m., Nov. 28th and at 8 p.m. we started

with all of the 3rd parts of "H" "O" and "E" of the First, in command of
Lt. Wilson Co. "K" "D" and "G" in commanding of Major Anthony.
Marched all night up Sand, to the big bend in Sanday, about 15 or 20 miles,
above where we crossed on our trip to Smoky Hill and came on to Black
Kettles village of 103 lodges, containing not over 500 all told, 350 of which
were women and children. Three days previous to our going out, Major
Anthony gave John Smith, Lowderbuck of Co. "G" and a government
driver, permission to go out there and trade with them, and they were in the
village when the fight came off. John Smith came out holding up his hands
and running towards us, when he was shot at by several, and the word was
passed along to shoot him. He then turned back, and went to his tent and
got behind some Robes, and escaped unhurt. Lowderbuck came out with a
white flag, and was served the same as John Smith, the driver the same.
Well I got so mad I swore I would not burn powder, and I did not. Capt.
Soule the same. It is no use for me to try to tell you how the fight was managed, only that I think the Officer in Command should be hung, and I know
when the truth is known it will cashier him.

We lost 40 men wounded, and 10 killed. Not over 250 Indians mostly
women and children, and I think not over 200 were killed, and not over 75
bucks. With proper management they could all have been killed and not lost
over 10 men. After the fight there was a sight I hope I may never see again.
Bucks, women, and children were scalped, fingers cut off to get the rings on
them, and this as much with Officers as men, and one of those Officers a
Major, and a Lt. Col. cut off Ears, of all he came across, a squaw ripped open
and a child taken from her, little children shot, while begging for their lives
and all the indignities shown their bodies that was ever heard of - women
shot while on their knees, with their arms around soldiers a begging for
their lives- things that Indians would be ashamed to do. To give you some
little idea, squaws were known to kill their own children, and then themselves, rather than to have them taken prisoners.

Most of the Indians yielded 4 or 5 scalps. But enough! for I know you
are disgusted already. Black Kettle, White Antelope, War Bonnet, Left
Hand, Little Robe and several other chiefs were killed. Black Kettle said
when he saw us coming, that he was glad, for it was Major Wynkoop coming to make peace. Left Hand stood with his hands folded across his breast,
until he was shot saying, "Soldiers no hurt me - soldiers my friends." One
Eye was killed; was in the employ of Gov't as spy; came into the Post a few
days before, and reported about the Sioux, were going to break out at
Learned, which proved true.

After all the pledges made by Major A- to these Indians and then take
the course he did. I think as comments are necessary from me; only I will
say he has a face for every man he talks. The action taken by Capt. Soule
and myself were under protest. Col. C— was going to have Soule hung for

saying there were all cowardly Sons of B— —s; if Soule did not take it back, but nary take aback with Soule. I told the Col. that I thought it murder to jump them friendly Indians. He says in reply; Damn any man or men who are in sympathy with them. Such men as you and Major Wynkoop better leave the U. S. Service, so you can judge what a nice time we had on the trip. I expect Col. C- and Downing will do all in their power to have Soule, Cossitt and I dismissed. Well, let them work for what they damn please, I ask no favors of them. If you are in Washington, for God's sake, Major, keep Chivington from being a Bri'g Genl. which he expects. I will send you the Denver Papers with this. Excuse this for I have been in much of a hurry.
Very Respectfully,
Your Well Wisher
(signed) Joe A. Cramer

(postscript)
John Smith was taken prisoner and then murdered. One little child months old was thrown in the feed box of a wagon and brought one days march, and there left on the ground to perish. Col. Tappan is after them for all that is out. I am making out a report of all from beginning to end, to send to Gen'l Slough, in hopes that he will have the thing investigated, and if you should see him, please speak to him about it, for fear that he has forgotten me. I shall write him nothing but what can be proven.

Major I am ashamed of this. I have it gloriously mixed up, but in hopes I can explain it all to you before long. I would have given my right arm had you been here, when they arrived. Your family are all well.
(signed) Joe A. Cramer

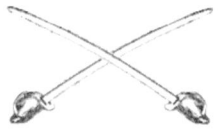

25

SPECIAL ORDERS
HEADDQUARTERS DISTRICT OF UPPER ARKANSAS
Fort Riley, Kansas, December 31, 1864
By order of Colonel James H. Ford:

Major E. W. Wynkoop, First Colorado Cavalry, is hereby relieved from duty at Fort Riley, Kansas, and will proceed without delay to Fort Lyon, Colorado Territory, and upon his arrival at that post will assume command. Major E. W. Wynkoop, upon his arrival at Fort Lyon, will make a thorough investigation of the recent operations against the Indians in that part of the District of Upper Arkansas, and make a detailed report of the same to these headquarters, with as little delay as possible...

Colonel Ford chewed on a soggy cigar as he rummaged through a stack of reports. He looked across his desk at Ned Wynkoop, who stood at attention.

"Sorry, Major," Ford said. "At ease. Have a chair."

"Thank you, sir."

"General Curtis finally made a decision about you."

"Firing squad?" Wynkoop sarcastically said.

"Oh, yeah, that would certainly put an end to this controversy," Ford chuckled. "No, you don't need to turn in your sword just yet. In fact, I'm sending you back to resume command at Lyon, effective immediately."

"Fort Lyon?"

"That's right." He handed the orders to Wynkoop, who quickly read.

"Well, I'll be god damned... sir. I reckon my military incompetence was just a passing fever. What changed the general's mind?"

"Obviously, that smooth tongue of yours," Ford said. "All hell's breaking loose in Washington over this Chivington business. Curtis is wading neck-deep in alligators because of it. You convinced him that you have a better idea of what's been going on down there than anybody, so you're gonna sort it out."

"May I assume General Curtis no longer intends to punish me for the Smoky Hill expedition?"

"Clean slate," Ford said. "He had no problem with the initiative you took, but what you did could have been deemed unmilitary and worthy of a court-martial."

"As I told General Curtis, I accept full responsibility," Wynkoop said. "The decision to go was mine, and mine alone."

"Well, that's all done now, Ned. The larger issue is this business at Sand Creek. You know, despite all indications of Chivington's abuse of power, some people think the Cheyennes had it coming."

"Not *those* Cheyennes, Colonel," Wynkoop said. "I won't belabor the point, just to say that Black Kettle's people were clearly prisoners under our protection. If someone at headquarters had paid better mind to our situation, maybe Chivington could have been stopped."

"Look, Ned, I know you're angry at both Curtis and Blunt, and just between you and me, you may be justified. Just take my advice and don't push. You're lucky you didn't lose more than your command."

"I'm a soldier, sir, not a politician," Wynkoop said. "If General Curtis had considered that and given me the benefit of the doubt before relieving me of my command at Fort Lyon, he might not be in this stew now."

Ford sighed. "In his defense, he's been trying to manage two wars coming at him from opposite directions. Do you really think Chivington would have reacted differently if you had been there?"

"I can't say how *he* would have reacted, but I guarantee I would have tried to stop him. At the very least, the soldiers under my command would not have accompanied him to Sand Creek. In fact, we would have honored our pledge to protect that village. If there were indeed any hostile Indians guilty of depredations there, Colonel Chivington had little success rooting them out. He was too busy slaughtering women and babies."

Ford angrily chewed his cigar as he read a letter to Wynkoop from Captain Soule that detailed the massacre. "Dear lord, this is disgusting," he said. "What kind of mongrel professing to be a human being would do something like this?"

"Chivington," Wynkoop said. "He scrounged up the worst kind of sick murderers to do his bidding. Did you read the letter from Cramer?"

"I did," Ford said. "It turned my stomach. If I didn't know those two like I do, I might not believe it. Soldiers wearing the uniform of the United States Army participated in a wholesale slaughter, disemboweled a pregnant squaw, shot little children begging for mercy – these are serious allegations."

"Soule and Cramer would not make them lightly, sir," Wynkoop said. "They're both highly disciplined officers who've seen their fair share of combat."

"That's what makes this Sand Creek affair so troubling. These charges are coming from loyal soldiers who rode with Chivington at La Glorieta."

"As did I, sir. Permission to speak freely?" Wynkoop asked.

Ford had to laugh. "When have you ever refrained? Go ahead."

"Frankly, sir, I don't think there is anything I could say to persuade your opinion. And, although General Curtis has gone out of his way to avoid me, I believe he would also agree that Colonel Chivington's attack on Sand Creek stinks to high heaven."

"I'm thinking of a place a bit lower than heaven, Major. I have to tell you, I'm hearing things about Chivington that are astounding."

Wynkoop sadly shook his head. "There was a time when I would have ridden into hell with the man. He made a good fight at La Glorieta, but he's never been able to duplicate the feat. While Grant grabs the headlines back east, he's been dwindling away, trying to exert his brand of muscular Christianity on the Indians and failing miserably. I don't know how a man of God – one who so vocally condemns slavery - could stand and watch any soldier under his command commit such inhuman acts."

Ford sighed and angrily crushed his cigar. "Well, whatever happened, there's gonna be shit to pay. You read his report. What do you make of it?"

"Tell me you believe he killed five or six hundred warriors at Sand Creek, and I'll tell you that Jeff Davis will succeed Lincoln as President. I rely entirely on Soule and Cramer's accounts. Cramer said that there were whites in that village – John Smith, Private Louderback. Hell, old One-Eye was paid by Anthony to supply information on Dog Soldier movements in Kansas. Those Indians at Sand Creek posed no threat whatsoever. Chivington knew where he could score a victory for his political career without risking his own neck. He's a murderer, plain and simple."

"What about the days-old white scalps he claims were found?"

"If he found fresh scalps, then where are the fresh white bodies they came from?" Wynkoop asked. "Were there any reports of whites being killed at that time - in that vicinity? I checked, sir. The answer is no."

"I find Captain Soule's refusal to fire interesting," Ford said. "In this letter, Cramer claims he refused as well, but Chivington only mentioned Soule in his report."

"If he reported more than one officer refusing to attack, it might lead to questions he doesn't want to answer," Wynkoop said. "Besides, with Soule, it was personal. Chivington has always trusted him like a son, and if I know Silas like I do, the confrontation they had at Fort Lyon must have been tantamount to supreme betrayal in Chivington's eyes. Soule has a heart of gold, but God help any man who dares rankle him. I've seen Silas whip men twice his size. Those two must have gone at each other like two cats thrown over a clothesline with their tails tied together."

"And the resulting yowls were heard clear back to Washington," Ford said.

"This just doesn't shake out right," Wynkoop said. "Anthony's report specifically said all the command fought well and observed all orders given. Yet, Soule and Cramer both admit they were clearly insubordinate at the fort, and they disobeyed orders under fire at Sand Creek. Then we have Chivington reporting Soule's refusal to obey orders, but he doesn't bring either him or Cramer up on charges. Colonel, I would charge *any* soldier who disobeyed me, unless, of course, I had something to hide."

Ford threw a sigh. "You're closer to the truth than you know, Major."

"What's that?"

"Chivington's enlistment expired last September..."

"What?" Wynkoop was incensed. "You can't be serious!"

"I'm looking right at it, Major. It's a tad difficult to file military charges against an officer in the United States Army when you're technically a civilian."

"Oh, this is rich," Wynkoop growled. "Forgive me for saying it, sir, but does anyone at headquarters have any idea what's been going on in Colorado?"

"Headquarters is far more concerned with affairs east of the Missouri, Ned. I'd say Chivington hasn't mustered out because the army's shorthanded on replacements."

"Shorthanded? Sam Tappan? Jake Downing? Me, for Christ's sake?"

Ford had to laugh. "A malcontent, a lawyer and a renegade crusader? There ain't a one of you on Curtis' short list, Major. I'm sure he figured replacing Chivington with one of you would toss him from the frying pan to the fire."

"Well, that's just dandy, sir. Essentially, we're talking about a civilian and a vigilante militia at the end of its 100-days commission conducting a massacre under sanction of the United States Army. They all go back to civilian life and leave us with five tribes on the warpath!"

Ford considered Wynkoop's argument. "Well, Ned, you've got your work cut out for you."

"I assure you, Colonel, I won't let you down."

"There's a lot of noise coming from Washington. Somebody down at Lyon is leaking information that has everyone squirming, from Curtis and Evans right down to Yours Truly."

"Respectfully, Colonel, Evans and Curtis made their own beds. I have no sympathy for them. They gave Chivington free reign to prosecute a war with an enemy they considered inferior and ignorant. We all got a lot more than we bargained for, and I fear we haven't even begun to suffer the wrath of the Cheyennes for killing Black Kettle."

"Well, here's some more news for your investigation. It appears Chivington's campaign for war hero hit another snag. Black Kettle isn't dead."

Wynkoop stopped short. "Sir?"

"He was spotted by scouts near the Smoky Hill."

"I hope you'll understand, sir, but I'm relieved to hear it. I consider the man my friend."

"In light of what happened, he may not feel the same way about you."

Wynkoop agreed. "I'm sure he thinks I betrayed him."

"So do the Dog Soldiers, Major. In addition to your investigation at Fort Lyon, I suggest you be certain to take all measures to fortify the post."

"Yes, sir."

"The eastern papers are screaming accusations that the army sanctioned a wholesale massacre of innocent women and children at Sand Creek. I suspect Sam Tappan is wielding his pen like a sword, since it's no secret he's been three years waiting in the weeds for a chance to ambush Chivington. I have it on good authority he pricked the right ears, and there's going to be a congressional investigation soon. The army will conduct an inquiry, as well, and that's why we need you to ask questions down at Lyon."

"How far do you want me to take it?"

"As far as it goes, no matter what is revealed. Just do me a favor. When you report back to me, don't write any letters to the Denver newspapers first."

"You don't have to worry about that," Wynkoop said.

"Ned, if we conclusively prove that Chivington knowingly attacked Indians to whom the army pledged its protection, this cannonball is gonna explode right in our face. The Third Cav is mustering out, along with Chivington and Anthony. The whole lot of them just escaped the reach of any military prosecution."

"You can't court-martial Chivington right now?"

"On what grounds? We don't know exactly what happened

down there, and we don't have any evidence yet. It's a sticky ball of grease, and Chivington just slipped away."

"Jesus Christ," Wynkoop said. He angrily threw his hands up. "Who the hell's in charge here?"

"If it's any consolation, I can tell you who isn't. That's why it's imperative that you take testimony from the Lyon soldiers immediately."

"What good will it do?" Wynkoop said. "There's no doubt in my mind that the army will simply accept Chivington's resignation and muster him out to avoid embarrassment. That bastard is going to walk away from this and probably win his next election campaign by a landslide."

"I wouldn't be surprised," Ford said.

Wynkoop boiled with frustration. "I'm sorry, sir, but I don't understand why I'm the only one here who thinks this is bullshit!"

"Oh, don't get me wrong, Major, I agree with you. Maybe what you don't understand is the fact that bullshit always rolls downhill. You're right, Chivington can't be touched by the military, and because he acted in behalf of the army, he is not under the jurisdiction of any civilian court. One thing I do guarantee is that once the public learns about the atrocities committed by Chivington's goons, Congress is going to go for the head of the snake, not the tail. I, for one, have no interest in dying on the cross for old Chiv. I want you to find out exactly what happened at Sand Creek, how many Indians were actually killed, and what happened after the attack."

"You mean, cover our ass, don't you?"

"That's a less-official term for it, yes. If we do prove his guilt, however, I don't think Chivington will escape this thing unscathed. He may never face prosecution, but the court of public opinion will slaughter him. So just do your job, Ned. Get to Lyon and interrogate everyone."

"Yes, sir. I'm particularly interested in what Soule has to say."

"You won't see Captain Soule. He and Cramer were sent to Denver, along with their companies."

"May I ask why?"

"Several reasons. Some of them are due to muster out, but we anticipate a few of them will be called to testify at the military hearing. Tom Moonlight is going to replace Chivington. He has legal experience, and he's sympathetic to the First Regiment. Moonlight is also aware of the threats Chivington made against Soule. He is going to assign Soule to the provost guard."

"Provost?"

"That's right. Soule knows exactly what happened from beginning to end. Since the attack, there's been more than just the accusations leveled at Chivington for how he prosecuted the battle. There was a lot of livestock captured at Sand Creek that hasn't been accounted for. We're hearing stories that Chivington and the boys of the Third Regiment may be conducting a profitable little enterprise on the side. One of Soule's first duties as provost marshal is to make a full accounting of the captured livestock. Plus, the assignment gives Soule certain liberties that might come in handy, should the need to protect himself arise. The Fort Lyon boys will be on hand to look out for him as well."

"Has Soule been threatened again?"

"Rumors are rumors, Ned, but under the circumstances, we're not going to ignore them. A reasonable man might infer Soule's defiance of Chivington as damning evidence against both Chiv and the Third Regiment. We need Soule in Denver, but once the investigation gets its head, that city is going to be a dangerous place for him..."

On January 10, 1865, a bill was passed in Washington by the House of Representatives, directing the Committee on the Conduct of the War to initiate an investigation into the Colorado Third Cavalry's attack on the Cheyenne Indians camped at Sand Creek. The Committee immediately went into action, collecting reports and compiling a list of witnesses to interview...

Hersa Coberly gently stroked Soule's auburn hair. He burrowed deep into her loving arms, watching the soft candlelight throw shadows on the wall. Her left hand found his, and their fingers intertwined.

"I'm broke as a pauper right now, darlin,'" he said, "but just as soon as I throttle the paymaster, I'm gonna put a ring on that finger."

Hersa giggled. "You can put a cigar band on it for all I care. Just get this finger covered up soon, mister."

"You don't like me smoking cigars."

"Well, maybe just one more for old time's sake."

"Dang. You made me quit smoking, drinking. I ain't got any more vices."

"Oh, I can think of a few sins you're still allowed."

"Well, come this spring, you're gonna make an honest man out of me."

"I already did that, but I can't wait to see it on paper. I just wish we could be married at the ranch."

"I know," Soule said. "But it's just too dangerous out there.

Besides, your brother Joe probably wouldn't stand for it. He thinks Chiv was right, and he ain't too happy that I'm not in his corner."

"Joe just can't let go," Hersa said. "The rest of us loved Papa just as much as he did, but killing those Indians at Sand Creek just wasn't enough for him. He says he's not gonna stop until every Indian is dead, but that won't bring Papa back."

Soule pulled her close. "I reckon if they'd killed my dad, I'd feel the same, but Joe didn't walk in me and Ned's boots. What happened out there was nothing short of a walk in hell. I swear, Hersey, sometimes I was afraid I was never gonna see your beautiful eyes again."

"Shh." Hersa put her hand on his mouth. "Don't ever leave me again, Silie. Promise me."

Soule mumbled through her hand. "I pomish."

They laughed and kissed. "Do ya love me?"

"More than a licorice stick," Soule said. "Believe me, that's something."

Hersa smiled. "You've been acting kinda funny since you got here. This is the first time you've been silly all evening."

"Been a lot on my mind..."

"It's what happened down there, isn't it?"

Soule nodded. "I'm sorry I told you so much, but I just can't stop thinking about it. With all the talk about the big hearing, the whole thing's coming back on me again."

"You can talk about it all you want, Silie. Maybe I can help."

"You help by being here, darlin'. I don't know what I'd do without you."

"Tell me what you're thinking," Hersa said.

Soule shook his head with a sigh. "I swear to you, in all my life, I ain't never been ashamed of myself – until I sat there on that ridge and watched those people get butchered."

"There wasn't anything you could do."

"I ain't so sure," Soule said. "Maybe I should have turned my men on those bastards. Maybe if me and Joe had taken a stand-"

"You were outnumbered, Silie."

"That don't matter. Hell, anywhere you go in life, you're outnumbered. I should have tried."

Hersa held Soule tighter. "It's such an awful world. I know many of those Indians are bad. Maybe I ought to hate them like Joe does, but I just feel sad for all of us."

"Same here, darlin', same here. Them Indians live in ancient times, and we live in the present. But once it boils down to human greed and cruelty, there ain't an ounce of difference between us. I should have found a way to stop Chiv."

"Oh, my Silas," Hersa said, "the great emancipator. It's like old John Brown telling you to leave him alone. You want to save the world, but don't you see? Maybe the world just doesn't care to be saved."

Soule gave her a sour look. "What makes you so smart?"

"I'm in love with you, aren't I?"

Soule gave it some consideration. "I reckon you *are* pretty smart."

"I love you, Silas Soule, and I want to spend my life with you."

"Yeah? Well, life ain't long, and it's getting shorter all the time."

"What do you mean?"

"Since I got here, I feel like I got a target on my back. Chiv's pull is strong around these parts, and the boys have heard talk that my life ain't gonna be worth a plugged nickel if I testify against him."

"Don't talk like that. Quit the army, Silie. Let's run away from here. I want to go and meet your family."

"I can't do that now, honey. I'd give anything to ride out of here tonight, but I ain't running from Chiv. I got my duty. Hell, I'm a damned marshal now."

"But there are people who want to kill you!"

"I know. I ain't too happy about it myself, but I got plenty of friends in Denver. If anybody has a mind to kill me, I'm gonna have something to say about it."

"How can you be so calm about this?"

Soule gave her that smile she so loved. "I reckon I'm just the same boy I always been. In fact, sometimes I still feel like I'm seventeen."

"I'm scared, Silie."

"Don't you fret. Once we get this hearing behind us, I'll get out of the army just as soon as I can. We'll get us that farm far away from here, and you and me will turn into old wrinkled folks with a slew of grandkids to tell stories to."

"You promise?"

"You betcha. I know I stand better than Chivington in regard to his great Indian fight. I'll just tell the truth, and everything will be alright..."

26

Major Wynkoop wasted little time when he returned to Fort Lyon in mid January. Although many of the soldiers and officers present at the Sand Creek attack were now in Denver, he immediately called for testimony from those still at the post, among them Private David Louderback, interpreter John Smith, Lieutenant James Cannon, civilian teamster Watson Clark and Indian agent Samuel Colley. On January 15, 1865, Wynkoop wrote a detailed report to Colonel Ford, which included a lengthy description of his council on the Smoky Hill with Black Kettle, and the subsequent peace council at Camp Weld. Wynkoop included the sworn affidavits of the men he interviewed at Fort Lyon, all denouncing Chivington's attack on Sand Creek:

The affidavits, which become a portion of this report, will show more particularly than I can state the full particulars of that massacre. Every one of whom I have spoken to, either officers or soldier, agree in the relation that the most fearful atrocities were committed that ever was heard of. Women and children were killed and scalped, children shot at their mothers' breasts, and all the bodies mutilated in the most horrible manner. Numerous eye-witnesses have described scenes to me coming under the eye of Colonel Chivington of the most disgusting and horrible character. The dead bodies of females profaned in such a manner that the recital is sickening, Colonel J. M. Chivington all the time inciting his troops to these diabolical outrages.

Previous to the slaughter commencing, he addressed his command, arousing in them by his language all their worst passions, urging them on to the work of committing all these atrocities. Knowing himself all the circumstances of these Indians, resting on the assurances of protection from the Government given them by myself and Major Scott J. Anthony, he kept his command in entire ignorance of the same, and when it was suggested that such might be the case, he denied it positively, stating that they were still continuing their depredations, and laid there, threatening the fort.

I beg leave to draw the attention of the colonel commanding to the fact established by the enclosed affidavits that two-thirds or more of that Indian village were women and children, and he is aware whether or not the Indians go to war taking with them their women and children. I desire also to state that Colonel J. M. Chivington is not my superior officer, but is a citizen mustered out of the U. S. service, and also that at the time this inhuman monster committed this unprecedented atrocity he was a citizen by reason of his term of service having expired, he having lost his regulation command some months previous.

Colonel Chivington reports officially that between 500 and 600 Indians were left dead upon the field. I have been informed by Captain Booth, District Inspector, that he visited the field and counted but sixty-nine bodies, and by others who were present that but a few, if any, over that number were killed, and that two-thirds of them were women and children. I beg leave to further state for the information of the colonel commanding that I have talked to every officer in Fort Lyon, and many enlisted men, and that they unanimously agree that all the statements I have made in this report are correct.

In conclusion, allow me to say that from the time I held the consultation with the Indian chiefs on the headwaters of Smoky Hill, up to the date of the massacre by Colonel Chivington, not one single depredation had been committed by the Cheyenne and Arapaho Indians. The settlers of the Arkansas Valley had returned to their ranches from which they had fled, had taken in their crops, and had been resting in perfect security under assurances from myself that they would be in no danger for the present, by that means saving the country from what must inevitably become almost a famine, were they to lose their crops. The lines of communication to the States were opened, and travel across the plains rendered perfectly safe through the Cheyenne and Arapaho country.

Since this horrible massacre by Colonel Chivington, the country presents a scene of desolation; all communication is cut off with the States except by sending large bodies of troops, and already over a hundred whites have fallen as victims to the fearful vengeance of these betrayed Indians. All this country is ruined; there can be no such thing as peace in the future, but by the total annihilation of all the Indians on the plains. I have the most reliable information to the effect that the Cheyennes and Arapahos have allied themselves with the Kiowas, Comanches, and Sioux, and are congregated to the number of five or six thousand on the Smoky Hill.

Let me also draw the attention of the colonel commanding to the fact stated by affidavit that John S. Smith, U. S. interpreter, a soldier and citizen were present in the Indian camp by permission of the commanding officer of this post, another evidence to the fact of these same Indians being regarded as friendly, also that Colonel Chivington states in his official report that he fought from nine hundred to one thousand Indians, and left from five to six hundred dead upon the field - the sworn evidence being that there was but five hundred souls in the village, two-thirds of them being women and children, and that there were but from sixty to seventy killed, the major portion of which were women and children.

It will take many more troops to give security to travelers and settlers in this country, and to make any kind of successful warfare against these Indians. I am at work placing Fort Lyon in a state of defense, having all, both citizens and soldiers, located here, employed upon the works, and expect soon to have them completed, and of such a nature that a comparatively small garrison can hold the fort against any attack by Indians.

Hoping that my report may receive the particular attention of the colonel commanding, I respectfully submit the same.

Your obedient servant,

E. W. WYNKOOP, Major, Commanding First Colorado Vet. Cav. and Fort Lyon

The United States Army, under extreme pressure from Congress and the eastern newspapers, acted quickly after receiving Wynkoop's report. Although Colonel Chivington was officially a civilian and immune to military prosecution, the army nevertheless ordered a special military commission to gather evidence and call witnesses in its own investigation into the Sand Creek affair. In addition to the hearings ordered by the War Department and the House of Representatives, the existing Joint Special Committee of Congress initiated a third inquiry shortly thereafter. The Joint Committee was established before the Sand Creek attack, for the purpose of monitoring the general treatment of all Indian tribes by military and civilian entities. Kansas and Colorado territories were under the supervision of Connecticut Senator Lafayette Foster, President of the Senate, Wisconsin Senator James Doolittle, and Representative Edmund Ross of Kansas.

The three dignitaries would journey to forts Lyon, Larned and Riley, and interview key soldiers and civilians during the Joint Committee's six-month Sand Creek inquiry. They would also take testimony from Governor Evans, Agent Colley and John Smith, who were interviewed in Washington. Foster, Doolittle and Ross were accompanied by General Alex McCook on their trip to Fort Lyon, where Major Wynkoop took them on a tour of the Sand Creek battlefield. The ravaged Cheyenne village was still strewn with decomposing Indian corpses, as the ashen-faced congressional members chillingly examined the bullet-ridden skulls of dead men, women and children. Wynkoop sent them home, confident that the carnage at Sand Creek made an indelible impression on the shell-shocked bureaucrats.

The other two inquiries by the army and Congress would include investigations at the three primary forts and in Washington throughout the winter and spring months. Much to Colonel Chivington's advantage, however, the lion's share of hearings would be held at Denver, where he was surrounded by Third Regiment supporters and the influential arm of Governor Evans' personal propaganda channel, the *Rocky Mountain News*. William Byers provided a constant barrage of criticism against the government inquiries, hailing Chivington and the Third Regiment as heroes that were being unfairly chastised for political purposes. Numerous conspiracy theories were implied as well, including accusations that John Smith and Agent Colley were trying to railroad Chivington in revenge for destroying their trade business with the Indians. Additionally, the *News* falsely reported that the Cheyennes killed at Sand Creek were the Dog Soldiers and Arapaho warriors that committed the summer depredations in Colorado and Kansas...

The military tribunal commenced in Denver on February 1, 1865, and three officers from the Colorado First Regiment were appointed to take testimony: Captain George H. Stilwell, a close personal friend of Chivington, Captain Edward A. Jacobs, believed to be the most impartial of the three, and Lieutenant Colonel Samuel F. Tappan, who upon numerous occasions had butted heads with Chivington in a power struggle over command of the District of Colorado. The three officers were selected because none had participated in the Sand Creek attack. As the highest-ranking officer under Colonel Moonlight, Tappan was appointed President of the Commission. Mindful that he might be walking into a bear trap, Chivington hired the services of Major Jacob Downing and Denver lawyer, Moses Hallett, to provide legal counsel...

A large crowd convened in the cold winter air outside the *Rocky Mountain News* office. Colonel Chivington and Major Downing held court.

"Give 'em hell, Chiv!" an onlooker yelled.

"The savages are already in hell," Chivington laughed. "Major Downing and I shall escort the rest of them directly, I assure you!"

The crowd cheered.

"Colonel, are you concerned that this military hearing might result in a court-martial?" William Byers asked.

"Of course not!" Chivington boasted. "Besides, I'm a civilian just like the rest of you. They have no power to court-martial me! I fully expect, however, that once the particulars of my glorious victory at Sand Creek are revealed, they will turn their sights on that traitor Captain Soule and the other yellowbellied cowards who've conspired against me!"

"But the focus of this military investigation is on *you*, Chiv," Byers said.

"Have I been arrested and charged with improprieties? No! This is simply an investigation to prove the idiots in the eastern press wrong. Those namby-pamby Indian sympathizers have no business interfering with our righteous cause!"

"What about the congressional investigations?" Byers said.

"Oh, this is not about Sand Creek," Chivington chuckled. "That's simply a feeble plan by partisan schemers who think they can undermine Governor Evans and myself. Those so-called 'high officials' are looking for Republican scalps, plain and simple."

"There's talk that they've already made their minds up to condemn you."

"So be it!" Chivington said. "That doesn't bother me. If they desire to become the servile dogs of brutal savages, that's their business. I think differently, and I acted accordingly!"

Another boisterous cheer arose.

"All that's fine, Chiv," Byers said, "but I see that you've retained a lawyer."

Chivington threw his arm around Downing. "Mrs. Chivington did not raise any imbeciles, gentlemen! If you must swim with barracudas, then it's best to ride the back of a sturdy shark. I've employed Major Downing because he is a brilliant lawyer, and he rode with me at the battle of Sand Creek. He knows what happened down there!"

"Major Downing," Byers said. "What do you make of these congressional inquiries?"

"It's an attempted lynching by bureaucrats who couldn't muster enough courage to carry water for Colonel Chivington. They're simply trying to line their political pockets at Chiv's expense, but they will fail, I promise you. As for the military commission, which is the only legitimate body qualified to investigate the Sand Creek battle, Colonel Chivington's deposition along with eyewitness testimony will exonerate both the colonel and the brave men who gallantly sent those redskin devils back to the stone-age where they belong."

"Why do you think Washington has suddenly taken an interest in our Indian problem, when they ignored it all summer?" Byers asked.

"If they weren't so preoccupied with destroying their political enemies," Downing said, "they would, to a man, agree that Indians are an obstacle to civilization and should be exterminated."

A crusty miner pushed through. "Hey, Chiv! I just joined up! The recruiter's office got more new volunteers than it can handle!"

"Excellent!" Chivington said. "Put me down for $500! You can use it for killing Indians and any heathen who sympathizes with them!"

Byers hollered over the cheering crowd. "So, Colonel, do you agree with Downing that Congress is simply trying to grab your glory?"

"Pure jealousy," Chivington said. "They're embarrassed. A brave company of simple volunteers managed to rid the country of those murdering savages, while they sat on their hands doing nothing!..."

On February 2, as the military tribunal was getting underway in Denver, six hundred Dog Soldiers swallowed Julesburg, Colorado whole, sacking the stage station, murdering everyone in sight, and burning the entire town to the ground...

27

HEADQUARTERS DISTRICT OF COLORADO
Colonel Thomas Moonlight, Commanding
TO:
Lieutenant Colonel S. F. TAPPAN,
President of Military Commission
SIR:

The commission, of which you are president, convened by Special Orders No. 23, current series, from these headquarters, in obedience to instructions from department headquarters, is convened for the purpose of investigating all matters connected with the action between Colonel Chivington and the Indians, known as the Sand Creek fight, to ascertain, as far as possible, who are the aggressors, whether the campaign was conducted by Colonel Chivington according to the recognized rules of civilized warfare, and whether based upon the law of equity from the commencement of Indian hostilities to the present time.

It is also important to understand whether the Indians were under the protection of the government, and by what authority, or through what influence, they were induced to place themselves under that protection; whether Colonel Chivington was knowing to this fact; and whether, or not, the campaign was forced upon the Indians by the whites, knowing their helpless condition; and whether the Indians were in a state of open hostility and prepared to resist any and all of the United States troops. Whether any prisoners were taken by Colonel Chivington's command, and the disposition made by the same. If the proper steps were taken by the colonel to prevent unnatural outrages by his command, and punish the transgressors, if such there were.

A special point in your investigation should be as to the amount, kind, and quality of property captured by Colonel Chivington and command; the disposition made of that property, and the steps taken by the colonel to protect the government and insure justice to all parties, and whether he gave this matter any special attention. Also, regarding the treatment of government property, such as horses and mules in the service, during the campaign, and until relieved from duty.

This commission is not intended for the trial of any person, but simply to investigate and accumulate facts called for by the government, to fix the responsibility, if any, and to insure justice to all parties. Colonel Chivington, under these circumstances, has not the right of challenge, and I have been careful to appoint a commission composed of officers not engaged in the operations they are called upon to investigate.

The commission will be sworn in presence of Colonel Chivington, under the 93d article of war, and he will be permitted to have such legal assistance as the commission may deem proper in the premises. The sessions may be public or private, as the members deem prudent and right. The commission has power to call for witnesses, and compel attendance. These instructions will be appended to the proceedings, and the whole forwarded through these headquarters.

I have been thus explicit, that the commission may have full sweep, and act without embarrassment...

The proceedings began with a lengthy objection by Colonel Chivington:

"I would most respectfully request the commission to delay their organization until I can prepare objections to their organization of the court as a commission, and to object to one of the members, on the grounds of prejudice open and avowed, as I have only this minute heard what the instructions of the colonel commanding were, and what the court intended to investigate."

Chivington wasn't finished.

"I would most respectfully request that the proceedings of this commission be public, and the daily or other papers be allowed, if they desire, to have reporters present..."

The Commission spent the next fifteen days arguing over Chivington and Downing's two objections. Chivington vehemently protested Colonel Tappan's appointment as President of the Commission, presenting two sworn affidavits from Third Regiment officers that accused Tappan of leading a conspiracy against Chivington.

Said Chivington, "I would most respectfully object to Lieutenant Colonel Tappan being a member of the commission, for the following reasons:

"First, Lieutenant Colonel Tappan is, and for a long time past has been, my open and avowed enemy.

"Second, Lieutenant Colonel Tappan has repeatedly expressed himself very much prejudiced against the killing of the Indians near Fort Lyon, Colorado Territory, commonly known as the battle of Sand Creek, and has said that it was a disgrace to every officer connected with it, and that he would make it appear so in the end.

"Third, I believe, from a full knowledge of his character, that he cannot divest himself of his prejudices sufficiently to render an impartial verdict, and is, therefore, not such a judge as the law contemplates when it directs that all men shall be tried by an impartial tribunal..."

Chivington presented two affidavits, one by himself, and the other by his former Adjutant, Captain Joseph Maynard, who rode with Chivington and the Third Regiment to Sand Creek. The affidavits declared that Tappan had openly criticized Chivington's attack on the Cheyennes and Arapahos, calling it a monumental blunder that would cost thousands of lives, and the government "a great deal of treasure." Chivington claimed that Tappan "is, and for a long time past has been, an avowed enemy of the said John M. Chivington; that the said Tappan has repeatedly stated that the Sand Creek affair was a disgrace to every officer connected with it; and upon one occasion said Lieutenant Colonel Tappan stated that he would make it appear so in the end."

Although the Commission denied the first motion to remove Tappan, Chivington and Downing relentlessly submitted new objections over the next two weeks, each time adding items for the Commission to consider:

John M. Chivington, late colonel first cavalry, Colorado, most respectfully objects that this commission has not power and authority to inquire concerning his official acts as specified in the order concerning this commission, for the following reasons:

1. That the subject matter which this commission is directed to investigate should be submitted to a court of inquiry, and not to a military commission.

2. That this court, although denominated a military commission, has been organized as a court of inquiry, using the forms prescribed for the organization of such courts.

3. That the instructions accompanying the order convening this commission clearly show that the duties of a court of inquiry are imposed upon this commission.

4. That the colonel commanding this district has no authority to convene a court of inquiry, or any tribunal which shall perform the duties of a court of inquiry, except by order of the President, or request of the officer accused.

5. That there are no charges or specifications filed with the commission, and that the order and instructions are couched in such general language that they do not apprise him of the nature of the accusations against him.

6. According to the provisions of General Orders, dated Washington,

D.C., 1864, the colonel commanding the district of Colorado, the number of troops in the district and under his command, are not sufficient to authorize the said colonel commanding to convene a military commission...

On February 15, the Commission denied all of Chivington's motions, including his request to bring in William Byers for the purpose of reporting the hearings in the *Rocky Mountain News:*

...the commission, not being able to determine who may be required as witnesses during this investigation, and believing that the exigencies of the public service do not demand, and that no one can be benefited by such publicity, decides that until further orders the sessions of the commission shall be private...

To Chivington's objections regarding the Commission's legal jurisdiction in the matter, a lengthy response was submitted with the following conclusion:

No one is arraigned before us on trial, no charges alleged and placed in possession of the commission; but the said commission is merely called upon to receive and methodize information only, and in this case to give no opinion on the same, as we are not required to make a report, save that of submitting the evidence in accordance with instructions, as the commission is instructed to collect evidence, information, and facts only...

To Chivington's charge of personal prejudice on the part of Colonel Tappan and his inability to impartially conduct the hearings, Tappan provided the following response:

In reply to objections of J. M. Chivington to my being a member of this commission, I desire to state, and have this statement made a part of the record:

The colonel misunderstood me to have said that, "I would make it appear so in the end," referring to my statement that the affair at Sand Creek was a disgrace to the officers connected with it. I said "it would appear so," not having any desire or expectation that I should ever be called upon to prosecute the matter, but confident government would take action on the subject, and the facts elicited would make it appear disgraceful.

The statement of Captain Maynard is substantially correct. A few days after the affair at Sand Creek I remarked to Captain Maynard that from what I could hear, the attack on the Indians at Sand Creek was the greatest military blunder of the age, and fatal in its consequences.

As to my alleged prejudice and alleged personal enmity, even if true, I

should not consider them at all influencing me in performing the duties
assigned me in this commission, especially after taking the oath required as
a member...

The motion to remove Tappan from the Commission was
denied. With all attempts by Chivington and Downing to stop the
military commission in its tracks exhausted, the hearing proceeded
on February 15.

The Commission called its first witness, Captain Silas S. Soule...

Colonel Tappan opened the questioning. "Your full name, age,
and rank in the army?"

"Silas S. Soule; twenty-six years of age; Captain, Company D,
Veteran Battalion First Colorado Cavalry, and Assistant Provost
Marshal General, District of Colorado."

"How long have you been an officer in the First Regiment
Colorado volunteers?"

"Since December 11, 1861..."

The commissioners asked Soule a series of questions regarding
Major Wynkoop's expedition to the Smoky Hill River in September.
Soule gave a full accounting of the meeting with Black Kettle and
the other chiefs, and their subsequent council at Camp Weld in
Denver. Soule testified that the chiefs expressed a sincere desire to
cease hostilities, and that Chivington and Governor Evans clearly
instructed them to bring in all Indians who wished to surrender to
Major Wynkoop.

"We returned with the chiefs to Fort Lyon," Soule continued.
"Major Wynkoop told them to bring in the Indians of their tribe
who were anxious for peace to Fort Lyon, and camp near the post,
and he would immediately send to General Curtis and see if peace
could not be made. He immediately sent Lieutenant Denison to
General Curtis. The Indians came in and complied with Wynkoop's
orders, and camped near the post."

"Did the Indians, in council, manifest a desire for peace, and a
willingness to comply with the conditions of Colonel Chivington?"
Tappan asked.

"They did."

"How many Indians came into the fort, and what tribes were
they?"

"There were one hundred and six lodges came into the post.
Arapahos and Cheyennes - mostly Arapahos."

"Were all the chiefs with them, those who had been to Denver?"

"Black Kettle, their Principal Chief, and Bull Bear went out to their tribes to bring in more Cheyennes, and brought in a number of Cheyenne families."

"State how long the Indians remained at Fort Lyon, and what was done concerning them."

"I should think that they remained at the post about two weeks, until Major Anthony came from Denver and relieved Major Wynkoop from command at Fort Lyon. Major Anthony told the Indians that they must give up their arms, and horses and mules, which belonged to the government or to the whites. This he told to Little Raven, then in command of the village near the post. Little Raven gave up three rifles, one pistol, and I think about sixty bows and quivers; nine horses and mules."

"Was the same demand made upon Black Kettle?"

"No; it was not made to my knowledge."

"What was the understanding with the Indians while in and about Fort Lyon?"

"That they were to be protected by the troops there until the messenger returned from General Curtis."

"Did a messenger arrive at the fort from General Curtis prior to the first of December, 1864?"

"There was not."

"Were you at Fort Lyon on or about the 27th of November? If so, what happened there on that day?"

Soule described his patrol's discovery of Chivington's troops on the trail to Fort Lyon. Tappan then asked if Chivington made inquiries about any Cheyennes or Arapahos still remaining at Fort Lyon.

"I said that there were some Indians camped below the fort," Soule answered, "but they were not dangerous; that they were waiting to hear from General Curtis. They were considered as prisoners; someone made answer that they wouldn't be prisoners after they got there."

"Did Colonel Chivington say anything to the Indians while in council near Denver? If so, what did he say?"

"Said his business was not to talk, but to fight; that he was a man of few words. He said but little. He gave them to understand that he was the man, and not Governor Evans, for them to talk to; that he left the matter with Major Wynkoop; that is about all I recollect of it."

"State what was done after the command of Colonel Chivington reached Fort Lyon."

"There was a guard stationed around the post, before the regiment arrived there - before I got in - with orders to allow no person to pass out. Major Anthony ordered myself and company to join the colonel's command with three days' cooked rations, and twenty uncooked. I joined Colonel Chivington's command that evening about 8 o'clock, in company with companies G and K, under Major Anthony. I immediately marched about north, marched all night, arrived at the village of Cheyennes and Arapahos just before sunrise. Major Anthony's battalion was ordered by Colonel Chivington to move across below the Indian camp to cut off a herd of ponies.

"Lieutenant Wilson, with a battalion of two or three companies, crossed the creek ahead of us and opened fire on the village. Major Anthony then moved our battalion to within about one hundred yards of the lodges and ordered us to open fire; some firing done, when the battery came up in our rear with the Third Regiment and prepared for action. Major Anthony ordered my company, which was directly in line of fire of the battery, to move down into the creek, with orders to move up the creek and for the purpose of killing Indians, which were under the banks.

"Before I got into the creek there were troops upon both sides firing across. It was unsafe for me to take my command up the creek, so I crossed over to the other side and moved up the creek. The battery and the first and third regiments kept up firing until all the Indians were killed they could get at; until about 2 o'clock. About 3 o'clock, I received orders from Major Anthony to accompany him with my company to escort a supply train on their way from Fort Lyon. I was not back to the battleground again that day. Met Colonel Chivington's command returning the next day; they went into camp with us, and the next day we marched to the mouth of Sand Creek, about eighteen miles from Fort Lyon. We started out that same night, and marched all night on the Santa Fe road, toward the States. We laid over the next day in camp; Colonel Chivington ordered me on a scout with twenty-odd men; I saw nothing more of his command until two days after, I think. I came across their camp, about eighty miles below Fort Lyon. We laid in camp, I believe, one day, and moved back in company with their command to Fort Lyon."

"Have you been at Sand Creek since; if so, what did you see there, and who went with you?"

"I went to Sand Creek on the last of December with about thirty men, accompanied by Captain Booth, Inspecting Officer and Chief of Cavalry, District of the Upper Arkansas. I saw sixty-nine dead Indians and about one hundred live dogs, and two live ponies and a few dead ones."

"Captain Soule, how long have you been Provost Marshal of the district?"

"Since about the 20th of January."

"How many horses, ponies, and mules have you taken for the government from private persons?"

"I don't know exactly. The guards have brought in a good many, and were turned in to the quartermaster."

"Do you know what became of the horses furnished the Third Regiment by the government, and the stock captured at Sand Creek by Colonel Chivington's command?"

"I do not; except I saw bills of sale of some signed by Captain Johnson, Third Regiment."

"What was the form of those bills of sale, and how signed, and to whom were they given?"

"I don't remember the form; I have one at the office, I think, given to a man on West Plum Creek."

"Do you know of any ponies that were captured at Sand Creek being driven north of Denver, fifty or a hundred miles, and left upon the ranch of Mason & Maynard, by Captain Johnson?"

"I have seen a note from Mr. Mason, stating that he, Mason, had sent a herd - that they were on their way to Denver."

Chivington stood. "I object to the answer on the ground that it is not responsive to the question and irrelevant to the subject matter of inquiry, and not evidence that the court should receive, being hearsay."

The commissioners conferred for a moment, and then Tappan spoke. "The Commission will sustain Colonel Chivington's objection. Captain Soule, have you any information in your possession as Provost Marshal that a herd of stock was left on Mr. Mason's ranch by Captain Johnson, and that it is there now?"

"I have information that a herd of stock was left there or sent there by Captain Johnson."

"I object to the question and answer because it does not adduce facts within the knowledge of the witness!" Chivington said.

"Let's move on," Stilwell said.

"Very well," Tappan said. "Captain Soule, at what time on the 28th of November did Colonel Chivington leave Fort Lyon, how far did he march to reach the Indian camp on Sand Creek, and what was his order of march?"

"He left camp about 8 o'clock in the evening, and arrived at the Indian camp between daylight and sunrise; distance about forty-five miles; marched in column of fours. Major Anthony's battalion I think was on the right. Lieutenant Wilson's battalion was in the rear of us, as near as I can recollect, between Anthony's battalion and the Third Regiment."

"Did you know before leaving Fort Lyon to join Colonel Chivington's command, that he was going to attack Black Kettle's band of Indians?"

"I heard so before the order was given, from Lieutenant Cramer."

"Did you protest to your commanding officer against attacking those Indians?"

"I did."

"Who was your commanding officer?"

"Major Anthony."

"Did you inform Major Anthony of the relations existing with Black Kettle's Indians?"

"I did. He knew the relations. I frequently talked to him about it."

"What answer did Major Anthony make to your protest?"

"He told me that we were going on the Smoky Hill to fight the hostile Indians. He also said that he was in for killing all Indians, and that he had been only acting friendly with them until he could get a force large enough to go out and kill all of them."

"On arriving near the camp of Black Kettle, what was the order of attack?"

"We went on a gallop in column of fours, for about two miles. Lieutenant Wilson's battalion went ahead, crossed Sand Creek, and opened the attack on the lower end of camp. Major Anthony's battalion took nearly the same as Wilson's and opened fire to the left, before we got to Wilson's battalion. The battery opened fire in rear of Anthony's battalion; they prepared for action in rear of Anthony's battalion, and moved forward before firing to about where Anthony's battalion had been. After that, I could see no order to the battle. The command was scattered and every man firing on his own hook on both sides of the creek."

"Did Lieutenant Wilson's battalion approach the camp in line?"

"They were in line when they opened fire."

"At the time Lieutenant Wilson's battalion opened fire, was Major Anthony's battalion in line? If so, from what point of the compass did he face the camp?"

"We were not in line when Wilson commenced firing, but were in line soon after, and opened fire from the south or southeast."

"At any time during the fight was a portion of Colonel Chivington's command under the fire of another portion?"

"They were."

"State how it was."

"The troops were on both banks of the creek firing across at

Indians under both banks, and if they over-shot they were liable to hit our own men."

"Did your squadron become separated from Major Anthony's battalion during the fight? If so, how did it happen?"

"It did when he ordered me into the creek. I kept my squadron together, and crossed over to the opposite bank, and followed up the creek one or two miles. I didn't see the balance of the battalion together till after the fight. I saw a number of Anthony's battalion, but not together."

"At the time of the attack, were there any white men in the Indian camp? If so, who were they?"

"John Smith, Indian interpreter, Fort Lyon; David H. Louderback, Private Company G, First Cavalry of Colorado, and a driver of Major Colley's; I don't think of his name."

"How came they there, and how did they escape?"

"They went out by permission of Major Anthony to do some trading with the Indians. It is a hard matter to tell how they did escape. Louderback escaped toward the command with some cloth or handkerchief on a stick. I would not swear it was white, but thought it was. I did not see how the others escaped. John Smith attempted to come to Anthony's battalion, but the fire was so hot he went back into a lodge."

"Did any of Colonel Chivington's command fire upon John Smith?"

"I think they did. I think they were fired on by Anthony's battalion and Wilson's."

"Did any of the Indians advance towards Colonel Chivington's command, making signs that they were friends?"

"I saw them advance towards the line, some of them holding their hands up."

"Was any demand made upon the Indians prior to the attack, and any attention paid to their signs that they were friends?"

"Not to my knowledge."

"Were the women and children shot while attempting to escape by Colonel Chivington's command?"

"They were."

"Were the women and children followed while attempting to escape, shot down and scalped, and otherwise mutilated, by any of Colonel Chivington's command?"

"They were."

"Were any efforts made by the commanding officers, Colonels Chivington, Shoup, and Major Anthony, to prevent these mutila-tions?"

"Not that I know of."

"Did you witness any scalping and otherwise mutilating of the dead during and after the engagement on Sand Creek?"

"I did."

"Did you see any officer engage in this business of scalping and mutilating the dead?"

"I cannot say that I did."

"Were any prisoners taken by Colonel Chivington's command? If so, what was done with them?"

"There were three squaws taken, the son of Colonel Bent, John Smith's son, and two children with the squaws. Smith's son was killed in camp. I took Bent's son with me and sent him to Fort Lyon. The squaws went to Fort Lyon at the time the command went back from Sand Creek. There were two other prisoners besides those - two children. They were kept by the Third Regiment. They are now in the mountains."

"Are you acquainted with the circumstances of Jack Smith's death?"

"Not of my own knowledge."

"On your second visit to Sand Creek, did you find that the dead had been scalped and otherwise mutilated?"

"I did."

"All of them - men, women, and children?"

"All, with the exception of Jack Smith and one squaw that was burnt in a lodge. I could not tell whether she was scalped or not."

"Did you discover any indications of rifle pits or earthworks that had been thrown up by the Indians prior to the attack on the 29th of November?"

"I didn't then see any that were thrown up by the Indians at that time. I saw holes under the banks in the sand that I think were dug the day of the fight."

"What was the object of the scout upon which you were sent with twenty-odd men?"

"To see if there was a camp of Indians on the Aubrey road about fifty miles south of the river, and to see if I could discover Indians anywhere south of the Arkansas River."

"Had the Indians committed any depredations in the vicinity of Fort Lyon, and on the road to Larned, during the three months prior to the 29th of November?"

"Not to my knowledge."

"Do you know what became of the stock and other property taken from the Indians on Sand Creek?"

"I know some of the stock and other property taken there is in the hands of persons that took it; members of the Third Regiment and First Regiment also."

"State who has the property, and describe it."

"I know of probably two hundred who have or had some of the property in their possession; nearly every man in the command had some. Lieutenant Antoby, Third Regiment, had a lot of stock. He had a number of ponies in his possession. Hank Lathrop, of the Third. He sold one pony, which he had in his possession on the way up. Lieutenant Hardin's wife had one pony given her by one of the Third Regiment. I think it was given by Lieutenant Antoby. Lieutenant Baldwin, of the Independent Battery, had some ponies from there. Captain Evans, Eleventh Ohio Cavalry, of Camp Collins, took five ponies from Mason's ranch, on Cache La Poudre. Major Anthony has trophies. Lieutenant Cannon, of the first New Mexico Volunteers, has got some Indian clothing. Major Anthony has, or had when I left there, an Indian shield, squaw's dress, and some other property of little value. I don't remember the articles. It's hard to enumerate these things. I know of a good many soldiers who have property of this kind. I have taken, as Provost Marshal, considerable of this stock, and turned it in to the quartermaster..."

The Commission concluded its questioning of Captain Soule at the end of the second day of his testimony. Although the general public and the press were barred from the proceedings, the entire city of Denver was aware of every word Soule had spoken, courtesy of unnamed sources. Soule's testimony severely indicted Chivington and the Third Regiment, implicating many in complicity with everything from war crimes to horse theft. Additionally, the commissioners never raised the issue of Soule's refusal to fire on the village. The question clearly presented a dangerous precedent for both sides. From the army's standpoint, a captain defying orders in battle might open the question of Chivington's lack of military authority, which, known to insiders, did not even exist due to the expiration of his commission two months before his expedition to Sand Creek. Chivington could not question Soule's defiance for the same reason, and because it might open the door to Lieutenant Cramer's letter written to Wynkoop after the attack, which claimed he also held his men back. Chivington might be able to accuse one officer of insubordination, but the defiance of two officers commanding companies independent of one another would clearly imply that Chivington's authority was questionable.

In the middle, Soule systematically cut both sides to ribbons with his frank and detailed testimony. Anger boiled over Denver, and Chivington indignantly aroused the ire of his supporters by accusing Soule of smearing the dignity and honor of the entire United States Army. He relished his opportunity to cross-examine Soule, which commenced the next day...

Chivington stood and wandered the council room, glaring at Captain Soule. "In what military district was Fort Lyon, and the place where the battle of Sand Creek occurred, at the time said battle took place?" he asked.

"District of the Upper Arkansas," Soule said.

"State, if you know, who had command of that district?"

"I think the district was in command of Major B. F. Henning, Third Wisconsin Cavalry."

"Do you know whether Major Wynkoop was ordered or directed by the commander of the district of Upper Arkansas, or any superior officer, to go out upon the expedition at the Smoky Hill River?"

"I don't know that he had any orders."

"State, if you know, whether Major Wynkoop was ordered to go out upon that expedition, or to treat with the Indians, by the Governor of Colorado, or the Commander of the District of Colorado."

"Not to my knowledge."

"Did or did not the Indians manifest any hostility towards Major Wynkoop's command upon that expedition?"

"They did when we met them. They met us in line of battle."

"What acts of hostility did the Indians show towards Major Wynkoop's command?"

"They were in line of battle; we were the same. They asked Major Wynkoop what he came there for, and he answered that we came there to talk. They asked Major Wynkoop why we came there with soldiers and cannon, in form of battle, if Major Wynkoop's intentions were peaceable. Major told them that he came prepared to defend himself in case of any treachery. They surrounded us, and marched about two miles, encircling our flanks and rear until we got to their camp. We met them two or three miles from their camp. While we were in, they were saucy. There were some cases of them putting their hands in soldiers' pockets to get tobacco.

"After we were in camp, they closed around us as though they meant to gobble us up. We expected an attack, until one of their chiefs, who went out with us from Fort Lyon, told the Indians that he had promised us protection, and if they fired on us, or attempted to kill us, he would join the whites and fight against them. One-Eye made a speech to them, and Black Kettle and One-Eye ordered us to leave and go a day or two's march nearer Fort Lyon, and go in camp and wait for them to bring in the white prisoners. During the council, Lieutenant Hardin, of the First, was officer of the day. He came in to the camp and complained to the major that the Indians were crowding in on him, and he could not keep them out. I think he said they had possession of the cannon, and were sitting on them. Then Major Wynkoop told the chiefs in council that they must keep their men out of camp, and One-Eye and others made speeches to the Indians. The Indians then left our camp."

"How far from the place where the council was held did Major Wynkoop's command march towards Fort Lyon on the day after the council?"

"On the day of the council we marched back about eight miles. The day after the council, we laid in camp, and the day after that we marched about twenty miles."

"Did the Indians commit any acts of hostility against the whites in the vicinity of Fort Lyon prior to the time when Major Wynkoop's expedition left there?"

"They had. They killed two men about two miles from the post. I don't remember the exact time, but I think about two weeks before Wynkoop's expedition went out. These men were on their way from Point of Rocks to Fort Lyon."

"Was there any whiskey, or other intoxicating beverages, used by the men or officers of Major Wynkoop's command on the day on which the council with the Indians was held?"

"I think there was. I saw some."

"State if you know whether any of the men or officers of Major Wynkoop's command were intoxicated at the time the council with the Indians was held."

"I will raise an objection here," Colonel Tappan said, "for this is not pertinent to the subject matter of this investigation. Some men in difficult situations become very much excited, and it would be unjust to accuse them of being intoxicated. The action of the officers on that occasion is a proper subject of investigation; but opinion of witnesses as to the impulses or influences under which they acted determines nothing."

Jacobs and Stilwell agreed, and the objection was sustained.

Chivington angrily continued. "Captain Soule, state, if you know, whether Major Wynkoop and other officers of his expedition acted as men, having full control of their reasoning faculties at the time the council with the Indians took place."

"I think they all did, except Lieutenant Hardin, who was excited."

"State if you know, whether the Indians of whom you have spoken in your direct examination, in council or elsewhere, stated by what Indians the captives of whom you have spoken were captured."

"They spoke of them as being captured by the Cheyennes."

"Did the Indians of whom you have spoken state how many white prisoners they then had in their possession?"

"They said they had seven."

"Did they or did they not promise to deliver to Major Wynkoop all the white captives they then had in their possession?"

"They promised to give them all up as soon as they could get them. They were sold in different tribes."

"State whether they did deliver all the white captives that they admitted were in their possession, and how many they delivered in accordance with their promise."

"They delivered four."

"Did the Indians, in council or elsewhere, state when and where they had captured the white prisoners of whom you have spoken?"

"I don't know as the Indians did."

"Did the white captives state where and when they were captured and by whom? If so, what statement did they make respecting the time when, place where, and Indians by whom they were captured?"

"They stated they were captured sometime in August, on the Little Blue River, by Cheyennes."

"Did or did not the Indians state that they had captured Mrs. Snyder a few miles below Booneville?"

"I believe they did."

"Did, or did not Major Wynkoop represent to the Indians in council that any person had power to make peace with them on behalf of the government? And if so, what statement did he make?"

"He told them that no one but the governor had the right; that he could not make peace with them."

"State, if you know, whether orders or directions were received by Colonel Chivington from Major General Curtis, commanding department of Kansas, at the time or before the council at Camp Weld was held, in relation to treating with the Indians. If so, state if you know what those orders or directions were."

"I don't know."

"Did or did not the Indians in council at Camp Weld, or elsewhere, represent that they had power to act for the Arapaho and Cheyenne tribes?"

"They did, I think."

"After Major Wynkoop's return to Fort Lyon from the Camp Weld council, did or did not the Indians represent that they would bring in the *entire* Arapaho and Cheyenne tribes to Fort Lyon?"

"They would if they could. They would bring in all who would comply with the orders of Major Wynkoop."

"Was there anything said by Major Wynkoop to the Indians after the Camp Weld council, as to furnishing provisions to those Indians who should come in and camp near Fort Lyon?"

"He furnished them provisions, but I did not hear him tell them he would furnish provisions."

"State as nearly as you can the quantity of provisions furnished by Major Wynkoop to the Indians."

"He furnished prisoners' allowance for ten days, I think, for five hundred Indians."

"At the time these provisions were furnished, had any communication been received by Major Wynkoop in reply to that sent with Lieutenant Dennison to General Curtis?"

"There had not."

"State, if you know, the number of Indians that came in and camped near Fort Lyon, in obedience to Major Wynkoop's orders."

"There were about one hundred and twenty lodges, or about six hundred Indians."

"When did Major Anthony assume command at Fort Lyon?"

"I don't remember the date; I should think about the first of November, 1864."

"Did or did not Major Anthony order or direct the Indians to remove from Fort Lyon, soon after he assumed command?"

"He directed or advised them to move out on Sand Creek. He could not furnish them provisions, and wanted them to remove where they could kill buffalo."

"State the number of Indians encamped near Fort Lyon, at the time Major Anthony required them to deliver up their arms, and the horses and mules belonging to the whites."

"I should think there were about six hundred Indians."

Where were Black Kettle and Bull Bear at the time Major Anthony required the Indians to deliver up their arms?"

"Out after the Cheyennes."

"Did Black Kettle and Bull Bear, or either of them, subsequently bring in other Indians?"

"They did."

"How many Indians did they bring in after that time?"

"I don't know; their camp was on Sand Creek. They were not allowed to come to the post with their village."

Were any steps taken by Major Anthony to secure all the arms the Indians had, other than the mere request that they should deliver them up?"

"There were steps taken to get all the arms from the band, besides the mere request."

"What steps were taken, as stated in your last answer?"

"He ordered me to count all the Indians in the village, and to take all arms that could be found."

"State, if you know, whether the arms received from the Indians were ever returned to them; if so, when and by whom?"

"They were returned by me, by Major Anthony's order, about the middle of November, 1864, I think."

"Did all the Indians of the Arapaho and Cheyenne tribes come in and camp near Fort Lyon, in compliance with Major Wynkoop's order?"

"They did not *all* come in. None of the Dog Soldiers came in, I think, and not all of the fighting men of the Arapahos. About forty or fifty, I should think, came in. They are not organized as their soldiers."

"Was there anything said in the council at Camp Weld about furnishing provisions to those Indians that should come in and camp near Fort Lyon?"

"There was something said, but I don't remember what it was."

"Were the squaws and children of the Arapaho and Cheyenne warriors among those Indians that came in and camped near Fort Lyon?"

"I don't know; I don't think the squaws came in without their warriors."

"What proportion of the Arapaho and Cheyenne Indians came in and camped near Fort Lyon?"

"I don't know; I don't know their strength; I think nearly all of the Arapahos in that section of the country."

Major Downing took the floor as Chivington sat down and stared at Soule. "Captain Soule, state your means of knowledge as to the understanding between the Indians and the officers at Fort Lyon, as to the protection to be furnished said Indians."

"I heard Major Wynkoop tell the chiefs that he would protect them until the messenger returned from General Curtis. Major Anthony and all the officers at the post signed a document to General Curtis, endorsing Wynkoop's action."

"State, if you know, whether Lieutenant Dennison, bearer of dispatches from Major Wynkoop, ever returned with orders from the latter officer."

"He returned after Major Wynkoop left, but I do not know whether he brought orders or not."

"How long after Lieutenant Dennison was sent as messenger to General Curtis, did Major Wynkoop remain in command at Fort Lyon?"

"I think about two weeks."

"By whom was Major Wynkoop relieved of the command at Fort Lyon, and by whose order was he relieved?"

"He was relieved by Major Anthony, by the order of General Curtis."

"At what time did the Indians remove from the immediate vicinity of Fort Lyon?"

"Shortly after Major Anthony's arrival. I should think it was about the middle of November."

"Who, if anyone, was present at the conversation held by you with Colonel Chivington, when you met him with the command above Fort Lyon?"

"I don't remember certain who they were. There were a number present. I think some of the soldiers of my command heard the conversation."

"Did Colonel Chivington in that conversation state to you the object of his expedition?"

"He did not, I think."

"State, if you know, whether any officer at Fort Lyon objected to joining Colonel Chivington's command; and if so, to whom such objection was made?"

"Objection was made to Major Anthony by officers at the post. I think objections were made at the post to Colonel Chivington, also by officers, and to several officers belonging to the expedition under Chivington."

"What are your means of knowledge respecting objections having been made to Colonel Chivington personally?"

"Lieutenant Cramer and someone else told me that day that they objected to Colonel Chivington personally, and I was warned by Major Anthony, Lieutenant Cramer, and some others not to go to the camp where Colonel Chivington was - that he had made threats against me for language I had used that day against Colonel Chivington's command going out to kill those Indians on Sand Creek."

"By whom was the plan of attack on the Indian village at Sand Creek arranged or directed?"

"By Colonel Chivington, I think."

"By whom were you ordered to move up Sand Creek after the battle began?"

"By Major Anthony."

"After you crossed Sand Creek, did you or did you not return to your superior officer for further orders? And did you receive any further or other orders during the progress of the fight?"

Soule did not take a pause. He artfully dodged the trap, throwing a cool glance at Chivington. "I met Major Anthony about 12 o'clock, and asked what I should do with my company. He told me to put them on guard over some wounded men and property belonging to our men and officers."

Downing pressed again. "Did you receive any orders other than those you have mentioned, during the fight at Sand Creek?"

"Not that I remember," Soule said, still looking at the furious Chivington.

"Did the squadron or company under your command remain together in rank and under your supervision during the fight?"

"They did."

"State, if you know, whether Colonel Chivington or any officer at the battle of Sand Creek ordered the men to disperse and conduct the fight without regard to order, or gave any order to the effect that the men should fight singly."

"Not that I know of."

"State, if you know, whether any company, battalion, squadron, or other military organization engaged in the battle of Sand Creek, remained in rank and conducted the battle as a military organization during the progress of the battle."

"Not to my knowledge," Soule said, "except what I took to be a squadron about three miles to the northwest of the Indian village."

"After the battle began, did the officers retain control of the men under their command?"

"I think not."

"What was the extent or area of the battleground where the battle of Sand Creek was fought?"

"I should think about four or five miles up the creek, and one or two each side."

"Were all the forces under the command of Colonel Chivington engaged in the battle?"

"I don't know."

"What part of the battlefield did you occupy during the battle?"

"I commenced at the lower end of the battleground, crossed the creek south, moved up the creek about two miles, crossed it to the north, and down the creek again to the village where the battle commenced."

"What forces were upon the northeastern bank of the creek

when you were there?"

"Men of the First and Third mixed together."

"What was the number of soldiers upon the northeastern bank of the creek when you were there?"

"I should think about four hundred."

"How long did you remain upon the northeastern bank of the creek?"

"Three or four hours."

"What time in the day did you cross from the northeastern to the southwestern bank of the creek?"

"Early in the morning at the commencement of the fight, and remained on the southwestern side till nearly noon."

"What time in the day did you cross from the southwestern to the northeastern bank of the creek?"

"Nearly noon - probably between 11 and 12 o'clock."

"Was the battle still progressing when you crossed, as stated in your last answer?"

"It was both above and below me."

"Did you see Colonel Chivington or communicate with him after the battle began, and before the close thereof?"

"I did. I saw him during the progress of and before the battle closed and communicated with him."

"What was that communication, and in what time in the day was it made?"

"It was about two o'clock. I asked him if I could send Colonel Bent's son Charles, who was taken prisoner with Jack Smith, to his home. Colonel Chivington said that his brother Robert did not care about having him taken back, and the colonel told me he guessed I better not take or send him back; and then, again, he said he had no objections."

"Did you see Major Anthony or communicate with him after the battle began and before the close thereof?"

"I did."

"What were those communications, and at what time in the day were they respectively made?"

"I think about twelve or one o'clock. I asked him what I should do with my command. He told me to put them on guard over some wounded men and baggage. I received orders I should think between two and three o'clock to get my command ready to go back that night with him to escort a supply train."

"Was the battle still progressing when you received the order from Major Anthony, about one o'clock in the day?"

"It was. The battle was still progressing when I received the last order."

"What time did you leave the battlefield?"

"I should think between two and three o'clock p. m."

"State if you know whether any of the Indians escaped from the battlefield on the day of the battle."

"I know I saw some escape."

"If you know, state whether orders were given by any officer at the battle of Sand Creek; or prior thereto, to the effect that Indians killed should be scalped or mutilated."

"Not that I know of."

"Do you state that Indian children were scalped or mutilated by soldiers at the battle of Sand Creek?"

"They were scalped I know; I saw holes in them, and some with their skulls knocked in, but cannot say how they were mutilated."

"Did you see any soldiers in the act of scalping or mutilating Indian children?"

"I think not. I saw soldiers with children's scalps during the day, but did not see them cut them off."

"To what company, regiment, or military organization did the soldiers mentioned in your last answer belong?"

"They belonged to Colonel Chivington's command."

"How many soldiers did you see with the scalps of Indian children?"

"I couldn't tell for certain."

"How high were the banks of Sand Creek at the place where the battle occurred?"

"All the way from two to fifteen and twenty feet."

"Where was the Indian camp with reference to Sand Creek - in the bend of the creek or on the banks thereof?"

"On the banks."

"On which bank of the creek was the Indian camp located?"

"On the northern banks."

"How high were the banks of the creek at the place where the camp was located?"

"The bank I should say was from two to five feet high."

"State if you know whether Colonel Chivington ordered portions of his command to occupy each bank of the creek."

"I don't know. I know that the regimental color-bearer of the Third, with the flag, was on the south side of the creek."

"How long after the battle began was it that the soldiers arranged themselves on each bank of the creek, so that those upon one bank were under the fire of those on the opposite bank?"

"Immediately after the battle opened - before I got across with my company."

"Do you know whether the soldiers who occupied the banks of the creek, in the manner stated in the last question, assumed those positions in obedience to the command of any officer?"

"I do not."

"Did they assume those positions in rank and by companies, or battalions, or in a disorderly manner?"

"In a disorderly manner."

"Did they not assume those positions for the purpose of driving the Indians from under the banks of the creek?"

"I suppose they assumed those positions to kill the Indians under the banks of the creek. They were not much on the drive."

"Were the positions of the soldiers upon the banks of the creek such that shots fired by those upon one bank at the Indians under the opposite bank would take effect upon the soldiers upon the opposite bank?"

"They were very apt to if they fired too high."

"Did you discover any Indians when you went upon the scout, immediately after the battle?"

"I did, what I supposed to be Indians."

"Where did you discover those Indians?"

"I discovered signal fires about forty miles south of the Arkansas, and about east of those, within about ten miles of the river, I came across what I supposed to be a village of Indians, in the vicinity of the signal fires to the east about eight or ten miles from the river."

"How near did you approach to the village mentioned in your last answer?"

"In less than a quarter of a mile."

"What reasons had you for supposing that it was an Indian village?"

"Their campfires were burning. The dogs barked at us. I heard the voices of Indians, and thought I saw Indians walking by the fire."

"What was the number of lodges in the village?"

"I could not tell; it was in the night. I did not think, from the appearance of the fires, that their lodges were up."

"How long before the battle of Sand Creek did the Indians remove from Fort Lyon?"

"I don't exactly remember; about two weeks."

"How long did the conversation between yourself and Colonel Chivington, when you met him with the command above Fort Lyon, continue?"

"Not long; a very few minutes."

"Did Colonel Chivington halt and remain with you while the conversation was being carried on?"

"He halted a moment. I rode on a little piece with him in the direction of Fort Lyon."

"How far above Fort Lyon is the place where this conversation took place?"

"About ten or twelve miles, at the head of the Big Bottom, near the watering place."

"State your means of knowledge as to permission being granted by Major Anthony to the persons who were in the Indian camp at Sand Creek to go to that place."

"The persons themselves told me the day before that they had permission. I also heard Major Anthony speak of these men having gone to the Indian camp."

"Give the names of the persons to whom such permission was granted by Major Anthony."

"John Smith, Indian interpreter, David L. Louderback, Company G, First Cavalry of Colorado, and teamster - I do not recollect his name."

"State if you know whether the authority given them by Major Anthony was verbal or in writing."

"I do not know."

"If you know, state how long the persons last named by you had been in the Indian camp."

"I think two days. They started, I think, the day Major Wynkoop started for the States."

"If you know, state what articles those persons were authorized to deal in, in trading with the Indians."

"I don't know."

"Do you state that any portion of Colonel Chivington's command fired on John Smith; and if they did so, was such firing done by command of any officer?"

"I think not. Firing was done, but not by orders of any officer. I heard Lieutenant Cramer sing out that it was John Smith, and tell him to come to Company K."

"Did you hear any plans suggested by officers at Fort Lyon after the battle of Sand Creek for prosecuting Colonel Chivington for the part he had taken in the battle?"

"I don't know that I heard any plan of prosecution. They all denounced him there."

"Captain Soule," Downing pressed, "did you hear *any* of the officers at Fort Lyon say that they would prosecute Colonel Chivington for the part he had taken in the battle of Sand Creek?"

"I don't know that I heard them say they would do it. I heard them say that he ought to be prosecuted, and that, when the facts got to Washington, he was liable to be, or words to that effect."

"Who were the officers who made these declarations?"

"It was the general talk among the officers at the post. I think I heard Major Anthony say so, and Lieutenant Baldwin, Lieutenant Cramer, Lieutenants Cannon and Minton, and Captain Hill. I don't remember all. Lieutenant Colonel Tappan, too, I think."

"Do you know whether Major Anthony made any statements to Colonel Chivington respecting the propriety at attacking the Indians on Sand Creek after Colonel Chivington's command arrived at Fort Lyon, and before the battle of Sand Creek?"

"I did not hear him make any."

Downing pushed harder. "Captain Soule, I'll ask again. Do you know whether Major Anthony made any statements to any persons as to the propriety of attacking the Indians on Sand Creek after Colonel Chivington's command arrived at Fort Lyon and before the battle of Sand Creek? If so, state if you know what those statements were."

"I talked to Anthony about it, and he said that some of those Indians ought to be killed; that he had been only waiting for a good chance to pitch into them. I reminded him of the pledges he had made them, and he said that Colonel Chivington had told him that those Indians he had pledged the soldiers and white men in the camp should not be killed; that the object of the expedition was to go out to the Smoky Hill and follow the Indians up. Anthony told me that I would not compromise myself by going out, as I was opposed to going..."

Chivington and Downing's relentless questioning of Soule had spanned four days, but they failed to put a dent in the brassy captain's testimony. Downing concluded the cross-examination with frustration, and the Commission then conducted a re-examination of Soule to address new questions raised by Soule's testimony. Tappan led the questioning with inquiries as to more details of Wynkoop's Smoky Hill expedition, obviously to address Chivington's implications that the Cheyennes who met Wynkoop's command were comprised of many Dog Soldiers who intended to kill the soldiers. Soule affirmed that Black Kettle was instrumental in controlling the warriors at the Smoky Hill, and prevented them from attacking. Tappan then re-directed questions regarding the Camp Weld Council, prompting Soule to reiterate that Black Kettle and the other chiefs clearly came to Denver with the intention of securing a peace agreement with Governor Evans. These same chiefs, Tappan's questions reaffirmed, were some of the Cheyennes and Arapahos killed at Sand Creek.

The re-direct of Captain Soule then turned to the question of the whites that were present in Black Kettle's camp at the time of Chivington's attack. Tappan sought to re-establish this fact to prove that the village was under the protection of Major Anthony's command at Fort Lyon. Further questions examined the helter-skelter nature of Chivington's attack that created a crossfire between the First and Third regiments...

"Did any of these officers appear to exercise a general supervision of the command and control it during the attack on Black Kettle's camp?" Tappan asked.

"I could not tell," Soule said. "I don't think they did."

"Did you hear Colonel Chivington, either prior to or during the attack on the Indian camp, make any remarks or give any orders to the command? If so, what were they?"

"I don't remember."

"Did you hear any officer converse with Colonel Chivington in reference to the disposal of Charles Bent or other prisoners?"

"I heard Lieutenant Dunn ask Colonel Chivington if he had any objections to having Jack Smith killed. Colonel Chivington said that he need not ask him about it; he knew how he felt about it, or words to that effect."

"Captain Soule, did you join Colonel Chivington's command with the understanding that all Indians to whom pledges of protection had been given should not be molested?"

"I think I did. I believed until after the firing commenced that we would not attack the village..."

The seven-day examination of Captain Soule mercifully concluded, and Soule wandered away from the council chambers weary but intact. He was well aware, however, that his stock in Denver was on a sharp decline. From this moment on, he would watch his back with greater caution than before...

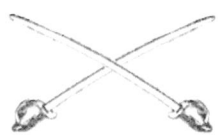

28

The combined investigations proceeded from February to April of 1865. The Military Commission called only First Regiment officers and soldiers that were at Fort Lyon at the time of Chivington's attack on Sand Creek. The questioning was intended to gather evidence pointing to improprieties during the attack itself, and afterwards, when the Third Regiment's stock and the horses captured from the Indians seemingly disappeared. In Washington, the investigation by the Joint Committee on the Conduct of the War concentrated primarily on Governor Evans' involvement in events leading up to the Sand Creek Massacre, and the historical relationship between Black Kettle's Cheyennes and the white civilians and soldiers that were acquainted with him...

On March 15, Governor Evans testified before the Joint Committee, presided by the Honorable Daniel W. Gooch, Acting Chairman. The questioning began:

"What is your present official position?"

"Governor of Colorado Territory, and Superintendent of Indian Affairs."

"Do you know anything of a band of Indians under the lead of a chief of the name of Black Kettle?"

"There is a band of Cheyenne Indians under a chief of that name, roaming over the plains."

"In what part of the country were they located, relative to the other bands of Indians?"

"The Indians that were with Black Kettle - I don't know that he was the leader of them entirely, but the Indians he went with, and was the chief among, were mainly roaming in the neighborhood of the Smoky Hill and Republican fork, and down on the south Arkansas. Sometimes they went up as far as the Platte."

"How many other bands were there?"

"There is a band up in the neighborhood of Fort Laramie, some of whose chiefs, the Shield and Spotted Horse, were with them."

"Was there any other band of the tribe of Cheyenne Indians than those on the Platte and those on the Arkansas?"

"Yes, sir, I think so," Evans said. "How far they were divided into bands it is rather difficult to say; and where each band is located is very difficult to say, because they range from away below the Arkansas to above Fort Laramie, or to Powder River. For years they have been in the habit of roaming back and forth over the plains."

"Will you give us the names of the head chiefs of the Cheyennes that you, as Superintendent of Indian Affairs, recognized?"

"There was Black Kettle, White Antelope, and Bull Bear among them."

"Having the supreme control of the Cheyenne nation?"

"No, sir; I do not think there was any such chief recognized. They had a party of about forty young men, called the Dog Soldiers, who several years ago took the control of the tribe mainly out of the hands of the chiefs. They were clubbed together as a band of braves, and the chiefs could not control them."

"What part of the country did Black Kettle and the Indians with him occupy during last summer?"

"From information which I have received I think they were mainly on the head of the Smoky Hill."

"How far from Fort Lyon?"

"Sometimes nearer, sometimes farther off," Evans impatiently said. "As I stated before, they are entirely nomadic, and they pass from one part of the country to another. The most precise information I have of their precise locality, at any particular time, is the report of Major Wynkoop, who went out and saw their camp in the latter part of August, or in the early part of September last."

"Where were they then?"

"At what is called Big Timbers, on the head of Smoky Hill."

"Have you any knowledge that they were north of Denver at any time during last summer? If so, state at what places they were."

"I have the information from the chiefs that during the summer they were on the Platte, in the neighborhood of Plum Creek, a little west of Fort Kearney; and on the Blue, east of Fort Kearney. They ranged away down into Kansas and Nebraska there during the summer."

"From whom did you derive this information?"

"It was either Black Kettle or White Antelope who told me so."

"At what time?"

"At the time of the depredations on the trains that were perpetrated in August last."

"I mean at what time did they tell you this?"

"They told me so on the 28th of September."

"You say they were down on Plum Creek at the time these depredations were committed?"

"They said the Cheyennes committed them."

"Governor Evans, what I want to know is whether you have information that Black Kettle, or any of the band that travel with him, had been north of Denver last summer. Did Black Kettle tell you that either he himself, or any of the band under his immediate control, had been there?"

"I inferred they had from his saying that the Cheyennes had committed those depredations. As a matter of course I told him they had committed them, because they had some white prisoners who had been captured there, and whom they claimed as theirs. He did not answer to that proposition. He said the Cheyennes committed the depredations east of Kearney. He did not say directly that they had been on the Blue. They gave up to Major Wynkoop the prisoners that were captured on the Little Blue, and then he said that the Cheyennes committed the depredations."

"Did Black Kettle say that *his* band had done it?"

"He did not say which band of Cheyennes. I inferred that they were his band because they did not speak of any other bands. These Cheyennes that range on the head of the Smoky Hill and Republican seem all to band together."

"What is the distance from their location about Fort Lyon to Fort Kearney, and from there to Little Blue?"

"I should have to guess at the distance."

"You have traveled that country frequently, have you not?"

"Not across in that direction."

"You have a general knowledge of that country and the bearing of it, and can estimate it from the route you have traveled, can't you?"

"It's at least from ninety to one hundred miles from Fort Lyon, and from Big Timbers to Fort Kearney would probably be 150 miles. I may be mistaken as to that."

"How far east of Denver is Fort Lyon?"

"It is southeast," Evans said.

"My question, sir, is how *far* east?"

"Something like 100 miles."

"What distance is Fort Lyon from Denver by a right line?"

"I suppose about 200 miles. It is about 250 miles the way they travel. It must be quite 200 miles on an air line."

"Where was it that Black Kettle was telling you about this?"

"At Denver."

"State the circumstances under which that conversation arose."

"He with other chiefs and headmen–"

"Please name them, Governor."

"I cannot give all their names."

"Well, state as many as you can remember."

"Black Kettle, White Antelope, and Bull Bear, of the Cheyennes; Neva and two or three others of the Arapahos. They were brought to Denver for the purpose of council by Major Wynkoop, after he had been out to their camp, brought there for the purpose of making a treaty of peace."

"You were acting as Superintendent of Indian Affairs?"

"Yes, sir."

"What propositions did you make to them, and what was the conclusion of that conference?"

"Gentlemen, Major Wynkoop's report is published in my report to the Commissioner of Indian Affairs..."

"That may be; but can you state it?"

"In brief, he reported that he had been out to their camp, and found them drawn up in line of battle. He sent in an Indian he had with him to get them to council instead of to fight; and he held a council in the presence of their warriors with their bows and arrows drawn. They agreed to allow these men to come to see me in reference to making peace, with the assurance that he would see them safe back again to their camp, as he states in his report or letter to me in regard to it."

"When you saw the Indians, what occurred?"

"The Indians made their statement, that they had come in through great fear and tribulation to see me, and proposed that I should make peace with them; or they said to me that they desired me to make peace. To which I replied that I was not the proper authority, as they were at war and had been fighting, and had made an alliance with the Sioux, Kiowas, and Comanches to go to war; that they should make their terms of peace with the military authorities. I also told them that they should make such arrangements, or I advised them to make such arrangements as they could, and submit to whatever terms were imposed by the military authorities as their best course."

"What reply did they make to that?"

"They proposed that that would be satisfactory, and that they would make terms of peace. The next day I got a dispatch from Major General Curtis, commanding the department, approving my course, although he didn't know what it was. But the dispatch contained an order that no peace should be made with the Indians without his assent and authority; dictating some terms for them to be governed by in making the peace."

"Did you communicate that fact to the Indians?"

"It was after the Indians had left that I received a dispatch,"

Evans said. "It came to the commander of the district; and a copy was sent to me for the purpose of giving me notice."

"Was anything further said in that conference with the Indians?"

"I took occasion to gather as much information as I could in regard to the extent of hostile feelings among the Indians, and especially in regard to what bands had been committing the depredations along the line and through the settlements, which had been very extensive."

"What did Black Kettle say in regard to his band; and what did the other Indians say in regard to their bands?"

"Black Kettle said he and White Antelope had been opposed all the time to going to war, but they could not control their young men - these Dog Soldiers; they have been very bad."

"These Dog Soldiers were on the Blue?"

"They were in his camp; they were his young men; Black Kettle was an old man."

"Where was his camp?"

"At the Big Timbers."

"Where Major Wynkoop found them?"

"Yes, sir."

"How do you know that fact?"

"By the statement that their warriors were there."

"Did Major Wynkoop make that statement to you?"

"Yes, sir; in his letter to me giving the circumstances under which he brought these Indians to me."

"Did Major Wynkoop report to you that the Dog Soldiers were in Black Kettle's camp?"

"He did not mention the Dog Soldiers; but the Dog Soldiers are warriors of the Cheyenne tribe."

"I understand that, Governor Evans, but you say there is no head chief that you recognized as such. I wanted to know if these Dog Soldiers belonged to the band under the lead of Black Kettle?"

"The Dog Soldiers belonged to the bands commanded by Black Kettle, White Antelope, and Bull Bear, which all run together. There is no known separation among them."

"Do I understand you, then, to say that the Indians indiscriminately occupy that country from below the Arkansas to the North Platte?"

"The Cheyenne Indians, the Sioux, and the Arapahos roam indiscriminately through there."

"Then there was no particular band that made their homes about the head of the Smoky fork?"

"There were a number of bands and tribes that hunted through there indiscriminately."

"What I want to know is the usual locality of Black Kettle's band."

"It was like all the rest," Evans said, now frustrated. "He goes where he thinks there is the best hunting; he ranges from one part of the country to the other."

"Do you know that the Indians known as Dog Soldiers ever were in Black Kettle's camp; and if so, at what time, and how do you know the fact?"

"I will not name them as Dog Soldiers."

"I mean the warriors known as the Dog Soldiers of the Cheyenne Indians. Have they ever been in his camp at any time that you know of?"

"Bull Bear, who was to see me, was the head of the Dog Soldiers himself, the head one of that band, a sub-chief. They said they left nearly all their warriors at this Bunch of Timbers."

"Where Black Kettle's camp was?"

"Black Kettle was in the camp!" Evans said. "You have the idea that Black Kettle had some particular camp. The distinction between White Antelope and Black Kettle, as an authority among the tribes, has varied at different times. The government has never recognized either of them as head chief that I know of."

"Governor Evans, you have omitted to answer the question whether you know of these Dog Soldiers, at any time or at any place, being in Black Kettle's camp or under his control!"

"I know the answer that Bull Bear gave when he came to Denver, sir. He was recognized as the leader of the Dog Soldiers. He, with Black Kettle and White Antelope, said that they left their warriors down at the Bunch of Timbers; and Major Wynkoop reports the same thing."

"But you inferred that the warriors referred to were the Dog Soldiers?"

"I did."

"At this conference, when Bull Bear told you this, what did he say in regard to war and peace?"

"He said he was ready to make peace. They spoke of some of their warriors being out. Their war is a guerilla warfare. They go off in little bands of twenty or thirty together and commit these depredations, so that there is scarcely ever more than that many seen in any of these attacks. They reported that some of their young men were out upon the warpath, or had been out, and they did not know whether they were in at the time. That, I think, was stated at that time, or in a communication that came from them a short time before this. I got a letter from Black Kettle through Bent. Upon which, Major Wynkoop went out to their camp, and either that or their statement at the conference gave me the information that a portion of their warriors were still out."

"How did Major Wynkoop know in regard to this letter or its contents?"

"It was brought in to Major Colley, at Fort Lyon, where Major Wynkoop was in command, by two or three Indians; and immediately upon their coming in, Major Wynkoop took these Indians, and went with them as guides."

"That was before you saw the letter?"

"Yes, sir; and they immediately sent me a copy of the letter."

"Did these Indians propose to do anything that you, as their superintendent, directed them to do in this matter, for the purpose of keeping peace?"

"They did not suggest about keeping peace; they proposed to make peace. They acknowledged that they were at war, and had been at war during the spring. They expressed themselves as satisfied with the references I gave them to the military authorities; and they went back, as I understood, with the expectation of making peace with 'the soldiers,' as they termed them - with the military authorities."

"Governor, why did you permit those Indians to go back, under the circumstances, when you knew they were at war with the whites?"

"Because they were under the control and authority of the military, over which I, as Superintendent of Indian Affairs, had no control."

"Did you make application to the District Commander there to detain those Indians?"

"No, sir."

"Why did you not do it?"

"Because the military commander was at the council."

"What was his name?"

"Colonel Chivington. I told the Indians he was present and could speak in reference to those matters we had been speaking about."

"Were any orders given to Major Wynkoop, either by yourself or by Colonel Chivington, in regard to his action towards those Indians?"

"I gave no orders, because I had no authority to give any."

"Did Colonel Chivington give any?"

"He made these remarks in the presence of the council: that he was commander of the district; that his rule of fighting white men and Indians was to fight them until they laid down their arms; if they were ready to do that, then Major Wynkoop was nearer to them than he was, and they could go to him."

"Do you know whether he issued any orders to Major Wynkoop to govern his conduct in the matter?"

"I do not. Major Wynkoop was not under his command, however. I understood that Fort Lyon was not in the command that Colonel Chivington was exercising at the time. It was a separate command, under General Blunt, of the military district of the Arkansas, as I understood it."

"Were the Indian chiefs sent back to their homes in pursuance of any orders given to Major Wynkoop, that you know of?"

"No, sir. I will say further, in regard to my course, that it was reported to the Indian Bureau, and approved by the Indian Bureau as proper, not to interfere with the military, which will appear in my annual report. I have no official knowledge of what transpired after this council, so far as these Indians are concerned, except that I notified the agent that they were under the military authority, and I supposed they would be treated as prisoners."

"How long have you been Superintendent of Indian Affairs there?"

"Since the spring of 1862."

"Have you any knowledge of any acts committed by either of those chiefs, or by the bands immediately under their control - any personal knowledge?"

"In 1862, a party of these Dog Soldiers-"

"I am not asking about the Dog Soldiers, but about Black Kettle's band."

"They are the same Indians! The Dog Soldiers were a sort of vigilance committee under those old chiefs."

"But I understood you to say, a few minutes ago, that the Dog Soldiers threw off the authority of the old chiefs, and were independent of them."

"I said that they managed the tribe instead of the chiefs," Evans said.

"What act of hostility was committed by the Dog Soldiers, in pursuance of the authority of any of the chiefs of the nation?"

"That I could not say, for I have no way of ascertaining what authority they have - only what I gather from the agent, who was intimate with them."

"What is the name of that agent?"

"Colley. He is familiar with those Indians, and said that the Dog

Soldiers were to blame for their ugly conduct."

"That is what I understand; and I wanted you, as Superintendent of Indian Affairs, to tell us if these Dog Soldiers were under the command of any chief that had control of them, and the name of that chief, if you know it."

"The identification of the chief that commands them is what I am not able to do, because they have in that band, or tribe, the chiefs that I have mentioned. Which of them is superior in authority, I am not advised."

"What was the general reputation of Black Kettle, as a hostile or a friendly Indian, during your control there as Superintendent of Indian Affairs?"

"Black Kettle has had the reputation of being himself a good Indian."

"Peaceably inclined, and well disposed towards the whites?"

"Yes, sir; and White Antelope more particularly. But I was going on to state in regard to their conduct. In the summer of 1862, a party of warriors of the Cheyennes came to Denver and called on me, and wanted something to eat."

"Can you designate what particular band they belonged to?"

"They were of the same band we are fighting about the Blue - Black Kettle, White Antelope, and Bull Bear's Indians, that range mainly down in the neighborhood of Smoky Hill. They came to Denver on a war expedition against the Utes. I advised them to cease their hostilities. When I went there I had an idea of trying to get everybody to live without fighting, the Indians among the rest. The Indians on the mountains and on the plains spent their time in chasing one another. I was in this delicate position: the Utes, who are a very warlike and dangerous tribe, had got a jealousy of the Indians on the plains and the whites who live on the plains also.

"The whites were constantly giving presents to the begging portion of the Plains Indians. The superintendency and the agency were constantly giving goods to them; and the Utes complained that the whites were fitting out the Plains Indians in their war parties against the Utes, which was true to some extent. The Utes said that when they chased the Cheyennes and Arapahos, which run together almost constantly, and the Sioux - there are parties of Sioux with the Arapahos and Cheyennes in nearly all their war parties. When the Utes would chase them down into the plains, they had to stop because the whites interfered, and they did not dare to go down into the plains. They were of the opinion that the whites were taking the side of the Indians of the plains; and they were on the point of going to war with us.

"I suggested to these Indians that it was better for them to make peace. I went with Colonel Leavenworth down to the camp of the Sioux, Arapahos, and Cheyennes, at a subsequent period, and tried to arrange with them. I had a Ute agent with me to make the arrangement to quit fighting. When this party came, in 1862, I mentioned these things, showing the advantages, and they promised me they would go back. I gave them some bacon and flour, and other things, for subsistence. They started under a promise that they would go back, and not go up to the Utes and jeopardize our safety with them. Instead of that, they started for South Park, the Ute battleground where they usually fight, and the next day or two afterwards, messengers came in from the settlers on the road, saying that the Indians were committing depredations - that they had cleaned out and outraged one landlord and insulted a woman. They had gone in and taken possession of several of these sparsely settled places; had made one woman cook for the whole party, and I think they had sent in for protection. Some six soldiers went up to protect the neighborhood, but when they got there, these Indians had gone back on the plains by another route."

"What was the name of the chief in command of that party?"

"I don't know; that was their first visit."

"Was it Black Kettle, or White Antelope, or Bull Bear?"

"I could not say it was not them, nor that it was. It was a party of warriors from the same party that Black Kettle, White Antelope and Bull Bear ranged with."

"Governor, although you had a conversation with them, and furnished them with supplies, and induced them to return, you do not know the name of the chief?"

"There were several chiefs," Evans said.

"Can you name *any* of them?"

"I cannot give the name; I might get it if I were in my office."

"As Governor of Colorado Territory, did you have any troops organized there last summer?"

"Yes, sir; I organized a regiment."

"For what term of service?"

"For one hundred days."

"Who was the colonel of that regiment?"

"George L. Shoup."

"Did you ever issue any orders to that regiment, or to any part of it?"

"No, sir."

"Were they organized as United States troops?"

"Yes, sir."

"Were they placed under the control of the district commander as soon as organized?"

"Before they were organized, for this reason: while the regiment was being raised, there was information come in of a camp of about 500 of these Indians; a report of which will be found in my annual report to the Commissioner of Indian Affairs. It came in this way: Elbridge Gerry lives on the Platte, sixty miles south of Denver. In the night, two Cheyenne chiefs came to him."

"What were their names?"

"It seems to me one of them was Crooked Neck. These Indians came in and notified Gerry to get out of the way. He was living on a ranch with a large amount of stock, and with a Cheyenne wife. He had Spotted Horse there with him under protection. Spotted Horse, a Cheyenne Indian of Fort Laramie, had been friendly all the time, and was there under protection.

"I think about 800 Indians were camped at the Point of Rocks on the Beaver," Evans continued, "which is about 120 miles east of Denver, composed of Arapahos, Cheyennes, Sioux, Kiowas, Comanches and Apaches. They said that their plan was to divide into small parties of about 200, going in about 40 miles below Gerry's. 100 going just above Gerry's to Fort Lupton; about 250 to the head of Cherry Creek, which is 25 or 30 miles south of Denver; and the remainder of them to go to the Arkansas, at Fontaine Qui Bouille. That these parties were to take a farmhouse, clean it out and steal the stock, and in this way commit the most wholesale and extensive massacre that has ever been known. I have no doubt it would have been so, but for the vigilance that was taken to prevent it.

"Gerry, who has been in my employ as a spy over the Indians, started the next morning. They got to his house about midnight, or 2 o'clock. Gerry started immediately in the morning with Spotted Horse, and got to my house at 11 o'clock; riding between 60 and 70 miles during the day, for the purpose of giving me this information. I immediately notified the District Commander, and put the recruits, which were supposed to be subject to my command under his command. He sent express in every direction to notify the settlers. I telegraphed, and also sent messengers. It so happened that a militia company had gone down there, and were near that, and that a militia company had gone to Fort Lupton.

"The Indians came in at these different points on the second night, skulking along under the bluffs, where their trails were seen. They found the settlements all alarmed, and went back again, except at the head of Cherry Creek, where they killed two or three and took quite a large number of cattle; and at Fort Lupton they killed one man. And before Gerry got back, they stole some of his horses and the horses of one or two of his neighbors, and ran them off."

"At what time was this?"

"It must have been early in August."

"At what time was this hundred-days regiment organized?"

"Early in September."

"At what time was it mounted?"

"Some companies were mounted before the regiment was full; others were mounted subsequently, as they could get horses."

"How were horses obtained, and from whom?"

"The quartermaster of the department."

"Do you know anything further than you have stated in connection with this attack upon Black Kettle and his band on Sand Creek? Did you issue any orders, or take any part in any transaction having in view any such attack?"

"I did not know anything about it," Evans said. "After I got to Washington, I got a letter from the Secretary of the territory, saying it was rumored they were going there."

"Whom did 'they' refer to?"

"Colonel Chivington and his force. I think he said it was surmised that they were going to Fort Lyon. It is proper for me to say that I understood they were going to make an expedition against the Indians, but I had no knowledge of where they were going."

"After Major Wynkoop left you in September, do you know what was done with these Indians?"

"I do not."

"Do you know what action the Indians took afterwards?"

"I do not."

"Do you know where they were encamped?"

"I accidentally heard - I had no official knowledge of the fact - that there were several hundred of them at Fort Lyon. The next day after this council I started for a place about 300 miles off, to hold a treaty with the Utes down on the Rio Grande, and was gone nearly a month."

"At what time did you start to come east?"

"I think I started on the 15th of November."

"You have not been back since?"

"No, sir."

"Was there any property accounted for to you, or to any officer of the government, so far as you know, that was taken at Black Kettle's camp?"

"Not any. I would say, however, that any property the army captured they would not be likely to turn over to me..."

Governor Evans was clearly on the hot seat with the Joint Committee on the Conduct of the War. He continued to reiterate the reasons for his conclusion that the Cheyennes were trying to unite all the Plains Indians in a war on the United States, and that Black Kettle and White Antelope, although claiming to be for peace, had no control over the Dog Soldiers. In a contentious exchange with Chairman Gooch, he repeated the entire incident at Gerry's ranch as justification for his request for the volunteer militia, but he offered little insight as to why Colonel Shoup's Third Cavalry ultimately ended up under Chivington's command 250 miles away at Sand Creek. The commissioners patiently listened to Evans' defense, but they were not impressed...

"Governor Evans," Chairman Gooch finally said, "with all the knowledge you have in relation to these attacks and depredations by the Indians, do you think they afford any justification for the attack made by Colonel Chivington on these friendly Indians, under the circumstances under which it was made?"

Evans squirmed. "As a matter of course," he said, "no one could justify an attack on Indians while under the protection of the flag. If those Indians *were* there under the protection of the flag, it would be a question that would be scarcely worth asking, because nobody could say anything in favor of the attack. I have heard, however - that is only a report - that there was a statement on the part of Colonel Chivington and his friends that these Indians had assumed a hostile attitude before he attacked them. I do not know whether that is so or not. I have said all I have had to do with them. I sup-posed they were being treated as prisoners of war in some way or other..."

Throughout his entire testimony, Governor Evans had displayed little understanding of the Cheyenne tribal, political, and military structure, and even less knowledge of who their chiefs were, or what bands they led. For a man holding the office of Superintendent of Indian Affairs, his testimony was embarrassing, to say the very least. And, as Governor of the Colorado Territory, Evans appeared wholly ignorant of why the regiment he personally raised to protect the Platte River had left the district to attack the government-pro-tected Indian camp on Sand Creek. Evans was drowning in a sea of inconsistencies and contradictions, and as his testimony concluded, he made a final attempt to snare a potential scapegoat:

"I had a letter from General Curtis, after I got here," Evans said, "saying he was troubled to know what to do with so many nominal prisoners of war at Fort Lyon, as they were so expensive to feed there. The subsistence of the fort was short, and it was a long way to get subsistence, and through a hostile country, and he was troubled to know what to do with them."

Chairman Gooch didn't buy it. "But from all the circumstances which you know," he pressed, "all the facts in relation to that matter, do you deem that Colonel Chivington had any justification for that attack?"

Evans continued to flail. "So far as giving an opinion is concerned, I would say this: That the reports that have been made here, a great many of them have come through persons whom I know to be personal enemies of Colonel Chivington for a long time. I would rather not give an opinion on the subject until I have heard the other side of the question, which I have not heard yet."

"I didn't ask for an opinion, Governor. Do you know of *any circumstance* which would justify that attack?"

"I do not know of any circumstance connected with it subsequent to the time those Indians left me and I started for another part of the country. It is proper for me to say that these attacks during the summer, and up to the time I came away, were of very frequent occurrence. The destruction of property was very great. Our people suffered wonderfully, especially in their property, and in their loss of life. They murdered a family some twenty-odd miles east of Denver. The attacks by hostile Indians, about the time I came away, were very numerous along the Platte. There was an attack as I came in, about the month of November. It was in the evening, about sundown, and I passed over the ground in the night in the stage with my family. And a few days afterwards, a party of emigrants returning from Colorado were murdered near the same ground, which was near Plum Creek. And for a considerable length of time, immediately after I came in, the attacks were very numerous and very violent, until the stage was interrupted so that it has not been running since, until within a few days.

"I started home and could not get there because there was no transportation. I came back here and shall return in a few days again. I mention this in order to do away with the impression that might exist that hostilities had ceased, and that this attack of Colonel Chivington had excited the recent hostilities.

"These Indians told me, when they were there, that the Sioux were in large force on the head of the Republican, and would make an attack about the time I expected to come in. I delayed my coming in a short time on account of what they told me, and when I did come in I found some Indians commencing their depredations, which they continued about the month following, both before and after the attack made by Colonel Chivington. General Curtis wrote to me that he did not think Chivington's attack was the instigation of the hostilities perpetrated along the Platte..."

The Joint Committee excused Governor Evans, for they'd heard enough...

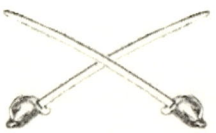

29

While the congressional inquiry continued in Washington, the commissioners of the military investigation traveled down to Fort Lyon, where Ned Wynkoop gave testimony...

"Major Wynkoop," Tappan said, "at the time of your assuming command of Fort Lyon in 1864, in what department and district was the post then located?"

"District of Colorado, Department of Kansas," Wynkoop replied.

"Who commanded the district at that time, and how far was district headquarters from Fort Lyon?"

"Colonel John Chivington commanded the district at that time. District headquarters was about two hundred and fifty miles from Fort Lyon."

"Was there a change of district lines while you were in command at Fort Lyon?"

"There was."

"State the time and manner of such change."

"I think the change was made about the middle of July 1864. Fort Lyon was included in the District of the Upper Arkansas, headquarters at Fort Riley, Kansas, Major General Blunt in command."

"Was there any other change in the district lines, or commander, while you were in command of Fort Lyon?"

"Yes. Major General Blunt left the district, and command was assumed by Major Henning, headquarters at Fort Riley."

"How far from Fort Lyon to headquarters, Department of Kansas, and District of the Upper Arkansas? And what facilities had you for communicating with department and district headquarters?"

"Distance to district headquarters was about four hundred miles; to department headquarters, about five hundred miles. The opportunities for communicating to district and department headquarters were very bad, in consequence of being obliged to cross the plains through a country which, during a large portion of the time, was troubled with hostile Indians; in fact, the only communication was by means of large bodies of troops."

"What tribe of Indians were at that time committing the depredations you speak of on the road?"

"It was my understanding the depredations were being committed by the Kiowas, Comanches, Sioux, Arapahos, and Cheyennes."

"How long did they continue to commit depredations on the road?"

"Up to within a couple of weeks of the 10th of September, 1864, the date of my consultation on the Smoky Hill. I heard of no depredations being committed between the 10th of September and the 29th of November, 1864, the date of Chivington's massacre at Sand Creek."

"Were any depredations committed by the Indians west of Fort Lyon, and in the vicinity of the settlements, prior to the 10th of September, 1864?"

"Yes. There were men killed in the neighborhood of Fort Lyon and further west in the vicinity of the Arkansas settlements."

"How long after you received the letter from Black Kettle and other chiefs in reference to certain prisoners did you start for the Smoky Hill with command?"

"Two days afterwards. I received the letter on the fourth day of September, 1864, and started on the sixth."

"Where were the white prisoners at the time of the council?"

"I don't know; when the Indians first saw me, they moved their village and left nothing but warriors behind, and I supposed the white captives to be with the village."

"Did Black Kettle and other chiefs in council say they were authorized to act for any other tribes than their own, in making peace with the whites?"

"They did not say they were authorized to act for other tribes," Wynkoop said, "but told me that if peace was made with the Cheyennes and Arapahos, the Sioux, Kiowas, and Comanches wanted peace also. Some of the chiefs said at the time, if they made peace and the whites wanted them to, they would assist in fighting the Kiowas and Comanches."

"In the council on Smoky Hill, was any reference made to a band of Indians called Dog Soldiers?"

"Yes, I spoke to Black Kettle and asked him if he could control a portion of his tribe called Dog Soldiers. I can't remember whether this conversation occurred at the council, but the conversation I have reference to took place with Black Kettle and Bull Bear, Chief of the Dog Soldiers, in case peace was made, whether they would submit to such terms as he might accept. He replied in the affirmative. I also understood from Bull Bear that the Dog Soldiers would indorse whatever Black Kettle and other chiefs might do, in reference to making peace with the whites."

"What did the chiefs say in council on the Smoky Hill, and Denver, they would do in order to secure peace with the whites?"

"I don't know of anything particular they said; they appeared willing to submit to anything the whites might impose on them. They also said at different times - I don't know exactly when and where - that they were willing to assist the whites in fighting the other Indians who were hostile; they also said that they were willing to go up to their reservation and remain there."

"Did you have a conversation with the rescued white prisoners in reference to their capture and treatment by the Indians?"

"I had a conversation with the oldest one, a young girl about sixteen or seventeen years old."

"By whom did they say they had been taken?"

"She stated that herself and two of the children were taken by the Cheyennes."

"Did she state the place and circumstances of her capture?"

"She did; she said that she was taken on the Blue River, from a ranch known as the Liberty Farm; that there were one woman and three children besides herself, taken at the same time and place, and I believe two men killed."

"On your return from the council on the Smoky Hill to Fort Lyon, did you make a report of what you had done? If so, state to whom you made it."

"I made two reports; one to Major General Blunt, commanding the district, the other to Governor Evans, of Colorado."

"How long after your return from the council on the Smoky Hill did you leave for Denver, and who accompanied you?"

"It was a few days after my return from the Smoky Hill," Wynkoop said. "I left for Denver with the Indian chiefs aforementioned in my testimony by an escort of about forty men, commanded by Lieutenant Cramer and accompanied by Captain Soule and John Smith, United States Indian Interpreter."

"At that time, had the settlers on the Arkansas left their farms on account of Indian depredations?"

"A large majority had. As I passed through the Arkansas valley, I found a great many farms deserted; both on the Arkansas and Fontaine Qui Bouille. I found the people congregated together at different points for mutual protection."

"On your arrival in Denver, to whom did you report?"

"I didn't report to anybody. I sent a message to the Governor of Colorado Territory that I had arrived."

"By whom was the council with the Indians convened at Denver?"

"Governor Evans."

"Why did you send a message to Governor Evans that you had arrived with certain Indian chiefs, instead of to the military commander?"

"Because Governor Evans was ex officio Superintendent of Indian Affairs, and because I was not under the command of the commander of the District of Colorado."

"Did you have a conversation with Governor Evans in reference to the Indian proposals for peace?"

"Objection," Major Downing said. "The question is leading."

"I'll rephrase," Tappan said. "Major, did you, while in Denver, have any conversation with any person or persons, holding an official position, in reference to the subject of your mission to that city?"

"I did."

"With whom did you have such conversation?"

"John Evans, Governor of Colorado and ex officio Superintendent of Indian Affairs."

"What was the purport of that conversation?"

"I told Governor Evans that I had come to Denver in accordance with the report I had made to him; that I had brought the chiefs with me and desired that he would see them and hear what they had to say. He stated that he did not think he could have anything to do with them officially, as these Indians had declared war against the United States, and he considered that the matter now rested in the hands of the military authorities. Besides, even if he could make peace with the Indians, he did not think it would be policy at that present time, for the reason that he had not punished the Indians sufficiently. He said that if he made peace with them under these circumstances, the United States government would be acknowledging themselves whipped.

"He also said that the Third Regiment had been raised upon representations made by him to the department that their services were necessary to fight these Indians, and that now, after they had been raised and equipped, if peace was made before they had gone into the field, they would suppose at Washington that he had misrepresented matters. But he finally consented to see the Indians and talk with them, and he set an hour and day for that purpose. He also said that he gave me a great deal of credit for rescuing those white prisoners, but that he would not have adopted the same means I had. He said that he, after finding out where their camp was, would have gone out and fought them and killed them, and made them deliver up the white captives. I reminded the governor then of the fact that all the force I could raise was one hundred and twenty-seven men, after leaving sufficient garrison at Fort Lyon, and that the Indians numbered upwards of two thousand."

"How long after the council in Denver did you return to Fort Lyon?"

"In about five or six days, I think."

"On your return, did you find the settlers on the Arkansas still absent from their farms?"

"Objection," Downing said. "Leading."

The commissioners conferred. "Overruled," Tappan said. "You may answer the question, Major Wynkoop."

"They had returned to their farms and were taking in their crops," Wynkoop said.

"What induced them to return to their farms?"

"Objection!" Downing said. "Calls for a conclusion."

"Overruled," Tappan said.

"Under an assurance from myself of safety," Wynkoop said. "Since I had the consultation with the Indians on the headwaters of the Smoky Hill, I told them that they could consider themselves in perfect safety until such time as I could give them warning to the contrary. I told them to return to their ranches and take in their crops, which they were doing upon my return from Denver."

"How long after your return to Fort Lyon did you commence issuing provisions to the Indians?"

"I don't know how long; it was in a few days after my return; there was a village of Arapahos that I first issued provisions to."

"Did you have any council with the Indians after your return to Fort Lyon?"

"I did. It was with Black Kettle and some of the chiefs I took up to Denver, together with Left Hand, chief of the Arapahos, and Little Raven, of the Arapahos, at which consultation some of my officers were present - also Colonel William Bent and John Smith."

"What was the object of the council and what was done?"

"I told the chiefs to bring in their villages, so that I could have them under my own eye until such time as I could hear from department headquarters. I also told Black Kettle that I wanted him to bring me in the three remaining white captives as soon as possible, which he promised to do, but said it would take some time; as they were off at a distance."

"How long after being relieved of the command of Fort Lyon did you leave for district headquarters?"

"I was relieved from command on the 5th of November, 1864, and started for district headquarters on the 26th of November."

"Did you receive any orders on your arrival at district headquarters?"

"I received an order placing me on duty at Fort Riley, and assumed command of the post."

"Did you make a report to the district or department commander after your arrival at Fort Riley?"

"I made a verbal report to the district commander at Fort Riley of my arrival. I also proceeded to department headquarters and had an interview with General Curtis."

"What explanations or report did you make to department commander?"

"I explained to him the facts that I have heretofore given in my testimony, but before I had finished, he intimated to me that he was aware of all the facts, and that he had censured me not for the course I had adopted with the Indians particularly, but for committing an unmilitary act by leaving my district without orders and proceeding to Denver City with the Indian chiefs and white captives to the Governor of Colorado instead of coming to himself. He asked what explanation I had to make. I told him that I had since become pretty well convinced that I had made a mistake, but that at the time I thought that Governor Evans was the proper person to refer that matter to, he being Governor of Colorado Territory and ex officio Indian superintendent. I also explained to him the isolated position of Fort Lyon, and how seldom the chances were for communicating with headquarters, and that in consequence, while in command at Fort Lyon, I felt it frequently incumbent upon me to assume responsibilities..."

The Commission closed its interview of Major Wynkoop, and Colonel Chivington immediately took the floor to begin cross-examination.

"Major Wynkoop, you stated that you received a letter signed Black Kettle and others, desiring to give up some white prisoners, and that they desired peace. Upon first seeing the Indians at the Smoky Hill, did they act in a friendly manner towards you, or did they not manifest a disposition to fight rather than treat?"

"The manner in which they were drawn up presented a hostile appearance," Wynkoop said.

"Then what induced you to believe they did not intend to *be* hostile?"

"In the first place, the fact of their not making an attack while having greatly superior numbers; and in the next, the fact of their delivering up the white prisoners which they had in their possession, and their chiefs entering my camp and delivering themselves over to me."

"After first seeing the Indians, were there not members of your command who expressed to you their fears of the Indians, and for certain causes threatened to return to Fort Lyon?"

"There were certain members of my command who expressed to me their fears that the Indians intended treachery, but they did not threaten in my presence to return to Fort Lyon."

"You say after meeting the Indians, you went into camp on the bank of a creek. Was not your camp on this bank surrounded on three sides by the creek, and was not the brush or willows very thick on the opposite side of the creek, and how far was the center of your camp to the brush?"

"The camp wasn't surrounded on three sides by the creek," Wynkoop said. "From the center of camp to the brush I should judge was from four hundred to six hundred yards. The brush or willow was thick on both sides of the creek."

"Will you describe your camp, and how your men were arranged - how large your guard, what their orders were, and if they were immediately on duty when you went into camp, and whether your men were permitted to leave camp when they pleased?"

"The camp was formed, cavalry in line, battery in the center, and wagons corralled in rear of the battery. My order to the officer of the day was to deploy the guard at certain intervals around the camp, and not allow any Indians to come into camp without my permission. They were on duty all the time, from the time they were mounted until they were relieved. The men were not permitted to leave camp when they pleased."

"Was this the camp first made after first seeing the Indians and in which your council was held?"

"It was the camp in which the council was held. It was made the day I first saw the main body of Indians. I had seen a few Indians the day before."

"What officer of your command was officer of the day on the day of the council and during the council, or at any time after first meeting the Indians? Did the Indians behave in a threatening manner towards you?"

"Lieutenant Hardin was officer of the day. I did not see them make any demonstrations that I considered hostile, except some of those who were present were apparently prepared for strife by having their bows strung and arrows in their hands. On the other hand, my men had their loaded carbines in their hands, prepared at any time to fight."

"Was your attention called to any threatening demonstration

made by the Indians during the council, and did not the officer of the day once during the council call to the men to fall in for the purpose of fighting the Indians?"

"While in the council, I was told that Lieutenant Hardin, for some cause or other, had formed the men in line, and that the Indians seeing it, had made a demonstration as though they were preparing for a fight. But nothing of this kind had taken place on the part of the Indians until our men had fallen in line."

"Did the Indians put any seeds or anything of that description into the vent of your howitzers?"

"I never knew of their doing so."

"During the council you state the Indians had among themselves, did not your interpreter inform you that the Indians meditated the destruction of your command?"

"He did not."

"At your first camp, where the council with the Indians was held, did not the Indians come into your camp, so that there were a great many more Indians in camp than soldiers of your command?"

"They did."

"Were not these Indians all armed, and did they not while in camp in many instances behave in a very threatening manner towards the soldiers of your command; and did not the Indians in some instances abstract the contents of the soldiers' pockets, taking such things as tobacco?"

"They were all armed. As I stated before, I did not see them act in a threatening manner. I never heard of their abstracting the contents of the soldiers' pockets."

"You stated that your command numbered one hundred and twenty-seven men; how many Indians, or about how many were in camp during the council, or at the time Lieutenant Hardin ordered his men to fall in?"

"I could not say positively about how many."

"Did Lieutenant Hardin ever inform you of the fact that seed had been placed in the vent of the howitzers by the Indians, or did you ever have any conversation with Lieutenant Hardin, or any other officer of your command, in regard to that fact?"

"I heard that some grapes had been dropped into the vent of the gun. That was the cause of a difficulty between the soldier on guard and an Indian. I understood that the soldier pushed the Indian off; that the Indian drew his bow and the soldier his revolver."

"In your conversation with the Indians in your camp, where the council was held, did you state to Black Kettle, One-Eye, or any other chief, that you were in the power of the Indians, and they could destroy you if they desired, or language to that effect?"

"I did not."

"Did the Indians state to you, at any conversation you had with them, that they could destroy you if they desired?"

"They did not."

Chivington continued to press. "In your conversation with the Indians, did you promise them subsistence or anything of that kind upon any conditions?"

"I did not."

"Was the cause of your moving toward Fort Lyon on account of the threatening demonstrations made toward you by the Indians, and the probability that if you remained there, there would be a collision between your command and the Indians?"

"No, sir. My object in removing toward Fort Lyon was for the reason that I had no occasion to go the other way."

"Was this the *only* reason you had in going toward Fort Lyon?" Chivington asked.

"The reason for moving my camp immediately to another locality was for the purpose of taking a better position, so that, in case the Indians did not accept the proposition I had made to them, and chose to be hostile, I would be in a better position to make a defense."

"Was there any act upon the part of the Indians that induced you to believe that they would not accept your proposition and would attack you? If so, what was that act?"

"I was induced to believe that my proposition might not be accepted from the fact that a portion of the chiefs composing the council appeared unwilling to deliver up the white prisoners, simply from my statement that I would endeavor to procure them peace. They desired an assurance of peace, which I told them positively I could not give them; and, as an officer, I took what I deemed to be the necessary precaution."

"Did John Smith at any time, state to you or any officer of your command that he would have to talk for your lives - that the Indians meditated the destruction of yourself and command?"

"He made no statement of that kind to me. I do not know of his making any statement to any officer of my command to that effect."

"Did Black Kettle or One-Eye at any time address the Indians assembled about your camp, and implore the Indians not to destroy yourself and command?"

"I did not know of their doing anything of that kind."

"Did they not state that the Dog Soldiers, they feared, could not be controlled?"

"No."

"Will you explain what the Dog Soldiers are, and how they are controlled?"

"I understand that the Dog Soldiers are a portion of the warriors of the Cheyenne tribe, and presume that they are controlled by the headmen."

"Did any of the chiefs, or did John Smith, at any time state to you that they feared the Dog Soldiers, as well as the Indian warriors generally, could not be controlled? And did not some of the Indian chiefs advise you to move toward Fort Lyon, fearing a collision between your command and the Indians?"

"They did not."

Colonel Chivington yielded the floor to Major Downing.

"Major Wynkoop," Downing began, "you stated in your direct examination that Colonel John M. Chivington said in Denver, at the council with the Indians, that he was the big war chief of this part of the country. Who was present when Colonel Chivington made this statement?"

"All those were present I believe that I have stated were present at the council."

"Did not Colonel Chivington manifest a desire for peace with the Indians, provided Major General Curtis would consent, and provided a peace could be made that would afford permanent security to the people of Colorado Territory? And did not Colonel Chivington state that he was determined the white people of Colorado should be protected in their lives and property, if he had to kill all the Indians on the plains? And was not all Colonel Chivington's conversation with you manifestly for the whites, regardless of the sympathies that others might have for the Indians?"

"I never heard him express himself in that way," Wynkoop smirked. "I never heard him make use of the expressions used in the latter part of your question. I had no conversation with him of importance, except what I had done and intended to do. He expressed no opinion particularly on the subject that I can remember, at any time that I was in Denver..."

Downing and Chivington continued to spar with Wynkoop, challenging his decision to feed the Arapahos at Fort Lyon and allow them to approach the post while camped nearby. Particular attention was given to a general field order issued by General Curtis on July 31, 1864, ordering post commanders to bolster protection of the forts, and to forbid any Indian prisoner to be brought in without a blindfold. The purpose of this order was to keep Indian spies from gaining valuable information regarding the size and strength of military forces. Chivington's obvious strategy in this matter was to imply that Wynkoop willfully disobeyed, but Wynkoop insisted he had never seen the order. Wynkoop's four-day examination under the Military Commission concluded on March 24...

Near Denver, Captain Soule and Captain George Price rode along the banks of Clear Creek with the boys of Company D. They were returning to Denver on a routine patrol that had taken them up the creek to Central City. Soule requested that Price, the District Inspector, accompany him, for he had general concerns he wished to discuss...

"Take it easy, Silas," Price said, "I didn't say I don't believe you!"

"Then, what do you mean – I'm jumping to conclusions?"

"I'm just saying that, to accuse any man of trying to kill you, you need proof."

"Proof? You want proof? I've been shot at three different times on patrol!"

"Gentlemen," Price said to the troops. "You've all been with Captain Soule when these shootings happened?"

The boys concurred.

"Seems like whenever I get out in the open lately," Soule said, "a random shot just happens to find its way to my vicinity."

"Hell, Sile," Price said, "a rifle shot ain't exactly a rarity in these parts – not with the Indians on the warpath."

"Have you seen any Indians around Denver lately, George?" Soule asked. "I ain't worried about them. The last time, somebody took a potshot at me right by Camp Weld!"

"Has anybody seen anything?" Price asked.

"Shit," Soule said, "a sniper can hide in a million places."

"I don't understand it," Price said. "I don't see why Chivington has it in for you more than Wynkoop, or Tappan, or Smith – hell, the entire First Regiment is out to crucify him."

"Yeah, but Tappan's on the Commission, and Wynkoop's out of range. Chiv publicly offered up $500 to anyone who plugs an Indian sympathizer, and guess who tops the list as an easy target."

"I don't know, Sile. If Chiv put a bounty on you, ain't nobody in this town could keep a secret. He'd end up in the calaboose in a heartbeat. Most people think he was just shooting his mouth off for the newspaper. And what the hell would killing you accomplish now? You already testified against him."

"That commission is a joke, George," Soule said. "My testimony don't mean a damned thing. The army's just puttin' up window dressing to distance themselves from the fact that Chiv hoodwinked them. Shit, they're wrapping up a pretty package that nobody's ever gonna open. Chiv's all puckered up because I stood up to him, instead of licking his boots like that sorry-assed lackey Anthony. He's out for revenge, plain and simple."

"Well," Price said, "officially, I have to say that you gotta come up with more evidence to prove that Chivington's trying to get you."

"He won't pull the trigger," Soule said. "That drooling flock of his is out to enforce his gospel. I'm gonna tell you this, with my boys here as my witnesses: If somebody *does* manage to kill me, Chivington will go into that hearing and attack me with both barrels. He'll make me out to be the devil of Sand Creek..."

30

The military hearings continued, and when called upon, Colonel Chivington presented a sworn deposition containing written answers to selected questions posed by the commissioners. Most other officers and soldiers called to the inquiry agreed to testify in person, while others also opted for written depositions...

Testimony of John M. Chivington:

"Since August, 1863, I was in possession of conclusive evidence of an alliance of the Sioux, Cheyenne, Arapaho, Comanche, and Apaches whose plan was to interrupt, or entirely prevent all travel on the routes along the Arkansas and Platte rivers and thereby depopulate this country.

"Last April, the Indians commenced depredations by entering isolated habitations in distant parts of the territory, taking what they desired and driving off stock. Indians have killed, wounded and cut to ribbons soldiers and settlers. Suffice it to say that during 1864, such atrocious acts were almost a daily occurrence along the Platte and Arkansas routes. The Indians became so bold as to murder and scalp a family consisting of a man, woman and two children by the name of Hungate within 15 miles of Denver. After seeing this, any person who could believe that these Indians were friendly, to say the least, must have strange ideas about their habits..."

Regarding the Camp Weld Council:

"...they said they had no power to make peace on such terms; that they would report to their young men and see what they would say to it. They stated that members of their tribe had committed most of the depredations. I promptly reported to General Curtis, and I was ordered to chastise these Indians, regardless of district lines..."

Major Scott Anthony (to the Joint Committee on the Conduct of the War):

"Major Wynkoop had some difficulty with the Indians. He had proposed terms of peace with them, which was not approved by headquarters."

"Were there orders issued disapproving his proposal?"

"There were several orders in regard to it," Anthony said.

"What I want is the departmental order disapproving of what

Major Wynkoop had done."

"I don't think I have those orders."

"Do you know who has them?"

"No."

"Did you ever see those orders?"

"Only so far as it related to his unmilitary conduct."

"I mean his attempt to pacify the Indians."

"I've never seen those orders," Anthony said. "I heard of them."

"Describe what you found when you took command."

"There were 652 Arapahos camped about a mile away. They agreed to do whatever I said. I said I was forbidden to feed them, and that they couldn't come within the limits of the post. I would treat them as prisoners of war if they surrendered their arms and stolen property. They turned over 20 head of stock, mules and horses, and a few arms - not a quarter of them what they stated they had. I fed them, returned their arms, and advised they go out to buffalo country where they could kill game to subsist upon."

"What authority had you for returning their arms and ordering them off?"

"My instructions were to act upon my own judgment. At the same time there were orders from General Curtis that they not be fed or clothed at the post."

"Were these orders issued after you took their arms?"

"Before that."

"Where did you get the authority for releasing them? Did you act upon your own judgment?"

"Yes, sir. I couldn't afford to feed them, and they were in buffalo country where they could hunt."

"Was Black Kettle with his band at the fort?"

"He came in and asked if I had any authority to make peace. I said I didn't. I said he might go to Sand Creek, or to Smoky Hill and remain there until I received word from General Curtis. I reported to headquarters that they were there, and there was a larger band about 100 miles from the post."

"Did you have reason to think Black Kettle intended to fight against the United States?"

"I had no reason to suppose it, beyond my general knowledge of the Indian character."

"Then why didn't you attack him when he was there?"

"I didn't consider it a matter of policy. I believed an attack would have caused a general Indian war, and I was not strong enough to defend the settlements..."

Colonel John Chivington:

"I had every reason to believe these Indians were either directly or indirectly concerned in the outrages which had been committed upon the whites. The character of the Indians in the western country for truth and veracity, like their respect for the chastity of women who become prisoners in their hands, does not inspire confidence in what they may say. Under the order of General Curtis to punish all hostile Indians, I ordered the Third Regiment to march in late November..."

Captain Silas Soule:

"On November 27th, I discovered some horsemen about 15 miles above Fort Lyon. We met them and found it was Colonel Chivington and ten to twelve companies of 100-Daysers. I told Colonel Chivington there were some Indians camped near the fort, but they weren't dangerous; that they were waiting to hear from General Curtis and they were being treated as prisoners. I was ordered to return to the fort with Colonel Chivington, and when we arrived, a guard was stationed around the post with orders from Chivington to allow no person to leave..."

Colonel John Chivington:

"When I reached Fort Lyon, I questioned Major Anthony about the whereabouts of hostile Indians. He said there was a camp of Cheyennes and Arapahos about fifty miles away; that he would have attacked before, but did not consider his force sufficient - that these Indians had threatened to attack the post, all of which was concurred in by Major Colley. I decided my course, resulting in the battle of Sand Creek, which has created the sensation in Congress through the lying reports of malicious parties..."

Major Scott Anthony:

"Major Anthony, did you tell Colonel Chivington the relations you had with those Indians?"

"Yes, sir."

"Did you approve of this attack upon them?"

"I did not. I didn't consider that they had surrendered to me, and my instructions were such that it was my duty to fight them wherever I found them, provided I considered it good policy to do so. I did not consider it good policy to attack this party on Sand Creek unless strong enough to go on and fight the band at Smoky Hill."

"Did you argue against making the attack?"

"I made a great many harsh remarks in regard to it. I did not so much object to the killing of the Indians as a matter of principle - merely as a matter of policy."

"You think the attack upon those Indians was impolitic?"

"Very much so..."

Lieutenant Clark Dunn, Third Colorado Cavalry:

"Lieutenant Dunn, upon your arrival at Fort Lyon with Colonel Chivington, did you talk with Major Anthony about the Indians camped at Sand Creek?"

"Yes, sir. He said they were hostile and not under the protection of the troops at Fort Lyon. He said it before the fight at Sand Creek and after it. He said he was damned glad we had come, and the only thing that surprised him was we had not come long before..."

Captain Silas Soule:

"Lieutenant Cramer told me that he and others objected to Colonel Chivington personally, and I was warned by Major Anthony and Lieutenant Cramer not to go to the colonel - that he had made threats against me for the language I had used against him..."

Lieutenant Joseph Cramer:

"I told Major Anthony I believed it to be murder to kill those Indians - that we owed them our lives for saving us at the Smoky Hill. I reminded him of the promises we made to protect them. Major Anthony said he didn't consider the promise binding, since he hadn't heard from General Curtis. I said I believed it was his duty to let those Indians know what was going on, and that an officer who would disregard his honor was a disgrace to the uniform."

"Did you make objections to Colonel Chivington?"

"Yes, I told him about the obligations that we of Wynkoop's command were under..."

John S. Smith, United States Indian Interpreter and Special Indian Agent:

"Did you tell Colonel Chivington the character and disposition of these Indians at any time during your interviews on this day?"

"Yes, sir."

"What did he say in reply?"

"He said he could not help it; that his orders were positive to attack the Indians."

"From whom did he receive these orders?"

"I don't know; I presume from General Curtis."
"Did he tell you?"
"Not to my recollection..."

Lieutenant William Minton, First New Mexico Volunteers:
"Some of the parties were endeavoring to press upon Colonel Chivington the injustice of going to attack that camp on Sand Creek, and explaining to him the particular circumstances in which the officers of this post and the Indians were situated. Colonel Chivington was walking the room in a very excitable manner, and he wound up the conversation by saying, 'damn any man who is in sympathy with an Indian'..."

Colonel John Chivington:
"In all my conversations with Major Anthony and Major Colley, I heard nothing of these statements that the Indians were under the protection of the government. I believed the Indians in the camp were hostile..."

Major Scott Anthony:
"Major Anthony, these were the very Indians that had taken up the position you directed them to take?"
"No, sir. I told them they should not remain on the road, but they might go to Sand Creek, or someplace where they could kill game."
"Did you not suppose that they understood, if they went there and behaved, they would not be attacked?"
"I don't think they thought that - I think they were afraid I was going to attack them, judging from things I heard like, they didn't like that 'red-eyed chief.'"
"Were there any whites in the Indian camp?"
"John Smith, Private David Louderback, and a teamster by the name of Clark. Smith was there as a spy. He asked to take some goods for trade, and I gave my permission..."

John Smith:
"I was called on by Major Colley to go pay them a visit and ascertain their numbers, their general disposition, and where other bands might be located."
"Why did he need this information?"
"Because there were different bands supposed to be at war. We knew they were at war, but this band had left the fort perfectly satisfied..."

James P. Beckwith, Indian Scout:

"Gentlemen," Colonel Chivington said, "I respectfully ask that, before this witness is sworn in, he be interrogated as to his belief in the existence in God, who rewards good and punishes evil."

COMMISSION: "James P. Beckwith, do you believe in the existence of a supreme being, of a god, by whom truth is enjoined and falsehood punished; and do you consider the form of administering an oath as binding upon your conscience?"

"I do," Beckwith said."

"Did you accompany Colonel Chivington's command to Sand Creek last November?"

"I started with Colonel Shoup as guide and interpreter; afterwards, Colonel Chivington took command..."

Colonel John Chivington:

"On the 29th of November, 1864, my command of 500 men of the Third Regiment, and 250 of the Colorado First attacked a camp of Cheyenne and Arapaho Indians at the Big Bend of the Sandy. We attacked at sunrise..."

Private David Louderback, First: Colorado Cavalry:

"A squaw came into the lodge and said there was a heap of buffaloes coming. A few minutes later, one of the chiefs said there were soldiers coming. We thought they were General Blunt's men from Fort Riley..."

John Smith:

"I saw Black Kettle hoist the flag, fearing there might be some mistake as to who they were..."

Robert Bent (from sworn deposition):

"When we came in sight of the camp, I saw the American flag waving and heard Black Kettle tell the Indians to stand round it..."

Sergeant Naman D. Snyder, First Colorado Cavalry:

"At the time of the attack, did you see any American flag?"

"Yes, at the lower end of the village..."

Sergeant Stephen Decatur, Third Colorado Cavalry:

"No, I saw no flag..."

Captain Presley Talbot, Third Colorado Cavalry:

"I didn't see any flags displayed by the Indians..."

Private George Roan, First Colorado Cavalry:
"I saw the stars and stripes waving over the camp..."

Lieutenant Joseph Cramer, First Colorado Cavalry:
"I saw a flag in the camp after the fight..."

John Smith:
"I started for the troops - I thought I could reconcile matters..."

Lieutenant Joseph Cramer, First Colorado Cavalry:
"John Smith came out, and someone hollered, 'shoot the old son of a bitch!' About the same time, Private Louderback came out with a white flag and was fired upon..."

Private David Louderback, First Colorado Cavalry:
"Colonel Chivington told me to come out - that I was all right. I went out, and a man fired at me. The colonel told him to stop firing and ordered me to fall in rear of the command..."

Captain Silas Soule, First Colorado Cavalry:
"Did any of Colonel Chivington's command fire at John Smith?"
"I think he and the others were fired on by Anthony's battalion and Wilson's..."

Major Scott Anthony, First Colorado Cavalry:
"I'm sure no man of mine fired. Smith started to run, and I supposed he imagined someone was shooting at him. If they were or not, I don't know - I didn't see shots fired at him. One of my men rode to bring him out. He was shot, and an Indian beat him over the head and killed him..."

Lieutenant Joseph Cramer, First Colorado Cavalry:
"George Pierce attempted to save Smith, but he was killed, I think, by the Third Regiment or Wilson's battalion..."

Major Scott Anthony, First Colorado Cavalry:
"The Indians - men, women and children - attempted to escape, and our artillery opened on them. Some took position under the bank in the bed of the creek..."

Colonel John Chivington:
"They had excavated rifle pits under the bank of Sand Creek, evidently designed to protect the occupants from the fire of an enemy..."

Corporal Amos Miksch, First Colorado Cavalry (from sworn deposition):

"There were no rifle pits except what the Indians dug into the sand bank after we attacked..."

Captain Silas Soule, First Colorado Cavalry:

"Wilson's battalion crossed the creek, and Anthony's battalion took nearly the same as Wilson's and opened fire. The 100-Daysers opened fire in the rear of Anthony's battalion. I was ordered down into the creek, as we were in the line of fire. After that, I could see no order to the battle. The command was scattered and every man fired on his own hook..."

Lieutenant Joseph Cramer, First Colorado Cavalry:

"They were shooting at each other. Several times, I ordered my men to cease firing as I was fearful of killing some of our own men..."

Sergeant Lucian Palmer, First Colorado Cavalry:

"I think, if the fight had been properly managed, it would have been an easy matter to take the squaws and children prisoners..."

Lieutenant Joseph Cramer, First Colorado Cavalry:

"Were the Indians in a line of battle?"

"Not that I saw."

"How did the Indians resist the attack?"

"By fighting back. They fought singly, or a few in a place when the ground would give them shelter. They fought bravely. A great many started towards our lines with hands raised, as if begging for us to spare them..."

Captain Silas Soule, First Colorado Cavalry:

"Did any Indians advance towards Chivington's command, making signs that they were friends?"

"I saw some holding their hands up."

"Did any officers appear to exercise a general supervision of the command and control it?"

"I couldn't tell, but I don't think they did..."

Major Scott Anthony, First Colorado Cavalry:

"Did the officers control their men?"

"There didn't seem to be any control."

"Were the men acting in defiance of orders?"

"I didn't hear any orders given that weren't obeyed. As a general thing the officers and men were just doing what they saw fit to do..."

"Major Anthony, state to the best of your knowledge, the number of Indians in the camp at the time of your attack."

"I thought at the time there were a thousand or more in the village; but, from information I have received since, I am satisfied that there were probably around 700..."

Colonel John Chivington:

"There were about eleven or twelve hundred Indians; about 700 were warriors, and the remainder were women and children. I am not aware that there were any old men among them. There was an unusual number of males, for the reason that the war chiefs of both nations were assembled there evidently for some special purpose..."

Major Scott Anthony, First Colorado Cavalry:

"Major Anthony, you're saying that 700 soldiers allowed 500 Indians to escape? Why did you not pursue them?"

"I don't know. That is the fault I found with Colonel Chivington at the time."

"Did he call off the troops?"

"No. The Indian warriors took their position right along the sandy banks of the creek, dug in, and fired upon us while the women and children tried to escape."

"And the Indians held you in check there for how long?"

"I think fully seven hours..."

Colonel John Chivington:

"State, to the best of your knowledge, the number of Indians killed, including men, women, and children."

"I judge there were five to six hundred..."

Major Scott Anthony, First Colorado Cavalry:

"I suppose it was about 125..."

Captain Silas Soule, First Colorado Cavalry:

"We saw 69 dead Indians..."

Sergeant Naman D. Snyder, First Colorado Cavalry:

"I saw 98..."

Colonel George Shoup, Third Colorado Cavalry:
"From my own observation I should say about 300..."

Lieutenant Joseph Cramer, First Colorado Cavalry:
"I estimated them at 175 or 180; I do not think there were that many..."

Private Amos D. James, First Colorado Cavalry:
"I counted 100 or a little over..."

Asbury Bird, First Colorado Cavalry (from sworn deposition):
"I should judge there were between 400 or 500 Indians killed..."

Captain Andrew J. Gill, Third Colorado Cavalry:
"I supposed at the time that there were about 500 killed..."

Corporal Amos C. Miksch, First Colorado Cavalry:
"I counted 123 dead bodies; I think that not over 25 were full-grown men..."

Sergeant Stephen Decatur, Third Colorado Cavalry:
"450 dead Indian warriors. I saw, comparatively speaking, a small number of women killed..."

Colonel John Chivington:
"Officers who passed over the field reported but few women and children dead..."

John Smith:
"I saw altogether 70 dead bodies, the greater portion women and children..."

Lieutenant James Cannon, First New Mexico Volunteers:
"My estimate of the number of Indians killed was about 200, all told..."

Colonel John Chivington:
"I can't state positively the number killed, nor can I state positively the number of women and children killed. I saw but one woman killed, and one who had hanged herself; I saw no dead children..."

Private David Louderback, First Colorado Cavalry:
"I didn't count them - I couldn't stand it - they were cut up too much..."

Captain Silas Soule, First Colorado Cavalry:
"Were the women and children shot down and scalped, and otherwise mutilated by any of Colonel Chivington's command?"
"They were."
"Were any efforts made by Chivington, Shoup or Major Anthony, to prevent these mutilations?"
"Not that I know of."
"Did you witness any scalping and otherwise mutilating of the dead after the engagement?"
"I did."
"Did you see any officer engage in this business of scalping and mutilating the dead?"
"I cannot say I did..."

Major Scott Anthony, First Colorado Cavalry:
"I saw nothing to the extent I have since heard stated. I saw a great many Indians and squaws that had been scalped; I don't know how many, but several."
"Were those men of your command?"
"Of Colonel Chivington's command..."

Lieutenant Joseph Cramer, First Colorado Cavalry:
"I don't recollect seeing one that *wasn't* scalped..."

John Smith:
"I saw the bodies of those lying there cut all to pieces, worse mutilated than any I ever saw before; the women cut all to pieces... scalped; their brains knocked out; children two or three months old; all ages lying there, from sucking infants up to warriors..."

Sergeant Stephen Decatur, Third Colorado Cavalry:
"I saw no mutilating or scalping by any of them..."

Captain Andrew Gill, Third Colorado Cavalry:
"I heard the colonel say 'that I wouldn't do any scalping.' This was to me privately, but I heard no orders given to prevent it..."

Major Scott Anthony, First Colorado Cavalry:
"I didn't see anyone mutilating any Indian, with the exception of one man who scalped a dead squaw while Colonel Chivington was standing by..."

Colonel George Shoup, Third Colorado Cavalry:
"I saw one or two men who were in the act of scalping, but I'm not positive..."

Corporal James Adams, First Colorado Cavalry:
"I saw some scalping done by officers of the Third Regiment and their men - there was one they called Major and another called Richmond..."

Lieutenant James Olney, First Colorado Cavalry:
"Lieutenant Harry Richmond, of the Third Regiment, scalped three women and five children while they were screaming for mercy..."

Lieutenant James Cannon, First New Mexico Volunteers:
"I don't know as I could tell you who did it - it was very near a general thing. I heard one man say he cut a squaw's heart out and had it on a stick..."

Major Scott Anthony, First Colorado Cavalry:
"I have since read reports about Indian bodies having been so badly mutilated, their privates cut off, and that kind of thing. I never saw anything of that, and I never heard of it until months after the fight..."

Lieutenant James D. Cannon, First New Mexico Volunteers:
"I heard of instances in which men had cut out the private parts of females and stretched them over the saddle-bows and wore them over their hats while riding in the ranks. These matters were a subject of general conversation and could not help being known by Colonel Chivington..."

Major Scott Anthony, First Colorado Cavalry:
"I did see some bodies that were mutilated, and one instance where three men repeatedly fired upon an Indian child until the little fellow dropped..."

Sergeant Lucian Palmer, First Colorado Cavalry:
"I saw several of the Third Regiment cut off fingers to get rings; I saw Major Sayr scalp a dead Indian - the scalp had a long tail of silver hanging on it..."

Corporal Amos Miksch, First Colorado Cavalry:
"I saw a major in the Third Regiment blow off the top of the head of a little boy. These men pulled out the bodies of squaws and pulled them open in an indecent manner. I saw some men unjointing fingers to get rings off and cutting off ears to get silver ornaments..."

Chivington stood and objected: "Corporal Miksch, did not the men who were cutting off fingers for rings tell you that they were simply obtaining trophies to preserve as reminiscences to bequeath to their children of the glorious field of Sand Creek?"

"No, sir," Miksch said.

"Were there not a great many wild dogs about the village that might have mutilated the bodies?" Chivington asked.

"Dogs could not mutilate the bodies as I saw them..."

John Smith:
"I saw some of the First Regiment committing some very bad acts, and I likewise saw some of the 100-days men in the same kind of business."

"Did you speak of this to Colonel Chivington?"

"No, sir. I had nothing to say about it, because at the time they were hostile toward me."

"Were any prisoners taken by Colonel Chivington?..."

Captain Luther Wilson, First Colorado Cavalry:
"One infant was picked up off the field. It was given to one of the squaws but afterwards died and was buried..."

Lieutenant James Cannon, First New Mexico Volunteers:
"I heard of a child being thrown in a feed box of a wagon, and after being carried some distance, left on the ground to perish..."

Captain Silas Soule, First Colorado Cavalry:
"There were three squaws and two children taken; also, Colonel Bent's son Charley; and John Smith's son..."

John Smith:
"My boy ran away with the Indians, but he came back to my lodge, which was surrounded by soldiers, and he stayed there the night. The next day, a soldier came up outside of the lodge and called me out..."

Private David Louderback, First Colorado Cavalry:
"There were several men talking to Jack Smith – called him a son of a bitch and ought to have been shot long ago. Jack said he didn't give a damn. When he said that, I thought it was time for me to get out of there, as men had threatened to shoot and hang me, too..."

James Beckwith:
"Jack was sitting with me. A shot came through an opening in the lodge, and he sprung forward and fell dead. We scattered, and I met a man with a pistol in his hand who said, 'The damn son of a bitch isn't dead - I'll finish him.' Says I, 'Let him rest...'"

John Smith:
"I heard a gun fired and saw a crowd run to my lodge. They said Jack was dead..."

Private David Louderback, First Colorado Cavalry:
"I said it was a damned shame they killed him. Some officer warned me about shooting my mouth off. I said I enlisted as a soldier, but I considered my tongue my own..."

Captain Silas Soule, First Colorado Cavalry:
"I think Lieutenant Dunn acknowledged that a man of his company shot him..."

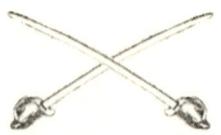

31

Agrand reception proceeded at the Planters House, honoring the marriage of Captain Silas Soule and Hersa Coberly, who had taken their vows earlier in a quiet morning ceremony at the private home of a friend. Hundreds of Huntsville and Castle Rock guests now mingled with soldiers of the Colorado First Cavalry, as Major Wynkoop toasted the happy couple.

"Ladies and gentlemen!" Wynkoop announced, raising his glass. "I'm greatly honored to stand before Silas and Hersa Soule. I shall reserve my own personal judgement regarding these two pranksters' decision to hitch their wagons together on April Fool's Day – at the bizarre hour of 8 a. m. - and shall assume this is not just an elaborate ruse to reunite the First Regiment for noontime libations!"

The crowd rolled with laughter.

"A simple matter!" Soule said. "The Third Cav boys were all invited to attend at 8 *p.m.!* It's a known fact that a hung-over sniper can't shoot straight before noon!"

"He's just using that for an excuse!" Hersa called over the laughter. "Fact is - I was kidnapped right out of my bed!"

Wynkoop laughed with the others. "Well, my dear, you're on your own! I've retired from the sticky business of rescuing damsels in distress!"

"Hear! Hear!" Joe Cramer yelled to the delight of the guests.

"Alright!" Wynkoop laughed, "on with the toast. To the happy couple - I am delighted to gaze upon Silas with the sincere hope that, at last, this maniacal Jayhawker will be tamed by such a sweet and honorable young woman!"

The guests gave a raucous cheer.

"To Hersa," Wynkoop said. "I wish you all the happiness that your heart desires. You are the sweet ray of love that captured Sile's Soule!"

The crowd drank the first toast as Hersa and Silas kissed.

"And to Silas," Wynkoop said. "Despite the fact that you are the most infuriating, annoying, *irritating* rapscallion this man's army has ever known..."

"Hear! Hear!" Cramer called as the crowd roared. Soule took a long, dramatic bow.

Wynkoop continued. "Not on this earth is there a more decent and honorable man. I am humbled to call you my friend, and I know that you will give Hersa all the love and happiness she deserves. I love you both!"

The crowd cheered and toasted the couple as Wynkoop embraced them. Soule suddenly planted a wet and terrible kiss on Wynkoop. The men bellowed and the ladies screamed as Wynkoop disgustedly shoved Soule aside.

"I want to kiss the bride, not you!" Wynkoop cried. He embraced Hersa and gave her a gentlemanly kiss.

"I'm next!" Cramer said.

"Me, too!" yelled Colonel Tappan.

"One at a time, boys!" Hersa laughed.

"Hey!" Soule said. "A little decorum here!"

The boys pulled Soule away, and Hersa disappeared in a sea of blue.

"Doesn't anybody want to kiss me?" Soule whined.

"I will!" Mattie Coberly hollered. Hersa's little sister advanced on Soule, but her big brother Bill separated the two.

"Welcome to the family, pard," Bill said, shaking Soule's hand.

"Thanks," Soule said. "I just wish your little brother would ease up on me."

Bill Coberly shrugged. "Joe's still smartin' from the past, Sile. We all are, but I know you did what you had to do. My little sis loves ya, and that's good enough for me." He winked. "But if you hurt her, I'll break your legs."

"Get in line," Soule laughed. He waded through the crowd and finally found Hersa, who was still passing out kisses.

"Boys!" Soule said, breaking into his Irish brogue, "I thank you all if ya relieve your lips from my beloved bride. I've still got a wee bit of kissin' to do me-self!"

"Who's he?" Hersa asked the boys.

"Ah – *begorra!*" Soule cried. "She's gone 'n forgot me already!"

"Step aside, Captain," Wynkoop said, moving in and taking Hersa's hand. "All the best to you, sweetheart. Sile is a lucky man."

"I'm the lucky one, Ned," Hersa replied.

Louisa Wynkoop stepped in and hugged Hersa, while Wynkoop and Soule shook hands.

"Thanks for coming up, Neddy," Soule said.

"I wouldn't have missed it for the world. To you, my friend, the luck o' the Irish."

The band struck up a lively two-step, and Soule took Hersa for their first dance together as Mr. and Mrs. Silas Soule. Wynkoop and Louisa followed, and the happy crowd then joined in...

Joe Cramer soon walked out to the Planters entrance, where Colonel Tappan had joined several armed guards patrolling the streets. Tappan and the men warily watched two horsemen, who'd been lingering at the end of Blake Street for some time now.

"What's going on, boys?" Cramer asked.

Tappan leaned against the doorway. "Those riders were here about an hour ago, but they rode away when the boys started towards them."

"Well, let's just go find out who they are," Cramer said.

"Don't bother, Joe," one guard said. "They don't seem to be of a mind to chat..."

April 1865 was perhaps the most significant month in the history of a nation still in its relative infancy. On April 9, General Robert E. Lee surrendered at the Appomattox Courthouse in Virginia, ending the brutal four-year War of Rebellion that claimed over a half-million American lives, and left over 400,000 wounded. Just five days later, President Abraham Lincoln was struck in the head by an assassin's bullet while attending the play, *Our American Cousin*, at Ford's Theater in Washington. A Confederate conspiracy to kill Lincoln, Vice President Andrew Johnson, and Secretary of State William H. Seward resulted in the death of only the president, but the nation's heart was shattered in its wake. The president's assassin, John Wilkes Booth, screamed *"Sic semper tyrannis!"* (Thus always to tyrants!) as he fired the fatal shot, delivering Lincoln and the Civil War to the ages. With Mary Lincoln by his side, the president lingered in a coma for ten hours until he succumbed at 7:21 a.m. on April 15.

Word of Lincoln's death rocked Denver City, leaving citizens already worn from four terrible years of strife with the Indians speechless and numb. Although the war in the States was over, the true Indian War was barely beginning on this beautiful plateau at the foot of the majestic Rocky Mountains.

The combined inquiries into the Sand Creek Massacre were yet in full swing, dividing Denver into two diametrically opposed camps. Although the initial dominant opinion in the city favored Colonel Chivington's raid on Black Kettle, the stories emerging from the Military Commission painted a disturbing picture of a large scale atrocity committed by the purported man of God. It was no secret that Silas Soule and Ned Wynkoop were at the center of the controversy, and many Denverites who first believed the Third Regiment justifiably attacked the Cheyennes could not help but wonder why such loyal soldiers – and staunch Republicans - would so vehemently oppose Chivington. Soule's reputation as a soldier and a man was unquestioned, and Wynkoop's fierce dedication to bringing peace to the territory was irrefutable. Yet, rumors leaking from the inquiry suggested that Chivington and Downing relentlessly attacked both officers' character, virtually accusing them of treason. As Denver mourned the death of their president, a tide of suspicion swelled over Colonel John M. Chivington...

APRIL 23, 1865

Soule and Hersa walked along Blake Street with Colonel and Mrs. Sam Tappan, and Joe Cramer and his young lady friend, having enjoyed dinner and an evening at the theater. Silas and Hersa bid their friends goodnight and turned toward their newly rented home on Curtis Street. The brisk April air was unseasonably warm tonight, but Hersa snuggled closely to her new husband.

"Honey," Soule said, "I didn't want to sound stupid in front of everybody, but since you already know I am, what the heck is an aria?"

Hersa laughed. "It's a song, silly."

"A song? Then why don't they call it a song instead of confusing me?"

"Because you're more fun when you're confused."

"I see." Soule wrapped an arm around his angel. "Boy, that fat lady sure had some pipes on her."

"Yes. She could sing, too."

Soule laughed. "Hey, *I'm* supposed to be the wiseacre in the family."

"We'll see about that."

Two couples approached, nodding as they passed.

"Good evening, Captain," said one gentleman. "Mrs. Soule..."

"Evening, folks," Soule said.

"Mrs. Soule," Hersa said. "I sure like the sound of that."

"My mother did a good job with it, so you're in good company."

"Amen, Mr. Soule, that I am." She felt so secure in his arms. "You're not tired of me, yet, are ya?"

"Well, I do miss sleeping with my nose in the dirt, swatting mosquitoes the size of raccoons, and eating hardtack morning, noon and night, but I doubt I could get tired of you, even if I make it to a hundred."

"You always have all the right answers, don't ya, slickie-boy?"

"Yes ma'am, I do."

They walked the almost deserted street, playfully taking a few steps together as if a band led them.

"So quiet tonight," Hersa said.

"Yeah. I reckon even this wicked town will be pretty tame for awhile, in light of what happened."

"I know. It seems, no matter what we do or where we go, it's hard to stop thinking about it. I just can't believe the president is dead. I can't begin to imagine what poor Mrs. Lincoln must be going through right now."

"Seems like every sunny morning ends up with a tornado," Soule sighed. "Makes you wonder if everything Lincoln accomplished will be for naught."

"I've always wanted to run away, but anymore I don't know where to run."

"Well, darlin', wherever it is, we'll run together." They heard drunken laughter roll from a saloon a block away. "Well, I guess *somebody's* gotten over their mourning period pretty quick. Hey, we could go down there and drink our troubles away."

"Not in a million years," Hersa said, pulling him away. "Besides, you don't drink. Remember?"

"Yeah," Soule sighed. "I sure been respectable since you came into my life."

"And you're gonna be even more respectable raising cattle, mister – that is, if I can ever pull you loose from the army."

"It won't be long now..."

They walked up to the front steps of the house. As they entered, a gunshot echoed outside in the distance.

"Aw, what the hell," Soule said. He peered out the doorway as a second shot rang out.

"What is it, Silie?"

"I reckon those boys at the saloon are hootin' it up." He checked his guns.

"What are you doing?"

"Well, old Chiv's accused me of being a cowardly drunken horse thief, so I might as well go shoot up the town, too."

"No, stop," Hersa said. "Don't go down there."

"Honey, I'm the marshal. I gotta go have a look."

"No, Silie!" She grabbed him. "I don't want you going there alone!"

"Don't fret, darlin'. It's just a few drunks getting spunky. By the time I get there, it'll be over. Besides, Joe's probably heading that way, too." He walked outside.

"Silie, I don't like this!"

"I have to do my duty, hon," Soule said. "You just stay inside, and I'll be back in a wink."

"Please be careful."

"I been careful all my life. I ain't gonna stop now." He walked to the road, but before he headed toward Arapaho Street, he suddenly turned back and looked at Hersa. "For me, there ain't nothin larger in this world than you. But Neddy's my best friend. If anything should ever happen to me, he'll always be there if you need him..."

Soule quickly moved along Curtis, and then west to Arapaho, cautiously scanning the darkness ahead. He heard a few muffled hollers coming from the direction of the saloon. A shadow suddenly scampered across the street and down a dark alley. Soule stopped and pulled his gun.

"Hallo, up there!" he hollered. "Who's there?"

He heard footsteps in the distance, but it was too dark to make out the shadows.

"This is the Provost Marshal!" Soule called. "Who's there?"

A craggy, drunken voice emerged. "Marshal? That you?"

"What's going on?" Soule said, aiming his pistol ahead. "Identify yourself!"

"Ain't nothing wrong here, Marshal! We was just celebratin'."

"Show yourselves, and put your hands up where I can see 'em!"

"Come on over and have a drink!"

"Ain't interested in that," Soule said, slowly walking forward. "What's all the gunplay?"

"Told ya! Just havin' some laughs."

Soule looked into the darkness, catching an inky shadow lurking near a corner of the alley. "Throw your gun down! Now!"

"I ain't lookin' for trouble, Marshal!"

"Well, you're gonna find some if you don't throw your gun into the street. Now, do as I say!"

"Shit! You gonna arrest me?"

"We'll talk about that after you drop your weapon and put your hands up. Come on, fella, you're waking up the whole town."

"Ain't nobody sleeps around here no more, Soule, thanks to you and your injun' lover friends!"

Soule stopped and aimed at the shadow, squinting in the darkness. "Charlie Squier, is that you?"

"Dunno, Cap'n," Squier replied. "Was me maybe an hour or two ago."

"Private, what the hell are you doing?" Soule scolded. "Ain't you got the good sense to know sooner or later somebody's gonna lock you up and throw away the key this time?"

"Ain't never had no good sense before, so why should I start now?" Squier mumbled. A second voice in the darkness joined Squier in drunken laughter.

Soule stiffened and gripped his pistol. "Alright boys, fun's fun, but I ain't joking now. Toss your weapons out where I can see 'em, and you boys come on so we can sort things out."

"Like you sorted it out for old Chiv?" Squier said.

"Private Squier, and whoever the hell else that is standing behind you, drop your arms and step out here in the light."

"So you can throw my ass in the stockade again?" Squier said. "You're right, they'll throw away the key. Whole fuckin' army wants my ass cashiered."

"It don't have to be that way, Charlie. Just toss your weapons, and I'll see you boys back to camp where you can sleep it off. Just that easy."

"Just that easy," Squier said. "Hear that, Billy? Old Injun lover Soule says it's just that easy."

"I ain't gonna say it again, boys," Soule said. "Drop your guns and step into the light with your hands up!"

Charley Squier suddenly jumped out, and both he and Soule fired simultaneously. Squier let out a painful yowl and rolled in the street, clutching his arm. Billy Morrow emerged from the alley and helped Squier to his feet. They clumsily disappeared into the darkness...

Hersa heard the shots as she stood on the front porch, pensively awaiting Soule's return. It seemed like an eternity of silence that followed, but then the night air came alive with voices that grew into hollers and screams. Hersa couldn't wait any longer. She ran down the porch and followed the clamour.

"Silie!" Hersa cried. She quickly ran down Curtis Street, and turned for Arapaho.

In the distance, several men hollered, as other people came from their houses to see what was going on. A large crowd gathered in the darkness as Hersa approached.

"Silie!" she cried. "Where is he?"

"Somebody get a doctor!" a man yelled.

"Oh no!" Hersa screamed. "Silie! No!"

Soule lay on the ground with a terrible wound ranging through his jaw and into his brain.

Hersa hysterically screamed, while someone tried to hold her as she dropped down to Soule. "Oh, my dear God! Please, no! Silie! Please help us!" She pulled his head into her lap, her dress soaked in blood.

Soule's wobbly eyes found Hersa as he clumsily reached to touch her face.

His hand grew weak and fell away as the sight of his loving Hersa drew away into the darkness. In another moment, Silas died in Hersa's arms...

Joe Cramer frantically shoved through the crowd. He fell to his knees and embraced Hersa.

"They killed him!" Hersa cried. "Joe! They killed him!"

Cramer bellowed in agony as he tucked Hersa's head to his chest. "God damn! No!" Consumed by rage, he quickly stood and lashed out at the crowd. "Who did this?"

"It was Squier!" a drunken man hollered. "I seen him and Morrow running down Lawrence! Look! There's a blood trail goin' that way!"

Cramer drew his pistol. "I want the son of a bitch!"

"I'm with ya!" the drunk cried, and several others pulled their guns and followed Cramer into the night.

Hersa sobbed as she rocked Soule in her arms..."

In a quiet, two-story home a block away, a large man stood at the open window. He listened to the impassioned cries of Hersa Soule for a moment, and then gently shut the window. He closed the lace curtains and climbed back into bed with his wife.

"What is it?" she asked.

"Some kind of trouble down the street," John Chivington said. "Probably just some drunken bummers on a bender. Go back to sleep, my dear..."

<h1 style="text-align: center;">32</h1>

A large funeral procession for Captain Silas S. Soule proceeded down Lawrence Street, following the services held for him at St. John's Church. Bound for Mount Prospect Cemetery on the east side of Denver, the procession was observed by hundreds of somber onlookers who now mourned a second United States hero assassinated in the past ten days. A military caisson rolled down the street, carrying Soule in a flag-draped coffin, followed by a horse with Soule's boots reversed in the stirrups. Eight military trumpeters marched behind the caisson, playing a somber funeral dirge, followed by carriages carrying Hersa Soule, with her mother, Sarah, and Mattie, William, and Joseph Coberly. Hersa vacantly stared ahead, softly weeping in William's sturdy arms.

Lieutenant Luther Wilson led a large military company of soldiers of the First Colorado Cavalry. The heartsick soldiers, many openly crying, maintained, as would be reported later in the *Rocky Mountain News*, "an appearance of style and discipline most 'military' indeed."

Excerpt from report submitted to the 38th Congress of the United States, by Benjamin Franklin Wade, Chairman, Joint Committee on the Conduct of the War, regarding Massacre of Cheyenne Indians:

...The treatment extended to those Indians by Major Wynkoop does not seem to have satisfied those in authority there, and for some cause, which does not appear, he was removed, and Major Scott J. Anthony was assigned to the command of Fort Lyon; but even Major Anthony seems to have found it difficult at first to pursue any different course towards the Indians he found there. They were entirely within the power of the military. Major Anthony, having demanded their arms, which they surrendered to him, they conducted themselves quietly, and in every way manifested a disposition to remain at peace with the whites...

...And then the scene of murder and barbarity began - men, women, and children were indiscriminately slaughtered. In a few minutes all the Indians were flying over the plain in terror and confusion. A few who endeavored to hide themselves under the bank of the creek were surrounded and shot down in cold blood, offering but feeble resistance. From the suck-

ing babe to the old warrior, all who were overtaken were deliberately murdered. Not content with killing women and children, who were incapable of offering any resistance, the soldiers indulged in acts of barbarity of the most revolting character; such, it is to be hoped, as never before disgraced the acts of men claiming to be civilized. No attempt was made by the officers to restrain the savage cruelty of the men under their command, but they stood by and witnessed these acts without one word of reproof if they did not incite their commission. For more than two hours the work of murder and barbarity was continued, until more than one hundred dead bodies, three-fourths of them of women and children, lay on the plain as evidences of the fiendish malignity and cruelty of the officers who had so sedulously and carefully plotted the massacre, and of the soldiers who had so faithfully acted out the spirit of their officers...

...It is difficult to believe that beings in the form of men, and disgracing the uniform of United States soldiers and officers, could commit or countenance the commission of such acts of cruelty and barbarity as are detailed in the testimony, but which your committee will not specify in their report. It is true that there seems to have existed among the people inhabiting that region of country a hostile feeling towards the Indians. Some of the Indians had committed acts of hostility towards the whites; but no effort seems to have been made by the authorities there to prevent these hostilities, other than by the commission of even worse acts...

Among the First Colorado Cavalry veterans who rode in Soule's funeral procession was Major Scott Anthony, whose expressionless face was somber and ashen...

...The testimony of Major Anthony, who succeeded an officer disposed to treat these Indians with justice and humanity, is sufficient of itself to show how unprovoked and unwarranted was this massacre. He testifies that he found these Indians in the neighborhood of Fort Lyon when he assumed command of that post; that they professed their friendliness to the whites, and their willingness to do whatever he demanded of them; that they delivered their arms up to him; that they went to and encamped upon the place designated by him; that they gave him information from time to time of acts of hostility which were meditated by other and hostile bands, and in every way conducted themselves properly and peaceably, and yet he says it was fear and not principle which prevented his killing them while they were completely in his power. And when Colonel Chivington appeared at Fort Lyon, on his mission of murder and barbarity, Major Anthony made haste to accompany him with men and artillery, although Colonel Chivington had no authority whatever over him...

Behind the military funeral procession, a long stream of carriages containing many city officials and friends of Captain Soule
followed, led by Governor John Evans...

...Governor Evans' testimony before your committee was characterized
by such prevarication and shuffling as has been shown by no witness they
have examined during the four years they have been engaged in their inves-
tigations; and for the evident purpose of avoiding the admission that he
was fully aware that the Indians massacred so brutally at Sand Creek were
then, and had been, actuated by the most friendly feelings towards the
whites, and had done all in their power to restrain those less friendly dis-
posed...

Colonel John M. Chivington, the former military commander of
the Colorado First Cavalry, and a man who once regarded Silas
Soule with as much love he would show his own son, was conspicuously absent from the funeral procession...

...As to Colonel Chivington, your committee can hardly find fitting
terms to describe his conduct. Wearing the uniform of the United States,
which should be the emblem of justice and humanity; holding the important
position of commander of a military district, and therefore having the honor
of the government to that extent in his keeping, he deliberately planned and
executed a foul and dastardly massacre which would have disgraced the ver-
iest savage among those who were the victims of his cruelty. Having full
knowledge of their friendly character, having himself been instrumental to
some extent in placing them in their position of fancied security, he took
advantage of their inapprehension and defenseless condition to gratify the
worst passions that ever cursed the heart of man. It is thought by some that
desire for political preferment prompted him to this cowardly act; that he
supposed that by pandering to the inflamed passions of an excited popula-
tion he could recommend himself to their regard and consideration. Others
think it was to avoid being sent where there was more of danger and hard
service to be performed; that he was willing to get up a show of hostility on
the part of the Indians by committing himself acts which savages themselves
would never premeditate. Whatever may have been his motive, it is to be
hoped that the authority of this government will never again be disgraced
by acts such as he and those acting with him have been guilty of commit-
ting.
There were hostile Indians not far distant, against which Colonel
Chivington could have led the force under his command. Major Anthony
testifies that but three or four days' march from his post were several hun-
dreds of Indians, generally believed to be engaged in acts of hostility

towards the whites. And he deliberately testifies that only the fear of them prevented him from killing those who were friendly and entirely within his reach and control. It is true that to reach them required some days of hard marching. It was not to be expected that they could be surprised as easily as those on Sand Creek; and the warriors among them were almost, if not quite, as numerous as the soldiers under the control of Colonel Chivington.

Whatever influence this may have had upon Colonel Chivington, the truth is that he surprised and murdered, in cold blood, the unsuspecting men, women, and children on Sand Creek, who had every reason to believe they were under the protection of the United States authorities, and then returned to Denver and boasted of the brave deeds he and the men under his command had performed...

Captain Soule was buried at the city cemetery on April 27, 1865. Three volleys were fired by a military honor guard, and the funeral procession slowly dispersed until Hersa Soule stood alone by her beloved husband's grave...

...In conclusion, your committee are of the opinion that for the purpose of vindicating the cause of justice and upholding the honor of the nation, prompt and energetic measures should be at once taken to remove from office those who have thus disgraced the government by whom they are employed, and to punish, as their crimes deserve, those who have been guilty of these brutal and cowardly acts.

Respectfully submitted,

B. F. WADE, Chairman...

The Sand Creek Massacre was investigated by two congressional committees and one military commission, resulting in a recommendation by the Joint Committee on the Conduct of the War to remove Governor Evans from office, and to try Colonel John Chivington and Major Scott Anthony before a military commission for violating the usage of civilized warfare and acts unbecoming officers. Because Chivington and Anthony had resigned their commissions prior to the hearings, however, the United States Army was powerless to prosecute them. With no further military action possible, the Military Commission officially concluded its inquiry on May 30, 1865. Under the heated pressure of President Andrew Johnson, who would soon burn in his own political fires, Governor Evans resigned in August 1865.

Judge Advocate General Joseph Holt, in a final attempt to fix official blame for the massacre, publicly accused John Chivington of "cowardly and cold-blooded slaughter." He recommended that the United States government publicly condemn the military's actions at Sand Creek. No such statement was ever issued. In 1870, however, President Ulysses Grant broke the military reticence on the matter of Sand Creek, and publicly stated:

"For the honor of humanity, it would be well could the record of their deeds be blotted out. The entire history of Indian warfare furnished no more black and damning episode than the massacre at Sand Creek..."

The massacre at Sand Creek ended any hope for peace between Plains Tribes and the government, as Arapaho, Kiowa, Comanche, Prairie Apache and Sioux warriors joined the Cheyenne Dog Soldiers in a long and bloody retaliatory campaign that lasted over five years. The war resulted in widespread death and destruction across northeastern Colorado, Kansas and Nebraska, until Tall Bull's Dogmen were defeated in 1869 at the battle of Summit Springs, Colorado. The surviving Dogmen scattered and joined the Northern Cheyenne and Sioux warriors above the Republican. Before the hostile Indians were eventually subdued in the late 1870s, this alliance scored one final victory at the Little Big Horn River in 1876, where they annihilated General George Custer's Seventh Cavalry, under the leadership of Sioux chiefs, Sitting Bull and Crazy Horse...

THE AFTERMATH

Nearly one-quarter of the Cheyenne Council of Forty-four was killed at Sand Creek, eliminating nearly all of the tribe's peaceably inclined chiefs. Disgraced in the eyes of the Plains warriors, Black Kettle would never again exert influence over the younger tribal chiefs, but he continued his efforts to make peace in behalf of the *Tsis Tsis Tas*. Pressured by Congress to compensate for the shameful actions of John Chivington's Colorado militia, the army appointed a special commission to propose a peace council with the Indians of the Upper Arkansas region. In the autumn of 1865, Black Kettle and other chiefs of the Cheyenne and Arapaho tribes met the commissioners: Major General William S. Harney; Colonel Christopher "Kit" Carson; William Bent; Major General John B. Sanborn; Judge James Steele, of the Bureau of Indian Affairs; Superintendent Thomas Murphy; and Indian Agent Jesse Leavenworth. Major Edward Wynkoop led the detachment to protect the commissioners.

This was the first time that Wynkoop laid eyes on Black Kettle since they parted as friends just three days before the massacre at Sand Creek. Although Wynkoop feared Black Kettle would hold him responsible for the attack, the noble Cheyenne chief greeted his old friend with understanding, having wisely ascertained that Wynkoop had not betrayed him. A contentious council ensued, but in the end the commissioners unofficially acknowledged military wrongdoing at Sand Creek and agreed to compensate the tribes through the Treaty of the Little Arkansas. Among the promises made under the terms of the treaty, parcels of reservation land below the Arkansas in Kansas were pledged to the chiefs who signed, and land and financial reparations were pledged to the families of those killed at Sand Creek. The United States Congress ratified the treaty but eventually distributed only goods and supplies worth less than half of the value promised. As for land pledged in the treaty, no reservation was ever established, for the Dog Soldiers refuted Black Kettle's efforts and continued to wage war between the Smoky Hill and South Platte. Again, the militant

Dog Soldiers and other warrior bands remained unbending in their pursuit of war against the whites, unearthing the fragile ground of peace upon which Black Kettle and other peaceably inclined Indians stood.

Black Kettle, ever patient, or as many Cheyennes believed - a glutton for punishment - once again agreed to yet another council with the government that involved Wynkoop, now an agent for the Cheyennes and Arapahos, and many of the old players from the Sand Creek era. The resulting Medicine Lodge Treaty of 1867 pushed the Plains Tribes further south to Indian territory in modern-day Oklahoma, on the Washita River, where Black Kettle and chiefs of the Kiowas and Arapahos agreed to make their winter camp.

On November 27, 1868, exactly four years after the Sand Creek Massacre, Lieutenant Colonel George Armstrong Custer's Seventh Cavalry led a surprise dawn attack on Black Kettle's village, and Black Kettle and Medicine Woman Later were among the first killed. After Custer's attack, the *New York Times* reported that "one of the most troublesome and dangerous characters on the plains had finally been exterminated."

Of Black Kettle, Edward Wynkoop countered in his eulogy address to the U. S. Indian Commission, December 23, 1868: "The whole force of his nature was concentrated in the one idea of how best to act for the good of his race..."

William Byers

For many years, William Byers insisted in his *Rocky Mountain News* that Colonel Chivington was a hero who acted correctly at Sand Creek, calling the massacre "the most effective expedition against the Indians ever planned and carried out." Byers condemned the Joint Committee's report as "a disgrace on the name of justice." Byers continued to revise Sand Creek history over the years, and by 1880, he denied that the Colorado Third Cavalry had scalped any Indians. He alternately blamed Smith, Colley, Wynkoop, Tappan, Soule and other First Cavalry soldiers of profiteering and jealousy, claimed that White Antelope was the murderer of the Hungate family, and he declared the Indians were actually the ones whose saddles were adorned with the severed breasts of white women.

Byers was not the only Chivington apologist in the western press.

The *Nebraska City News* said: "We warn Indians and niggers to beware of his (Benjamin Wade's) example. We are in favor of the Reverend Colonel Chivington and a religious extermination of Indians generally, together with senatorial, congressional or other sympathizing committees..."

In 1868, the *Pueblo Chieftan* called the Indian "treacherous, chewing, lying, drunken, sneaking, bloodthirsty, brutal, ungrately, and has all these and every other bad quality in the superlative..."

An 1870 *Golden Transcript* editorial called for "an utter and uncompromising war of extermination upon every hostile tribe..."

Byers remained in Denver, surviving numerous scandals, including cheating on his wife, and he amassed a fortune in business partnerships that promoted the growth of Denver. He died in 1903...

John Evans

Governor John Evans forever maintained he had no prior knowledge of Chivington's planned attack on the Indians at Sand Creek, but his decidedly good name and reputation would forever share the burden of the tragedy. Despite a vigorous public defense of his position, his gross mismanagement of relations with the Indians and inability to understand the nature of deceitful, hardball politics effectively destroyed Governor Evans' political career. For Denver, however, Evans' ouster from the political arena was a silver lining to the black cloud of Sand Creek.

Dr. Evans' ineptitude in politics was far outweighed by his brilliance and vision in the private business sector. Evans founded the University of Denver, to this day among the most prestigious private universities in the country. He put up his own funds to help build churches and encourage new businesses to move to a city that, in the aftermath of Sand Creek, was entirely cut off by vast Indian war parties and written off by many. For several years after the massacre, Denver was proclaimed "too dead to bury" by its rivals in Cheyenne, Wyoming, but the relentless drive of John Evans and other die-hard Coloradoans kept the critically wounded city breathing through the 1860s. At the end of the decade, Denver's fate dramatically turned when Evans and his partners persuaded voters to approve a bond issue that gave birth to the Denver Pacific Railroad, a 100-mile line that connected Denver to Cheyenne. Once again, just when the Mile High City was on the brink of extinction, she defiantly stood up and challenged all comers.

Little did Wyoming businessmen know at the time, the relatively short Denver Pacific tie was the first strand of a railroad web that eventually turned the town of Cheyenne into a secondary route. Evans and the astute business moguls of Denver subsequently connected their city to rail lines from all directions of the country, creating a primary hub for mining interests to transport and refine their product. Evans established the Denver Tramway Company with his son, William, and partners William Byers, Henry Brown and Roger Woodbury. The company built Denver's first network of electric trolleys that connected all parts of the city and employed thousands of citizens. Denver's commerce and population exploded throughout the remainder of the next two decades, as it became the largest industrial center between St. Louis and California.

From its wild and violent beginnings, when Ned Wynkoop and a band of Jayhawkers staked their claims along Cherry Creek, the little mining camp called Denver rose from obscurity and evolved into a 21st Century metropolis of two million people. This, largely due to the tireless efforts of John Evans, who once wallowed in the ignominious shadow cast by a huge, ruthless opportunist by the name of Chivington...

Bull Bear

Dogman Chief Bull Bear rose to prominence among the militant warriors after the betrayal at Sand Creek. Among but a few Dogmen in favor of peace before the massacre, Bull Bear relented afterwards and led some of the most vicious attacks on white settlements and wagon trails during the five-year retaliation. At times, however, he considered Black Kettle's overtures to peace with the whites, participating in the ill-fated and futile Medicine Lodge Treaty of 1867. By then, Bull Bear was considered among the most prominent Cheyenne chiefs, far surpassing Black Kettle in political power and influence. Despite his outrage over the Sand Creek Massacre, Bull Bear reconciled with Ned Wynkoop, and maintained a civil rapport with the Tall Chief. His friendship with Wynkoop did not quell the warrior spirit after Sand Creek, however. He continued to resist the white infringement upon the Dogmen's self-proclaimed spiritual rights to the Smoky Hill country, until the death of his cantankerous compatriot, Tall Bull, at Summit Springs in 1869.

Tall Bull's defeat sounded the death knell of the Dogmen, and Bull Bear was forced to wander north toward Sioux country, where he clearly saw the handwriting on the wall. After Black Kettle's death on the Washita, the former Dogman warrior knew the Indians' reign over the great plains had come to an end, and he soon agreed to take his family to the newly established Darlington Agency reservation near Fort Reno in modern-day Oklahoma. There, Bull Bear put his children in white schools and ultimately adopted the Christian faith. A relentless survivor, Bull Bear grew less defiant with age, and the once fearsome Dogman lived peaceably among the whites until his death in 1904...

Scott J. Anthony

New York native Scott Anthony lived for a time in Rhode Island and later moved to Kansas at the age of 25 to take up the Union cause in 1855. The cousin of woman's suffrage leader, Susan B. Anthony, the young abolitionist's roots were planted deeply in political issues, and he soon joined a vigilante militia to fight against pro slavery raiders. The Colorado gold rush drew Anthony to Denver, where, like many, he soon abandoned dreams of wealth to fight at La Glorieta with the Colorado First Cavalry. After becoming entangled in the controversy surrounding Sand Creek, Anthony angrily resigned from the army and moved to Montana to escape the ignominy of his association with John Chivington. He returned to Denver in 1869 and established a successful real estate business, later serving as Director of Evans' Denver Tramway Company for ten years. Anthony harbored a deep bitterness for Chivington, but his resentment apparently waned in later years, for he served as a pallbearer at the Fighting Parson's funeral. Scott Anthony died in Denver in 1903 at the age of 73...

Joseph Cramer

Disillusioned and angry over the murder of his friend, Silas Soule, Lieutenant Joseph Cramer resigned from the military and escaped the wrath of the Chivington apologists in Denver. He returned to his roots in Kansas, where he was elected Sheriff of Dickinson County. His health deteriorated a few years later, and he fell seriously ill from complications caused by an old injury he received in service. Cramer died in 1870 at the age of 31 and was buried in Solomon, KS...

John Smith

John Smith continued to work for the government as an Indian interpreter, participating in both the Little Arkansas and Medicine Lodge treaty negotiations.

His 20-year journey through the tumultuous decades of white/Indian acrimony came to an end shortly after Smith arrived in Oklahoma to assist the establishment of the new Darlington Agency. It was there that Smith and George Bent brought the emerging influential Cheyenne Peace Chief Stone Calf, who came to great prominence in waging political battles for the benefit of the *Tsis Tsis Tas*. John Smith died in 1871 at the age of 61...

Jacob Downing & George Shoup

Chivington's closest supporters, Jacob Downing and George Shoup, also resigned from the army shortly after Sand Creek. Although second in command of the Third Regiment at the Sand Creek Massacre, Shoup seemed to fall through the cracks of accusations and scandal, and mustered out of the army unscathed. He ventured to the great northwest and successfully ran several businesses while advancing his political career. He became the first Territorial Governor of Idaho in 1889, appointed by President Benjamin Harrison, and spearheaded the movement to admit Idaho into the Union. He was elected Governor of the new state in 1890, and later represented Idaho for two terms in the U.S. Senate. He died at Boise in 1904.

Jacob Downing remained in Colorado and amassed a fortune in ranching, real estate and horse breeding. Among the most revered and honored Denver pioneers, Downing was active in many civic and charitable organizations and made enormous contributions to the development of Denver. Perhaps more than any other Chivington supporter, Jacob Downing never waned in his defense of the Colorado Third Cavalry's attack at Sand Creek. He often railed against Indians in public forums, and he never

shied away from extolling the virtues of exterminating the red man when Bill Byers needed copy. Downing died in 1907...

Little Raven

Arapaho Principal Chief Little Raven kept his demoralized clan alive through the winter of 1865. The Southern Arapahos' relationship with its Cheyenne cousins deteriorated in the aftermath of Sand Creek, leaving the smaller Arapahos vulnerable. Although Little Raven's name was often confused with his warrior son, the elder chief had always maintained a peaceful attitude with the whites, and, like Black Kettle, he never strayed from his endeavor to keep the peace. Raven's personable manner with his old friends helped him maintain a dialogue with the government in the  aftermath of Sand Creek. He visited President Ulysses Grant and received a peace medal before his death at Oklahoma in 1889. In a belated but sincere gesture, the City of Denver named a street in 1994 to honor the great Southern Arapaho chief...

Left Hand (Niwot)

Left Hand was among the most prominent Arapaho chiefs that endeavored to keep the peace with the white settlers. An amicable and intelligent man, Left Hand spoke Cheyenne, Lakota and English fluently. He had befriended the Denver settlers during the Pike's Peak Gold rush years, having once appeared on stage with Ned Wynkoop in a local theatrical production in which he made an impassioned plea to refrain from talk of fighting Indians. Severely wounded at Sand Creek, Left Hand was among the injured taken away from the battlefield. He died a short time later near the Smoky Hill River. It has been estimated that Left Hand was in his early 40s at the time of his death, and he left a wife and several children. His brother Neva survived him, but as in the case of many Indians, there is very little documentation to account for the whereabouts of Neva after Sand Creek.

Another Arapaho chief by the name of Left Hand emerged as a prominent leader in later years, but most historians agree that the latter chief was no relation to the Left Hand killed in the Sand Creek Massacre. The latter Arapaho Chief, Left Hand, who upon Little Raven's death became Principal Chief of the Southern Arapahos, is not to be confused with the Arapaho peace chief who played a prominent role in saving the lives of Laura Roper and her fellow captives...

Bent Family

William Bent

When William Bent sold his trading post to the army, he was set upon the path to Sand Creek, where his family was destroyed.

Charley Bent disappeared after the Sand Creek attack. He became a murderous renegade, and once made an unsuccessful attempt to kill his father. He was killed by Pawnees in 1868.

Robert Bent, forever hated by Cheyennes for his role in the Sand Creek Massacre, continued to work as an army interpreter and scout until his death in 1889.

George Bent recovered from his wounds at Sand Creek and joined the Dog Soldiers in their bloody reign of vengeance after the massacre. He married Black Kettle's niece, Magpie, and continued to live with the Cheyennes his entire life. George became the best known of the Bent family, eventually compiling a half-century of Cheyenne history published by noted historian, George E. Hyde. George Bent died in 1916.

George Bent

William Bent's Cheyenne wife, Yellow Woman, survived the Sand Creek Massacre, but was soon killed by General P. E. Connor's troops. His family destroyed, and cut off by the Cheyennes he so loved, Little White Man died alone in 1869...

Laura Roper & the Indian Captives

Laura Roper and her three fellow captives, Ambrose Asher, age 7, Daniel Marble, age 9, and three-year-old Isabel Eubank rode with Wynkoop's command to Denver in September 1864. Their extraordinary and horrifying experience epitomized the brutal nature of ancient Indian customs in warfare, and represented the tragic collateral damage suffered by the many unfortunate whites captured by Indians during the twenty-year war on the plains.

Daniel Marble, Laura Roper, Isabel Eubank, Ambrose Asher

Laura, the strong-willed teenager who defiantly stood up to her Dogmen captives, spent several weeks in Denver, living with a local family and answering numerous requests by the papers to relate her story to the world. She wrote to officials in Nebraska City, seeking any information they might have regarding the fate of her family. In short order, Laura received a letter from her elated mother, who'd nearly given up all hope for Laura's survival. Laura was overcome with relief to learn her entire family had escaped the Dogmen raid on the Little Blue. She was soon put on a heavily guarded wagon train bound for Fort Kearney, Nebraska, and then took a stage to Nebraska City, where a tearful reunion of the Roper family brought Laura's long ordeal to a happy conclusion. Joseph Roper, with a bellyful of pioneer life, immediately took his family back to Pennsylvania.

Laura spent several years fielding requests for interviews by the ravenous press, dutifully relating her story but declining offers to write her memoirs for a book. In time, the fervor subsided, and

Laura went on to marry, raise children, and live a long and happy life. In 1918, at the age of 70, Laura finally put her remembrances to paper – this time at the request of her children and grandchildren. Laura passed away in 1929 at Enid, Oklahoma.

The fate of Lucy Eubank* and her infant son, William Joseph Eubank, was less merciful. Lucy, Isabel, baby Willie, and nephew Ambrose Asher were the only Eubank family members that survived the brutal Dogman attack on Liberty Farm. It was a simple and wicked twist of fate that separated Lucy and William from Isabel, whom the warriors mistakenly believed to be Laura Roper's child. Laura and Isabel's good fortune to fall into the hands of the humane Arapahos, Left Hand and Neva, was in stark contrast to Lucy's horrible captivity with the brutal Sioux murderer, Two Face.

Mrs. Eubank and her baby were held for more than a year before being ransomed by Two Face near Fort Laramie. Union soldiers rescued Lucy and William, and executed Two Face and his renegade band. Sadly, however, Lucy never saw Isabel again. Her daughter, who was adopted by a Denver physician, died within months of her release, reportedly of injuries or illness brought on by her ordeal with the Indians. Over the years, Lucy rarely discussed her experiences as a Sioux captive, but at the time of her rescue she bitterly alluded to physical and sexual abuse by the renegade warriors. Suffering from severe emotional scars the rest of her life, Lucy married twice, losing both husbands to death after just a few years. Lucy thereafter lived with her son and his family until her death in 1913. William, who was mercifully too young to recollect his captivity, began to contact historians after his mother's death, seeking information about his murdered family and the horrid details of the Dogman attack on the Liberty Farm. While living in Greeley, Colorado, Eubank was put in touch with Laura Roper, and the two former Indian captives met in an emotional reunion, 62 years after the hideous day on the Little Blue River...

Ambrose Asher was returned to family members and grew up in Illinois. He married and had five children, but died of malaria in 1894 at the age of 37. Daniel Marble was the son of William Marble, who was killed on Plum Creek during the same time of the raids on the Little Blue. Before he could be returned to his mother, Daniel died of typhoid fever not long after he was released and brought to Denver by Major Wynkoop...

---

* Some accounts refer to the spelling 'Eubanks,' or 'Ewbanks,' while Laura Roper's written accounts, along with personal letters written by William J. Eubank Jr, used the spelling: Eubank.

Samuel Tappan

Samuel Tappan moved to New York City after Sand Creek, and became a political activist in the Indian reform movement, serving many years on the Indian Peace Commission. Tappan adopted one of three Indian children who survived the Sand Creek Massacre, but the young girl died of tuberculosis at the age of sixteen. Tappan died in Washington D.C. in 1913, and is buried at Arlington National Cemetery...

Samuel R. Curtis

West Point graduate Samuel R. Curtis was considered among the most successful generals in the Civil War. His most notable achievements included the solidification of Union control in Arkansas at the Battle of Pea Ridge, and his turning back Confederate General Sterling Price's Missouri raid at the Battle of Westport in 1864. Curtis retired to Iowa shortly after the war. He died of a sudden illness in 1866 at the age of 61...

Edward W. Wynkoop

The storied life of Edward Wanshaer Wynkoop rivaled any of his more famous counterparts, but unlike Kit Carson, George Custer or Ulysses Grant, Wynkoop had no desire to seek political office or garner glorious headlines. Beyond the naming of a street in the city he helped found, Wynkoop quietly slipped into the footnotes of Western American history. At the urging of friends, he once attempted to write a book about his remarkable career, but the inherently unpretentious pioneer abandoned the manuscript before it was completed. The opening paragraph of his aborted 1876 auto-biography summed up his life in a few simple but revealing words:

If this narrative should ever be read by any besides my personal friends and relatives I have an apology to make for what must be inevitable in simply detailing the experiences of the humble writer viz the frequent use of the personal pronoun...

The personal pronoun "I" rarely found a comfortable place in Ned Wynkoop's vocabulary. Indeed, the tall and imposing Pennsylvanian was impulsive, emotionally brash, easily agitated, and sometimes downright arrogant in his youth, but the young boy who always stepped in to stop a schoolyard brawl forever carried that most admirable quality of temperance throughout his life. He was the first to take responsibility for his mistakes, and although sometimes the proverbial bull in a china closet when it came to military protocol, Wynkoop impressed his superiors more often than confounded them. If nothing else, history will forever remember Ned Wynkoop as the consummate arbitrator with a keen insight to human nature; a man, much like his Cheyenne friend Black Kettle, who sought the high road to peace, no matter the unfavorable odds or petulant opposition.

After being fully exonerated by all three Sand Creek inquiries, Wynkoop was appointed to the service of the War Department at the rank of Brevet-Lieutenant Colonel, where he served as Agent for the Cheyenne and Arapaho tribes for the remainder of the decade. Wynkoop's highly regarded negotiation skills were put to the supreme test under the most volatile circumstances. On many occasions after the disaster at Sand Creek, Wynkoop boldly faced Tall Bull, White Horse, Bull Bear and other Dogmen chiefs in councils, earning their respect, and in the case of Bull Bear, rekindling their friendship. Sadly, his efforts to end the Indian Wars were continually undermined by both the brutal Dog Soldiers' refusal to relent in their vicious Sand Creek retaliations, and the government's inherent indifference to the plight of the only true indigenous inhabitants of the United States.

Wynkoop spent four futile years arranging councils and proposing peace treaties, only to see them either broken, or rigorously amended by Congress, which served to drive a deeper wedge between Indians and whites. The Medicine Lodge Treaty of 1867 would be Wynkoop's final failure, for he realized too late that the friendly Indians of the Plains might again pay the ultimate price for the hostility of their warrior brethren and the hypocrisy of the United States government. In essence, Wynkoop was still the boyhood referee, but in this case he stood between two immovable bullies determined to fight to the death with no regard for the innocent red and white lives caught in the middle. In the end, Wynkoop chose to step away rather than die on his own sword. Clearly sensing the potential for future Chivington massacres, he angrily tendered his resignation to the Commissioner of Indian Affairs, stating that he refused to once again be a party to the "murder of innocent women and children."

Perhaps Wynkoop's resignation was more the product of inside information than intuition, for Custer led the dawn attack on Black Kettle's peaceful village camped at the Washita River on the very day Wynkoop stepped down. Custer's swift and brutal strike, followed by a hasty retreat from harder fighting up river, rang eerily familiar to Chivington's hit-and-run attack on Sand Creek. The Cheyennes later identified the dead as Black Kettle, Medicine Woman Later, 20 warriors and 40 Indian women and children, but Custer's subsequent reports eventually inflated the number to 300 Indians killed. Fearing another Sand Creek debacle, the United States Army buried the dead Indians and revealed only sketchy and inconsistent casualty statistics to the public. A bold and vocal preemptive propaganda campaign followed, as the army dispatched its most articulate and loyal officers to strike down the inevitable comparisons of Washita to Sand Creek by the eastern press. Wynkoop, Tappan and a host of other Indian sympathizers were summarily smeared and ridiculed for their efforts to bring peace to the Plains.

Angry and disillusioned, Wynkoop left government service in 1868. He moved his wife and children back to Pennsylvania and struggled in the family's iron business for several years before the call of adventure once again beckoned. In 1874, he ventured to the Black Hills to prospect for gold. Wynkoop's return to the West reinvigorated his life, as he participated in the gold rush and led a small detachment of volunteers charged with protecting the vicinity from Indian war parties. Two years later, George Armstrong Custer, in a bid to run for president after one final victory over the Indians, was cut to ribbons when he attacked a Sioux camp on the Little Big Horn River. The Sioux warriors and Cheyenne Dogmen reclaimed the area, and Wynkoop hastily retreated on a perilous journey back to Pennsylvania with four friends.

He then took his family to Colorado, and subsequently to Arizona and New Mexico, back in the employ of the government. He served as Adjutant General of the New Mexico Territory, and later as warden of the federal penitentiary. Throughout the remainder of his life, Wynkoop harbored bitter hatred for John Chivington, not only for Sand Creek, but also for the murder of his close friend, Silas Soule. Although witnesses clearly placed Private Charles W. Squier at the murder scene - and Squier himself later openly boasted of killing Soule - Wynkoop adamantly insisted that Chivington ordered the assassination. Chivington did publicly offer a $500 bounty to anyone who killed an Indian or those who sympathize with them, but his offhand comment to a partisan crowd was passed off to the political bluster of the times. First Regiment officers had testified to hearing Chivington make threats against Soule at Fort Lyon, and although it was never proven, Wynkoop and Samuel Tappan forever maintained that Soule's assassination was sanctioned by the Fighting Parson.

A harsh life on the prairie had taken its toll on Wynkoop, and by the age of 55, he endured many maladies stemming from the numerous injuries and wounds suffered as a young man. The man whom George Bent once called the Cheyenne and Arapaho's best friend died of Bright's Disease at Santa Fe in 1891, survived by his wife, five sons, and three daughters.

Louisa Wynkoop moved back to Denver after Ned's death. She lived with her son, Frank Murray Wynkoop, and his family – just five doors down from John Chivington's home on Stout Street.

Chivington's career in politics but a shattered memory, he had returned to Denver after several tumultuous decades in exile back East. Perhaps in attempt to ease his conscience, Chivington was among signers of an affidavit in support of Louisa's application for a pension upon Ned's death. Their son Harman Wynkoop reportedly rejected a later Chivington attempt to mend fences, telling the Fighting Parson he would forever share his father's disdain for Chivington and his men. Frank Wynkoop claimed he once had an encounter with the old man, in which Chivington whispered to him, "Young man, your father was right in condemning that Sand Creek massacre..."

James D. Cannon

In the summer of 1865, Lieutenant James Cannon, of the First New Mexico Volunteers, helped apprehend Captain Soule's confessed murderer, Charles Squier, after receiving a tip that Squier was hiding out in Las Vegas, New Mexico. Two days after Cannon brought Squier back to face a military court-martial in Denver, he was found dead in his hotel room at the Tremont House after a night of drinking and gambling in a local saloon. Witnesses reported hearing a commotion in Cannon's room that night, raising speculation that yet another Chivington enemy had been murdered – possibly by poisoning. A post-mortem exam concluded that a lethal combination of alcohol and morphine caused Cannon's death. A man dying of an alcohol/drug overdose was not an uncommon occurrence in the wild and wooly pioneer town of Denver, but to this day Chivington's supporters and detractors continue to debate over the circumstances of James Cannon's death...

Charles W. Squier

The history of Private Charles W. Squier's life still lurks in the shadowy darkness from which he emerged to bushwhack Captain Silas Soule at 15th and Arapaho Street in Denver. Charles Wesley Squier was linked to the family of Joel Squier, a Methodist minister from Bethlehem, New York, first in Gary L. Roberts' classic 1984 doctoral theses, *Sand Creek – Tragedy and Symbol*. Professor Roberts reported that Charles Wesley Squier, born in 1836, had served as a captain in the 74th New York State Volunteers in the Civil War. Captain Squier abruptly resigned his commission in 1864, fraudulently citing family hardship when he in fact was a disillusioned malcontent unable to commit to the Union's cause. He drifted west, working briefly for the railroad and ultimately ending up prospecting for gold in the Rocky Mountains. Court documents show that the confessed killer of Captain Soule, Private Charles W. Squier of the Second Colorado Cavalry, had been previously tried and convicted in November 1864 for the attempted murder of Mariano Medina, a Mexican immigrant and well known Colorado pioneer and mountain man. Squier's conviction was soon overturned, however, because the case was tried in a federal, rather than county court. Apparently destitute and out of work, Squier enlisted in the Second Colorado Cavalry in December of 1864 but was soon arrested again, this time for an undocumented crime, but records state he was jailed until April 1865. During this time Squier undoubtedly met Williamson Morrow, another Second Cavalry recruit and Squier's accomplice in Captain Soule's murder.

After his arrest for the murder of Captain Soule, Private Squier was held in a Denver jail throughout the summer of 1865, awaiting an October trial by military court-martial. According to the Roberts dissertation, Squier received legal assistance during this time from several military officials, and most interesting, noted journalist and editor, Ephraim George Squier, the half brother of Charles Wesley Squier of New York. E.G. Squier attempted to call in favors to ensure his black sheep brother be accorded a fair trial. The elder Squier feared for his brother's life in light of the raging controversy over Sand Creek and the open hostility reportedly displayed by vengeful First Cavalry soldiers and local friends of the popular Captain Soule. On October 5, Private Squier escaped from jail, just days before his trial, aided by conspirators that picked the jail lock and chiseled off Squier's shackles. Two conspirators were arrested during the jailbreak, but Squier and the other man made a clean getaway. Again accusations of a Chivington conspiracy to murder Soule arose, now expanding to the rescue of his killer from the gallows. More than likely, however, Squier escaped with the help of his brother's considerable reach. For over 100 years, historical accounts of the Sand Creek Massacre reported that Squier fled to California and was never seen again, but Professor Roberts uncovered two alleged 'sightings' of Squier in subsequent years.

In the 1890s, a retired soldier in a California home for veterans reportedly made a deathbed confession to the murder of Captain Soule. Witnesses stated that the dying man claimed he was hired by Chivington to kill Soule, but no documentation of the alleged confession exists. Roberts also uncovered a 1902 claim by a Sand Creek veteran of the Colorado First Cavalry, who reported that Soule's killer was living in Washington state. A Charles Squier was indeed found in Washington, but he was not the same man. The true chapter to the mystery of Private Charles W. Squier lies in the records of the Squier family papers, held at the New York Historical Society archives that were chronicled in historian Tom Bensing's 2012 biography, *Silas Soule: A Short, Eventful Life of Moral Courage*. Bensing traced Squier's path along an arduous year-long journey back to New York, where the fugitive was eventually harbored by his long-suffering but loyal brother, E.G. Squier. The murderer drifted from job to job, attempting at one time to re-join the army and later unsuccessfully seeking passage to Central America.

Squier's saga ended in 1869, when after five years of drifting through the shadows and evading arrest for the murder of Silas Soule, fate finally brought the killer to justice when Squier's legs were crushed in a railroad accident. He succumbed to gangrene and was ironically hailed as a war hero by the Eastern press apparently unaware of the fugitive Squier's dark history west of the Mississippi.

Hersa Coberly Soule

In the short span of nine months, Hersa Coberly Soule's father was killed by an unidentified band of Indians (most likely Kiowas or Arapahos), and an assassin's bullet struck down her husband. A bride for just three weeks, 21-year-old Hersa was shattered by the murder of Silas Soule. She was taken under the wing of Soule's friends, Sam Tappan and Ned Wynkoop, who escorted her to Lawrence, Kansas in August 1865, where she lived with Soule's brother, William Lloyd Garrison Soule and his wife, Mary. Hersa remained there for a time to mourn her beloved "Silie," and to find a new direction for her life.

In a letter to Soule's sister, Annie, Hersa wrote:

I like Will and Mary very, very much, but I don't think Will is much like Silas. He is not full of fun, but his eyes and hair are very much like My Silies'. But I have no doubt but he is as good, and I love him dearly, but oh dear Annie, no one can feel as I do; he was my future hope, and some time when I look at Will and I see the very same eyes, I think oh can it be, I want to throw my arms around his neck and say tis true you're with me yet my own dear Silie. The thought is almost maddening to me sometimes, and I go to my room and stay for hours and read to get it off my mind. Oh, I am afraid I shall make them unhappy. I would rather die than so. I think because it is my fate to be unhappy, it is not right that I should make others unhappy on my account...

Hersa forever regarded the Soule family as her own, but as time passed, she eventually returned to Colorado to be near her mother and brothers and sister. In 1870, Hersa met a veteran soldier, miner, and civil servant, Alfred E. Lea, whom she married the following year in Boulder, Colorado. Their oldest son, Homer, born in 1876, suffered a fall in his infancy that caused a permanent and debilitating curvature of his spine. In 1879, Hersa took Homer to Kansas City to have the child examined by a medical specialist, but the prognosis was grim. The young boy was destined to live out his life with unrelenting pain and a severe handicap.

Homer Lea, however, overcame the odds and went on to attend Stanford University, where he fed his voracious appetite for Chinese history. At 23, he traveled to the Far East and joined the forces of Kang Yu-wei in a failed attempt to suppress the Boxer Rebellion. Lea later served as an advisor to Sun Yat-sen and participated in the recruitment and training of Chinese revolutionary guerillas to be smuggled into China. He was appointed Chief of Staff when Sun Yat-sen finally turned China into a republic in 1911, but he died of a stroke within a year. An extraordinarily gifted military scholar, Homer Lea wrote two significant books, *The Valor of Ignorance*, which predicted the rise of Japanese aggression in the Pacific; and *The Day of the Saxon*, which foretold the rise of Hitler's Third Reich. The radical ideas of Homer Lea received little attention in his lifetime, but later attracted the attention of many military leaders, among them General Douglas MacArthur.

Hersa would never see the accomplishments of her son, however. In the late 1870s, she reportedly suffered from a recurring streptococcus infection, malignant erysipelas, a common open-wound infection easily treated by modern medicine, but often fatal in the days before the development of antibiotics. The untreated infection damaged Hersa's lymphatic system, and she passed away in 1879 at her mother's home in Denver. She left her grieving husband, young Homer, and two daughters. Hersa was buried just a short distance from Silas Soule's grave at Riverside Cemetery.

Inscribed on her headstone: *"Resurgam"* (Latin: "I shall rise again") and, *"My lambs shall lie down with me."*

Silas S. Soule

Captain Silas S. Soule's fate was sealed at Sand Creek on a cold November morning in 1864, along with the Cheyenne and Arapaho villagers who died at the hands of John Chivington's vengeful Colorado militia. The military commission never questioned Soule about his refusal to attack the Indians that morning, nor did Chivington bring it up during cross-examination. After Soule was murdered, however, Chivington presented a deposition to the Commission, sworn by freighter Lipman Meyer, accusing Soule and Lieutenant Cannon of cowardice, theft and drunkenness

during the days following the Sand Creek Massacre. Other witnesses for Chivington attempted to implicate Soule in a conspiracy with John Smith and Sam Colley to profit from the Indian War. Soule's ominous prediction voiced to Captain George F. Price, regarding his fear of being murdered and then vilified by Chivington in the hearings, were subsequently presented in a deposition by Price, a former adjutant and friend of Chivington. Upon the Commission's receipt of Price's deposition, Colonel Tappan filed a motion to dismiss Meyer's testimony as irrelevant, hearsay, and an obvious attempt to turn the blame for Sand Creek on Soule. The Commission sustained Tappan's objection.

Undaunted, William Byers pitched in to help his friend Chivington. Byers dutifully reported Soule's murder as a moral tragedy, and he cried out for justice against the killer. Regarding Soule's funeral, however, Byers couldn't help but take one final shot at the body. Of the Reverend H. H. Hitchens' eulogy to the fallen warrior, Byers said:

"He refrained from speaking on private character, he said, because that custom of publicly overhauling private character, in the pulpit, for either praise or censure should be foreign to occasions of this kind..."

A different quote of Reverend Hitchens' eulogy, provided by Colorado State Historical Society contributor C. A. Prentice, reported a slightly different interpretation:

"It is of Captain Soule as a soldier that I may say something without fear of encroaching upon that sacred private memory that belongs alone to his widow, his mother and his friends. It is from the testimony of others that I must speak. By his commanding officers I am told he was a good soldier, and how much does that short objective involve? It involves all that can be said of a soldier. It implies that he had no fear of work, of fatigue, of suffering, of danger, of death. And was it not so? Did he not in the darkness of the night, almost at the midnight hour, go out to discharge his duty as commander of the Provost Guard of this city? Did he not go when he had every reason to believe that the alarm which called him out was only to decoy him into danger? Did he not go when he knew positively that his life was threatened, and that weeks ago five shots had been sent at him with deadly intent? Did he not go, feeling so certain that his doom was sealed, that he took farewell of his young wife, telling her what she must do in case he returned no more alive?

"Yes, and there is the spirit of the soldier, and the good soldier, too; he did his duty in the midst of danger, did his duty in the face of death, and fell by the assassin's hand..."

Twenty years after Soule's death, the City of Denver reclaimed the city cemetery and cleared the graves to make way for Cheesman Park. The army relocated Soule's remains to Denver's Riverside Cemetery with other deceased military personnel. At the time of Soule's death, his fellow soldiers of Company D took up a collection to erect a large monument to honor their fallen comrade, but today his grave is now marked by a simple military headstone that reads: S. S. Soule, Company D, First Colorado Cavalry. His grave looks across the quiet cemetery, where Hersa and her sister, Mattie, are buried side by side in the shadow of a large, opulent monument honoring Governor John Evans...

John M. Chivington

John Milton Chivington's timely retirement from the service insulated him from military and civil prosecution for his role in the Sand Creek Massacre, but his political career nevertheless disintegrated. He was never questioned or officially accused of complicity in the assassination of Captain Silas Soule, but even his most ardent supporters could not ignore, nor condone the murder of a Union officer. Whether by innuendo or blatant accusation, most Denverites on both sides of the Sand Creek issue suspected that Chivington had a hand in Soule's assassination, thus unraveling the Fighting Parson's presumption of innocence in the entire Sand Creek affair. A small, hard-core contingency of Chivington supporters, led by the *Rocky Mountain News*, would continue to grasp at straws in his defense, but Chivington's behavior over the next few years would rattle even the myopic William Byers.

Although the Methodist Church at first supported Chivington's actions at Sand Creek, Chivington was ultimately pressured to resign his position as presiding elder. He fled Denver, first to California and then Nebraska, but it seemed that the Indian spirits would follow him and dispense the justice that the government never delivered. In 1866, Chivington's son, Thomas Chivington, drowned in the North Platte River while trying to rescue passengers from an overturned stagecoach, and several months later Chivington's two-year-old granddaughter drowned in the Missouri River when she fell from a riverboat. The following year, Chivington's wife, Martha, suddenly took ill and died. Chivington then stunned his supporters in 1868, when he married Sarah Chivington, his widowed daughter-in-law, in an attempt to make a claim on his late son's freighting business. The claim yielded a mere $360, and Chivington abandoned his daughter-in-law bride shortly thereafter, prompting William Byers to write:

"What he will do next to outrage the moral sense and feelings of his

day and generation remains to be seen; but be sure it will be something..."

That may be the first time William Byers ever printed the truth. Shunned by the Methodist Church for his moral turpitude, and facing numerous legal charges ranging from assaulting a woman to extortion, Chivington fled to Canada, later emerging in Ohio, where he was flogged by voters in an unsuccessful political run for the Ohio State Legislature. Around the same time, he was arrested for assaulting his third wife, Isabella Arsen, who accused Chivington of beating her when she discovered that he had forged her signature on a promissory note to secure a loan. Isabella later dropped the charges and reconciled with her husband.

Bankrupt and disgraced, Chivington returned in 1883 to the only place where he could get a handout – Denver City, where he was invited to speak at a Denver Pioneer Society celebration. Renewed by the supportive crowd, Chivington railed against the military and government for condemning him, concluding his impassioned speech by declaring "I stand by Sand Creek!"

Chivington was elected Sheriff of Arapahoe County, but later charged but acquitted of perjury. He later joined the Denver County Coroner's office, but was soon arrested for stealing $800 from a corpse in his charge. He confessed to the crime and agreed by court order to return the money to the dead man's family in lieu of prosecution. The Chivington home later burned down, and investigators suspected - but were unable to prove - that Chivington set the fire in order to collect the insurance.

In 1892, Chivington filed an "Indian Depredation" claim of $30,000 against the Sioux Nation for loss of horses. Chivington died of palsy in 1894 before his claim was resolved, but the Indian spirits of Sand Creek took one last opportunity for revenge. The special investigator assigned to review Chivington's Indian Depredation claim was Samuel Tappan, who denied the claim.

Chivington was buried in Denver's Fairmount Cemetery, after a grand funeral that attracted "thousands" to Trinity Methodist Church, according to the *Rocky Mountain News*. William Byers declared Chivington "one of Colorado's greatest heroes." The Reverend Dr. Robert McIntyre said of Chivington, "I never in my life knew a man who so represented the soldierly element in Christianity as did the man whom we are here to honor...We shall not look upon his likes again."

In 1996, the United Methodist Church issued an official apology to the Cheyenne and Arapaho people for the Sand Creek Massacre, led by the Reverend Colonel John Milton Chivington...

By the very nature of ancient Indian culture, most historical data predating the 20th Century is provided through the interpretation of white historians, for Indian history was related by storytellers and passed on in the oral tradition prior to the 1900s. It is impossible to identify every Cheyenne and Arapaho person who died at Sand Creek, particularly the women and children. The following list was compiled from Roberts' *Sand Creek – Tragedy and Symbol*, official military records, and the 1982 issue of the *Northern Cheyenne Tribal News*, which provides a partial list of Cheyenne and Arapaho casualties at Sand Creek:

Bear Feathers
Bear Man
Bear Robe
Bear Skin
Big Child
Big Head
Big Louse
Big Man
Big Shell
Big Smoke
Big Wolf
Black Horse
Black Wolf
Blue Crane
Blue Horse
Bob-Tail Wolf
Buffalo Woman
Cohoe
Crow
Crow Necklace
Cut Lip Bear
Cut Nose
Dog Coming Up
Feather Head
Foot Tracks

Forked Stick
Full Bull
Heap Of Crows
Hog
Kills Bear
Kingfisher
Kiowa Wolf Mule
Lame Bear
Left Hand
Loser in the Race
Man On Hill
Morning Star
(or Dull Knife)
Mound Of Rocks
Old Little Robe
One Eye
Red Arm
Red Paint
Sitting Bear
Skunk
Spanish Woman
Spirit Walking
Spotted Crow
Standing Bear
Standing Water

Tall Bear
Tall Bull
(not the Dog Soldier Chief)
Tall Wolf
The Man
Turtle Following
   His Wife
Two Lances
Two Thighs
War Bonnet
White Antelope
White Beaver
White Calf
White Crane
White Faced Bull
White Hat
White Man
Wolf Mule
Wood
Wooden Leg
Wounded Bear
Yellow Shield
Yellow Wolf

Army casualties at Sand Creek, compiled from the Colorado State Archives as follows:

Aldrich, Joseph W. – 1st Colo. Cav. Private

Berkheimer, Jesse – 3rd Colo. Cav. Private

Conner, Joseph - 3rd Colo. Cav.

Douglas, John A. – 3rd Colo. Cav.

Duncan, John R. – 3rd Colo. Cav.

Foster, Henry C. – 3rd Colo. Cav.

McDermott, Patrick C. – 3rd Colo. Cav.

McFarland, Robert - 3rd Colo. Cav.

Medino, Francis – 3rd Colo. Cav.

Parkes, John – 3rd Colo. Cav.

Pierce, George W. – 1st Colo. Cav.

Pierson, Oliver – 1st Colo. Cav.

Shortly after the Sand Creek Massacre, the United States Army scoured the site and removed all evidentiary artifacts and remains in an apparent futile attempt to close the books on any further investigation of the incident. Although the Cheyennes collected some of their relatives' remains after the battle, many of the victims' bodies were taken by the army and used for forensic study of the effects of gunshot wounds on the human body. The remains were later donated to the Smithsonian Institution. In the late 20th century, the government finally acquiesced to the Cheyenne and Arapaho Nations' demand for their return for proper ceremonial burial in Oklahoma...

For more than 130 years, the Sand Creek Massacre site lay in relative obscurity within the sparsely inhabited ranching lands of southeastern Colorado. Throughout the latter 1900s, Sand Creek Ranch owner William Dawson maintained the central area where the Indians were attacked and welcomed Cheyenne and Arapaho visitors to conduct sacred ceremonies to honor their ancestors that perished there.

In 1998, the United States Congress passed the Sand Creek Massacre National Historic Site Study Act, introduced by Colorado Senator Ben Nighthorse Campbell, a Northern Cheyenne Chief. The National Park Service (NPS) was authorized to study the Sand Creek site, enlisting help from the Colorado Historical Society, property owners along the Big Sandy, and most importantly, people of the Cheyenne and Arapaho tribes from Oklahoma, Wyoming and Montana. The study included extensive research and examination of the area to pinpoint the precise location of the massacre, which was ultimately determined to be exactly where white and Indian historians always knew it was – on the Dawson ranch. The two-year study resulted in the passage of Public Law 106-465 on November 7, 2000, authorizing establishment of a Sand Creek Massacre National Historic Site, which encompasses a proposed 12,500 acres of land in Colorado's Kiowa County. Since the passage of the bill, the National Park Service has engaged in purchasing the private lands for the purpose of establishing the site. The flash point of the attack, an area that encompasses the bluffs overlooking Sand Creek and the bowl where the Cheyennes and Arapahos were camped, was purchased from Mr. Dawson in 2004.

The Sand Creek Massacre National Historic Site is now open to the public. Updated information on the Sand Creek Massacre National Historic Site can be found at *www.nps.gov*

Visit www.kclonewolf.com for extensive research notes and bibliography regarding the Sand Creek Massacre.

Selected Reading about the Sand Creek Massacre
and Related History

Books

Abbott, Carl, Stephen J. Leonard & Thomas J. Noel. *Colorado, a History of the Centennial State*. Boulder, CO: Colorado Associated University Press, 1982.

Afton, Jean; Halaas, David F.; Masich, Andrew E.; with Ellis, Richard N. *Cheyenne Dog Soldiers, A Ledgerbook History of Coups and Combat.* Denver: Colorado State Historical Society and the University Press of Colorado, 1997.

Alberts, Don E. *The Battle of Glorieta: Union Victory in the West*. College Station: Texas A & M Press, 1998.

Ambrose, Stephen E. *Crazy Horse and Custer.* New York: Doubleday, 1975.

Athearn, Robert G. *William Tecumseh Sherman and the Settlement of the West*. Norman: University of Oklahoma Press, 1956.

Baker, James B. ed., and LeRoy R. Hafen, assoc. ed. *History of Colorado*. Vol. I., Denver: Linderman Co., Inc., 1927.

Beardsley, Issac Haight. *Echoes from Peak and Plain, or Tales of Life, War, Travel, and Colorado Methodism*. Cincinnati: Curtis and Jennings; New York: Eaton and Mains, 1890.

Beckwourth, James P. *The Life and Adventures of James P. Beckwourth*. Ed. by T. D. Bonner. New York: Alfred A. Knopf, 1931.

Bensing, Tom. *Silas Soule: A Short, Eventful Life of Moral Courage*. Indianapolis, IN: Dog Ear Publishing, 2012

Berthrong, Donald J. *The Cheyenne and Arapaho Ordeal, Reservation and Agency Life in the Indian Territory*. 1875-1907 Norman:University of Oklahoma Press, 1976.

_____ *The Southern Cheyennes* (The Civilization of the American Indian Series, 66) Norman: Unversity of Oklahoma Press, 1975.

Billings, John D. *Hardtack and Coffee, or the Unwritten Story of Army Life*. Lincoln: University of Nebraska Press, 1993 (1887).

Blackman, Frank, ed. *Kansas – a Cyclopedia of State History, Embracing Events, Institutions, Industries, Counties, Cities, Towns, Prominent Persons, etc*. Cincinnati: Standard Publishing Co., 1912.

Brady, Cyrus T. Indian Fights and Fighters. Lincoln: University of Nebraska Press, 1971.

Breakenridge, William M. *Helldorado*. NY: Houghton Mifflin CO., 1928.

Brill, Charles J. *Conquest of the Southern Plains; Uncensored Narrative of the Battle of the Washita and Custer's Southern Campaign*. Oklahoma City: Golden Saga Publishers, 1938.

_____ Custer, Black Kettle, and the Fight on the Washita. Norman: University of Oklahoma Press; Red River edition (April 2002)

Broome, Jeff. _Dog Soldier Justice: The Ordeal of Susanna Alderdice in the Kansas Indian War._ Lincoln, KS: Lincoln County Historical Society, 2003.

_____ _Cheyenne War: Indian Raids on the Road to Denver 1864-1869._ Denver, CO: Aberdeen Books, 2013

_____ _Custer into the West._ (Custer Trails Series, Volume 11) El Segundo, CA: Upton & Sons, 2009.

Brown, Dee. _Bury My Heart at Wounded Knee._ New York: Holt, Rinehart and Winston, 1970.

Byers, William N. _Encyclopedia of Biography of Colorado: History of Colorado_ Chicago: Century Pub. & Engraving Co., 1901.

Cahill, Kevin. _Sand Creek, a Novel by Kevin Cahill._ Bloomington, IN: Author House, 2005.

Carroll, John M. _General Custer and the Battle of the Washita: The Federal View._ Byron, TX: Guidon Press, 1978.

_____ ed. The Sand Creek Massacre: A Documentary History. New York: Amereon House, Sol Lewis, 1973.

Catlin, George. _Catlin's Letters and Notes on the North American Indians._ North Dighton, MA.: JG Press, 1995.

Chalfant, William Y. _Cheyennes and Horse Soldiers: The 1857 Expedition and the Battle of Solomon's Fork._ Norman: University of Oklahoma Press, 1989.

Coel, Margaret. _Chief Left Hand._ Norman: University of Oklahoma Press, reprint 1990.

Coffin, Morse H. _The Battle of Sand Creek._ Waco, TX: W. M. Morrison, 1965.

Collins, Dennis. _The Indians' Last Fight, or The Dull Knife Raid._ Girard, KS: Press of the Appeal to Reason, 1915.

Collins, Hubert E. _Warpath and Cattle Trail._ New York: William Morrow & Sons, 1928.

Colton, Ray C. _The Civil War in the Western Territories._ Norman: University of Oklahoma Press, 1984

Connell, Evan S. _Son of the Morning Star: Custer and The Little Bighorn._ San Francisco: North Point Press, 1984.

Cook, Edward M. _Justified by Honor: Highlights in the Life of General James William Denver._ Falls Church, VA: Higher Education Publications, Inc., 1988

Craig, Reginald S. _The Fighting Parson, The Biography of Colonel John M. Chivington._ Los Angeles: Westernlore Press, 1959.

Crawford, Samuel J. _Kansas in the Sixties._ Chicago: A. C. McClurg & Co., 1911.

Criqui, Orvel A. _Fifty Fearless Men: The Forsyth Scouts & Beecher Island._

Marceline, MO: Walsworth Publishing Co., 1993.

Custer, George A., Quaife, Milo Milton ed. *My Life on the Plains.* New York: Promontory Press, 1995.

Cutler, Bruce. *The Massacre at Sand Creek: Narrative Voices.* Norman: University of Oklahoma Press, September 1997.

Czaplewski, Russ. *Captive of the Cheyenne: The Story of Nancy Jane Morton and the Plum Creek Massacre.* Kearney, NE: Morris Publishing, 1993.

Dixon, David. *Hero of Beecher Island: The Life and Military Career of George A. Forsyth.* Lincoln: University of Nebraska Press, 1994.

Dodge, Col. Richard Irving. *Our Wild Indians: Thirty-three Years' Personal Experience Among the Red Men of the Great West.* New York: Archer House, Inc., 1959 (1890).

_____ *The Plains of the Great West and Their Inhabitants.* New York: Archer House, Inc., 1959 (1877).

Dorsey, George A. *The Cheyenne.* Field Columbia Museum Publication 99, Anthology Series, Vol. 9, No. 1 Chicago: March 1905.

_____ Traditions of the Arapaho. Lincoln: University of Nebraska Press; Reprint edition, December 1997

Dorsett, Phyllis F. *The New Eldorado: The Story of Colorado's Gold and Silver Rushes.* New York: Macmillan, 1970.

Dunn, J.P., Jr. *Massacres in the Mountains: A History of the Indian Wars of the Far West, 1815-1875.* New York: Archer House, 1958.

Dunn, William R. *I Stand by Sand Creek: a Defense of Colonel John M. Chivington and the Third Colorado Calvary.* Ft. Collins, CO: Old Army Press, 1985.

_____ War Drum Echoes. Fort Collins, CO: The Old Army Press, 1979

Edington, Thomas and John Taylor. *The Battle of Glorieta Pass: A Gettysburg in the West, March 26-28, 1862.* Albuquerque: University of New Mexico Press, 1998.

Ellenbacker, John G. *Tragedy at the Little Blue: The Captivity of Laura Roper and Lucinda Eubank.* Niwot, CO: Ryder-Soderlum, 1993.

Epple, Jess C. *Custer's Battle of the Washita and a History of the Plains Indians Tribes.* New York: Exposition Press, 1970.

Forsyth, George A. *Thrilling Days in Army Life.* New York: Harper & Brothers, 1901.

Fremont, John Charles. *Narrative of Exploration and Adventure.* Ed. by Allan Nevins. New York: Longmans, Green & Co., 1956.

_____ Report of the Exploring Expedition to the Rocky Mountains. Ann Arbor, MI: University Microfilms, 1966.

Gardiner, Dorothy. *The Great Betrayal.* Garden City, NY: Doubleday & Co., Inc., 1949.

Garrard, Lewis H. *Wah-to-yah and the Taos Trail.* Norman: University of Oklahoma Press. 1955

Goodrich, Thomas. *Scalp Dance: Indian Warfare on the High Plains 1865-1879.* Mechanicsburg, PA: Stackpole Books, 1997.

Goodstein, Phil. *The Ghosts of Denver: Capitol Hill.* Denver: New Social Publications, 1996.

Greene, Jerome A. *Washita: The U.S. Army and the Southern Cheyennes, 1867-1869* (Campaigns & Commanders) Norman: University of Oklahoma Press, 2004.

Greene, Jerome A.; Scott, Douglas D. *Finding Sand Creek - History, Archeology, and the 1864 Massacre Site.* Norman: University of Oklahoma Press, 2004.

Grinnell, George Bird. *The Fighting Cheyennes.* Norman: University of Oklahoma Press, 1956.

_____ *By Cheyenne Campfires.* Lincoln: University of Nebraska Press, 1971.

_____ *The Cheyenne Indians, Their History and Ways of Life* (2 vols) Lincoln: University of Nebraska Press, 1972.

_____ *Beyond the Old Frontier.* NY: Charles Scribner & Sons, 1913.

Hafen, LeRoy R. *Colorado and its People.* New York: Lewis Historical Publishing Co., 1948.

_____ ed. *Overland Routes to the Gold Fields, 1859.* Glendale, CA: Arthur H. Clark, 1942.

_____ *Relations With the Indians of the Plains.* Glendale, CA: Arthur H. Clark, 1959.

_____ with Francis Marion Young, ed., *Fort Laramie and the Pageant of the West, 1834-1890.* Glendale, CA: Arthur H. Clark Co., 1938.

_____ ed., *Pike's Peak Gold Rush Guidebooks of 1859.* Southwest Historical Series, Vol. IX, Glendale, CA: Arthur H. Clark Company, 1941.

_____ ed. *Colorado Gold Rush.* Southwest Historical Series, Vol. IX, Glendale, CA: Arthur H. Clark Company, 1941.

Hall, Frank. *History of the State of Colorado.* Chicago: Blakely Printing, 1889.

Hall, Martin H. *Sibley's New Mexico Campaign.* Austin: University of Texas Press, 1960.

Halaas, David Fridtjof and Andrew E. Masich. *Halfbreed, The Remarkable True Story of George Bent, Caught Between the Worlds of the Indian and the White Man.* Cambridge, Mass: Da Capo Press, 2004.

Hardorff, Richard G. *Cheyenne Memories of the Custer Fight.* Lincoln: University of Nebraska Press, 1995.

Hatch, Thom. *Black Kettle, The Cheyenne Peace Chief Who Sought Peace but Found War.* Hoboken, N. J.: John Wiley & Sons, Inc., 2004.

_____ *The Blue, the Gray & the Red, Indian Campaigns of the Civil War*. Mechanicsburg, PA: Stackpole Books, 2003.

_____ *The Custer Companion, A Comprehensive Guide to the Life of George Armstrong Custer and the Plains Indian Wars*. Mechanicsburg, PA: Stackpole Books, 2002.

Heitmann, Francis B. *Historical Registry and Dictionary of the United States Army. Vol. 1.* Washington DC: Government Printing Office, 1903. Urbana: University of Illinois Press, 1965.

Herskovitz, Robert M. *History of the Arkansas Valley, Colorado*. Chicago: O. L. Baskin, 1881.

Hill, Alice P. *Tales of the Colorado Pioneers*. Denver: Pierson and Gardiner, 1884.

Hoebel, E. Adamson. *The Cheyennes: Indians of the Great Plains*. New York: Holt, Rinehart and Winston, 1960.

Hoig, Stan. *The Sand Creek Massacre*. Norman: University of Oklahoma Press, 1961.

_____ *The Battle of the Washita*. Lincoln: The University of Nebraska Press, 1979.

_____ *The Peace Chiefs of the Cheyennes*. Norman: University of Oklahoma Press, 1980.

_____ *The Western Odyssey of John Simpson Smith*. Glendale, CA: Arthur H. Clark Co. 1974.

_____ *People of the Sacred Arrows*. New York: Dutton Books; 1st ed edition, 1992.

_____ *Tribal Wars of the Southern Plains*. Norman: University of Oklahoma Press, 1993.

Hollister, Ovando J. *Boldly They Rode*. Lakewood, CO: The Golden Press, 1949 (1st Ed. 1863).

_____ *History of the First Regiment of Colorado Volunteers*. Denver: Thos. Gibson & Co., 1863.

Howbert, Irving. *Memories of a Lifetime in the Pike's Peak Region*. New York: The Knickerbocker Press, 1925.

_____ *The Indians of the Pike's Peak Region*. New York: The Knickerbocker Press, 1914

Hutton, Paul A. *Phil Sheridan and His Army*. Lincoln: University of Nebraska Press, 1985.

Hyde, George E. *Life of George Bent*. Norman: University of Oklahoma Press, 1968.

Inman, Colonel Henry. *The Old Santa Fe Trail. The Story of a Great Highway*. New York: The Macmillan Co., 1897.

Jablow, Joseph. *The Cheyenne in Plains Indian Trade Relations, 1795-1840*. New York: J. J. Augustin, Inc., 1951.

Jackson, Helen Hunt. *A Century of Dishonor*. Boston: Roberts Brothers, 1887.

Jauken, Arlene Feldmann. *The Moccasin Speaks: Living as Captives of the Dog Soldier Warriors Red River War 1874-1875.* Lincoln, NE: Dageford Publishing Inc., 1998.

Johnston, Terry C. *Black Sun: The Battle of Summit Springs, 1869.* New York: St Martins, 1973.

Jones, Douglas C. *The Treaty of Medicine Lodge: The Story of the Great Council Treaty as Told by Eyewitnesses.* Norman: University of Oklahoma Press, 1966.

Keim, B. Randolph De. *Sheridan's Troopers on the Borders: A Winter Campaign on the Plains.* Philadelphia: David McKay. 1885.

Kelman, Ari. *A Misplaced Massacre: Struggling over the Memory of Sand Creek.* Cambridge: Harvard University Press, 2013.

Kelsey, Harry E. Jr. *Frontier Capitalist, the Life of John Evans.* Denver: Colorado State Historical Society and Pruett Publishing Co., 1969.

Keenan, Jerry. *Encyclopedia of American Indian Wars, 1492-1890.* Santa Barbara: ABC-CLIO, 1997.

Kinsley, D.A. *Favor the Bold, a Soldier's Story.* NY: Promontory Press, 1988.

Kraft, Louis. *Sand Creek and the Tragic End of a Lifeway.* Norman: University of Oklahoma Press 2020

_____ *Ned Wynkoop and the Lonely Road From Sand Creek.* Norman: University of Oklahoma Press, 2011.

_____*Custer and the Cheyenne: George Armstrong Custer's Winter Campaign on the Southern Plains.* El Segundo, CA: Upton & Sons, 1995.

Kroeber, Alfred L. *The Arapaho.* Lincoln: University of Nebraska Press, 1983.

Lavender, David. *Bent's Fort.* Lincoln: University of Nebraska Press, 1954.

Leckie, William H. *The Military Conquest of the Southern Plains.* Norman: University of Oklahoma Press, 1963.

Lee, Wayne C. & Raynesford, Howard C. *Trails of the Smoky Hill: From Coronado to the Cow Towns.* Caldwell, ID: Caxton Printers Ltd., 1980.

Llewellyn, Karl N. & Hoebel, E. Adamson. *The Cheyenne Way: Conflict and Case Law in Primitive Jurisprudence.* Norman: University of Oklahoma Press, 1941.

Longstreet, Stephen. *War Cries on Horseback: The Story of The Indian Wars of The Great Plains.* Garden City, NY: Doubleday & Co., 1970.

Luchetti, Cathy. *Children of the West: Family Life on the Frontier.* New York/London: W.W. Norton & Co., 2001.

Mails, Thomas E. *Dog Soldier Societies of the Plains.* New York: Marlowe & Co., 1973.

_____ *The Mystic Warriors of the Plains.* Tulsa, OK: Council Oak Books, 1972.

_____ *Dog Soldiers, Bear Men and Buffalo Women: A Study of the Societies and Cults of the Plains Indians.* Englewood Cliffs, NJ: Prentice-Hall, Inc., 1973.

Marquis, Thomas B. *Wooden Leg, A Warrior Who Fought Custer.* Lincoln: University of Nebraska Press, 1931.

Masich, Andrew E. & Halaas, David F. *Cheyenne Dog Soldiers: A Courageous Warrior History* [AUDIOBOOK] (CD-ROM)

McCarter, Margaret Hill. *The Price of the Prairie: A Story of Kansas.* Chicago: A.C. McClurg & Co., 1910.

McMechen, Edgar Carlisle. *Life of Governor Evans.* Denver: Walgren, 1924.

Mead, James R. Jones, Schuyler ed. *Hunting and Trading on the Great Plains 1859-1975.* Norman: University of Oklahoma Press, 1986.

Mendoza, Patrick. *Song of Sorrow: Massacre at Sand Creek.* Denver: Willow Wind Publishing Co., 1993

Meredith, Grace E., ed. *Girl Captives of the Cheyennes: A True Story of the Capture and Rescue of Four Pioneer Girls 1874.* Los Angeles: Gem Publishing, 1927.

Michno, Gregory F. *Battle At Sand Creek: The Military Perspective.* El Segundo, CA: Upton & Sons, 2004

_____ *The Three Battles of Sand Creek: The Cheyenne Massacre in Blood, In Court, and as the End of History.* El Dorado Hills, CA: Savas Beatie LLC, 2016

_____ *Lakota Noon: The Indian Narrative of Custer's Defeat.* Missoula, MT: Mountain Press Publishing Company, 1997

_____ *Encyclopedia of Indian Wars: Western Battles and Skirmishes 1850-1890.* Missoula, MT: Mountain Press Publishing Co. 2003.

_____ *Deadliest Indian War in the West: The Snake Conflict, 1864 - 1868.* Caldwell, ID: Caxton Press, 2007.

_____ **& Michno, Susan** *A Fate Worse Than Death: Indian Captivities in the West 1830-1885.* Caldwell, ID: Caxton Press, 2007.

_____ *Forgotten Fights: Little-known Raids and Skirmishes on the Frontier, 1823 to 1890.* Missoula, MT: Mountain Press Publishing Co. 2008.

Monnett, John H. *The Battle of Beecher Island and the Indian War of 1868-1869.* Niwot, CO: University Press of Colorado, 1992.

Mooney, James. *The Ghost Dance.* North Dighton, MA: JG Press, 1996.

Mumey, Nolie. *History of Early Settlements in Denver, 1859-1860.* Glendale, CA: Arthur H. Clark, 1942.

Nankivell, John H. *History of Military Organizations of Colorado.* Denver: W.H. Kistler, 1935.

Neihardt, John G. *Black Elk Speaks: Being the Life Story of a Holy Man of the Oglala Sioux.* New York: Simon & Schuster, 1932.

Nye, Wilbur S. *Plains Indians Raiders.* Norman: University of Oklahoma Press, 1968.

O'Donnell, Jeff. *Blood on the Republican.* New York: M. Evans & Co., 1992.

_____ *Luther North, Frontier Scout.* Lincoln: J & L Lee, 1995.

O'Neal, Bill. *Fighting Men of the Indian Wars.* Stillwater, OK: Barbed Wire Press, 1991.

Paul, R. Eli ed. *The Nebraska Indian Wars Reader.* Lincoln/London: University of Nebraska Press, 1998.

Perkin, Robert L. *The First Hundred Years – an Informal History of Denver and the Rocky Mountain News.* New York: Doubleday & Co, 1959

Perkins, LaVonne. *D.C.Oakes - Family Friends & Foe.* Denver: Stony Ridge Press, 2009.

Pitzer, Henry Littleton. *Three Frontiers. Memories and a Portrait of Henry Littleton Pitzer as recorded by his son Robert Clairborne Pitzer.* Muscatine, IA: The Prairie Press, 1938.

Powell, Father Peter John. *People of the Sacred Mountain: A History of the Northern Cheyenne Chiefs and Warrior Societies 1830-1879.* San Francisco: Harper & Row, 1981.

_____ *Sweet Medicine: The Continuing Role of the Sacred Arrows, The Sun Dance, and the Sacred Buffalo Hat in Northern Cheyenne History.* Norman: University of Oklahoma Press, 1969.

Propst, Nell Brown. *The South Platte Trail, the Story of Colorado's Forgotten People.* Boulder, CO: Pruett, 1989.

Rickey, Don Jr. *Forty Miles a Day on Beans and Hay.* Norman: University of Oklahoma Press, 1963.

Rister, Carl C. *The Traffic in Prisoners by Southern Plains Indians, 1835-1875.* Norman: University of Oklahoma Press, 1940.

Roberts, Gary L. *Sand Creek, Tragedy and Symbol.* Norman: University of Oklahoma; University Microfilms Intnl.,1984. Available at the Denver Public Library Western History Department - call: C970.3 C428rob

_____ *Massacre at Sand Creek: How Methodists Were Involved in an American Tragedy.* Nashville, TN: Abingdon Press, 2016.

Robinson III, Charles M. *Satanta: The Life and Death of a War Chief.* Abilene, TX: State House Press, 1997.

Ryus, William H. *The Second William Penn. Treating with the Indians on the Santa Fe Trail, 1860-66.* Kansas City, MO: Frank T. Riley Publishing Co., 1913.

Sabin, Edwin L. *Kit Carson Days.* Vol. II. New York: The Press of the Pioneers, 1935.

Sandoz, Mari. *Cheyenne Autumn.* (McGraw Hill, 1953.) Lincoln: University of Nebraska Press, 1992.

_____ *Crazy Horse: The Strange Man of the Oglalas.* NY: MJF Books, 1942, 1992 by arrangement with University of Nebraska Press.

_____ *The Horsecatcher.* Lincoln: University of Nebraska Press, 1986.

_____ *Hostiles and Friendlies: Selected Short Writings of Mari Sandoz.* Lincoln: University of Nebraska Press; Reprint edition (February 1992)

_____ *These Were the Sioux.* Lincoln: University of Nebraska Press; Reprint edition (September 1985)

Sanford, Mollie Dorsey, *Mollie: The Journal of Mollie Dorsey Sanford in Nebraska and Colorado Territories, 1857-1866* Lincoln: University of Nebraska Press, 2003.

Schultz, Duane. *Month of the Freezing Moon – The Sand Creek Massacre – November 1864.* New York: St. Martin's Press, 1990.

Seger, John H. *Early Days Among the Cheyenne and Arapaho Indians.* Norman: University of Oklahoma Press, 1956.

Sheridan, Phillip H. *Personal Memoirs of P.H. Sheridan, Vol. II* New York: Charles Webster & Co., 1888.

_____ *Record of Engagements with Hostile Indians Within the Military Division of the Missouri, 1868-1882.* Facsimile ed. Fort Collins, CO: Old Army Press, 1972.

Sides, Hampton. *Blood and Thunder: The Epic Story of Kit Carson.* New York, NY: Anchor, 2007.

Skogen, Larry. *Indian Depredation Claims, 1796-1920.* Norman/London: University of Oklahoma Press, 1996.

Smith, Duane A. *The Birth of Colorado - a Civil War Perspective.* Norman: University of Oklahoma Press, 1989.

Smith, Duane A.; Ubbelohode, Carl; Benson, Maxine. *A Colorado History.* Boulder, CO: Pruett Publishing Co., 1972

Sparks, Col. Ray G. *Reckoning at Summit Springs.* Kansas City: Lowell Press, 1969.

Stands In Timber, John. *Cheyenne Memories: Second Edition.* New Haven: New Haven: Yale University Press; 2nd edition, 1998.

Stoekel, Carl, and Ellen Battelle. *Correspondence of John Sedgwick Major General.* New York: The DeVinne Press, 1903.

Stone, Wilbur F. ed., *History of Colorado.* Chicago: S.J. Clarke, 1918.

Svaldi, David. *Sand Creek and the Rhetoric of Extermination.* Lanham, MD: University Press of America, 1989

Thayer, William M. *Marvels of the New West.* Norwich, Conn.: The Henry Bell Publishing Company, 1888.

Trenholm, Virginia C. *The Arapahoes, Our People.* Norman: University of Oklahoma Press, 1973.

Turner, Don. *Custer's First Massacre: The Battle of the Washita.* Amarillo: Humbug Gulch Press, 1968.

Utley, Robert M. *Frontiersmen in Blue: The United States Army and the Indian, 1848-1865.* Lincoln: University of Nebraska, 1967

_____ *The Indian Frontier of the American West, 1846-1890.* Albuquerque: University of New Mexico Press, 1984

_____ *Frontier Regulars, The United States Army and the Indian, 1866-1891*. Lincoln: University of Nebraska Press, 1973

Vestal, Stanley. *Warpath and Council Fire: The Plains Indians' Struggle for Survival in War and Diplomacy 1851-1891*. New York: Random House, 1948.

Ware, Captain Eugene F. *The Indian War of 1864*. New York: St. Martin's, 1960.

Weingart, Richard. *Sound the Charge: The Western Frontier: Spillman Creek to Summit Springs*. Englewood, CO: Ajacqueline Enterprises, 1968.

Weist, Tom. *A History of the Cheyenne People*. Billings: Montana Council for Indian Education, 1977.

Wellman, Paul I. *Death on Horseback: Seventy Years of War for the American West*. Philadelphia/New York: J.B. Lippincott Co., 1947.

Werner, Fred H. *The Summit Springs Battle, July 11, 1869*. Greeley, CO: Werner Publications, 1991.

_____ *The Sand Creek Fight*, November 29, 1864. Greeley, CO: Kendall, 1993.

West, Elliott. The *Contested Plains: Indians, Goldseekers, & the Rush to Colorado*. Lawrence: University Press of Kansas, 1998.

White, Lonnie J. *Hostiles and Horse Soldiers*. Boulder, CO: Pruett, 1972.

Whitford, William Clark. *Colorado Volunteers in the Civil War*. Denver: State Historical and Natural Historical Society of Colorado, 1909.

_____ *The Colorado Volunteers in the Civil War, The New Mexico Campaign in 1862*. Glorieta, NM: Rio Grande Press, 1971.

Whitlock, Flint. *Distant Bugles, Distant Drums: The Union Response to the Confederate Invasion of New Mexico*. Boulder: University Press of Colorado, May 2006.

Williams, Ellen. *Three Years and a Half in the Army: or History of the Second Colorados*. New York: Brentano's, Inc., 1931.

Willison, George F. *Here They Dug Gold*. New York: Brentano's, 1931.

Wooster, Robert. *The Military and United States Indian Policy, 1865-1903*. New Haven, CT: Yale University Press, 1988.

Wynkoop, Edward W. *The Tall Chief, the Autobiography of Edward W. Wynkoop*. Christopher Gerboth, ed. Denver: Colorado State Historical Society, Monograph 9, Essays and Monographs in Colorado History, 1994. (Available at the Colorado History Museum book store - 13th & Broadway, Denver)

Zamonski, Stanley W. and Teddy Keller. *The Fifty-Niners: Roaring Denver in the Gold Rush Days*. Frederick, CO: Platte'n Press, 1983.

Zornow, William Frank. *Kansas: A History of the Jayhawk State*. Norman: University of Oklahoma Press, 1957.

Government Records

"War of the Rebellion" - United States War Dept. The War of the Rebellion: A Compilation of the Official Records of the Union and Confederate Armies. Four series, 128 volumes. Washington: Government Printing Office. 1880-1901

 "Sand Creek Massacre" – United States Congress, Senate. Report of the Secretary of War, Sand Creek Massacre, Sen. Exec. Doc. No. 26, 39 Cong., 2 sess. Washington, Government Printing Office, 1867

"Massacre of the Cheyenne Indians" - United States Congress, House of Representatives Joint Committee Report on the Conduct of the War, 38 Cong., 2 sess., Washington, Government Printing Office, 1865.

United States Congress, Senate. *Indian Affairs, Laws and Treaties.* Vol. II. Sen. Exec. Doc. 319, 58 Cong., 2 sess. Edited by C.J. Kappler. Washington. Government Printing Office., 1904.

Congressional Globe, 38 Cong., 2 sess. Washington. Office of John C. Rives, 1865.

United States Interior Department. Bureau of Indian Affairs. Reports of the Commissioner of Indian Affairs for the years 1851 through 1865 (separate volumes for each year). Washington. Government Printing Office, 1852-66.

"The Chivington Massacre" – United States Congress, Senate. Reports of the Committees, 39 Cong., 2 sess. Washington Government Printing Office, 1867.

Manuscripts, Articles, Collections

Adams, Blanche V. *The Second Colorado Cavalry in the Civil War.* Colorado Magazine, Vol. VIII, May 1931.

Anderson, Robert. *The Buffalo Men, a Cheyenne Ceremony of Petition Deriving from the Sutaio.* Southwestern Journal of Anthropology 12, no. 1, Spring 1956.

Anderson, Harry H. *Stand at Arikaree.* Colorado Magazine 41, Fall 1964.

Anthony, Scott J. *Papers of Scott J. Anthony 1830-1903.* Library, Colorado State Historical Society.

Ashley, Susan R. *Reminicenses in the Early Sixties.* Colorado Magazine 8, 1936.

Bancroft, Hubert H. *Hubert H. Bancroft Collection.* University of Colorado Library, Western History Collections.

Barry, Louise. *The Ranch at the Great Bend.* Kansas Historical Quarterly, 1973.

_____ *The Ranch at Little Arkansas Crossing.* Kansas Historical Quarterly, 1972.

_____ *The Ranch at Cimarron Crossing.* Kansas Historical Quarterly, 1973.

_____ *The Ranch at Cow Creek Crossing.* Kansas Historical Quarterly, 1972.

Bennett, William Charles, Jr. *Reminiscences of Edward W. Wynkoop 1856 -1858.* Heritage of Kansas, XI, No. 3, 1978. (Special thanks to Christopher Wynkoop)

_____ *Edward W. Wynkoop, Frontiersman, 1856-69.* MHQ: The Quarterly Journal of Military History, Vol. 14, Is. 2, 2002.

Bent, Charles. *The Charles Bent Papers.* New Mexico Historical Review 30, no. 2, April 1955.

Bent, George. *Papers, Manuscript 1904-1918.* Western History/Genealogy Department, Denver Public Library.

_____ *Letters to George E. Hyde – MS XXI,* Colorado State Historical Society, Denver, CO.

_____ *Three Letters to Colonel Tappan – Feb. 3, 1869; March 25, 1889; April 16, 1889.* Colorado State Historical Society, Denver, CO.

_____ *Letters.* New Haven, CT: Yale University Collection of Western Americana, Beinecke Rare Book and Manuscript Library.

_____ ed. Hyde, George E. *Forty Years With the Cheyennes.,* The Frontier. October 1905 – February 1906.

Bent, William. *Nine letters to A. M. Robinson, Jan. 1859 - Feb. 1860.* Relative to the Upper Arkansas Agency. Records of the Bureau of

Indian Affairs, National Archives, Washington D.C.

Blackmar, Frank W. ed. *The Rescue of John Doy. Excerpt from Kansas: a cyclopedia of state history, embracing events, institutions, industries, counties, cities, towns, prominent persons, etc.* Chicago: Standard Publishing Co., 1912.

Blake, Henry. *Henry Blake Diary.* University of Colorado Library, Carnegie Branch.

Blunt, James G. *General Blunt's Account of His Civil War Experiences.* Kansas State Historical Collections, No. 3, May 1932.

Broome, Jeff. *Indian Massacres in Elbert County, Colorado: New Information on the 1864 Hungate and 1868 Dietemann Murders* Denver Westerners Roundup, VOL. LX, No. 1, January-February 2004.

_____ *Death at Summit Springs: Susanna Alderdice and the Cheyennes.* Wild West, October 2003.

Brown, John. *John Brown Papers, 1826 – 1948.* Kansas State Historical Society.

Burkey, Elmer R. *The Site of the Murder of the Hungate Family by Indians in 1864.* Colorado Magazine 12, no. 4, July 1935.

Burlington Weekly Hawk Eye (Burlington, Iowa) - *List of killed and wounded in the engagement of November 29th 1864, on Big Sandy Creek, Colorado Territory.* (Special thanks to Al and Donna Rothe.)

Campbell, W.S. *The Cheyenne Dog Soldier.* Chronicles of Oklahoma, 11, January 1921.

Carey, Raymond G. *The Puzzle of Sand Creek.* The Colorado Magazine, Vol. XLI. No. 4. 1964.

_____ *Collection.* Penrose Library, University of Denver, Denver, CO.

_____ *Colonel Chivington, Brigadier General Connor, and Sand Creek.* Denver Westerners Brand Book. Vol. XLI. Denver, CO, 1960.

_____ *The Bloodless Third Regiment.* Colorado Magazine, Vol 38, No.4, 1961.

Case, Frank M. *Experiences on the Platte River Route in the Sixties.* Colorado Magazine, August 1928.

Cheetham, Francis T. *The Early Settlements of Southern Colorado.* Colorado Magazine, February 1928.

Chivington, John M. *The First Colorado Regiment .* Denver, Colorado, October 18, 1884. Colorado State Historical Society, Denver, CO.

_____ *Papers, Manuscript of John M. Chivington 1862-1892.* Western History/Genealogy Department, Denver Public Library.

_____ *The Pet Lambs.* Denver Republican, April 20-May 18, 1890. Denver Public Library

Clark, Olive A. *Early Days Along the Solomon Valley.* Collections of the Kansas State Historical Society, 1926-28.

Clarke, Charles E. *The Chivington Massacre, A Participant in the Battle Denies That It Was a Massacre.* Colorado Miner, Georgetown, Clear Creek County, Colorado, Saturday, 14 October, 1876, Page 1. (Special thanks to Christopher Wynkoop)

Cobb, Frank M. *The Lawrence Party of Gold Seekers.* Colorado Magazine 10, no. 5, September 1933.

Coberly, Carroll H. *Carroll H. Coberly Papers (MSS #125).* Colorado State Historical Society.

Collings, Ellsworth. *Roman Nose: Chief of the Cheyenne.* The Chronicles of Oklahoma, Vol. 42, No. 4, 1964-65.

Connelley, William E. *The Treaty Held at Medicine Lodge.* Kansas Historical Collections 17, Winter 1926-1927.

Cox, C. Jefferson. *Summit Springs.* Denver: Denver Westerner's Roundup, Vol. 26, No. 3, March 1970.

Craig, Reginald S. *Tall Bull's Last Fight.* Denver: Denver Westerner's Roundup, April 1968.

Cramer, Joseph A. *Letter to Major E.W. Wynkoop, December 19, 1864.* Rocky Mountain News. "Sins of Sand Creek," September 15, 2000.

Davis, Theodore. *A Summer on the Plains.* Harper's New Monthly Magazine, Vol. 36, No. 18, 1868.

Dawson, Thomas F. *Dawson Scrapbooks.* Colorado State Historical Society, Denver, CO.

_____ *Colonel Boone's Treaty with the Plains Indians.* The Trail, Vol. XIV, July 1921.

Dawson, William F. *Ordinance Artifacts at the Sand Creek Massacre Site: A Technical and Historical Report.* Unpublished, 1999. Click link to National Parks Service Index, find article under "O" and download - NOTE: PDF file, Adobe Acrobat required.

Denver Daily News. *The Latest From Ft. Lyon, December 12, 1864.* List of killed and wounded soldiers at Sand Creek.

Dormis, John T. ed. *The Chivingtons.* Masonic News-Digest 36, June 28, 1957.

Dorsey, George A. *The Cheyennes: The Sun Dance.* Field Columbian Museum Pub. no. 103, Anthropological Series 9, no. 2, Chicago 1905. FIELD MUSEUM MAIN LIB. GN558.C53 D66 1971

_____ *The Cheyenne, Ceremonial Organization.* Field Columbian Museum Pub. no. 99, Anthropological Series 9, no. 1, Chicago 1905.

Ediger, Theodore A. *Some Remembrances of the Battle of the Washita.* Chronicles of Oklahoma 33, Summer 1955.

Ellenbecker, John G. *Oak Grove Massacre, (Oak, Nebraska), Indian Raids on the Little Blue River in 1864.* Marysville, KS: Marysville Advocate-Democrat, 1927. (Special thanks to Christopher Wynkoop).

Ellis, Elmer. *Colorado's First Fight for Statehood, 1865-1868.* Colorado

Magazine, Vol. VIII, January 1931.

Englert, Kenneth E. *Raids by Reynolds*. 1956 Brand Book of The Denver Westerners. Boulder, CO, Johnson Publishing Co., 1957.

Evans, John. *Collection, Indian Affairs*. Colorado Division of State Archives and Public Records.

_____ *Dictations*, Bancroft Collection, Bancroft Library, University of California, Berkeley CA

Field, Matthew C. *Sketches of Big Timbers, Bent's Fort, and Milk Fort 1839*. Colorado Magazine, May 1937.

Filipiak, Jack D. *The Battle of Summit Springs*. Denver: The Colorado Magazine, Vol. XLI, No. 4, 1964,

Fisher, John R. *The Royal and Duncan Pursuits: Aftermath of the Battle of Summit Springs*. Nebraska History, Vol. 50, No. 3, Fall 1969.

Flynn, Arthur. J. *Creating a Commonwealth*. Colorado Magazine, Vol. I, July 1924.

_____ *Furs and Forts of the Rocky Mountain West*. Colorado Magazine, March 1932.

Foreman, Carolyn T. *Col. Jesse H. Leavenworth*. Chronicles of Oklahoma. 13, 1935.

Gage, Duane. *Black Kettle: A Nobel Savage?* The Chronicles of Oklahoma, Vol. 45, No. 3, 1967.

Garfield, Marvin H. *The Military Post as a Factor in the Frontier Defense of Kansas*. Kansas Historical Quarterly, Vol. 1, No. 1, Nov. 1931.

_____ *Defense of the Kansas Frontier, 1864-1865*. Kansas Historical Quarterly, Vol. 1, No. 2, February 1932.

_____ *Defense of the Kansas Frontier, 1866-1867*. Kansas Historical Quarterly, Vol. 1, No. 4, August 1932.

_____ *Defense of the Kansas Frontier, 1868-1869*. Kansas Historical Quarterly, Vol. 1, No. 5, November 1932.

_____ *The Indian Question in Congress and in Kansas*. Kansas Historical Quarterly, 1933.

Godfrey, General Edward S. *Medicine Lodge Treaty 60 Years Ago*. Winners of the West, no. 6, March 30, 1929.

Goertner, Thomas G. *Reflections of a Frontier Soldier – The Sand Creek Affair as revealed in the Diary of Samuel F. Tappan*. Thesis presented to University of Denver, 1959.

Gower, Calvin W. *Gold Fever in Kansas Territory: Migration to the Pike's Peak Gold Fields, 1858 -1860*. Kansas Historical Quarterly, 1973.

_____ *The Pike's Peak Gold Rush and the Smoky Hill Route, 1859 -1860*. Kansas Historical Quarterly, Summer 1959.

Green, James. *Incidents of the Indian Outbreak of 1864*. Publications of the Nebraska State Historical Society 19, 1919.

Grinnell, George Bird. *George Bird Grinnell Papers*. Southwest Museum Library, Los Angeles, CA.

_____ *The Cheyenne Medicine Lodge*. American Anthropologist 16, no. 2, April-June 1914.

_____ *Coup and Scalp among the Plains Indians*. American Anthropologist 12, no. 2, April-June 1910.

_____ *Early Cheyenne Villages*. American Anthropologist 20, no. 4, October-December 1918.

_____ *Great Mysteries of the Cheyenne*. American Anthropologist 21, no. 4, October-December 1910.

_____ *Social Organizations of the Cheyennes*. International Congress of Americanists, 13th sess. New York, 1902, Easton, PA, 1902.

_____ *Some Early Cheyenne Tales*. Journal of American Folklore 10-21, nos. 78 & 82, July-September 1907, October-December 1908.

_____ *Bent's Old Fort and Its Builders*. Reprint from a chapter in Beyond the Old Frontier. NY: Charles Scribner's Sons, 1913.

Hadley, C. B. *The Plains War in 1865*. Proceedings and Collections of the Nebraska State Historical Society, 2nd Series.

Hafen, LeRoy R. *When Was Bent's Fort Built?* Colorado Magazine 31, no. 2, April 1954.

_____ *The Last Years of James P. Beckwourth*. Colorado Magazine, Vol. V, August 1928.

_____ *The W. M. Boggs Manuscript About Bent's Fort, Kit Carson, and the Far West and Life Among the Indians*. Colorado Magazine, Vol. VII, March 1930.

_____ *The Early Fur Trade Posts of the South Platte*. Mississippi Valley Historical Review, December 1925.

_____ *Colorado Mountain Men*. Colorado Magazine, January 1953.

_____ *Lewis Ledyard Weld, and Old Camp Weld*. Colorado Magazine, v. 19 November, 1942.

Hagerty, Leroy W. *Indian Raids Along the Platte and Little Blue Rivers, 1864-1865*. Nebraska History 28, no. 4, October-December 1947.

Halaas, David Fridtjof. *All the Camp was Weeping: George Bent and the Sand Creek Massacre*. Colorado Heritage, Summer 1995.

_____ *America's Blurred Vision: A Review Essay on Indian-White Histories*. Colorado Heritage 3, 1983.

_____ *Worlds Apart: Indians and Whites in Nineteenth-Century Colorado*. Denver: Colorado Historical Society, 1984.

Hall, J. N. *Colorado's Indian Troubles as I View Them*. Denver: The Colorado Magazine, Vol. XV, No. 4, July 1938.

Harrison, Emily Haines. *Reminiscences of Early Days in Ottawa County*. Kansas State Historical Collections, Vol. 10, 1907-1908.

Harvey, James R. *Interview with Elizabeth J. Tallman. Pioneer Experiences in Colorado*. Colorado Magazine, Vol. XIII, July 1936.

Hickman, Russell K. *A Little Satire on Emigrant Aid - Amasa Soule and the Descandum Kansas Improvement Company*. Kansas State Historical

Quarterly, November, 1939 Vol. 8, No. 4.

Hill, Nathaniel. *Nathaniel Hill Inspects Colorado Letters Written in 1864*. Colorado Magazine, Vol. XXXIV, January 1957.

Hodder, Haile Riley. *Crossing the Plains in War Times*. Colorado Magazine, July 1933.

Hoopes, Alban W. *Thomas S. Twiss, Indian Agent on the Upper Platte, 1855-1861*. Mississippi Valley Historical Review, Vol. 20, 1933-34.

Hornbeck, Lewis N. *The Battle of the Washita*. Sturm's Oklahoma Magazine 5, no. 5, January 1908.

Howbert, Irving. *Irving Howbert Manuscript Collection*. Colorado College Tutt Library Special Collections and Archives.

_____ *Howbert Family Collection*. Pioneer Museum of Colorado Springs, Starsmore Research Center.

Hoyt, A. W. *Over the Plains to Colorado*. Harper's New Monthly Magazine, June 1867.

Hull, Myra E. ed. *Soldiering on the High Plains: The Diary of Lewis Byram Hull, 1864-66*. Kansas Historical Quarterly, February 1938.

Hundall, Mary Powers. *Early History of Bent County*. Colorado Magazine, Vol. XXII, November 1945.

Isern, Thomas D. *The Controversial Career of Edward W. Wynkoop*. Colorado Magazine 56, Winter-Spring 1979. (Special thanks to Christopher Wynkoop)

Justus, Judith P. *The Saga of Clara Blinn and the Battle of the Washita*. Journal of the Little Big Horn Associates, Vol. 14, No. 1, Winter 2000.

Kansas Historical Quarterly. *Topics in Kansas History: War Essay on the Plains Wars*.

Keeling, Henry C. *My Experiences with the Cheyenne Indians*. Chronicles of Oklahoma, Vol. 3, No. 1, April 1925.

Kelsey, Harry. *Background to Sand Creek*. Colorado Magazine 45, no. 4, Fall 1968.

Kingman, Samuel A. *Diary of Samuel A. Kingman at Indian Treaty in 1865*. Kansas Historical Quarterly, 1932.

Kirwin, John S. *Patrolling the Santa Fe Trail: Reminiscences of John S. Kirwin*. Kansas Historical Quarterly, 1955.

Kraft Louis. *Edward Wynkoop: A Forgotten Hero*. Research Review: The Journal of the Little Bighorn Associates 1, June 1987.

_____ *Ned Wynkoop & Black Kettle*. The Journal of the Little Bighorn Associates.

_____ *Ned Wynkoop's Early Years on the Frontier*. Research Review: Journal of the Little Big Horn Associates v 6, No. 1, Jan. 1992.

_____ *Ned Wynkoop and the Explosion on Pawnee Fork*. Military Heritage, Volume 2, No. 1, August 2000.

_____ *Between the Army and the Cheyennes*. MHQ: The Quarterly

Journal of Military History, Volume 14, No. 2, Winter 2002.

Kroeber, A.L. *Cheyenne Tales.* Journal of American Folklore 13, no. 50, July-September 1900.

Lambert, Julia S. *Plain Tales of the Plains.* The Trail, January-September 1916.

Lecompte, Janet. *Sand Creek.* The Colorado Magazine. Vol. XLI. No. 4. 1964.

_____ *Charles Autobees.* Colorado Magazine, Vol. XXXVI, July 1959.

Lubers, H.L. *William Bent's Family and the Indians of the Plains.* Colorado Magazine 13, January 1936.

Mardock, Robert. *The Plains Frontier and the Indian Peace Policy, 1865-1880.* Nebraska History 49, Summer 1968.

Marlatt, Gene Ronald. *Edward W. Wynkoop, An Investigation of His Role in the Sand Creek Controversy and Other Indian Affairs, 1863-1868.* M.A. Thesis, University of Denver, (1961) Denver Public Library; Colorado Historical Society; University of Denver, Penrose Library.

Mead, James R. *The Little Arkansas.* Kansas State Historical Society Collections, X, 1907-08.

Mellor, William J. *The Military Investigation of Col. John M. Chivington Following the Sand Creek Massacre.* Chronicles of Oklahoma 16, no. 4, 1938.

Michno, Gregory F. *The Real Villains of Sand Creek.* Wild West, December 2003.

_____ *Cheyenne Chief Black Kettle* Wild West, December 2005.

Milavec, Pam. *Alias Emma S. Soule: Corrected Historical Fictions Surrounding Silas Soule and the Sand Creek Massacre.* Denver: Denver Westerners Roundup, July-August, 2005.

Morse, O. E. *An Attempted Rescue of John Brown from Charlestown, VA Jail.* Kansas State Historical Society, Vol. VIII, 1902-1904.

Mumey, Nolie. *John Milton Chivington, the Misunderstood Man.* 1956 Brand Book of the Denver Westerners.

Myers, J. Jay. *The Sand Creek Massacre.* Wild West, December 1998.

Nichols, David H. *Papers.* University of Colorado Library, Western History Collections.

North, L. H. *My Military Experiences in Colorado.* Colorado Magazine, March 1934.

Orahood, Harper A. *Papers.* University of Colorado Library, Western History Collections.

Peck, Robert M. *Recollections of Early Times in Kansas Territory.* Kansas Historical Collections 8, 1903-1904.

Perkins, LaVonne. *Silas Soule, His Widow Heresa (sic), and the Rest of the Story.* Denver: Denver Westerners Roundup, Vol LV, no.2, Mar-Apr, 1999.

Perrigo, Lynn I., ed. *Major Hal Sayre's Diary of the Sand Creek Campaign.* Colorado Magazine 15, 1938.

Peterson, Karen D. *Cheyenne Soldier Societies.* Plains Anthropologist 9, no. 25, 1964.

Pierce, James H. *The First Prospecting in Colorado.* The Trail 7, no. 5, October 1914.

_____ *With the Green-Russell Party.* The Trail 13, no. 12, May 1921.

Prentice, C. A. *Captain Silas S. Soule, a Pioneer Martyr.* Denver: Colorado Magazine, vol.4 May, 1927; reprint November/December 1935.

Pyle, L. Robert. *Cheyenne Chief Tall Bull.* Wild West, Vol. 15, No. 1, April, 2002.

Reckmeyer, Clarence. *The Battle of Summit Springs.* Denver: The Colorado Magazine, Vol. VI, No. 6, 1929.

Rees, D.S. *An Indian Fight on the Solomon.* Kansas State Historical Collections, Vol. 7, 1901-1902.

Robinson, Charles M. III *Kiowa Chief Satanta* Wild West, August 1999.

Rocky Mountain News (weekly-daily)

_____ Two Articles: *Appeal to the People, authorizing the organization of civilian militias, under the rules of militia law, to fight hostile Indian bands.* August 10, 1864. *Proclamation* – After receiving approval from the War Department, Governor John Evans calls for volunteers to join the Colorado Third Regiment to fight Indians for a period of 100 days. August 13, 1864.

_____ *To Fight Indians* – Rocky Mountain News editorial urges Colorado citizens to form militias at the request of Governor Evans; to organize under the rules of militia law, and fight hostile Indian bands. August 10, 1864.

_____ *The Reynolds Band* – Editorial defends the killing of five members of the notorious James Reynolds Gang by Colorado soldiers. September 9, 1864.

_____ Rocky Mountain News Editorials After the Sand Creek Massacre, including: *The Battle of Sand Creek* – praises the Colorado third regiment. December 17, 1864. *The Third* – 3rd Regiment soldiers not paid for their service at Sand Creek. December 29, 1864. *The Fort Lyon Affair* – Indignation over criticism of the Sand Creek attack. December 30, 1864. *Its Effect* – The consequences of a congressional investigation. December 31, 1864.

_____ *Arrival of the Third Regiment - Grand March Through Town* - Details Third Regiment return to Denver after the Sand Creek Massacre. December 22, 1864.

_____ *High Officials Checkmated* – Letter to editor criticizes "High Officials" rumored to be pushing for an investigation into the Sand Creek Massacre. January 4, 1865.

_____ *The Homicide Last Night.* Report of the murder of Captain Silas S. Soule, April 24, 1865 p. 2 c. 1.

_____ *Captain Soule's Funeral.* Obituary of Captain Silas S. Soule, April 27, 1865 p.2 c.1.

_____ *He Kept The Faith* - Obituary of Colonel John M. Chivington. October 8, 1894.

_____ *Scenes at Sand Creek* - Interview of Captain John McCannon in 1881, detailing his experiences and opinions regarding the Sand Creek Massacre. January 26, 1881.

_____ *Sins of Sand Creek.* The recent discovery of two letters written by Captain Silas Soule and Lt. Joseph Cramer, to Major Edward Wynkoop, detailing their experiences at the Sand Creek Massacre. September 15, 2000.

Rocky Mountain PBS. Video documentary: *Tears in the Sand.* "Rocky Mountain Legacy."

Root, George A. *Extracts from Diary of Captain Lambert Wolf.* Kansas State Historical Quarterly, Vol. I, 1931-31.

Sanford, Albert B. *Life at Camp Weld and Fort Lyon in 1861-62.* Colorado Magazine 7, May 1930.

Sayre, Hal. *Papers. University of Colorado Library,* Western History Collections.

Schlesinger, Sigmund. *The Beecher Island Fight.* Collections of the Kansas State Historical Society, 1919-1922, Vol. XV, 1923.

Seabrook, S.L. *Expedition of Col. V.E. Sumner Against the Cheyenne Indians, 1857.* Kansas Historical Collections 16, 1923-1925.

Sheridan, Phillip H. *Papers.* Manuscript Division, Library of Congress, Washington D.C.

Shields, Lillian. *Relations with the Cheyennes and Arapahos in Colorado to 1861.* Colorado Magazine, August 1927.

Sievers, Michael A. *Sands of Sand Creek Historiography.* The Colorado Magazine, Vol. XLIX. 1972.

Smiley, Jerome C. ed., *History of Denver: With Outlines of the Earlier History of the Rocky Mountain Country,* Denver. The Denver Times, The Times-Sun Publishing Company, 1901.

Sorenson, Alfred. *General Carr's Campaign – The Battle of Summit Springs.* Manuscript Collections, Kansas State Historical Society.

Soule, Hersa. *Letter to Annie J. Soule, August 6, 1865.* From the private materials of Byron Strom, Anne E. Hemphill Collection.

Soule, Silas S. *The Letters of Silas S. Soule – Recounting His Experiences in the Colorado Territory - 1861-1865.* Western History/Genealogy Department, Denver Public Library. Excerpts: Two letters to Sophia Soule (mother) regarding the Sand Creek Massacre.

_____ *Letter to Major E.W. Wynkoop, December 14, 1864.* Rocky

Mountain News. "Sins of Sand Creek," September 15, 2000.

Sparks, Col. Ray G. *Tall Bull's Captives.* Trail Guide of the Kansas City Westerners, Vol. VII, No. 1, March 1962.

Spring, Agnes Wright. *Cheyenne Girl and White Man's Ways.* Frontier Times, Vol. 44. No. 5. Western Publications, Inc. Austin, TX. 1970.

Stanley, Henry M. *A British Journalist Reports on the Medicine Lodge Peace Councils of 1867.* Kansas State Historical Quarterly, Vol. 33, No. 3, 1967.

Stuart, J.E.B. *Dairy.* Microfilm, Kansas State Historical Society, Topeka, KS.

Tappan, Samuel F. *Unpublished Autobiography.* Topeka, KS: Kansas State Historical Society.

_____ *Diary.* Microfilm, Colorado State Historical Society, Denver, CO.

Taylor, Alfred A. *The Medicine Lodge Peace Council.* Chronicles of Oklahoma 2, no. 2, June 1924.

Taylor, Morris F. *The Mail Station and the Military at Camp on Pawnee Fork, 1859 -1860.* Kansas Historical Quarterly, 1970.

Templeton, Andrew J. *Papers.* Pioneer Museum of Colorado Springs, Starsmore Research Center.

Unrau, William E. *The Story of Fort Larned.* Kansas Historical Quarterly 23, no. 3, August 1957.

Vasicek, Donald L. *The Sand Creek Massacre. Film documentary.* Winner: 2005 American Indian Film Festival Documentary Short Film Competition; 2005 IndiGathering Documentary Short Film Competition.

Watson, Elmo Scott. *The Battle of Summit Springs.* Chicago Westerners Brand Book, Vol. VII, No. 7, September 1950.

Wellman, I. *Some Famous Kansas Frontier Scouts.* Kansas Historical Quarterly, 1932.

Welty, Raymond L. *Supplying the Frontier Military Posts.* Kansas Historical Quarterly, 1938.

_____ *The Policing of the Frontier by the Army, 1860-1870.* Kansas Historical Quarterly, 1938.

White, Lonnie J. *Indian Raids on the Kansas Frontier, 1969.* Kansas Historical Quarterly, No. 4, Winter, 1972.

_____ *White Women Captives of the Southern Plains Indians.* Journal of the West, Vol. III, No. 3, July 1969.

_____ *The Battle of Beecher Island: The Scouts Hold Fast on the Arickaree.* Journal of the West 5, January 1966.

_____ *From Bloodless to Bloody: The Third Colorado Cavalry and the Sand Creek Massacre.* Journal of the West 5, 1967.

Wilson, Hill P. *Black Kettle's Last Raid – 1868.* Kansas State Historical Collections, Vol. 8, 1903-1904.

Woodward, Arthur. *Sidelights on Bent's Old Fort.* Colorado Magazine, October 1956.

Woodward, George A. *Experiences with the Cheyenne Indians.* A Monthly Review of Military and Naval Affairs, Vol. 1, No. 2, 1968.

Wright, Arthur A. *Colonel John P. Slough and the New Mexico Campaign.* Colorado Magazine 39, 1962.

Wynkoop, Christopher H. *Edward Wanshaer Wynkoop.* Extensive online collection of information about Major Wynkoop's life and his experiences both before and after Sand Creek. The Wynkoop entries below are a few samples of the larger collection that includes manuscripts, newspaper articles and personal recollections.

Wynkoop, Edward Estill. *Edward Wanshaer Wynkoop.* Collections of the Kansas State Historical Society 13, 1913-1914.

Wynkoop, Edward Wanshaer. *Wynkoop's Unfinished Manuscript.* Colorado State Historical Society, Denver, CO. See also, *Tall Chief: The Autobiography of Edward W. Wynkoop*

_____ *The Battle of the Washita: An Indian Agent's View.* Chronicles of Oklahoma, Vol. 36, No. 4, Winter, 1958-1959.

Wynkoop, Frank Murray. *Data Concerning Col. Edward W. Wynkoop.* Colorado College Tutt Library Special Collections and Archives.

_____ *Intimate Notes Relative to the Career of Colonel Edward Wynkoop.* Museum of New Mexico History.

_____ *Reminiscences of Frank Murray Wynkoop.* Colorado Historical Society, Edward W. Wynkoop Papers, Mss 695, FF 5, December 12, 1953.

Zwink, Timothy A. *E. W. Wynkoop and the Bluff Creek Council, 1866.* Kansas Historical Quarterly, No. 2, Winter, 1977.

PRIMARY SAND CREEK MASSACRE RESOURCES

www.KClonewolf.com

Western History/Genealogy Department Collections, Denver Public Library.

Colorado State Historical Society Collections

Colorado College Tutt Library Special Collections

Kansas State Historical Society Collections

Museum of New Mexico, History Library Collections